Ask Larry

Also by LARRY TOWNSEND:

The Construction Worker
2069 Trilogy
Mind Master
The Long Leather Cord
Man Sword
The Faustus Contract
The Gay Adventures of Captain Goose
Chains
Run, Little Leather Boy
The Scorpius Equation
The Sexual Adventures of Sherlock Holmes

A RICHARD KASAK BOOK

Ask Larry

LARRY TOWNSEND

First Richard Kasak Book Edition 1995

First Printing June 1995

ISBN 1-56333-289-2

Cover photo by Susan McNamara
Cover Design by Dayna Navaro

Manufactured in the United States of America
Published by Masquerade Books, Inc.
801 Second Avenue
New York, N.Y. 10017

Contents

Doing the "Leather Notebook" Column for Drummer Magazine

FOREWORD

In 1979, when I first started doing "The Leather Notebook" *column for* Drummer *magazine, we were still in our age of political innocence. The "movement" had been gaining momentum for a good ten years, and AIDS had yet to become the deadly, destructive force that staggered us backward—almost into our closets—before we were able to recover our equilibrium—those of us who survived the initial onslaught. But this period, from 1979–80 to 1992, saw an enormous evolution in attitudes within the gay community in general, and very particularly within the leather/SM subculture.*

Initially, the changes, had to do largely with our sexual practices. We either altered our behavior or we contracted a disease that was going to kill us—in those early days, sooner rather than later. But any factor evoking changes as basic and profound as this had to create other very serious changes as well. For some it was bitterness and resentment, a searching for the source of our misery, and a need to place the blame somewhere away from ourselves. For all of us there was the terrible trauma of seeing friends and acquaintances disappearing all around us. Then came the strong reaction, a banding together to combat this unseen enemy as best we could—determination growing out of a variety of motivations: anger, fear, guilt.

With all of these newfound sentiments, there seemed to be a new degree of self-awareness. Suddenly people who had been afraid to form serious relationships were looking for a single partner and a monogamous living arrangement. Others simply abstained from having sex with any partner. Many guys were infected, but finding they could survive and lead a relatively normal life for varied, extended periods of time. For them, "quality of life" assumed new meaning. But HIV positive or not, sexual behavior was changed and was changing, while the ability of the average gay man to live within the safe-sex rules went from a grudging acceptance of an inconvenient new mode to a matter-of-fact reality of existence.

It was against this dynamic, evolving background that I wrote my column, trying to answer the questions that a wide variety of gay men and/or leathermen were asking. Most of these were not directly AIDS-related, of course, but within this climate it was impossible that they be completely divorced from the ever-present threat. This was often more on my part, as the respondent, than on theirs as questioner, because I always had to bear in mind the potential harm I could do if I neglected to take the health crisis into account. In a way, it was a relief when someone asked me about social conduct or clothing, philosophy, or other nonsexual activities.

In 1982 I went to New York to negotiate the contract for The Leatherman's Handbook II, and it was here that these momentous changes were thrown into sharpest focus for me. I had already written that I believed AIDS (or GRID in those days) was a communicable disease, and advised that all of us cool it until the medical establishment came up with an answer—something we all expected to see happen quickly, despite the obvious indifference of the government. A great many people, including some vocal spokespersons from within the medical establishment, told me I was wrong, that cancer—including gay cancer—was not communicable. Then I embarked on my sojourn—my first visit to the Big Apple in twenty years.

In New York, I became a prophet in a foreign land, so to speak, and was accorded all sorts of courtesies, including a gold pass to The Mineshaft and a number of playtimes given in my honor. I also stopped in Houston on my way home, and much the same situation prevailed there. On these occasions I did little more than watch, as did the friends I was visiting in both areas. A year later, those of us who had not participated were still around; the guys who had been putting on the unprotected sex shows for us were all either dead or dying (the ones with whom I had maintained contact, and thus knew what was happening to them). It was a lesson I have never forgotten.

The second lesson to come out of this took longer to mature, but certainly provides on interesting insight. When I learned that one of my hosts in NYC had come down with AIDS, I was so shocked and upset I called him immediately, spoke to him for a long time, and afterward found myself in a really depressive state for quite a long period. When he died a few weeks later, I could hardly believe it. Such things just didn't happen to young men in their thirties. A few years later, when a man who had been a much closer friend died, I was deeply distressed and I cried for him, but the sense of abysmal horror wasn't there. I, like so many within our community, had become used to having death lurking all around us, and no longer had it in me to be surprised by the ravages of this wretched disease. It was the evolution of a basic attitude, reflecting the human need to erect barriers for protection against emotional depletion.

Likewise, there has been a considerable evolution within Drummer *itself over the period I did* "The Leather Notebook" *column for them. I started when the magazine was owned by John Embry, and John Rowberry was editor. It was subsequently acquired by my friends Tony DeBlase (Fledermaus) and Andy Charles. Although these were very different men, with quite diverse attitudes toward the written word, they all left me alone to do my own thing, while battling their windmills on other plains. I left* Drummer *and transferred my flag—so to speak—to* Honcho *after Tony and Andy sold out to the guys from Amsterdam.*

In trying to draft the structure of this book, I had originally been concerned with noting precise dates and trying to keep my questions and answers in a tight chronological order. I eventually had to give up on this for a couple of reasons. John Embry started the practice of putting out the magazine with no dateline, merely a volume number. I think this happened because of the difficulty in meeting specific deadlines. I know that there were more likely to be ten issues per year than twelve. This was fine, and no one seemed really to care, except that it does provide problems when one tries to go back and pick up publishing dates. I made the mistake of not dating my copies of the columns as I submitted them, so I am partly to blame for my own inability to always tell you exactly when I said it.

Then, the one bone of contention I had over this long stretch of time: editorial freedom. My original agreement with the two Johns (Embry and Rowberry) was that they not edit what I said, in such a way as to alter my meaning. Correcting my notoriously bad spelling was okay, and if they really didn't like something I said they were free to drop the item from the column, but not to change it. This worked well in the initial stages, but as other guys replaced Rowberry, and eventually John Embry, I did find my comments either changed or cut from time to time. Usually one protest stopped the practice—until the next editor came along. At any rate, the questions and answers given here are all from my original copies of the text I submitted and may therefore vary slightly from something you remember reading. You may also notice that my comments within each chapter will gradually begin to reflect health concerns that were not as obvious in the earlier answers—this being a reflection of the attitude changes occasioned by the encroaching health crisis. (I have maintained a fairly consistent chronological order to the questions and answers within in chapter.)

I have had people say to me (or write to me), asking why I tended to answer so many of the questions I received as seriously as I did. After all, they ask, some of these things are so silly that it's hard to imagine why someone would actually be concerned about them. But that's the whole point of a column like this. It provides a forum for a guy to ask his question(s) with whatever degree of anonymity (and naïveté) he wishes and have it answered without his having to expose himself to the jaundiced eye of a more sophisticated or less sympathetic adviser.

Of course, there were the correspondents who wrote to bait me with questions they expected would provoke a barbed response—and sometimes they got it, especially if I felt it would add some spice to the *fabric of words. But even for them, a perfectly straight-faced answer was often the most effective. It was all largely instinctive on my part, I suppose, but—whatever—it seems to have worked. The column ran for about twelve years in* Drummer *and is still going in* Honcho. *In this book, I have gathered up the most interesting, significant, and/or amusing items from those first twelve years, organized them into thirteen fairly broad categories, and tried to title the resulting thirteen chapters accordingly—again, with no attempt actually to date them. To help the reader decipher all of this, I've used three typefaces: italics for remarks I am making "today," boldface for the answers I originally gave to the questions submitted, and regular type for the questions as sent in by the readers. These questions, by the way, are generally in exactly the form submitted, although I sometimes had to cut them down owing to space requirements, and I occasionally felt compelled to straighten out the syntax, or to clarify what I thought the writer was trying to ask. So read on, and I will continue to regale you with further pearls of wisdom, as written then and now. And if some of the subjects do not always seem to fit as well into the category where I placed them as in another, just scratch it up to my subjective judgment—and my mood on the day I wrote it. It's my book, damn it!*

CHAPTER 1

Finding a Partner

This is the problem that has beset more readers than any other, and has resulted in my most difficult mental gymnastics to come up with some sort of intelligent—or at least helpful—answer for each of so many divergent situations. If the guy sent a picture, it made my task a bit easier, although sometimes it merely helped me better understand why the writer was single. Here are some typical and atypical examples:

Dear Sir,

    I have just finished reading your book, and I am writing to you for some advice. I am twenty-five years old, studying in a Roman Catholic seminary—still five years short or ordination as a priest. Although I have been actively gay since my early teens, I have never gotten into the SM scene, but I have always wanted to be a "bottom," to serve as a slave. I've answered a *Drummer* ad and have made contact with a guy in a nearby city, but I am hesitant to take this next step...with him, or with any other opportunity that might present itself. I'm concerned, on the one hand, with the potential physical danger, and on the other with the long-term decision I will have to make. Is there a future in being a slave? Am I being foolish to even consider this in light of my entire life's orientation? Any thought you might be able to give me would be greatly appreciated.

Seminary Student

Dear Student,

Although I have known a number of clergymen (Catholic and otherwise) who have been involved in male-to-male SM, each has had to make his own unique compromise with his conscience. At this point, I would be doing you a disservice if I suggested that you cast aside all your previous hopes and plans, to plunge headlong into the world of leather-SM. You haven't even tried it yet, and I assure you that the reality is going to be quite different from whatever masturbatory fantasies you have experienced. Why don't you follow through with your present contact and go from there. You seen to have time on your side. You also seem intelligent enough to weigh the alternatives and make your own decision before the final commitment—vows, etc. There are, of course, a number of gay religious groups: Dignity, which is Catholic, the MCC, and a large number of smaller denominations. You might look into these, not so much with an eye to a transfer of allegiance, but in the beginning simply as a place to meet and talk with other guys who have confronted your problem and dealt with it in their own way—however successfully, you will have to judge for yourself.

Interesting in looking back on this one. I wonder what decision this guy made. His letter arrived in 1983, so he's now had over ten years to find his way. With all the recent furor over priests "molesting" their charges, it does give one pause. Of course, it has always seemed preposterous to me that any organization—church or otherwise—should try to force a healthy male to refrain from any form of sex. It only makes for many games of naughty-naughty, and lord knows how many gallons of jism expelled each year via Merry Palm.

Dear Larry,

I enclose a photo. In addition to one side of my face being disfigured by a birth defect, I'm also quite skinny (a condition I prefer in other people), and due to a natural (not dietary produced) deficiency I have a blotchy complexion on my chest and back. In short, I'm hardly a "cutie." Although "lookism" is supposed to reign supreme, I do manage to trick (not enough), but never in my preferred role/scene— Greek passive in bondage. The men who want to trick want me as Top, or as bottom limited to French, no bondage. I find this strange, because my ass is in far better shape than the rest of me. I can't see why Tops should object to my admittedly un-hot looks in this one respect and not in the others. Comments? Ideas?

Tony, Alberta, Canada

Dear Tony,

Admittedly, your face is not your fortune, but as in the case of almost anyone who does not qualify as a Colt model, there always seems to be "someone out there" who is going to respond positively to the very qualities that you perceive as a turn-off for others. Many guys who are not able to attract the partners they want strictly on the basis of their physical attributes, are able to do so by letting the other guy get to know him well enough to respond to the person within the shell, rather than just the exterior flesh. It's easier said than done, of course, but if any guy begins to perceive his sex partner as more than "a piece of meat for the evening," he also tends to relate better to that other person's needs. I really don't know what else to suggest to you; but from your letter you seem to have a good mind, and that could prove your salvation. I don't mean to give you a bullshit answer; but, as I'm sure you already know, yours is not an easy problem to solve.

Dear Larry,

Drummer has been a magazine that I have enjoyed from the first, as one of the best expressions of our unique lifestyle. I very much get off on most of your material, and I've also learned a lot.

Recently, I answered a number of ads from Masters, as I am definitely and seriously in need of a strong and long-term Master. (And I'm not a bad catch.) Despite your (*Drummer's*) best efforts in forwarding mail to me, over 60 percent of the people approached never even bothered to reply. This is very discouraging, and if I didn't know better it might make me thing we're a bunch of phonies, J.O. effeminates, not men enough to follow up on earnest applications—at least with a "Thanks, but I don't like your looks," or *something*.

Would you, Sir, have any suggestions on how a sincere, genuine, experienced slave can match up with a real man? I must tell you that a few honest Masters have responded, fortunately. Word of mouth by good Masters and friends may also help. But your experienced advice is sought in my deadly earnest search. Thanks.

Sincere and Willing, VT

Dear Sincere,

It seems I've heard this song before. Your batting average sounds about average. When a guy runs an ad, especially as a Master, he will generally get a flood of replies, because (as has been said, written and sung many times) a good Top is hard to find. He can generally pick and choose from the responses. Nor, would I suspect, is Vermont the most fertile territory for your search. If you've already gotten it on with a few good Tops, I'd say you haven't done badly. There are a lot of guys reading these pages who'd be more than gratified to find just one. And since you've found more than one, I can't help but wonder if you're really as good a bottom as you think you are. Why haven't these good "honest Masters" come back for seconds?

This may have been a classic example of a pushy bottom trying to assume the mantle of "slave," when he really doesn't understand what the term implies. As such, I should perhaps have included it in Chapter 11, where we'll get more involved in that particular controversy. But, I'll give him the benefit of the doubt and leave him here among the honest seekers.

Dear Mr. Townsend, Sir:

I have a small problem. I'm a real Daddy's Boy. As a youngster, I always fantasized about older men, like my father's friends, so I know it's my place. The problem is, whenever I meet a hot "Dad," I always end up Top. I'm nineteen years old, about 5'11", a pretty stocky build and I've been told I'm very handsome—that I carry myself well for someone my age. According to *Drummer* articles, I'm a blue-collar man (auto painter), so I always learn something new from your great mag. I plan on going to Southern California this summer to look for work and to live, and hopefully to find a tough, hard-ass, hairy Dad who knows his place on Top. Where do they hang out?

R. R., AZ

Dear R. R.,

Boy, you guys sure know how to ask the difficult questions! You can't get into a California bar until you're twenty-one, but you probably wouldn't find your Daddy there, anyway…except that you might meet someone who would introduce you to someone, etc. There are a number of leather clubs and bike clubs which have meetings, runs, etc.—again with a twenty-one-year age rule (although some might be eighteen—you'll have to check). So, now I've told you where you probably can't go. While you're still underage, your best bet is to frequent places with lots of gay patrons, such as stores and restaurants in West Hollywood, Silverlake, etc. Try to make friends with some other young guys first and go from there. Once you get settled with a place to live, a job, and some routine to your life it becomes a matter of encountering the right guy—maybe in a gym. No one can tell you where you're most apt to find him, or when. You merely increase the odds in your favor by meeting more people and cultivating more friendships.

I answered that one almost ten years ago, and even then told the kid to poke around West Hollywood. Today the number of gay businesses and cafés has burgeoned to a point where an attractive young guy should have little trouble making as many contacts as he wants, even if he is too young for the bar scene. Of course, most

Daddy types avoid the discos, which are the most popular hunting grounds for the younger set; but there are plenty of bar/restaurants, coffee shops, markets and other stores where the clientele is gay and cruisy. You just have to keep your eyes open.

Dear Larry,

I would like to comment on "Sincere and Willing, VT" (Issue 75), and relate my own experience in placing an ad in *Drummer*. With the heading "Pig Wanted," I received a potpourri of approximately eighty responses: fifteen from England and Central Europe, one from Australia, twenty from Canada, and the rest from the USA. Several were from guys who lived a great distance from me, but just wrote for the joy of acknowledging another pig out there. Because of where I live, many wrote that they would be passing through. I was shortly able to distinguish which were the serious letters (i.e., those which were legible and not stuck together). Surprisingly, only six guys totally understood the ad and responded accordingly. Only five did not receive a response from me. Others received a letter and photo, thanking them for their interest. For whatever reason, only twenty-five continued with any correspondence, thus indicating our mutual seriousness. I fully enjoyed responding to all of these guys, but also realize that it was becoming very time consuming and a bit expensive. So, on the basis of my experience, I think VT had a very good response to his letters, and think he might have been expecting more than any series of letters could achieve. Contacts don't always work out in the bars or clubs; why expect it to be any different with *Drumbeat*?

D. LePorc, Vancouver, B.C.

Dear Porker,

Your responses were quite interesting. I'm glad to see that the *Drumbeat* ads are drawing so well. I guess in any such situation there is going to be more chaff than wheat. But, as "they" say, it only takes one—unless you're a real pig, and then maybe it takes two or three…or four…five…twenty?

Advertising for one's paramour is a practice of long standing, dating back at least to the time of early settlement in America, and later in Australia. It has always seemed an "iffy" business to me, although I must confess to having played the game—also with mixed results. It's just too easy for a guy to lie in a letter, to send a fifteen-year-old photo, etc. But if you like to whip ass, that might offer an excuse to administer a proper punishment. Every cloud, as "they" say.

Dear Larry,

I am a twenty-two-year-old, living in the not-so-popular city of Detroit. I have had interests in SM since I first met my (now) ex-lover, even though at that time I really didn't think or know that it was SM. I have not led a very intelligent life. I've made a lot of bad decisions and have ended up regretting them. I even once was in the process of becoming a slave, and I fouled that up, too. My question is: should I try to become a slave again? I've been reading through the classifieds of a recent *Drummer*, and have seen a few ads requesting slaves and I have been thinking of answering them. I feel that if left on my own I won't go anywhere. I need the training and discipline from someone else to straighten me out. Can you give me any advice on what I should say and do to be accepted? I am fairly healthy, but do not work out. I also smoke. Is it conceivable that a Master can help me overcome my addiction to cigarettes? Any advice would be appreciated.

J. R., Detroit

Dear J. R.,

It has been my experience that very few guys are ready to become slaves until they have had fairly extensive experience as bottoms. Otherwise, they don't know what they are getting into, either physically or psychologically. Even then, a genuine Master/slave relationship is going to happen only when the right two people come together. When you're ready for the ultimate commitment—which may still be a long way off—you should also be experienced enough to know it. At twenty-two you've got plenty of time, and you are certainly entitled to a few mistakes. Hopefully, you'll learn by them.

This kid sounded so depressed and disoriented I sent him a personal message, but never heard back. His uncertainties are so typical of many guys his age that I always have the feeling that nothing I say is going to help. He just has to plod along at his own pace and—with any luck—learn as he goes. This degree of introspection seems preferable, at least, to the happy-go-lucky types who hit the bars every night and never stop to think about the direction of their lives.

Dear Larry,

I am a latent homosexual and a bottom, and have just come out. I go to an adult bookstore here, and there are always three or four or more young guys (some queens) hanging around there cruising. There are also holes in some of the booths. What are they cruising and waiting for? I am an older person (fifty) and am curious about it. Am I supposed to pay them or whatever to go down on them, or what? Actually, I would like a well-hung one to fuck me, but is all this safe? I am afraid of AIDS. Please answer me. PLEASE!

Chuck, Las Vegas, NV

Dear Chuck,

I don't know much about the hustler scene in Las Vegas, but I've never heard of play-for-pay through a glory hole (holes between booths in bookstores or public johns). If you see a guy who looks interesting, why not just ask him if he'd like a drink, or make some other innocuous suggestion, and see how he responds. If he wants money, he's going to ask for it. Be careful, though, not to make the first real sexual overture. It could be a vice-squad trap. I don't know what you look like, but a guy at fifty looking for young numbers may well be expected to pay.

As for "safe sex," any act involving the exchange of body fluids is suspect. With a hustler there is a higher risk, as with anyone who has multiple partners. While you're at the adult bookstore, why not buy a copy of *Damron's Guide* or *The Gayellow Pages* and check out the bars in your area? Your chances of health risk should be less with non-pros, although these days there is no guarantee with anyone.

Dear Larry (Sir),

I'm twenty-three. 6'2", brown eyes. I was recently discharged from the navy after serving my full four years, during which I had one long affair with an officer who introduced me to bondage and SM. I've now moved to the desert, where there are many gay men, but most with lovers. Also, I have only found a few "real men." I have a lot of sexual energy, and while I've been told I'd make a good "Daddy," I'd much prefer to be the "son" first. Except for the navy, my experience is limited—just one spree in Los Angeles (Silverlake), during which I had my left nipple pierced and got a small tattoo on my ass. As a result of my military experiences, I am very much into uniforms. At the moment I'm working at a job with no future, just to pay the rent and put food in the fridge. So my question is: "How do I go about finding a "Daddy" (not a "sugar daddy").

Respectfully,
Confused and Bewildered, Palm Springs

Dear Confused,

At your age, most of us were in the same space as you. As you have already discovered, you are probably hunting in the wrong forest. I'm sure this letter will get plenty of responses, but whether they will be any better than you'd get from an ad is hard to tell. I would suggest that L.A. or San Francisco is going to be more productive for you, but also more dangerous in several respects. You sound young and vulnerable; the big cities can eat you alive if you aren't prepared—emotionally and financially—to cope. Neither is this the time to go out and have a lot of experiences, trying to find the right guy. Let's see what kind of responses you get, and we can go from there.

I wasn't able to be much help to this guy, although I did forward a few letters to him. He wrote some months later and was still in

Palm Springs. Interesting that he should have gotten there in the first place, if he didn't want a Sugar Daddy. With all the retired gay men in the area, it would certainly be a fertile hunting grounds for a guy with that in mind.

Dear Larry,

When people run ads, like in *Drummer*, they use abbreviations that I guess everyone is supposed to understand. But I don't know what most of them mean. I assume W/M means "white male," and I guess FF means "fist-fucking." But I don't understand: W/S, B&D vs. B&B, TT, etc. And what does "safe sex" mean? I really think you should publish some kind of glossary.

Reader, Miami, FL

Dear Reader,

You're probably right, and maybe the *Drummer* editors will take heed. I have to confess that some of the more esoteric abbreviations confuse me, too; but I guess the people who are supposed to understand them do. Of the ones you mention, W/S means "water sports" (as in piss); B&D is "bondage and discipline," whereas B&B means "boots and britches" (uniforms). TT now means "tit torture," although a few years back it sometimes meant "testicle torture," and I've even seen it used to mean "toilet training." So, you see the aficionados can sometimes be confused, too. As for "safe sex," that means the guy wants to do it, following the guidelines that are supposed to guard against exchange of bodily fluids.

Dear Larry,

I have a problem I hope you can help me with. Next year I turn thirty, and for the past few years I have been looking for a Daddy. Right now I feel that my age is not helping me. Whenever I see a guy whom I consider "Daddy material" (over thirty, hairy, beefy-muscular, etc.) he isn't interested in me. (I'm short, stocky, with a beard.) To be truthful, if I were to find a Dad, I would want to be a son, not a slave. I don't want to be kept nude in a house, wearing a dog collar and be subjected to all that this implies. Yet I would want him to be boss, and I would be willing to do pretty much what he wanted me to—including sessions at the gym to get my body into the shape he might want it to be. I would even give his big, hot, sweaty body a tongue bath after our workouts. Is there any hope for me? I just desperately want to find a Dad.

Tony, NYC

Dear Tony,

Although most successful Daddy-type relationships that I have observed seem to have started when the "son" was a little younger than you are, they frequently extend well beyond that point. And there certainly are relationships that start when Sonny is well past thirty. I really don't think age is your problem. But as you have undoubtedly observed, most guys who want to be Daddies are seeking partners who at least appear to be younger and less experienced than themselves. Beards tend to make a guy look older than he is, especially if he is also of a more robust build. If your present appearance isn't working, why not change it? Work out, lose some weight, and shave off your beard. If it doesn't work, you can always grow it back. If you want the relationship so badly, this would seem a reasonable concession. I don't know what sort of approach you are using with your potential Daddies, but you might also give this a little thought. If you come on to a guy who is about your own age (and who may like to think he looks younger) with a big "Take me, Daddy!" you are only asking for rejection.

I've seen some really inexplicable combinations, playing this Daddy/son game. In essence, it's role-playing taken to a relatively extreme degree, and the core of the relationship's success is the ability of each partner to perceive the situation as his imagination would have it be. It happens occasionally that Sonny is older than Daddy, or that Daddy is actually the bottom. But I don't see that it makes much difference. There are no rules that need be observed— just two guys who enjoy what they're doing. And isn't that the essence of any successful relationship?

Dear Mr. Townsend,

I would like to pose a question similar to those you have previously answered, but with a little different subject in mind. I am totally average: age thirty, 5'7", brown eyes, dark hair. My strength comes from within the mind and soul, which transcends and extols my outward appearance. I am not an intellectual; neither am I a moron, for I adapt to whatever situation I find myself subjugated. This allows me to become an animal, human, or if you wish, vegetable. Yet I am still the same being. My only concern is that I don't become crippled or killed in the course of action (sane sex). And the only hindrance I feel that would jeopardize a relationship is that I am self-reliant and supportive. I am not impressed by the material objects of others. The only thing I want from a man is to be able to serve, with both of us being satisfied together. This, along with honesty and integrity. My experiences lately have been of Masters who either have slaves of their own, or live outside my area. While we're together, the moment is enjoyable. I am complimented on having the proper attitude and for being a hot man. But then the same question arises every time: Why don't you have a lover? Could you give me the answer?

jeff, Seattle

Dear jeff,

There are a great many reason why guys who would like to have lovers don't have them. Seattle isn't so much of a gay desert that you should be lacking the opportunity to find someone, so you've probably let a good prospect or two get away from you. Remember that a long-term relationship has to have more than just sex to sustain it. I'm assuming you don't want to be a real live-in slave, but rather a bottom in a partnership. When you meet a guy who seems to be lover material, why not extend the contact beyond the bedroom? Have dinner with him, or suggest going away for a weekend. Establish a social as well as a sexual rapport; and if it builds from there, let nature take its course. Remember, if you want a real long-term relationship, you (as well as your partner) will have to give more than just your (his) body.

I remember when I answered this guy, I had the feeling that he was an extremely aggressive man, which probably meant a "pushy bottom." Although some Tops like this, most do not. Over the years I have become ever more aware of the real antagonism that can result from a bottom with an attitude.

Dear Larry,

A few years ago, I had a very torrid affair with a guy who really turned me on. At the time I would have loved to become his permanent slave, but he was too flighty and not ready to settle down. Now he has come back into my life and wants to pick up where we left off. Unfortunately, he has gotten quite heavy, and I no longer find him attractive. (I would guess that he has gone from 175 to over 250.) Our previous sex was the best I ever had, however, and I still fantasize about our sessions when I jack off. I know I could really respond to him if it weren't for all that fat. I'm afraid to say anything, though, because it just isn't the right thing for a slave to say to a Master. What should I do?

Frustrated, Midwest

Dear Frus.,

I think if you told him exactly what you've told me, and if you told him in a properly contrite, supplicating manner, you might encourage him to do something about his weight. He is probably as unhappy about it as you are, and this might be the motivation he needs. After all, you have nothing to lose, and the chances are he already suspects the reason for your reluctance to rekindle the old flame. On the other hand, there is always the blindfold.

Dear Larry,

In most accounts of SM relationships, it seems possible for the Top to be of almost any age; however, the bottom is generally young—and usually considerably younger than the Top. I know that this makes a better story, whether dealing with real or fictional characters, but I wonder how this translates into real life. Because my own experience in leather/SM is quite limited, especially in the area where I live, I wonder how it is in San Francisco or New York, where the population of leather guys is much larger. Are there many situations where the bottom is an older man? Older than his Top? Or is this such a rare occurrence that a guy over 40 might as well forget it?

One older bottom, WI

Dear Older,

If you're only in your forties, there's lots to hope for. I know one famous (or infamous) bottom who must be pushing 75, has had open-heart surgery, and still takes his licks regularly, and heavily. Being retired, he has the time to travel, and he certainly makes the most of it! Naturally, most Tops in this youth-oriented culture are going to fantasize on a young, virile bottom, with glowing youthful skin and a beautifully molded ass. But when it comes to actually doing the deed, he is most likely to accept something considerably less breathtaking. And yes, I do know of several relationships where the bottom is older than the Top. Although these are sometimes a pay-for-play situation or a long term live-in deal where the older guy is footing the bill, it isn't always that way. And believe it or not, there are a lot of young guys who really get off on the idea of tying Daddy up and whipping the shit out of him. You might also remember that being a good bottom requires just as much skill as being a Top— albeit the reverse role. If you're a good bottom, able to take what the Top wants to give you, the chances are you will be in demand over the pretty boy who whines and wants to tell his Master what to do to him.

Dear Larry,

I am normally a Top—late forties, over six feet—and I have bottomed out only four or five times in my life. However, I have one long-standing fantasy I would really like to have fulfilled: namely, I want to be the recipient of a fraternity-type initiation. I would prefer that this be done by a guy who is younger than I am. After running a number of ads in *Drummer* and other publications, I have

still been unsuccessful in finding a partner. Short of paying for the service, do you have any suggestions?

Name and location withheld

Dear Withheld,

If you are like most men with long-standing fantasies, you have probably honed your mental images into a specific scenario that can never be fulfilled unless you spell it out, step by step, before the start of the scene. This is one of the classic dilemmas for an M, because he either wrecks the Top-to-bottom relationship by appearing to take over the direction, or else lets the Top do his things and ends up being unfulfilled. That is the problem which has existed—or will exist even after you find a willing and capable partner. As to the initiation scene, itself, there are some real difficulties in pulling it off. The genuine action usually takes place in a frat house, where there is plenty of room and a good number of participants. There is also the underlying "college-boy" mentality that most of us can remember only vaguely. It is certainly going to be hard to duplicate all this if you hire a street hustler to play Pledgemaster. So, how do we solve all these problems? The fact that you are normally a Top should be the most intriguing factor you have going for you. Many younger guys are turned on by the concept of "working Daddy over." You might even consider turning one of your own bottoms into Pledgemaster for the occasion—thus making the humiliation all the greater. It might also provide the opportunity for a greater structuring of the scene you want played out. I really don't know what else to suggest, since finding the partner still has to come about as a result of your own efforts. I do know that the Chicago Hellfire Club has a fantasy committee on their Inferno run to help just such cases as yours. There may be other clubs trying the same thing, but I do not know for sure.

It's too bad the genuine frat boys don't realize what a potentially fantastic fund-raising situation they have. Can you imagine the response they'd get from the SM community as a whole (gay and otherwise) if they offered to treat a few paying guests to a real hell-week trip?

Mr. Townsend, Sir,

   i am writing to you in hopes that you can help me, SIR. i am twenty-six year old, 5'11", 175 pounds, SIR. Currently married, going on six years. i am not happy. i need to be a slave, to surrender myself totally to a Master. i want to be kept in bondage, naked, existing only to please my Master, SIR. Bellingham affords little chance to meet a Master, and i don't know about "through the mail" as to do this would leave so much to chance. i would enter the leather world mostly a novice. i am willing to give myself totally to a man who would mold me into exactly the kind of slave he wants. i would be willing to do anything for such a man, SIR. What should i do? i want so badly to be a slave and owned by somebody, by body being used solely for my Master's pleasure. How, SIR, can i find a Master who wants me?

                              Your humble slave, Bellingham, WA

Dear humble,

   If you're really as sure of yourself as your letter indicates, you don't seem to have much choice but to slip your current traces and seek greener pastures—perhaps in Seattle? California? But remember, there is a serious health crisis out there. Don't let someone subject you to any high-risk behavior just because you are so anxious to please. Like playing the stock market, there are no guarantees, but you can't win if you don't take the risks. (And I mean the risk of giving up your current security, in addition to gambling with your health.)

   Perhaps the most difficult person to advise is one like this guy, who has apparently experienced none of the things he thinks he wants so badly. In his state of blissful ignorance, he is willing to give up everything he has in the belief that he is going to find Utopia as envisioned in his masturbatory fantasies. I often wonder how many of these men discover that it hurts to get whipped, and bondage can be uncomfortable, and Masters can be very demanding; and only then realize that this lifestyle isn't for them. It isn't at all like the easy turn-on, turn-off of a JO session where you control the time you keep the ropes on your wrists and ankles, or the leather harness around your cock and balls. Some guys take to SM without ever looking back; for others, the reality is not at all what they want. I hate to see a guy give up his comfortable life until he knows, even if he thinks he's miserable with what he's got.

Dear Mr. Townsend,

I am thirty-seven, a bottom, and have been interested in leathersex since my early teens. While I have had lengthy (six-month) involvements with Tops over the years, I have never been able to forge any kind of long-term relationship which combines the qualities of affection and an "equal partnership" in areas outside the sexual arena, with a leathersex component. I either find myself a third with an already-established couple, or (more commonly) find that my partner wants only an anonymous "fuck buddy." What is it that keeps people from combining affection into a scene? Or is it just me? I have seen other people seeming to enjoy the type of relationship I really crave, but there is no way for me to see into the most innermost parts of these situations, so I don't know if everything is really as it appears on the surface—to me, as an outsider.

David, Toronto, Canada

Dear David,

As I have maintained from the time of my earliest writings on the subject of SM relationships, there is no way to predict one person's or couple's behavior on the basis of somebody else's behavior. People are simply too different. Because you have been unable to establish the type of relationship you really want does not necessarily mean that such relationships do not exist. By your own account, you apparently found one or more that lasted for six months. In some ways, I think the most fortunate thing that can happen to a "relationship-seeking" bottom is for him to be taken in hand early on and trained by an experienced Top. This way, he comes to accept the real-life standards of his first Master and, in doing so, he finds a fulfillment that he probably would not have found later on, when his fantasies have had time to conjure up an impossibly perfect situation. In other words, you have to reach a point where you stop seeking an unrealistically idyllic relationship, and settle for something that really exists. As for affection—sure, affection is very much a part of any long-term relationship (or should be). But by its very nature, an SM relationship calls for affection to be displayed differently from the standards we are taught to expect as we grow up. We are weaned on "love Hollywood style," which provides a wonderful blackboard on which people can sketch their sexual/emotional fantasies. Yet these are often as unrealistic for anyone else as they are for us. Maybe that's why our divorce rate is so high, and why you are certainly not alone in your quest for that Mr. Right. If you really want a long-term relationship, you are probably going to be forced to accept something that is not quite as perfect as your fantasies.

Dear Larry,

For years I have been attracted to the leather scene and to the look and feel of leather. I have read and been intrigued by your books and have tried to get into SM, both as a Top and a bottom. What I have found is that I remain attracted to leather, enjoy having sex in leather, but I just don't enjoy pain—either inflicting it or as a recipient. I don't know if I just haven't found the right person(s) or what. I guess my question is: Am I unique, or are there others out there with similarly limited interests? I go to the Eagle and Spike in NYC. I'm a big (6'3", 200-pound) masculine-looking guy, and I get approached by a lot of men and often go home with someone. I frequently feel that I have presented myself in one way and then don't deliver, although I try to be as up-front as possible with people in the bar.

R. A., NYC

Dear R. A.,

Giving or receiving pain is not the only way to enjoy SM, and there are a lot of guys—especially now in the current health crisis—who have gotten more heavily into bondage without using the whips and other toys which can abrade the skin and require careful disinfecting between usages. Try a gray hankie in your back pocket (whichever side your mood for the night dictates) and see what happens. You might also remember that a little light belting across the ass really doesn't hurt very much; so if it's the pain and not the particular fetish that bothers you, who not let the guy know you're really enjoying the sight of his bound and helpless condition?

Dear Larry,
I have answered at least two dozen ads in the hope of meeting a mutual partner that could become a friend. Out of all this I've received only two replies. Why do all these guys put ads in if they don't intend to respond? Oh yes, not everyone has photos available to send out all over the place. My scene is not wild, wild, and yes, I'm forty+ and am told I look like Magnum P. I. I just wish either the ad was not phony or the guy placing the ad [wasn't either]. Thanks.

F. M., Lowell, MA

Dear F. M.,
Meeting someone through an ad is an "iffy" proposition at best. Many guys who run an ad—or respond to one—are looking for a fantasy they aren't ever going to find. For this reason, very few advertisers are looking for "forty+," especially without a photo. That's just the way the old pickle squirts. Read on.

Dear Master Larry, Sir:
Sir, i want to thank you. i took your advice and now have found my Master at last. Sir, i did have one bad experience, though, when my ad first came out in *Drummer*. i traveled all the way to the Midwest by plane to be with Him, and when i got there it was an all different story, Sir. He wanted a little boy slave, and i'm not a little boy. But that wasn't the worst part. He had a wife and also had two young guys living with Him, as well as a guy about my age, Sir. i had paid my own way out there, figuring it was to be a full-time Master-slave relationship, and finding it was all a lie, Sir. But i got lucky and found a real leather MAN

and a true Master, and i found him through the same *Drummer* ad. i am afraid i will lose a friend if you print this letter, but i want other slaves to know what i went through, Sir.

slave, New England

Dear slave,

What can I say? A happy ending makes its own statement.

Typical for a dizzy slave, this guy mentions "my age," but never tells us what it is, so the picture he paints isn't as clear as it might be. He may have expected that I would be able to match him up with some previous correspondence, but I had neither the time nor the energy. Slaves!

Dear Larry,

How about some advice? I'm twenty-six, and a bit above average looking. I always seem to date someone for three to six months, and then I want to move on. I really want to find the right guy to spend the rest of my life with, and I've really tried. Once I made a complete change in my life for a guy I thought was the right one, only to have it all come apart after six weeks. I really dream of a hairy Daddy with a nine-inch rod to ram into me and let me know he's boss. On the other hand, I have a lover right now who is loving and considerate, but doesn't have much in the way of a cock. I guess I'm floating between two powerful forces—love and lust—and I don't which I really want.

Nick, in the mountains of TN

Dear Mountain Man,

Oh, the universality of the lovers' dilemma! You are expressing the same doubts and concerns that fill the lines of ancient Greek tragedies, Shakespearean dramas, and half of Hollywood's greatest—albeit, your phraseology is a bit more basic. And, of course, none of these great minds has ever solved the problem. I would expect there is no universal answer. You will just have to find the best compromise you can; i.e., a guy who can give you something from both your categories of need. But you might remember that he is also seeking something, and maybe you are *his* compromise.

Dear Larry,

   I am an old cocksucker, retired now and moved back to my roots in Kentucky. There are many friends (both gay and otherwise), in addition to family, available to keep going socially, and I am not lacking for things to occupy my mind and my time. In fact, I've gotten into university-level classes, and I'm so busy I have less free time than I had when I was working. But I do miss the opportunity to get down on my knees in a good working glory hole, and get my face stuffed full of big, hard, uncut meat. I'm a little reluctant to do much in my own area, but a trip across the state line once in a while would not be out of the realm of possibility. My question: If all I want to do is suck cock, how much danger am I in, healthwise? Isn't there a lesser chance of meeting an HIV-positive man in this part of the country? I've never contracted anything in all my years of service to mankind and don't want to start now. Still, the juices are flowing, and my lips sometimes ache for the old feeling of smooth, slick velvet sliding down my throat.

                                                   A. C., Louisville, KY

Dear A. C.,

   Good for you! You've certainly got the right spirit. As to the danger: Yes, it's there. We can't deny it. As I've commented before, statistically speaking, cocksucking is a low-risk form of behavior. There is probably a greater chance of your being arrested than of contracting AIDS, although this would be true anywhere. But both dangers are present. You can reduce the health risk by: (1) not taking the guy's load, or (2) washing your mouth out with a good swig of vodka immediately afterward. It also helps to be sure you don't have any kind of open sore in your mouth or on your lips. Some guys even go so far as to slip a rubber on the guy's dick. I don't know if you'd be willing to do that, but it's the only completely safe answer, even in the backwaters of Appalachia.

Sir,

I really don't know how to put all this down, but here goes. I'm twenty-three, and somewhat into leather—pierced nipple, harness, armband, etc. I've also been a waiter in one of the two so-called leather bars in the area. I'm head-over-heels for a twenty-one-year-old boy, and I'd like us to grow up together, with me as Top and him as my "puppy." The main problem is that I have emotions for him, but his insecurities are holding him back. So, it's obvious I have to hold back until he comes around. But I can't sometimes, because I have the desire to find a Daddy for myself; and unfortunately in Detroit the chances are slim. I need a Daddy to teach me how to be a man physically, mentally, and emotionally. I was told once that you can't be the best Top without being the bottom first. And I want to be the best Top for my boy. But then, again, if I have the right Daddy and grow into the right kind of man, I might someday meet the right boy to serve me and want to do it. Bars aren't the answer because there aren't any worth the name in Detroit, and personal ads are always full of lies. Can you offer me any help?

Ponyboy, Detroit, MI

Dear Ponyboy,

As I see it, you have more than one set of conflicts, and the only way you are going to start resolving any of them is to try for a better grasp on your own reality. On the one hand, you want to be a Top, which is a role you are ill equipped to handle. On the other, you want a Daddy to teach you the ropes, from which experience you might well benefit. In your opening phrases, you imply an emotional involvement with your twenty-one-year-old friend, and in the end you seem willing to forsake him with the hope of finding another young partner sometime in the future, when you are better equipped emotionally to handle him.

On a purely academic level, I'd say your best bet is to find the Daddy (or Top or Master) and let him guide you toward a greater degree of maturity. As you point out, from the practical standpoint, this may not be possible. But what about your feelings for this young man you already seem to love? You know, it is one of the great accidental triumphs in life to meet a person whom you can love and who can love you in return. If you've really found him, don't throw away the opportunity. Stop being so selfish and try to adapt your needs to mesh more closely with his. Once the relationship is established it can evolve—gradually, perhaps—into something more attuned to your fantasies. You might even be able to bring in a third person at a future time—assuming you can find him—and let him play with both of you. In any event, you've got plenty of time for trial and error, and in the end that's the only way any of us make it through life.

I had several friends chastise me for wasting so much space on an obvious (to them) young jerk, who didn't have enough on the ball to know who he was, much less where he wanted to go—and who might actually have been pulling my leg. But I always try to give a correspondent the benefit of the doubt. I think he was just a confused kid, whom I hope made it into some kind of satisfactory relationship.

Dear Sir,

I am interested in many aspects of the leather scene; however, I am also shy, and want to meet someone who would expand my limits and become by best friend and partner. I am a guy with Klinefelter's syndrome, and because my body lacks the male hormone testosterone, I have begun—after twenty years—to take a weekly 100 mg. dose. My body is developing some muscle tone, but my doctor says it may take at least eighteen months to see a real change. I find myself attracted to a muscular male. I am a nice-looking guy: forty-five years old, 6'4", 230 lbs, salt/pepper hair, brown "bedroom" eyes, black mustache and beard, somewhat hairy, small endowment and balls, nonsmoker, light drinker, no drugs, HIV neg. I would appreciate your comments. I do respond to ads, and will continue to do so. If you print my name, please use my first and middle names only. I still live in the same city as my folks, and they are not aware of my lifestyle.

John M., Roanoke, VA

Dear John,

Although you tell a good portion of your life story, you do not indicate how much sexual/SM experience you have had. I suspect this had been somewhat limited. At least, I detect a modicum of naïveté in your initial statement. Be that as it may, you present an unusual problem. At the present, you apparently have a body with a somewhat feminine delineation—and there are a lot of guys who like that. However, at the same time you are in the process of trying to change yourself into a more masculine mode. This sounds great, too, except that the guys who like you one way may not be as attracted to your other persona. I'd suggest that you not worry so much about finding your life's partner right at the moment. Whether via an ad in *Drummer* (or whatever local publications you have in your area), or personal contact, you should probably experience a little more before you try to get serious with anyone. If the right guy is going to come along, it is most likely to happen unexpectedly—and he is not going to be the image of your fantasies. Just as you're looking for someone to compromise in picking you, you should expect to do the same.

Dear Larry,

I'm a twenty-eight-year-old guy with above-average looks (facially), and I work out regularly, so I have a good body, normal endowment, etc. However, I'm HIV positive, and have been for about five years. I still have no symptoms and get regular checkups to make sure. (T-cells still above 1500.) Naturally, I want to have sex once in a while, and I don't have any problems finding partners. I'm into leather, light SM, bondage, etc., and I'll take either side. I always insist on playing by safe-sex rules, but I don't tell my partner that I'm positive anymore, because when I did, I had a couple walk out on me. Since I play it safe anyway, I don't see where I'm doing anything wrong. But I have been told otherwise. What do you think?

Positive in Houston, TX

Dear Positive,

Yours is a moral dilemma shared by all too many in our community. Those of us who are a little more sophisticated simply assume than any previously unknown partner is HIV positive and behave accordingly—regardless of anything he says. Statistical surveys have shown that an overwhelming proportion of guys will lie to get the sex partner(s) they want. The fact that you are ethical enough to be concerned about it marks you as a person with enough sense of responsibility to abide by the safe-sex rules. That being the case, I don't think it matters what you say. The only important exception might be if your prospective partner asks you outright, when he is going to be Top. In that situation, he might take you at your word and do something he shouldn't, when you can't do anything to stop him.

The letters from these seekers, spaced over more than ten years, express some interesting consistencies. But I don't know how reflective they are of our community as a whole. It strikes me that they are from men who have yet to find a life partner and are still looking. Many within the SM subculture have found what these guys are still hunting, and our next chapter will concentrate more on their questions and problems.

I would remind you, again: in reading these chapters, you should bear in mind that I start with the oldest in each (around 1980–81). Thus the increasing concern with AIDS as we progress through the individual time frames becomes manifest—then it diminishes and starts over in the subsequent chapter(s).

CHAPTER 2

What to Do With Him Once You've Found Him (And How to Keep Him)

Oh, what a problem this can be! It's amazing how many difficulties a guy can encounter in trying to keep himself and his sex partner happy and together—to say nothing of the nearly impossible task of pleasing a lover. Here are a few of the situations that came to my attention. Let's start at the beginning, with a very young one (too young, actually, for Drummer*):*

Dear Sir,

I am a boy, age sixteen, and would like to ask you a few questions. My brother, age fourteen, and I enjoy putting our brother Phil, age twelve, into bondage. We do this at night most of the time, while our mother is away at work and we are alone. Our dad is dead. So far we only tied Phil to his bed, bent over a bar stool, and to a tree out in the woods behind our house. I want to know some new positions we can tie him in. Is it possible to hang him up without hurting him? If so, what position would be best? By his wrists, or upside down by his ankles? I hope you don't think my brother and I are crazy for doing things like this to our younger brother, but Phil likes being tied up. I also would like to know if you agree with me that Phil should be stripped naked when we tie him up. Hope to hear from you soon.

Beginner

Dear Beginner,

As is always the case when a guy in your age range writes to me for advice, I am torn between the desire to help someone who probably needs it more desperately than an adult, and the awareness of the constraints placed upon us by laws and customary moral standards. Because the law requires that a boy's gonads remain dormant until the magical age of eighteen (or twenty-one), it likewise condemns any adult who presumes to offer technical guidance in any sexual area—especially one such as bondage.

If you were an adult, I might advise that the safest form of suspension is accomplished by using all four extremities, especially with a young subject, whose cartilage can be easily damaged. I might also comment that a naked bondage subject is usually more interesting than one who is clothed. However, because you are too young, I can't tell you these things, and I should also discourage you from reading about them. So, quit reading this mag, kid; come see me when you're eighteen (or twenty-one, if that's the law in your locale.)

Despite my evasive answer, the Drummer *editors chickened out on this one, and to my knowledge it never got published. They didn't want to acknowledge that any underage person could possibly be reading this material—all of which is really too bad. There are many sexually precocious youths who could benefit greatly from adult advice, which might well prevent them from making some terrible mistake that could cause permanent physical or emotional damage. When I was that age, what I wouldn't have given for the opportunity to read something like* The Leatherman's Handbook! *It's only thanks to good luck and a healthy constitution that I didn't do some severe damage to myself or to my equally inexperienced partners, strictly through ignorance.*

Dear Sir,

I am thirty-four years old, and I met a great guy. Started going out with him and things were (are) going well except that he likes his tits squeezed, and he tries to pat my butt. I love SM; I have leather. I was wondering if I should get titclamps for him, also start playing (lightly) some scenes with him? Or should I just wait and see. His fantasy is to get fucked by a guy (me) in chaps.

Dizzy in Leather, NYC

Dear Dizzy,

What's your problem? If you're into leather, and if you like SM, why do you even hesitate? It sounds to me as if you've found exactly what many of our readers are breaking their asses to find. And if his "patting your butt" means he'd like to use those clamps on you...well, why not just ride the whirlwind?

A lot of guys hold back from their initial SM engagements for several different reasons, one of the most common being fear of the unknown—another being the deep-seated guilt we are conditioned to have when our longings tend toward the bizarre or unusual. It's such a shame there are so many forces in our society that try to prevent us from enjoying our own sexuality, often making us feel guilty even when we finally decide to go ahead and do it, anyway. Here's a classic case of a guy who apparently has it offered to him on the proverbial silver platter, and he's still afraid to reach out and take it. Shades of our puritan forebears!

Dear Larry,

My lover and I have been together six years. Both of us are interested in SM, and as we grew to know each other, we mutually communicated these feelings. While we did not have a Master/slave relationship outside the bedroom, I was usually Top, and we enjoyed our scenes very much.

About two years ago, that changed. While having sex, I shoved the blunt end of a whip into his mouth and broke a tooth. When he started to bitch, I lost control and beat his ass bloody—a nonsexual act that rendered the scene a total failure. Since then I have tried to talk to him about it, but

he refuses to communicate, and our sex life has become
nonexistent. On weekends he'll get on his skins and go to
the bars, where he has been getting involved in progres-
sively heavier scenes—he comes home smelling of piss and
covered with welts, etc. Often, I'll find he's taken our toys
into the bathroom and locked himself in, jacking off in
front of the mirror.

Once a month we have a true rape scene, which is fun for
me, but not enough. Things can't go on this way, but I
hate to throw out six otherwise-great years. Can you offer
any insights or suggestions? Please, no name or city.

Disaffected, East Coast

Dear Dis.,

Too often, I think, we find ourselves hanging on to a relationship long after we've lost it because we remember how
good it was or how good we thought it was going to be. When
your sexual partner prefers Merry Palm to the real thing, it's time
to look elsewhere. Six years may seem a lot to lose, but it's best
to cut your losses before it becomes ten or twelve.

*Interesting, that I answered this one as I did. It was 1983, just
before we realized what AIDS was going to do to our community
and to the status of relationships. I think I might well advise differently today—specifically, that the partner with the superfluity of
outside contacts is dangerous (and was when this was written,
although we didn't know how dangerous). However, a six-year
relationship, even if it is to become asexual, has a greater value
today than it did ten or twelve years ago. I might suggest that
"Dis" opt for that, if he could reconcile his other feelings, and if he
could ever merit his partner's trust again. My feeling on that
score, however, is that if the guy really didn't trust him anymore,
he wouldn't have permitted the rape scenes. That being the case, I
would suspect that the guy's sexual attraction had faded to a dull
glimmer.*

Dear Master Larry,

When Master Sam, a burly, macho Italian, is using his
wide leather strap across my ass, i use my tube sock to

muffle the whines, whimpering, screams and moans from the painful application to my burning flesh. But, Sir, how can i stop the tears and crying from the pain? Master gets irritated at my crying/tears, and he seems to extend the deserved punishment into something that is almost more than i can handle. My feeble explanations only merit a slap across the face. i am a lazy and disobedient slave, so i am not complaining about my punishment. Master Sam lays the leather generously and crisscrossed to produce a juicy red rump. But neither of us wants the tears to flow. Sir, any suggestions?

Respectfully,
jason, a slave, CA

Dear jason,

The only way to stop the tears is psychological. you must come to a mental set wherein you command yourself not to shed tears. you must start by learning not to cry out or whimper while you're getting your ass reddened, since that entire complex of responses ties in with the tears. It will not be easy, but if it's so important to you, give it a try. Personally, I like to hear the cries and see the tears. How else can a man know he's doing his best?

When I answered this one, I half-expected to get a letter from some quasi-professional, telling me that tears can be controlled physically, perhaps with some drug. So far, after ten years, nothing has come in.

Dear Mr. Townsend,

For the past eight years I have been involved in the FF scene. For the first three years, I had two regular weekly bottoms, both of whom were heavy Tops on the home front, but came to me to release their fantasies without shattering their images with their "home" slaves. After three years of this, one of the men asked me to become his slave, provided I would take care of his "fist" needs on command. This worked well for a couple of years, until Daddy began feeling the need to fist me. He went through some obvious

emotional turmoil over this, during which he became needlessly aggressive and wouldn't allow me to offer any advice,
even when he wasn't able to do a proper insertion. When I
tried to offer some guidance on the basis of my own past
experience, he really roughed me up...split lip, etc. Our
relationship is now somewhat uncertain, solely because of
Daddy's inability to Top me in an FF scene. I know it has
to do with guilts and fears stemming from childhood and
his racial/religious (Italian) background. I want him inside
me, but I am afraid of what happened before. Can you give
me any advice as to getting suggestions across without
another broken lip or nose?

Sad in Sheepshead Bay

Dear Sad,

   You're in much the same position as the psychological counselor who sees (or thinks he sees) exactly what his client's
problem is, but can't maneuver the guy into discovering it for
himself. I find Daddy's violence a bit disturbing because he is
probably on an even heavier guilt trip than you realize. But I
think you basically understand the situation. You are in an
unusual Top/bottom/Master/slave relationship, however, and
despite your both willing it otherwise, Daddy can not be the
complete Master until he resolves this FF role dilemma—at
least not within his own mind. If he follows the classic pattern,
he will be able to contain the guilt over being what he is only
by being Master/Top in every aspect of your relationship. You
might, if you handle it delicately enough, convince him to let you
teach him the techniques he lacks by both of you working
together, topping a third person. This is assuming that his inability to fist you truly stems from his not knowing how—and not
from some other emotional blockage. In any case, you are dealing with a fairly complex psycho/emotional problem. It might
be more than you can handle without some professional assistance.

   *When one partner gets physically violent, it is always tempting
to tell the recipient of the abuse to break it off and, if necessary, to
head for the hills. However, in male-to-male SM relationships*

(even more commonly than in heterosexual abuse situations) there is the possibility that the abused partner actually wants this to happen. I remember a friend some years ago showing me the terrible bruises and lacerations he had received the night before when he had submitted to a Hell's Angel and had barely survived to tell about it. He got a hard-on as he related the details to me—obviously happy as a pig in shit!

Dear Larry,

Although I try to practice it as safely as possible, I am very much addicted to fisting, and just find myself behaving like a caged animal if I can't feel a strong, probing hand up my ass every so often. In keeping with this, I have been insisting that my Top use lots of lubricant (much more than they usually do), to make sure I don't get torn up. A friend of mine has been telling me that this can cause other problems, particularly appendicitis if the lubricant (especially a "hot" variety) gets into the appendix. Is this really something I should worry about?

Hot Bottom, Houston, TX

Dear Hot,

Whatever else the lubricant may do, it is highly unlikely to affect your appendix. The anus is at one end of the colon; the appendix is at the other, attached just past the point where it joins the small intestine. If you are using one of the sterile water-soluble lubricants it isn't going to do any harm. The dangers of fisting—as I'm sure you are well aware—come from other sources. The large amount of lubricant could cause you to lose a larger amount of the "good bacteria" you need in your bowel for it to perform its normal functions. It's the same problem the enema guys have. You should drink lots of fruit juice and eat a little yogurt to help them along.

Advising a guy on anal activities can be tricky, and I always tried to read between the lines to gain an idea of his degree of experience—or his sanity. Remember that sticking foreign objects up the old poop-chute is far and away a more common practice that anyone short of an emergency-room doctor can possibly real-

ize. For this reason I seldom tried to discourage it, merely did my best to help the guy do it with minimal risk. Here's a little different variation:

Dear Larry,

I have been a fan of yours and of *Drummer*'s for more years than I'd care to admit, but I've never seen any comments from either source on my main area of activity, or worry. I'm very much into enemas (which I know both of you have written about), but my concern is: Can this be considered "safe sex?" The scenes I've been involved with over the last three or four years have not involved such things as asslicking or exchange of body fluids. And, of course, all the voided material simply goes down the toilet. Would you give me your opinion, please, and any suggestions? I really don't want to stop if I don't have to.

Ward, K. C.

Dear Ward,

Since the enema has never been my scene, I may overlook some aspect of the action more apparent to the aficionado. With that disclaimer in place, I would say that you are probably not in any more jeopardy than in a vanilla scene of sucking and fucking (using rubbers, etc.). I assume you are not using the same nozzle on different guys, nor letting any material back up into a tube so that it could get transferred from one gut to another. Of course, any assplay involves the chance risk of contact between fecal material and any open wound on your hands, arms, etc. This is a universal danger, however, and certainly not confined to your specialty. As enema nozzles are cheap compared to Bardex equipment, I might also remind you of the danger in using this more expensive paraphernalia on more than one person. A frequent wash-up might also be a good idea. And be sure you flush the toilet!

Dear Larry "SIR":

I am a twenty-three-year-old slave, living in Los Angeles—as yet unowned by any Master. I am writing to you because

I don't know where else to turn. I am not new to the leather/SM scene. I have experienced a good deal of what this culture has to offer and have evolved into a very dedicated bottom/slave. The problem is that in this area it has been nearly impossible to find a Master interested in more than a night or weekend fantasy. I am very serious about my need to serve and be trained in the strictest sense by a capable, experienced Master. I am looking for a dead serious commitment. How does someone like me move into the circles of DEAD SERIOUS SM relationships in the L.A. or California areas? I don't believe I can find this Master in the personals or in the bars on Saturday nights. I am twenty-three, 5'9", blond hair—high and tight, an ex-marine, bodybuilder, blue eyes, 7 1/2" thick, 18" neck, 19" biceps, 52" chest, 30" waist. College graduate, I am very physical and athletic and great-looking. Please write soon and help me learn how I can move into the world of servitude.

Slave R, Los Angeles, CA

Dear Slave R,

I am going to devote a good portion of this column to answering you because I feel that your problem is an absolutely classic example of the problems a great many people have in fulfilling their SM desires. Unlike so many others, you have the physical attributes to make you a desirable quantity. So the reason you are failing is not because you're too old or too homely to attract the sort of man you wish to meet. Neither, by the tone of your letter, are you a shrinking violet who is afraid to approach another guy.

Because you were local and sounded so great, I made personal contact with you. We had an hour or so of conversation before I took you down to my dungeon and did a little further "research." I subsequently referred you to a friend of mine who is a very active, experienced Top because I wanted to see how you might do with him. Both sessions left a good deal to be desired, and I would like to share my thoughts on this with you and—since you wrote to me through *Drummer*—with our readers.

First, let me note that you did not make any deceptive claims as to your physical attributes. You were exactly what you said you were in this respect. In speaking with you, I felt that you made all the correct responses, except that even before we went into a scene, I picked up on the first problem—one which is very common to bright, educated young men. This is the tendency to intellectualize your past and projected experiences. I am very cognizant of this tendency, because I went through it myself at your age and had one hell of a time forcing myself to overcome it. You simply can not respond on a basic, physical (animal?) level when your mental process is set on this other wave length. It holds you back from a full participation in the scene. Your body is there, but your mind is elsewhere. And, despite any claims to the contrary, a Top is not looking for a gentleman or an intellectual encounter session; he wants a physically attractive, responsive subject.

Secondly, you claimed a quasi-slave status, or at least orientation. You are not a slave; you are a bottom. But as a bottom, you again manifest another classic syndrome of the bright, basically aggressive young man. You want to submit in the respect of being bound and subjected to a degree of humiliation. But you are unwilling to relinquish control of the interaction. There are certain things you want done to you; but beyond this relatively narrow range, you resist the Top's direction. This happened first in our session; and, because I thought it might just have been me, I referred you to my friend. He reported the same responses.

This, again, is not an insurmountable problem, but it is one you will have to address before you achieve the type of relationship you seem really to desire.

Then there is the "roadblock" of your appearance. It's all to your advantage in attracting the Top, but once the contact is made you've got to forget how beautiful you are. The weapon that wins the cruising battle becomes overkill when you permit its attendant vanity (however justified it might be) to impinge upon your relationship with this man to whom you have supposedly submitted. When you tell your Top that you are going to do something you wish to do because you are "younger, bigger and stronger than he is," you are completely shattering the

Master/slave facade. Coming in the first session, as happened with my friend, it can turn him off so completely that he really won't care whether or not you come back. In fact, his comment to me was "Sure, he's beautiful, but I've got two other guys coming to me who are just as gorgeous. Who needs to put up with this bullshit?"

So there you have it in a nutshell. You have what it takes to get the Top interested, but if you want more than one-night stands (and marginally satisfactory ones, at that), you must look to yourself and reevaluate these facets of your own personality and the responses which they manifest. A good Top is not easy to find, and for that reason he can generally be just as selective as you in picking the partner with whom he is going to establish a relationship. It's really a matter of suppressing your own ego; i.e., subordinating it to that of the Top. This is the difference between a real slave and just another bottom. I can see many positive qualities in your personality. Don't think I am selling you short. If I didn't think the potential was there, I wouldn't be laying it out in such detail.

I hope "Slave R" eventually met the guy who could teach him to be the kind of sex partner he really wanted to be. He was a nice, personable kid, very bright, and certainly a gorgeous hunk! He had everything going for him except the ability to submit. And an ex-marine, at that. You know the basic masochism had to be there.

Naturally, his letter and my answer stirred up a lot of controversy; but strangely enough, the most interesting letters were not addressed to me, but to the Drummer *editors, and run in the "letters from the readers" columns. However, they did spark an interesting reply from my friend, to whom I had referred "Slave R."*

Dear Larry,

When you referred "Slave R" to me several months ago, I had no idea that the encounter would generate so much controversy. Now that it has, I may as well put in my two cents worth as the "other Top." M.C.'s well-conceived letter ("Malecall," *Drummer* **# 100) makes some valid points and gives an overview of a fantasy/lifestyle which—although**

"not in the majority" according to M.C.—is, I'm sure, shared by a significant number of *Drummer* readers (at least the fantasy part). This TOTAL dominance may be exactly what Slave R was looking for, in which case he has probably contacted M.C. by now. If so, I'd be eager to know the outcome. During my acquaintance with R, it was made very clear that any "servitude" would be subject to availability after considerations of employment, schooling, and several other commitments. I have no problem with this as I am not available for "a scene" or "play" twenty-four hours a day, either. Would M.C. deprive R of his bright future and present pleasures to be replaced with the satisfaction of a sexual/psychological need for complete dominance? If not, it is hard to imagine the mental contortions which would maintain the conviction of total dominance/submission when the submission is subordinated to a multitude of prior decisions and obligations. At any rate, I enjoyed R, both personally and sexually, and wish him the very best in discovering what he wants.

Top B, Los Angeles, CA

Dear Top B,

You've said it just about the way it is, I think. R is a nice kid—and a very bright young man. I like him, and it was certainly not my intention to hurt him by my previous comments. We all face the need to order our priorities in life, and especially during our twenties we are torn between the urgings of brain and balls. It's a fortunate man indeed who can balance these and satisfy both sets of needs. "Living in Leather" is—and must remain—an unobtainable dream for the vast majority of leather/SM men. The practical considerations of earning a living, getting an education, or simply fulfilling the social and familial obligations that life heaps upon us make it impossible to follow our genital urgings 100 percent of the time. In fact, for a great many guys—especially during the current health crisis—the opportunity to express these "leather lusts" comes only in the form of fantasy. And, when all is said and done, isn't that what we (*Drummer*, Yours Truly, etc.) are here for?

Interestingly, our next letter is from a bottom who is unhappy to find the same attitude in his Tops and in himself, as Top B and I found disturbing in Slave R—although this guy's fantasies go a little above and beyond.

Dear Sir:
I'm twenty-six, and I've been into SM sex for about eight years—usually as the bottom, and I have fairly extensive experience in this. When I think of what leather means to me, it boils down to surrendering my will to the dominance and strength of another man, absorbing his power and "floating" on the response and feelings. Over time, however, I have found myself becoming overly analytical of my sexuality, to the point where it interferes with my enjoyment of a scene. On the one hand, I want my Top to "do it," not talk about it; on the other, I have some very particular things I'd like him to do (or let me do to him), but I'm afraid that if I try to tell him, I'll break the mood of the scene. As the submissive partner, I can't very well tell my Top; "Just shut up and do it," or go into a lengthy dialogue as to what I would like to have happen. And some of the things I'd like are not easy to describe to a newly found Top. For instance, I love to eat ass. Nothing turns me on more than having a big butch fucker sit on my face with my nose up his butt-hole while he jerks off. I also like being forced to smell his farts while he shoves my face into his crack. But I can't go around and say that to someone who is calling the shots. I'm also scared that if I get up the courage to tell him about my fetishes, he'll either think I'm sick or trying to tell him what to do. How can I get into it without words? I feel as if the only way I'll be happy is to learn to communicate telepathically, and I know that's impossible.

Bottom, Houston, TX

Dear Bottom,
To speak or not to speak, is that the question? (Sorry, Will!) You've got the same problem that most of us have, whether we're Tops or bottoms. We find a guy who turns us on physi-

cally, and we get into a scene with him. We want to have a good time, and we want him to have a good time, but we're afraid to fuck it up by saying the wrong thing. How many poor scenes might have been good—and how many good scenes might have been better—if the right words had just been spoken at the right time?

First things first: If the Top is turning you off by talking too much, you can often just tell him so, but phrase it as a compliment: "It's okay, I trust you, Sir; you don't have to reassure me." Or catch him at the beginning of the scene and simply lay it out before he's had a chance to talk and therefore can't perceive your comments as criticism of him. If he's a good Top, he should give you a chance to state some limits and tell him of any physical problems you have that are relevant to a scene. Just work the request into this. As to telling him what you'd like to do, I've found myself responding more positively to a bottom who phrases it so that it sounds more like a general surrender. In your case you might say something like: "...and I'm really turned on to you, Sir. You could even sit on my face, etc." If he picks up on it, you're in; if he doesn't, there's not much more you can do. (Although in light of the current health crisis, are you sure you want to do this? If such a request should prove a turnoff for the Top, it could very well be because you scare him. "If this guy is willing to do this with me, how many others has be done it with? Am I going to get more than just a sex scene from him?" At this particular time in our gay experience, guys who seem willing to engage in unsafe sex are understandably subject to rejection.)

Dear Mr. Townsend,

I am more or less of a novice in SM—twenty-four years old, with my first leathersex about two years ago. I'm no Adonis, but I seem able to attract the type of Tops I want. My problem is that I have also seen a number of my friends shot down by the current epidemic; and although I enjoy almost anything short of mutilation, I am really afraid to let a strange Top take full control for fear he won't observe all the safe-sex rules. Harping on this at the beginning of a scene—much less questioning the guy to make sure he knows what his limitations must be—can really fuck up the dominance/submission relationship. If it were not for the fact that I may literally be putting my life on the line, I wouldn't be so concerned about it. (I mean to say that I have very few other limits insofar as things he can do to me.) Can you offer any helpful advice? I would imagine a lot of your other readers are in the same situation.

Name Withheld

Dear Withheld,

A sensible Top will know the rules and abide by them, so I think your biggest problem is selecting a guy who isn't gone on drugs, or so infatuated with his own ego that he isn't going to have a concern for you. With this kind of man, you should be able to establish the "rules of the game" well ahead of time; i.e., in the bar or wherever you meet, long before you ever enter the play area. There is also the situation which I have found—and discussed at length with several good Tops—in which they have been tested regularly for AIDS antibodies and have always been negative. Their feeling is that whereas they will generally stay within the rules set forth by the medical establishment, they do not look ón themselves as potential threats to their bottoms. For this reason, they may appear more casual than they really are to the men with whom they are playing. Although I would not recommend that anyone simply ignore the rules, I can see a certain validity in a man's feeling and projecting his own healthy condition. Bear in mind that the major dangers lie in anal sex, SM sex which draws blood, and water sports. You might concentrate on these as your limits. It has always been the bottom's right to state these, and you are not exceeding privilege by doing so. And if in doubt...well, there's always Merry Palm.

Since the time of this letter, I've had a number of people telling me that water sports really are not particularly dangerous, assuming an intact skin on the bottom, and no fluid into the face. (We're discussing piss scenes, in case there is some question.) My feeling is twofold. First, it's too easy for urine to splash into the face, or to find

*some skin abrasion that may have previously gone unnoticed.
Secondly, too many guys get carried away and after a good, hot piss
scene will progress into some other activities while the urine is still
on the skin. An additional word of caution: Even with an HIV
negative Top, don't let the urine get into your eyes. A gonorrhea
infection can cause permanent blindness, while other microbes
can cause a variety of other serious infections that have nothing to
do with AIDS.*

Dear Larry,
  **I have two questions I hope you can answer: (1) I'm
fairly small and am afraid to get fucked because I'm afraid
I'll be injured. How can I tell if a cock is too big for me? (2)
There are electric shockers on sale in stores where I live. Can
a person use these on himself? Thanks!**
                                                C. H., Tulsa, OK

Dear C. H.,
  The dangers of getting fucked are difficult to assess because
they will vary so greatly from one person to another. It is not so
much the size of the anal opening that determines this, as the
length (depth) between the opening and point at which the
anal canal turns to connect with the colon. Most damage from
ass-fucking occurs because the invading cock hits the top, so to
speak, and stretches the tissues, sometimes tearing them. As a
general rule, I would say that an average-size cock probably
won't do any damage unless the guy gets too violent. Unfortunately, you probably won't find a doctor in your area who
can take a look and advise you; although, if you could, this
would give you a better answer. As to the "shockers," I assume
you mean cattle prods. These come in various strengths and
are intended to be used on animals with hides considerably
thicker than yours. The power of the prod is usually determined
by the number of batteries ("C" cells, mostly) that it holds. If
you're going to play with one, don't exceed three cells, and
don't use the 9-volt battery model, even though it is smaller than
the others and looks less lethal. It isn't. Don't use it above the
waist, and then only on large muscles (butt or upper thighs). It

is much more fun to use it on someone else (or have him use it on you), but everyone to his own taste.

Since answering this one, I have seen some pretty heavy use of cattle prods in a variety of scenes—and have used one a few times myself when the damned slave needed to be reminded of his status. Now, or course, they have come out with "stun guns" that are intended as defensive weapons to ward off would-be attackers. The most powerful of these can really knock a guy on his ass! A friend of mine had one bottom who wanted to be stunned into unconsciousness when he arrived and subsequently wake up in full bondage for a heavy session. I know they did this several times without any apparent ill aftereffects, but I don't think I'd recommend it as a standard part of your game plan. Most people are squeamish about electricity, anyway, and these big guns pack an enormous wallop. I'd be afraid of causing a cardiac arrest, especially with a bottom whose medical history is unknown to me. (There I go being supercautious again!)

Dear Larry,

I am a bondage enthusiast as either Top or bottom. I also have an underwear fetish, in that I like to look at guys' briefs, as well as smell them—especially if they have been worn for a few days. In my last couple of encounters, the Tops have used their underwear on me as gags. I find this a big turn-on, but I am now wondering if it falls within the limits of "safe sex." All other aspects of my scenes are discussed beforehand to assure that we do not engage in unsafe practices. What's your opinion?

David, NY

Dear David,

The name of the game in safe sex is no exchange of body fluids. This includes (for sure) blood, semen, urine and fecal materials. It may also include (debatably) saliva, sweat, and tears. Although orally ingesting these fluids is considered a lower risk than blood-to-blood or anal contamination, there is still that smaller degree of danger. On the other hand, the AIDS virus will not survive for very long outside a warm, moist environment. If being gagged with a pair of dirty shorts is really important to you, I'd suggest that you toss them into a corner for a couple of days before allowing them to be used on you.

And if you get your Top to go home without his shorts—and he's any good—it might be an effective way to get him back for a second session. Especially if they're Calvin Kleins; them puppies are expensive!

Dear Larry,

A good bottom is hard to find! Because of our current health crisis, safe sex is the order of the day. I work with my bottoms in this regard. On the other hand, they generally don't work with me. I'm a rough-'n-ready guy, and safe sex does pose limitations which are emotionally and psychologically hard to deal with. I find most of the desirable bottoms unwilling to cooperate with the Top in order to bring pleasure to both. Several Tops and Masters I know just don't have sex anymore because of the bad attitude of bottoms in general. I usually don't, either. In the past, Tops were hot, always ready to go, in control, and very responsible. Our health crisis has changed that; even the hottest Tops need help to cope with the change in sex styles. If the bottoms don't start showing some responsibility, too, they won't have a Top to be with. Is it too much to ask a bottom to be aware of his responsibilities, or is a bottom just a bottom?

Clifford, San Francisco, CA

Dear Clifford,

Although your tone is almost bitter, and your attitude more pessimistic than I like to hear, you are really stating the case for a lot of us. It has also been my experience that Tops, who are at lower risk then bottoms, tend to be (generally speaking) much more wary of unsafe behavior. I would also go a step further and state my own feeling that I am really afraid of a bottom who has "been around"; i.e., a guy who has the experience to make him a more interesting sex partner. I keep trying to picture the number and types of men he has been with over the previous five years. In effect, I'm having vicarious sex with each of them when I make it with this little M. So, when I roll on that rubber, it's really more for my own protection than his.

Sir:

i am a white male, forty-two years old. i placed a *Drummer* ad that was answered by a New York City Master. After a couple of letters back and forth, he started telling me that just because i was a beginner in leathersex wasn't going to stop him from using me any way he wanted, and that because i was his slave he could rent me out to other people; i would be bound and whipped until i was bleeding, etc. Well, i told him i wasn't into being disfigured, and that i thought our correspondence had gone just about far enough. i didn't want to be his slave, and we should forget the whole thing. He wrote back that he had contacts all over the world who would see that he got what he wanted—that once i had become his slave, he was the only one who could break the relationship. His tone scared me because some of what he wrote sounded like a death threat; so i went to the police to see what i should do. Sir, i have read your books, and i don't see anything in them to justify what this man wanted to do to me. i am interested in finding a Master i can please, but not in being killed. Am i wrong, Sir?

W, Vermont

Dear W,

It's unfortunate that you were not experienced enough to know that a Master-slave relationship played by mail is really more of a game than anything else. Some Tops get carried away, expressing fantasies in their letters that they never would—or could—actually enact. I doubt you were ever in any danger, and it's too bad you had to consult the authorities. If I know my cops, all you accomplished by this was to give them a good story to pass around at their periodic bull sessions.

This was one of several letters I received on this subject, and in each case I have been surprised at the naïveté of the bottom. But, if the through-the-mail Top can be convincing enough, I guess this is going to be the inevitable—although hopefully occasional, result. Another concrete example of "It takes all kinds..."

Dear Larry,

I really want to fuck a nice, tight little ass—to lie on top of it and pound my cock into a warm, grasping hole. I haven't done this in four or five years. You know why. But I've gotten to a stage where I need it so desperately, I could even bring myself to do it with a rubber (which I hate). But how safe do you think they really are? Various articles seem to be telling us that a condom is the best thing to use if you can't go without the sex. Well, I can't go without much longer, but I don't want to take a big risk. What's the problem? Are they apt to leak? Or break? Why is there the implication that they just aren't quite 100 percent safe?

Horny, Dallas, TX

Dear Horny,

Because they may *not* be 100 percent. A good brand-name condom is not likely to leak, but it can break. There is also the chance of passing the virus in some other way. Just recently *(Jan 1988—ed.)* the CDC in Georgia has been in dispute with the Masters and Johnson people over the possibility of saliva acting as a medium for transmission. On the other hand, if you're doing the fucking, you are at minimal risk inside your rubber. A little care in the selection of a partner can also greatly reduce the danger.

In reading over this answer, I find it a little naïve by more current standards. Contemporary theory (1994) is that saliva is an unlikely medium of HIV transmission, and tends to kill it. Also, the guy doing the fucking has always *been at minimal risk. It's my comment about selection of partner that bothers me today. Just because the guy looks healthy should not lull you into a sense of security. And "social status" is no guarantee, either. Every casual trick should be presumed HIV positive.*

Dear Larry,

I have a sort of strange question, but I hope you won't

just laugh at me. I'm a bottom (not a slave), and I have a regular Master who really likes to work me over, and who usually ends up fucking me. (We're both antibody negative, etc., so no problem there. We're also monogamous.) My problem is that I have a terrible time with my guts. I just can't seem to empty myself completely, and I'm always afraid I'm going to dirty my Master. I have tried taking an enema before I go to meet him, but he always likes to get together early, have dinner, then come home and play. Even if I eat very lightly, I have problems. I even get gassy sometimes, and the long time span between our initial meeting and our sex is difficult. I don't want to discuss this with my Master because I'm sure it would be a real turnoff for him. What would you suggest?

Name withheld, West Coast

Dear West,

You may have a mild spastic condition of the colon, which tends to be a physical condition brought on by the emotional tension (excitement) of your impending sexual encounter. Or you may just need a "softener" to help you eliminate more completely early on. In either case, it is a problem that your doctor should be able to solve for you. I note you live in a small town; but even if you don't want to tell all, you can tell your medico enough that he can prescribe a remedy. The condition isn't unique, and it may be the forerunner of a more serious condition that you can prevent if you get treatment now.

Our autonomic nervous system can often play havoc with our normal daily existence, to say nothing of our sexual behavior. It's the same neural network that causes some men to be impotent (or women frigid), that makes us "piss shy" in a public john, or that makes your normally substantial endowment shrink to insignificance in the shower room at the gym. Because these problems (in the above and other forms) are so common and so annoying, there are many kinds of medications on the market to control them, and there are many shrinks making their living(s) by helping people overcome them via counseling and/or psychotherapy. If you have experienced any of these syndromes, don't think you're unique, or even one of a tiny group of victims. The problems are very common, and for this reason you should not be afraid that seeking professional help is going to mark you as some sort of freak or deviate.

Dear Larry,

Although I try to observe the rules of safe sex, I am still getting my share of the action. I've found, however, that most guys I have gone with are interested in having only one ejaculation. Then, as far as they are concerned, the scene is over. I am good for at least a couple more shots, and often come home and jack off afterward because I'm not fully satisfied. Am I oversexed, or what? Shit, I sometimes leave to go home with my cock still hard and ready, while my partner has pooped out and fallen asleep.

C. H., Decatur, GA

Dear C. H.,

You are apparently what Kinsey called a "high-performance male." There is nothing wrong with you, nor with your sex-buddies. I'd suggest you let your partner know that you like to come more than once, and get yourself off an extra time or two before he does. I doubt anyone is going to have serious objections.

What a wonderful, rare find it is for a dedicated cocksucker to get his face stuffed full of good stiff meat, take a hot creamy load, then feel the guy's hands clamp tightly against the back of his head, because the rigid prong is about to deliver another blast—or two! Oh, if "they" could only find a cure, so we could enjoy these pleasures once again! Well, as my most-qualified world-class cocksucker friend has told me, "When the great day comes, the Little Sisters of the Poor may have to wheel me into the tearoom, but I'm going to get my lips around another few dicks before I go." His is a display of true courage and devotion.

Dear Larry,

About a year ago i became the slave of lovers who are both Masters. i have been very happy serving them. At the beginning they explained that they enjoyed fisting and that i would be expected to eventually take their fists. They have worked my hole on a regular basis until i can now take an arm almost to the elbow. At that point it seems to hit rock bottom. Now they have told me they intend to keep expanding my fuckhole until they can lock their fingers, hold hands, and double-fist me. i would never complain unless i felt they were physically damaging me. My question is: Is there a limit to how big my fuckhole can get, and if it gets that big, will it cause me any problems? i feel proud to take what my Masters want to give me, and i have no problems so far.

slave r. j.

Dear r. j.,

I'm always hesitant to put myself in the position of advising a slave to dispute his Master's will. Nine out of ten times the Top knows what he's doing, and if he threatens to do something destructive to the bottom, it's often more for effect than reality. But it is that tenth instance that sometimes worries me. In your case, it sounds like they are trying for greater width in opening you up, without necessarily going for greater depth. That being the case, the worst they'll probably do is leave you with a sagging pucker-string. Of course, there are physical risks in fist-fucking, as I'm sure you already know. If your Top is experienced, sane, and sober, you will usually have little to worry about, although accidents can still happen to the best of us.

Fisting questions were always a tricky proposition because the scene is fraught with dangers, even under the most ideal circumstances. Most frightening to me was the tendency for people to use drugs during a session, which rendered them less aware of their behavior at the very time when they should be most alert. This kid doesn't mention that aspect of his scenes, so perhaps it wasn't a problem. His description of his paired Masters sounded ominous, but it was hard to tell at long distance. They might have been okay, but they might also have been a pair of maniacs. Then, interestingly, I got a letter from him a couple of years later (October 1991):

Sir Larry Townsend,

I doubt that you remember me, but my name is Casey. I used to go by r. j. until my Masters renamed me. I hope I'm not wasting your time, but my problem is not the type you would take to your mother. In my first letter I expressed some concerns about how big my Masters wanted to make my fuckhole.

In June my two Masters told me that they had decided to break up. I had been with them for over three years. I was devastated. I blamed myself for a while about the breakup. I thought that maybe if I had been a better slave, they would still be together. In the settlement and split-up, I became the property of Master Ed, and we moved out of the house and into an apartment.

Yesterday Master Ed told me that someone offered to buy me and that he really needed the money, so they worked out a deal. He must be someone who knows me because, as far as I know, Master Ed never exhibited me to anyone for the express purpose of selling me. But since the breakup he has been playing with me with other people. I am writing this letter very quickly because my new Master is coming over tonight to pick me up.

I never told them, but I loved both my Masters. Since serving them, I have never been happier or more fulfilled in my entire life. I felt I had found my reason to exist. I'm ashamed to admit it, but I cried all last night over this. I feel like the best part of my life is over. My stomach keeps turning over and over, and I don't know what to think. Everything came to an end so suddenly. Their breakup, my being sold. I still love them both.

I trust Master Ed. He said my new Master will pay him half of the money tonight and if I work out for him, the other half in six months. It's not like I couldn't just walk away, but I really feel that I am Master Ed's property, and that if he wants to sell me, it's his business.

I'm so upset and sad right now I can't think straight. Please, what do you think I should do? I don't want Master Ed to think I'm questioning his authority and right to do what he wants with me, but everything is happening so quickly. I never thought about them breaking up or me getting sold.

Confused, but loyal slave,
Casey, AKA r. j., San Francisco, CA

I advised Casey to go along with the arrangement, and see if the situation was one he could live with. (Although he did not give me time to answer him before the fateful moment arrived, I did send him a note, for whatever help that might have been.) Naturally, a slave can always terminate the relationship, and Casey seemed perfectly aware of this. I never heard from him again, so I don't know how he finally resolved his ownership. He was obviously a good slave, and many of those I quote and advise in Chapter 11 would do well to try understanding his attitude.

Dear Larry,

In several stories that I have read recently there have been scenes involving armpit shaving or licking—worship, if you will. I find this particularly exciting because it has always been one of the activities that really turned me on (either doing it, or having it done to me.) I hope that this trend continues to grow as it should, since it has to be completely safe sex, and once a guy tries it he is going to keep going after it. Of course, fucking an armpit has to be the ultimate, and again completely safe. Have you ever tried it? Do you know of any clubs or organizations devoted to this practice?

Aarom Pitt, Cleveland, OH

Dear Aarom,

Your letter, as well as your pseudonym, certainly tweak my funny bone. However, despite my reluctance to "rise to the bait" of a put-on, I'm going to answer you. I know that armpits do have a fetish attraction for some guys. There is hair to be shaved or whatever; there is usually an odor; and an armpit can be manipulated to form a surrogate asshole or pussy. But no, I don't know of any clubs devoted exclusively to this activity. As to my own experience in the area, I have to admit that it is quite limited. I recall one unhappy circumstance a number of years ago, of getting a mouthful of underarm deodorant; and another, when a guy tried it on me and almost tickled me to death. But if you dig it, more power to you; and if someone writes to tell me about a club in your area, I'll pass it on.

As my earlier comments note, I have always (in my own mind) associated armpit action with tickling and "tickle torture," mostly because I'm so ticklish I can't stand to have anyone tongue my pits. I'm told that this is unfortunate—although not unusual—because there is a whole catalog of activities that guys get into with armpits. But there is also a whole new popularity of the tickling scene. I guess if you can't play it straight-faced in one, you can get hysterically turned on by the other. Here's another guy's observations on the subject:

Dear Mr. Townsend,

Tit torture and tickle torture are near and dear to my heart. They have always been the center of what I enjoy doing to other people, long before the current health situation. I need help in getting the right "flagging" colors. I finally found one listing that gave dark pink for tit torture. I have not found a listing that gives tickle torture a color. Is there one?

I am finding that a big soft bushy mustache, a rough moist tongue, and sharp ridged teeth to be extremely effective in subduing ticklish people. It is incredible how many supposedly "undiscovered" areas can be found, in addition to the usual ones. The same goes for tit torture. The sharp-ridged teeth give one so much more "control" over titclamps. Teeth don't slip off, and they give an infinite variety of pressure instantly to subdue reluctant people.

Robert, Rocky Hill, CT

Dear Robert,

The wearing of colors (hankies) to display one's interests has been a subject for much tongue-in-cheek advice. Several of the most widely circulated lists have resulted from a couple of guys sitting down and trying to tag every conceivable activity with the most outlandish hue imaginable. I think I have seen one person wearing dark pink in all of my travels, and I suspect its greatest effect was to cause a few people to ask the wearer what it symbolized. Whatever color you or I might decide to assign to tickle torture would probably work in much the same way. And, at this point, there really aren't many colors left. I might also add a word of caution in the tickle situation. If you tie the guy down and go at him without proper preliminaries, you can end up with an hysterical bottom, totally turned off to the entire scene. Not always a good way to go.

Breaking in a novice is not always easy—especially in tickle torture; and if you're looking for this kind of action, do your best to find an experienced Top who seems to have a reasonably patient nature. Of course, this need not apply solely to tickling situations. Here's another rather typical dilemma for the novice—not realizing how much his fantasized abuse is going to hurt, or how much damage it can do:

Dear Larry,

For a long time—years, that is—my fantasy was to be tied up and worked over by a real Master, but to be bound in a very specific way. I wanted to be standing up in the center of a room, or at least far enough away from any wall or other obstruction that the guy could reach me from any angle. Then I wanted to have my hands spread wide apart, suspended from the ceiling by a pair of ropes or chains. (But with my feet still on the floor.) I wanted to be left there for maybe a couple of hours, or even more, while my Master really worked me over with a leather strap, went into some extensive tit-and-ball torture, etc.

I was only recently able to find someone to do this, when I made a trip to Chicago. It was very exciting at the start of the session; but as it went on, my arms and finally my whole body began to get really fatigued. After a little over an hour, the pain from just the bondage got so bad I was begging him to let me down, which he eventually did. Now, a week later, the little finger on my left hand is still numb, although he used leather cuffs on my wrists, so I didn't really get cut or anything. Do you think I've got some kind of permanent damage? I'm afraid to go to my regular doctor because I don't know how to explain what happened to cause the problem.

Frightened slave, Des Moines, IA

Dear slave,

By the time you receive my answer (which I'm sending directly, so you get it before all the delays in publication), hopefully your problem will have cleared up. If not, you'd better bite the bullet and go to a doctor. Long-term bondage can damage a nerve, although in the situation you describe, it would be unusual for the condition to be more than temporary; i.e., to last more than a couple of weeks. Nerves that lie close enough to the surface of the skin to be pinched during a relatively light bondage session have a great regenerative capacity. But there is a lesson to be learned from this—perhaps more than one. First, it's not a good idea to tie someone up for too long a time with his extremities raised significantly above the level of his heart. Secondly, it doesn't hurt to remember that a good JO fantasy can often become a very different ball of wax in reality. Bondage can be exhausting to muscles that are not used to it, and the heavy whipping of your imagination can really hurt when it actually happens to you. (If you do need to see a doctor, tell him you wrapped a rope around your wrist in the course of moving a heavy piece of furniture. The resulting damage would be about the same.)

Dear Larry,

In response to your request for details from the armpit lovers, my Daddy and I have always had a great affection for each other's pits. When we met five years ago, after I fell for his handsome face, eyes, and lips, I recall being turned on next by snuggling up under his thick leather jacket, where his naked torso was dripping in sweat. Later, I spent the evening sleeping with my face buried in his big, delicious pit.

Nothing in the world makes me feel more content and inspired then a good long whiff from my Daddy's underarm. Now he orders me to stop using deodorant a week or more before we meet for a scene. We then have two pacifiers for each other: our cocks and our overhead embraces. It takes about four days to work up a real sweet pit aroma and peter breath; alas, about the time our visits must come to an end. These are not stale smells we're talking about! Sweat is the essence of fresh and living manhood which our fastidious society forces us to mask. Though this practice does not seem to lend itself to organized clubs, as your reader inquired, I can see a role for groups in love with sweaty and dark, tender areas—without going into the hard-core realm of raunch, scat, and cheese. Even if you aren't playing with pits *themselves*, Larry, haven't you ever judged a man by the pleasure of his body odor?

Bob, Austin, TX

Dear Bob,

Of course, the odor of the guy you are sizing up for a night's adventure is an important component of his positive or negative valence. Whatever part of him appeals to any of your senses is going to be determinant to your level of desire. Whatever blows your skirt, as "they" say. But I notice you turn thumbs down on raunch, scat, and cheese. You'd have lots of argument on either of the three scores, so who's to say who's right? Or is there a right?

Dear Larry,

I have been in a monogamous relationship for over seven years. My partner and I are HIV negative. Our sexuality has evolved greatly over the years, and we have recently branched out to include other men as playmates. Several of these guys want us to sit on their faces for prolonged rimming sessions and feeding. My question is, how safe is it to be the Top in a scat scene? It seems to me that this role would be risk-free. Is feeding fecal material or food from the rectum any more dangerous than simple rimming? Please advise me of your opinion.

Anxious to dish it out, San Francisco, CA

Dear Anxious,

There obviously can be no danger to the donor in any activity where no part of his body is penetrated. I suppose one could make the farfetched case of an asshole with an open sore coming into contact with a similarly injured tongue—the latter belonging to an HIV-positive man. However, despite my reluctance to place a stamp of "safe sex" on any activity I consider dangerous, I frankly can't see any risk to you or your friend in what you'd like to do. As to what you might pass to your guests...well, that's another story. I hope you're playing safe with all these third parties. HIV+ seems to be frighteningly common in the Bay Area. And by-the-by, if you're getting it on with third parties, you are *not* involved in a monogamous relationship.

Dear Larry Townsend,

I don't know what to do. I've broken up with another lover—the fifth in six years. And again I don't know what went wrong. Yeah, it was the same explanation: "You're really nice, but I'm not ready to settle down." Or "You're one of the best friends I ever had, but I don't like you sexually any more. I hope we can still be friends." (Ha! Fat chance!) I don't know what I'm doing wrong. With the last one, we just came back from an RSVP cruise and he said, "I don't want to date you any more. I need space."

I'm thirty-two, a bottom looking to settle down with a Top. I love intense sex bondage, spanking scenes, dildos, fisting, etc. I'll even go for three-ways. The men I meet are generally into being Top, but after a couple of weeks, months, our sex life peters down—a lot. Then I realize what will be said in another couple of weeks: "You're really nice, but..." I've enclosed a picture. What do you think?

D. P., Chicago, IL

Dear D. P.,

In any relationship that's going to last, it is necessary for each partner to be mature enough to recognize his own failings as well as those of his partner. In order to land five lovers over the space of six years, you must have something going for you—several somethings. On the other hand, you're obviously doing something wrong. You may be attracted to guys who are not emotionally equipped for a long-term situation, in which case the only fault lies in your selection of a partner. Or, as a bottom, you may not be playing the role you should—too submissive? Or the opposite—too pushy and directive when your Top is trying to take control? Maybe it isn't the sex; something else may be responsible for the breakups. There are so many possible variables that it's impossible to make a definitive assessment from long distance, on the basis of the information you've supplied. You have got to be very introspective and willing to do a careful mental evaluation of what's happened in these past failed relationships, and above all to be willing to accept your own shortcomings. In the long run, they are the only ones you are going to be capable of changing. (In your photo, you look like a Top. Do you ever play that role? Might that be something your partners would have liked? Lots of guys switch these days.)

In reading back over the letters and responses I chose for this chapter, I am struck by two very poignant aspects. First is the increased concern with safe sex as we progressed toward the end of the decade—a situation we will see, to a greater or lesser degree, in each chapter of this book. Secondly, there is the attendant concern of so many guys to maintain the relationship they have started. I think this is more prevalent now that it might have been in preceding periods (the 60s and 70s, for instance). But even so, the underlying lust is undiminished, merely forced into a more careful mode of expression. We are not yet losing our sexuality, merely our careless attitude toward its joys and responsibilities.

CHAPTER 3

Social Behavior, SM and Otherwise, Including Etiquette, Customs, Rules and "Life-styles"

Most leatherguys find it impossible to "live in leather" except for very special times and places. For the fortunate few who can more fully determine their own lifestyles, to the most restricted, closeted, would-be leathermen, come a variety of questions on how to behave in any number of circumstances.

Of course, SM has its own sets of rules, customs, and etiquette, so we must consider these, as well. Here are a few who wrote to ask, and my answers.

Dear Sir,

I'm sure you have better things to do than answer questions from this straight "fag hag" [sic], but the only sure answer I would receive is from a gay male—preferably one such as you, who is not unused to giving advice. My gay male roommate and I have been cohabiting for over a year. We have ironed out all our rough spots, except for one particular behavior in him that I just can't handle. Although I understand and appreciate a male's having a higher level of sex drive than most women, I can't understand why his mind is constantly on his crotch—so much so that it is beginning to cause friction between us. He "steals" my car at night so he can cruise the bars and train stations, etc., while I'm sleeping. He seems to have no sense of responsibility when it comes to getting himself a trick. (And "leather" is not the problem, since I am into this, where he is not.) Oh, yes, he's had lovers before who have caused him to domesticate himself temporarily, but he always had to get something on the side during these relationships. I wonder if there's a way to explain to this roommate of mine that there is more to life than sucking cock. Have you any suggestions?

Distracted roomie, Springfield, IL

Dear Distracted,

Since you're not his momma, his mistress, or his wife, there isn't a hell of a lot you can do about this guy's sexual proclivities. Some men (gay or otherwise) have this itch, and, for them, there is only one way to scratch it. Any woman who maintains close friendships with us has to be aware of that. Except for his unauthorized use of your car, the only harm he seems to be doing to you is to upset your sense of order and social priority. My logical conclusion, then, is that your real concern is for his well-being. And that places you in the same situation as so many of us who see our friends doing things that we fear will cause them injury, but over which we have no control. Isn't that one of the essentials of the human social dilemma? I'm sorry to offer so little encouragement, but I think your choice is either to live with it, in the hope he will mature and outgrow the excessive needs, or break it off.

Then, a few issues later, I got a another letter from a woman who was responding to a comment I had made to still another woman sometime before. It was about this point I began to realize that there are more women on the fringe of our scene than most of us had imagined. Again, social changes have come about in many of our major population centers. Women are to be found in most gay organizations these days, and very few bars or other social gathering places would try to exclude them. But in 1983–4, the following was the about the way it was:

Dear Larry,

I recently saw a letter in your column from a woman who is into the leather/SM scene and spends a lot of time in men's bars. I want to thank you for not writing an immediate, disapproving response. Gay men who are part of this scene are incredibly lucky, compared to the woman who has no leather bar, leather-oriented bath, shop, or magazine like *Drummer*. Only now, are there a few support groups forming and a few books coming into print, but they are not much help on a Saturday night, when you want to go out with like-minded folks and maybe find a partner for the evening.

I've spent a lot of time in gay men's leather bars simply because there is no other space available. I deeply appreciate the sensitive and caring gay men who have made me welcome, socialized and played with me. I've learned more about SM and sex in general from them than I could possibly describe. As for the occasional gay man who is hostile or rude, I have this to say: Where do you want me to go? I am not interested in ruining anybody else's fantasy trip, but I think a guy who has to focus on my presence to the exclusion of all the hot men in a space is ruining things for himself. I never press myself on anybody who isn't interested (and anyway, my primary sexual interest is in other women), but I do feel good about myself and like having a good time wherever I am, in a gay men's or lesbian bar.

And there's one final thing to think about. Given that the basic dynamic of SM sex is a power exchange, expressed in an infinite variety of ways, does gender matter as much in SM as it does in vanilla sex? I think most SM people have a tendency to respond to power wherever they find it, in men or women, though of course we all have our usual gender preferences.

Pat Califia, NYC

Dear Pat,

Thanks for your comments. It's certainly a many-sided issue. (For the benefit of those who do not know her, Pat is a contributor to a number of gay publications. It was she who reviewed *The Leatherman's Handbook II* for the *Advocate*. Sit on my face for ignoring women, indeed!)

Since this exchange of letters, Pat has become very well known in both the gay and lesbian SM arenas and has written extensively in both.

Dear Larry,

Why is it, when gay guys get together, they call each other girls' names, or say "Let's go, girls!" We are not female, and I see this even in leather bars, all across the country. Some guy in leather called me "Mabel" the last time I was in a San Francisco bar, and I almost decked him. I am not feminine at all. I'm over six feet tall and quite muscular, and I really resent this implication of being into a female role.

Ron is the name, NYC

Dear Ron,

Oh, you are right on! The next asshole who calls me "Loretta" is going to need a new set of choppers. I think this comes from our generic past, when gay men were cast into a feminine stereotype and perceived themselves as such. It's a reflection of that past, and I find it much more common among the older set. In fact, I consider it a failing of the brain.

Of course, the shrinks tell us that hypersensitivity on this issue is a reflection of our own uncertain sexual identity—and perhaps some guilt as a result. Be that as it may, I agree with those who enjoy having a cock and balls between their legs, not a pussy; and I prefer to be called by a name that reflects that condition.

Dear Larry,

I just read an article in *Mandate* called "Macho Delusions" that says some pretty dumb things about *Drummer* and quotes you several times. The guy seems to be trying to put down leather and SM and everything to do with it, but at the same time he claims to be into the scene himself. In case you haven't seen this bullshit, I'm sending you my copy, torn out of their mag, because I'll never want to refer to it again. I'd like to see your response, Sir, as I'm sure you could flush this guy away.

H. C., Baltimore

Dear H. C.,

I don't know that there is too much to flush away in this article. It reminds me a bit of something you might see in the *National Inquirer*—big headlines promising a grand exposé, but little of substance in the copy. The main point Rutledge seems to be making has to do with the elitist attitude on the part of many leatherguys. He claims it's become "that dreaded social phenomenon—a lifestyle." Then he wanders off on several other tangents, never explaining what's wrong with a lifestyle, and generally hedging each subsequent statement until the sharp edge is gone. There follows a series of half-baked references to self-righteousness, reincarnated Nazis, and out of context quotes from Luke Daniels, John Preston, Yours Truly, etc. I would try to answer this, but I can't find a thread of logic leading to any justifiable conclusion. The article does a good enough job of disproving itself that no one else needs to try. I think, as leather-guys, we have developed a certain sense of community; and because there have been so many new adherents over the past few years, many outsiders may perceive us as threatening. Why a guy who claims to be into leather should respond this way, I really don't know. Maybe he's as confused as his article.

My late friend John Preston, who was also belittled by this jerk, sent me a note in response to my comments. His advice: "Don't pick a fight with someone smaller than you are." That was always his attitude toward ineptitude, particularly the twits some magazines assign to review leather stories—fluffs who claim to have leather wings, but who don't understand half of what they're reading. It's offensive, but that's the world we live in. Then another loyal fan was heard from:

Dear Larry,

I was amused to note in your last column that you tried to answer that clown who did the dumb article in *Mandate* about the evils of being devoted to leather. I agreed with you as far as you went. But you missed the most important point by not picking up on the asinine remark about our trying to achieve a "leather lifestyle." Now, I'm about as much into leather/SM as it's possible to get. I'm in my forties, have been a slave, and am now more or less of a Master. I always wear leather to the bars or clubs, and I hardly ever have sex that isn't at least symbolically SM. But I also work a good job, own a home, drive a decent car, and have an active social life that includes dining out in some "better" restaurants, going to shows and the opera, etc. When engaged in these activities I don't wear leather, nor does anyone else I know. So, what's that "leather lifestyle" shit? Maybe you've got one, or the guys who put out *Drummer* do. But if someone doesn't make his living in, by and for the leather crowd, how the fuck can he have a "leather lifestyle?"

Living with no lifestyle, CT

Dear Living,

I was hoping no one would ask me this one because some guys I'm rather fond of have already put their (collective) foot in it by claiming this elusive "Leather lifestyle." And they have exactly the same problem you have—or I have, or any of us have. However much we may enjoy leather and SM sex, there are times and places where the costume and attitudes are inappropriate. The problem becomes even more apparent if you try to analyze the leather group, as I did with the survey in *Handbook II*. Although this as not a scientifically controlled sampling, the figures I obtained were so lopsided that they have to be at least somewhat indicative of "who's out there." I came up with about 40 percent advanced university degrees in my sample group. Less than 4 percent had failed to at least graduate from high school, and a comfortable majority were college graduates. This group of men are nearly all in their thirties and up, so it would be logical to expect that they would (as a group) be doing well financially. We might also expect a fairly high level of social awareness, diverse intellectual interests, along with business/professional activities that preclude their "living in leather." Still, many of us consider ourselves to be "leatherguys," regardless of whatever else we have to do in our lives outside the area of leather/SM. For this reason, then, I think "leather lifestyle" is a foolish term to use, simply because it implies an exclusive condition that very few men are able to achieve. And don't ask me to define what it should be. I'm not that much of a masochist.

I probably would not have bothered reprinting these two letters, except that they did stir up my most poignant answer to this "leather lifestyle" nonsense. The original article was really not worth all the hoopla, as my comments were far kinder than the author deserved. And, lest I be misunderstood, let me make it clear that I see nothing wrong with a guy living in leather all the time, if he is able to do it. I simply feel that he must be such a rare individual that very few other men could emulate him. Here's one who seems to have come close:

Dear Larry,

In regard to the letter you answered dealing with "Leather lifestyle," I think it is important to note that there are quite a few of us who *do* live in a leather lifestyle—far more than merely putting it on for bars, etc. Leather smells best when it is worn daily; otherwise it is no more than drag. I made a major career change a number of years ago in order to accommodate this particular lifestyle—with most satisfying results. I am completely self-employed and wear leather when I feel like it. In honesty, there is one exception: when I perform chamber music, because some of the other musicians felt it inappropriate. As a sane-sadist I have freedom to take time, anytime, to chain a man up and do with him as I choose—and I do. My clients and students are well aware of my lifestyle and accept it, although I will admit I have lost a few. You answered that there may be times when a leather lifestyle is inappropriate. I would concede, otherwise; I would wear my chaps when performing Mozart. I am a long way from saving my lifestyle for those cherished evenings in a bar. I know it is often difficult for men to make the change; but believe me, it is worth it.

Rev. Paul, MN

Dear Rev.,

I think you are saying much the same thing I did, although you are trying to expand the limits of my logic. First, I did not say that there were times when the leather lifestyle was inappropriate; I said there were times when the attire and attitudes (affect) were inappropriate. A true leatherman is going to hold this orientation within him at all times. My argument is not with the ability of a man to be honestly committed to this way of life. Rather, I dislike the term "Leather lifestyle" because it conjures up the image of a man who literally lives in leather. Even in your unique professional situation, you have to admit that you can't do this all the time; for a man who must earn his living in a situation where others determine the appropriateness of his dress and affect, the situation becomes impossible. We might also return to the old problem of defining the difference between "Leatherman" and an "SM'er." They often are synonymous, but not always, not by a long shot. Hence my dislike for the term. I simply feel it is misleading and inaccurate. All of us who are involved in this scene carry the love or the lust within us for most of our waking hours and sometimes in our dreams. But for many in our group, the central fetish isn't leather; it may be ropes or chains or steel shackles, or simply a dominant/submissive relationship, wherein leather is a secondary consideration.

"'Nuff said!"

Dear Larry,

What does it mean when a guy wears a chain on his boot? Does it make a difference if it's on the right of left, like the wearing of keys, etc.? I was told that wearing it on the left meant he was gay, on the right he was not. Your clarification would be appreciated.

Stan, Salt Lake City

Dear Stan,

Chains on the boot have never been a universal signal, and I'm sure the significance will vary from place to place. Ten years ago, at least in California, it meant that the guy wanted to "buddy-ride" on a bike—right meaning he was sexually bottom, left indicating Top. More recently, I've seen guys wearing boot chains just because they liked the appearance, although the left for Top and right for bottom still seemed to prevail. In your area, at this time, it could very well mean what your friend told you it meant.

Except that the heterosexual vs. homosexual code seems unlikely, since a straight man would probably be unaware of the signals being sent by a gay man.

Mr. Townsend:

I have a problem which I'm sure is pretty common, and I'm sure a lot of guys would be happy if you would address it in your column. Although I'm into SM action, where I function most satisfactorily as a Top—the role I prefer—I am very self-conscious about my voice. I know I sound "nelly"; and sometimes in the middle of a scene, I am almost paralyzed at the sound of my own voice. This is a problem of course, that haunts me outside my gay relationships, as well, because I'm sure I come across as "faggoty" when I'd just as soon be innocuous as to my sexual preference. I don't think the rest of my appearance is especially effeminate, so if I could just control my voice, I would lead a much more comfortable existence.

Tom, Montana

Dear Tom,

This is a problem you share with many guys, although I think you are probably more self-conscious than you need to be. Just the fact of your recognizing the situation is probably helping you, subconsciously, to correct it, except in times of heightened stress or emotion. If your voice is naturally high-pitched, it is going to be more difficult to modify than if it is only the tonal inflection. Still, you can go through the same basic exercises as many actors do, when they practice facial expressions or posture in front of a mirror. In your case, dealing with sound, you could devise your own training program and work at it for a few minutes every day. Place your hands in front of your ear, when you do this, because it allows you to hear yourself more accurately, without the "echo effect." Write yourself some short scripts and practice them. Use a tape recorder, if that's easier. To lower the pitch of your voice, you have to train yourself to speak more from the diaphragm. Since this is a basically a singing technique, you might want to check the library for some books by the better-known vocal coaches. A friend of mine who had the same problem actually started taking singing lessons in order to master these techniques, and it really seemed to "butch up" his act.

Dear Larry,

My Master and I have been together for five years (well past your estimated average time), although I have to admit that our relationship has cooled down a bit since its early days (sexually, but not otherwise). My question has to do with the results of our being together so long. Both his family and mine are aware of our situation, at least from the standpoint of our being lovers. I don't think they suspect the specifics of our sexual behavior. However, I am very much the slave at all times. When his parents or mine come over for dinner, Master requires me to serve the food and clear the table. Although I am not normally allowed to sit at the table with Him when we are alone, He does permit this during these special times. He still imposes certain restrictions on me, though, and punishes me later if I say something to contradict him in front of the "folks." It makes for a very tense situation, at least for me, and my mother has asked me several times if everything is all right between Master and me. I can't explain why I have so little to say when she is there, and I don't want her to think I'm unhappy. And I'm not; I just don't know how to handle this one.

Slave Bobby, NYC

Dear Bobby,

Although I usually refer these questions on etiquette to Dear Abby, the answer to this one is so obvious that even I feel equipped to answer it. Master, as well as you, are clearly in the closet as far as your folks are concerned, at least as applies to your SM relationship. Tell Master that Mommy is getting suspicious, and suggest that you put on a little more convincing act for the old folks in the future. After all, the worst he can do is punish you for it. And isn't that why you tied up with him in the first place?

When I made the comment about Dear Abby, I was being facetious, but I note that in recent years she has started answering questions that come close to this, so times change even here. Good for her!

Dear Larry,

There seems to be a continuing trend away from having things "natural," and this bothers me. For instance, I really like the odor of a man's body, but every time I meet a guy who turns me on (if I'm successful in getting him into the sack), I discover a body that smells of soap and deodorant, and sometimes even (ugh!) cologne. I also flip out on the smell and taste of a cock that hasn't been scrubbed clean after a normal day's sweat and whatever. I don't mean that I'm into anything really filthy and stinking, but just that nice male odor that builds up in a day or two of being left alone. I don't think I'm weird in this, because I've talked to a lot of guys who agree with me. But still, most of them shower and spray their armpits before they go out cruising because they're afraid they'll smell bad. I'd appreciate your comments.

J. K., Salt Lake City, UT

Dear J. K.,

I hear you, and to some extent agree with you. But you're seeking a rather fine line between that "just right" smell and the two conditions that lie close on either side of it: pristine cleanliness vs. raunch. I'm sure you'd find plenty of takers for either, although with a substantial majority who would rather have you fresh and soapy smelling than otherwise. It really boils down to the problem of the one-night stand, doesn't it? If you've never made it with the guy before—maybe haven't even met him until you get together to do it—you (or he) cannot anticipate his unknown partner's preferences when he prepares himself for his night of hunting. If you make a date for a return engagement, that's the time to try setting the stage (or the crotch) for your ultimate desire. Otherwise it's a matter of being safe rather than sorry, since—as noted above—a majority of our brothers like 'em clean. (Procter & Gamble must hate you!)

Wonderful how tastes change with time and space. In Germany and Italy, until quite recently, body odors were a part of any sex scene, sometimes due to their lack of American-style preoccupation with scented soap and deodorants. In France and sometimes in Spain, you are likely to find even very masculine guys wearing cologne. I remember in some of my more esoteric readings, it was said that Louis XIV disliked having sex with anyone who had bathed within the previous two or three weeks. And Napoleon was reputed to have dropped a note to Josephine from the battlefield: "Plan to be home in two weeks. Don't bathe."

Dear Larry,

My lover and I have been together for almost ten years, although we are both just short of thirty. We have not had any outside sexual contacts for over five years, and we've both tested negative several times. I mention this only because I don't think the disease problem has anything to do with my question. My lover is really hot for "risky" sex. He is constantly trying to get me to suck him off in a park or public john, or to have some kind of a wild orgy at night in some deserted location. I keep telling him that it just scares the shit out of me to do this. I don't see any reason to risk arrest or other embarrassment when we have our own home (house and yard) where we could do any of these things without having to worry about the vice squad. Can you: (1) explain why he does this? and (2) offer any suggestions to cool him off on the idea? Thanks.

Scared, Washington State

Dear Scared,

One night in the slammer will certainly cool him off, to say nothing of what it'll do to your pocketbook(s). These seemingly crazy sexual urges are unusual, but certainly not unique. (At least while you're doing these things with him, you know he isn't doing them with anyone else.) For many guys, the lure of danger definitely heightens their sexual enjoyment and stimulates the sensual centers in the brain more strongly than the sex itself. That's the "why" in your equation. As to how you're going to stop him—or at least slow him down—I almost hesitate to make a suggestion. If I were in your boots, I'd probably set him up with a realistic phony bust that would scare him badly enough to get him off the public-sex kick for a while. But you'll have to figure out how to do that one. Of course, the way our recent Supreme Court decisions have been going, we are not completely out of danger doing these things in our own bedrooms.

The outdoor settings and potential danger have always held a strong attraction for many of us. I used to enjoy taking a hunky young number up the hill to a vacant lot above my house, throwing him down across the hood of the car, and fucking him silly. It was exotic and dangerous, but hot and exciting! How did Oscar Wilde put it? "It was like feasting with panthers. The thrill was half the excitement."

Dear Larry,

I have a very heavy interest in wearing rubber gear, and have been this way since the age of twelve (and I'm now sixty-eight). There are a lot of rubber guys out there who don't know each other. Why don't you start a *Rubber Notebook*, knowing as I do that many heavy rubber guys would be grateful for such a page in *Drummer*? PS—I have a *Drummer* son and two slaves.

Fred, MA

Dear Fred,

Since the pages of *Drummer*'s classifieds are open to men of various persuasions, there is nothing to stop rubber guys from using them the same as leathermen do. That is one of the best sources for meeting other guys, and the reason I make referrals so seldom. As for a column specifically for rubber, why worry about it? This column might just as well be titled something to do with SM or rubber. The problems that guys have, or questions they want to ask, apply pretty well across the board. I haven't kept track, but I would estimate that only 10 percent or so of the questions I answer have to do specifically with leather. Rubber certainly has its own distinctive smell and feel, but the things you're doing in it are not that different from the many exotic activities that are done, or tried, in leather. In fact, I wish more leather guys would get into it, since it forms such an effective shield to prevent the exchange of body fluids.

Dear Larry,
   On a trip to London last year, I found several old German insignia in a flea market. My favorite is one of an eagle with its wings pointed obliquely upward, as if he is about to land. He is holding a swastika in his talons. I was loudly denounced for wearing this on my leather jacket when I went to a club meeting several weeks ago. I have two questions. First, do you know what the badge would be—I mean, from which agency or branch of service? Secondly, do you think it's wrong for me to wear it? I'm certainly not a Nazi, but I think they were hot men sexually.
                                         Name Withheld, Dayton, OH

Dear Withheld,
   Because of the aura of cruelty associated with Nazism, there is a decided mystique about their uniforms and insignia—particularly in SM circles. However, we still live in an age when the memories of Nazi atrocities remain vivid in the minds of people who lived through the time of their ascendancy. For this reason, I feel it is in bad taste to wear the swastika or any other obviously Nazi insignia in public. (After all, they did in a lot of homosexuals along with millions of Jews, Slavs, Gypsies, and just plain Volk who didn't agree with them.) In a private scene, if it turns on everybody concerned, it becomes a matter of your own choice.

As to the identity of your souvenir, it is probably a Luftwaffe cap insignia.

It's not hard to explain the fascination so many guys have with Nazi materials. The symbolism is very sadistic, and it certainly is a fetish unto itself. It's too bad the racial/ethnic overtones make it so unacceptable socially. Those black SS uniforms with their high boots were particularly sharp, and some of the guys who wore them were handsome by any standards. I've often wondered if French military insignia carried a similar negative image in England or the rest of Europe after Napoleon. I also find it strange that we aren't as violently negative toward Soviet Russian materials. After all, Stalin was easily as anti-Semitic and homophobic as Hitler. In fact, he is reputed to have done in at least twenty million of his own people. That's about three times as many as the Nazis. But I don't see many guys going bonkers over Russian uniforms as fetish pieces. Yet the Russians have been notorious torturers since the advent of human settlement in the steppes. Guess it took the right kind of press to make sex symbols out of one gang of bastards at the expense of another. Then there were the Red Chinese, but I guess that's really another story.

Dear Larry,

May I have your opinion, please, on a question I have had for some time? I am a bottom, attracted to strong, dominant men. I entered into my first live-in relationship at nineteen, wherein my partner made all the decisions regarding our daily life, weekends, etc. I kept house, cooked meals, but generally followed his lead in every major decision. Then, when we were moving into a new house, he mentioned that two teachers had occupied the property before us, and he wondered if they were into giving "hacks" (spanking). I replied jokingly that if he felt he needed one, I would gladly provide it. From this, developed our little fetish, where—after sucking his cock and getting him very aroused—I would lead him to the couch or a kitchen chair, have him spread his legs and lean over the back of it, and proceed to paddle his bare ass, using a wooden spoon, a ruler, or a piece of kindling which he had retrieved himself. We both enjoyed this, but I never entered him—quite the contrary; the spankings usually resulted in my getting some of the most passionate fuckings I've ever had. My question, in view of articles/stories I have read in your publications and in *Drummer:* Does this kind of situation fit in with any sort of SM lifestyle? Is it reasonable to seek a partner who will enjoy my spanking him, yet be able to assume the role of Top in the other aspects of our relationship? Thank you for any insight you can provide.

M. H., San Francisco, CA

Dear M. H.,

In structuring your own sexual relationship, you must be concerned with your desires and those of your partner—and to hell with the opinion of anyone else. Whereas I might argue with you over the definition of terms in trying to describe what you or someone else is doing, I would never suggest that my standards or anyone else's be the determining factor in your sexual behavior (except possibly in matters of safety). If you are asking me whether your spanking activities—which place you in the role of Top—are in conflict with the rest of your behavior, in which you are a bottom, I'd have to say that they are. But this is merely a matter of definition. In effect, you are playing a very common game of switching roles. You are simply doing it in an individualistic way. I would classify it as marginal SM behavior, only because the rest of your sexual activity is garden-variety vanilla. I'm sure there are plenty of guys who would dig your scene, although most who tumble to it will probably want to expand the horizons a bit. If so, why not give it a try? You might both enjoy it.

This guy sounded so naïve, it was hard not to make a stronger case for his going after what he obviously wanted—a more fleshed-out B&D scene. But, I have a feeling that if he (they) kept going in the direction they appeared to be headed, they probably got there eventually. Theirs is an almost classic case, of course, of a man being dominant in his "normal" (social-business) life, but desiring to be mastered in the place of sexual exchange. It's much more common than most of us realize—more obvious, perhaps, in hetero-

sexual exchanges, where a man enjoys being submissive to a woman. We often see it when a big guy lets a smaller man tie him up and top him—or when an obviously stronger, or more experienced guy kneels down unexpectedly before his young and/or novice partner and bows his head in token of a desire for subjugation. After all, that's why "they" call it perversion.

Dear Larry,

I have a rather strange "social" question for you. I'm a bottom, and I live next door to the guy who is more or less my "Master." That is to say, we aren't officially in an exclusive relationship, but we play often and both of us are afraid to stray very far afield because of the health crisis. He is a few years older than I am, and outside of our sexual encounters, he seems to enjoy "mothering" me. He is always giving me food that he has prepared, and frankly, he is a terrible cook. I mean, he gives me big bowls of tuna salad that is so awful the cat won't eat it, and if I feed his meat loaf to the dog, it gives him diarrhea. I really like the guy and certainly enjoy having sex with him. I don't want to hurt his feelings, but how can I stop this flood of unwanted kindness? Please don't identify me by name or area of residence.

Anonymous, USA

Dear Any,
 Don't you have a garbage disposal?

Dear Larry,

I've gotten myself into a situation, and I'm not sure how to get out of it. I'm forty, a professional, with a good job that requires my maintaining a degree of discretion in my personal life. A couple of years ago, I picked up a kid off the street, and he has been living with me ever since. He was seventeen at the time I met him, and not really a street hustler, because he had just come into town from his home in a rural area. Supposedly, we had a monogamous relationship, something I emphasized as essential if he was to remain in my home. As a result of a doctor friend's recommendation, we both had the AIDS antibody test last week. I was negative, but the kid was positive.

Now I'm in a real dilemma. Our relationship was not really "lovers," but more of an older guy keeping a younger one for his sexual favors. Only now I'm afraid to touch him, and I'd really like to break it off—especially as his being positive has to mean he has been tricking outside the house (or maybe in it when I'm away)—something he promised never to do. On the other hand, I don't want to be like the roommates you read about, who throw out their friends because they have AIDS. I've discussed this with a couple of friends, and both think I'm crazy to continue letting the kid live with me. What do you think? I really want to be fair, but I don't want to get AIDS.

R., San Diego, CA

Dear R.,

If your little friend did indeed come in to you from a rural setting, where an HIV infection is well-nigh impossible, then his exposure to the virus would almost have to be conclusive evidence of his stepping out on you. That would seem to break the covenant, as I see it, and justify your tossing him out. The fact that he tests positive does not mean he's sick, or is necessarily going to be sick in the near future. He has violated your trust. You aren't deserting a lover in a time of need.

This letter came in when the plague was in an earlier stage, so I felt fairly confident in the theory of a rural setting being an unlikely place to contact HIV. Now, of course, with high-school kids fucking like minks, there's no guarantee. I had a couple of people tell me that my advice in this instance was harsh, but so be it. We only go around once in this world, and if someone betrays you, then it's time to look out for Number One.

Dear Larry,

In reading a number of your things, including the two *Handbook*s, I get the impression that you feel it is okay to mistreat another human being, but not an animal.

Am I reading you correctly? If so, how do you justify this?

Martin, Los Angeles CA

Dear Martin,

I do not feel that it is okay to mistreat another human being unless that person wants to be mistreated. There is a great deal of difference between consensual SM and rape, and if you are not able to distinguish that difference you don't belong in the scene. Animals, like small children, are unable to perceive the finer points which make it possible for one adult to enjoy dominating or submitting to another.

It is interesting, though, that your neighbor is much more likely to turn you in for beating your dog than doing the same to your lover. I don't see that this is necessarily wrong. The lover can fight back; the poor beast can't (or won't). Yeah, I guess I have to admit it. I have a much softer place in my heart for animals than for humans. Their devotion is unqualified and uncomplicated, and they don't argue.

Dear Larry,

I have been invited to a couple of SM sex clubs a few times. Most of the men who attend come as couples, and the scenes I've watched have been good. And I have picked up some good ideas, although I have not been invited to "join in" yet. Up to now I have hesitated to start my own scene and only watch. (I usually don't hesitate to approach someone on a one-to-one basis in other circumstances.) Now I have been invited again. What is the proper etiquette for attending these meetings, but not actively participating? Any advice?

Thor, San Francisco, CA

Dear Thor,

In all probability, the reason you're being invited to the club parties is in the hope that you *will* participate. I don't think there need be any great anxiety over it if you don't, but you may not be invited again. The general rule in trying to join a scene is simply to ask the Top if you can help him, or if he'd "do that to me, too." If he says no, there's nothing lost, but the fact that you have attempted to join in may well encourage someone else to approach you. After all, if the guy wasn't interested in fun and games, he wouldn't be there.

Ah, faint heart ne'r won fair cock. Most of us are just not pushy enough in these situations. When I look back on all my own encounters—and there were quite a few—the instances I remember best were the ones where I failed to speak up in time. It's like the fisherman's proverbial "one that got away."

Dear Sir,

i have been with my Master for eight years. We have had a very good and honest relationship. My Master is into very heavy cock and ball torture, which i love and am able to take during long sessions in the playroom. i am very well hung, with large balls and a long thick cock. We are both professional men and hold good jobs. Every morning before we leave for work, my Master puts a harness on my cock and balls, which is very tight because of my huge size. i am expected to wear this harness all day, but because of its being so tight i remove it as soon as i am at work, and replace it just before i leave for home. My Master believes i wear it all day because He put it on me and ordered me to wear it. i don't like this lie between us and don't know how to tell Him the truth. i don't want to endanger a great eight-year relationship, but i'm afraid i'll do myself some serious, permanent damage if i obey. Please help me. i know he will listen to your advice. We get *Drummer*. Thank you, Sir.

slave tim

Dear slave,

Your Master is certainly going to be justified in punishing you for your disobedience, but he should also be responsive to the possibility of doing you some physical damage. In his boots, I'd whip your ass until it glowed, but I'd buy you a bigger harness.

Dear Larry,

I'm twenty-six, and sexually active in quasi-SM–type sex. I have recently been approached by a small filmmaker who wants me to star in a new flick (tape) he wants to do. Although he is not asking me to do anything I don't normally do, and he assures me he will observe all the safe-sex guidelines, I'm concerned that I might get infected with HIV. After all, I don't know ahead of time who he is going to pair me with, and I'm not all too sure that once he gets me on the set, he might not try to embarrass me into doing things without the proper precautions. What do you know of the practices generally accepted as standard on a porn filming? Would I be within my rights to walk out on the whole thing if I didn't like what they are asking me to do?

Actor, Los Angeles, CA

Dear Actor,

Your body is yours to do with as you please. If you really want to do this tape, I'd say to go ahead and do it, but make sure your producer understands ahead of time that you will insist on safe sex in every aspect of the filming. Then, if he fails to keep his promise, get out. Reading between the lines of your letter, I'm not sure if you have some fear that you may be physically restricted and unable to cut out. If that's the case, insist that some trusted friend also be present, to get you out of any situation you can't handle yourself. I will say, though, that all the gay producers I know anything about are very concerned with health safety. You'll notice the use of condoms and germicides in most new tapes being released today.

There is also the commonly observed rule that no sex takes place with one of the partners in bondage. They may simulate it, but they do not show actual penetration. This fairly well eliminates the danger of an actor's being put into bondage and forced into unwanted sex acts. I will say, though, that I have been appalled, when on several recent video shoots, to see the number of guys who get their faces right down in the crack and eat ass. One director shrugged when I asked him, saying; "The kid loves to do it, so I let him." That's as it may be, but—from my own experience—another very popular porn rimmer, who was scheduled to do some stills for one of my books a couple of months ago, had to cancel for health reasons. At last report, he's still alive, but just barely. I know he has hepatitis. He may or may not have AIDS. Don't forget that the old diseases can still kill you just as effectively as they could prior to the HIV epidemic.

Dear Larry,

Here's a social question for you. I'm a twenty-eight-year-old Caucasian bottom. I really dig getting my ass and tits worked over, and just about anything else you can do these days that's reasonably safe. I'm not an Adonis or anything, but I have my fair share of takers when I go out barring. Recently, there has been a big black Top hanging out in my favorite watering hole, and he is determined that I'm going to bottom out to him. I've made it with a couple of black studs, so I don't think I'm especially prejudiced, but I really don't turn on to this guy. He's kind of fat and otherwise not very attractive (to me), and the few times I've been close enough to him to notice, he has bad breath. But he just won't take no for an answer, and a couple of nights ago, he made a small scene, accusing me of being "an uptight WASP," etc. I have been going to this bar for several years and really like the place, but short of not going there, I don't know what to do.

Tim, NYC

Dear Tim,

Maybe your tormentor will read this and take the hint. If not, tell him to fuck off! If he thinks you're prejudiced, that's *his* problem.

I've seen this happen to several guys over the years. A "minority" person will get the hots for a white guy who couldn't use him stuffed, and try to shame him into having a scene. Nine times out of ten, it isn't racial prejudice that's causing the rejection. God knows there are plenty of whites who don't turn on other whites. It's not a private club, either, despite all the latter-day bullshit about initiation rites. We still get to pick and choose our sex partners, and

in the few situations where race does play a part in the selection—
tough shit. It's your body; don't give it to someone you don't want,
just because you feel you "should." (Unless, of course, he's an old
Maestro who deserves your tender young endowments in appreci-
ation for all the good advice he's given you over the years.)

Dear Mr. Townsend,
In a recent issue of *Drummer Leather Notebook* you quote
a letter from a slave who has to wear a cock harness which
his master puts on him every morning (although he takes it
off again). Would you please describe the kind of harness he
meant, as i would be very interested in getting one for
myself to present to my Master, and so have the pleasure of
being made to wear it. And i wouldn't take it off again!
M. F., Hamburg, Germany

Dear M. F.,
My correspondent did not describe the harness he was
supposed to wear, but I would expect it was probably a snap-on
leather strap that went around the base of his cock and balls,
probably with some sort of ball spreader or separator attached.
There are any number of varieties on the market, even some
that can be locked in place, or which have a waist harness in
addition to the genital straps. I'd suggest you look over the
available items in any of several shops in the *Repperbahn* area,
or get hold of a good mail-order catalog.
And, of course, I sent this guy a set of my flyers. You don't catch
the old Maestro napping—not in these days of flagging commerce.

CHAPTER 4

SM Techniques—How to Do It, Where and When, and What Equipment to Use While You're at It

Although those of us who have opted for a leather/SM mode of expression, and like to feel we have achieved an uninhibited freedom that permits the release of our most basic lusts and desires, we still—on occasion—find ourselves seeking new outlets for our energies and imaginations. It never hurts to look into the other guy's experience(s), and to ascertain where he did it exceptionally well, or where he failed. There are lots of men "out there" who know the ropes very well, indeed—many of whom learned the hard way. It behooves us to seek them out and to hear what they have to tell us. Let's explore a few assorted questions that came into me under this general heading:

Dear Larry,

I know that catheters up to FR30 are regularly sold by various specialty stores and mail-order businesses. But I recently read an article that indicated they go up to FR45. Is it possible for the usual suppliers to get them in this size, or is it a restricted item—or such an unusual item that the wholesalers don't stock them? I'd also like to know if they are made without a hole in the business end, or at least with a smaller hole, but still with a hollow tube. Of course, I can't find any kind of catheter on the home market.

R. J., England

Dear R. J.,

To properly answer your question, let's first take a quick look at the definition of the word "catheter." The term applies to any flexible or solid tube, used to draw fluids from any part of the body (or to put them in). The FR numbers are merely the French system, by which the diameter of the catheter is measured in metric increments. The regular latex catheters, sold by most businesses that cater to the "kink" market, go from FR8 (the smallest) to FR52. However, somewhere along the line (usually somewhere in the twenties), the suppliers and manufacturers change the nomenclature in their catalogs from "urinary catheter" to "rectal tube." Yet the shape of the item is the same, or almost the same. It simply has a larger length and diameter as the numbers get bigger. Since the FR30 catheter is about as big around as your little finger, there aren't many dicks that can accommodate it, and most medical catalogs label it as a rectal tube (or rectal catheter).

To answer your question specifically: Yes, FR45 is available, but most places don't carry it because it's "in the middle" vis-à-vis urinary/rectal use. I've never seen a catheter without a hole at either end, but then it wouldn't be a catheter, would it? The size of the holes vary from one manufacturer to the other; but if you're going to get this specific, you'd better make friends with a surgical supplier who has the time and interest in finding your exact desire.

Strangely enough, the English seem more into these larger latex appliances than Americans. Despite my having far fewer Brits than Yanks on my mailing list, when I offer a new rectal toy, I often sell as many in England as in the US. With this strong orientation, I'm surprised that the British "chemist" (pharmacist) doesn't stock a good varied supply of enema/rectal tubes and tips. Guess it's not quite proper, don't you know? In the United States, however, it can be a problem to find catheters of any size, because most pharmaceutical suppliers won't sell them to "civilians" (i.e., nondoctors.) They are in an "iffy" category, however, not specifically banned from sale to us in most jurisdictions, but still considered questionable and something that might be put on the proscribed list at any time—for sure if the powers that be discover that people are buying them in any quantities for recreational purposes. (Remember, you aren't supposed to enjoy *using medical equipment.)*

On quite a different subject, we have another Brit advising us, in response to some of my previously published comments—this time concerning another of their specialties: flogging.

Dear Larry,

In reading your comments about flogging in England, I would like to offer a few corrections. This is a prime interest of mine, so I have done quite a bit of research on the subject. As far as I can ascertain, no public floggings have taken place in the British Isles in this century; but flogging as a judicial punishment was still used, mainly for minor crimes of violence (mugging, etc.) until 1948, when it was abolished on the mainland, but retained in the Isle of Man and the Channel Islands. As to the method, men over eighteen took it strapped to a wooden or metal frame, across the back. Boys seventeen and under were birched across the buttocks while being held against a table by two or more prison officers. The actual number of lashes was usually quite low, commonly six to twelve, but with such force that blood was usually drawn on the first stroke and the victim would often pass out.

In the Channel Islands, flogging remains on the statute book (as does hanging), but has not been used since the 1950s, and probably won't be, since the European Court ruling concerning the Isle of Man. There it was abolished for men over twenty-one in 1970, but retained for younger offenders. In 1980 one young man who had been birched took his case to the European Court of Human Rights and

won. The Court declared birching to be "a cruel and degrading punishment, contrary to the European Charter of
Rights."

Reader, Ontario

Dear Reader,

Oh, for the good old days! I certainly thank you for your
comments, much of which had to be cut due to space limitations.
Still, I could not help but think, as I read your letter, that the
incidence of corporal punishment seems to bear a direct, inverse
correlation to the increase in violent crimes. But I guess the
learned gentlemen on the bench know what they're doing.

*And if you believe that, you'll believe that pigs can fly and
chickens have lips! As I write this, I am looking at an article in the
L. A. Times, regarding an American brat who was apprehended
in Singapore for spray painting cars. At this point, he's been
sentenced to get a few strokes across the ass with a cane (whipping
variety, not to be confused with a walking stick), and to spend
four months in jail. The whole American administration is up in
arms, trying to protect the poor kid. I wonder how it might reduce
our own local acts of graffiti-vandalism if we had a similar law
on our books. Unfortunately, we'll never know, although it would
certainly be the most legitimate and effective application of SM that
I can think of.*

*But, since we have more space here, I'd like to give you a little
more of this gentleman's letter. After his comments on the changes
in the Channel Islands, following the case brought before the
E.C.H.R., he adds:*

"In jails, floggings occurred quite frequently up to 1964,
when they, too, were abolished. I once met a prison officer
who started work in 1962 when floggings were still in use
and witnessed several. The method was much like I have
already described: the victim standing up stripped to the
waist, strapped by wrists and ankles to a large tubular metal
frame bolted to the floor, and around his waist strapped a
thick leather belt about 6" wide to cover the kidney area. The
whip used was a braided leather variety about four feet

long made of six or seven thin leather strands around a steel wire core. Usually six or twelve lashes were given, full strength and making quite a bloody mess, which was cleaned up with a cloth soaked in strong antiseptic. According to my source, of the five or six prison officers usually present, most of them had hard-ons and quite often the victim did as well. Incidentally, it was always across the back. I do not believe adult men were ever birched on the buttocks in an English jail. It was the evidence of the sexual connotations of flogging that played a large part in its being abolished in 1964. When the equipment was disposed of at the end of that year, my friend took home the kidney-protection belt, which he now has, and five years ago I was privileged to have it strapped on me prior to receiving twelve hard lashes.

"Since I've been here (Canada) I've hardly met anybody else who's into heavy whipping. In fact, whipping seems to be going out of fashion in favor of FF, scat, WS, piercing, and more extreme activities. I have subscribed to Smads for a year, but found little to my taste and some that I find nauseating (mutilations, etc.) I've been corresponding with a guy in Alabama and hope to meet him soon for some mutual exploration."

Yes, the times they do change, and not always for the better. But the Brits still know how to handle a nice firm bum! (The mention of "Smads," incidentally, refers to a newsletter that specialized in SM ads, published by a friend of mine, Ron, out of New York City until his untimely death on the mid-1970s. He had cancer that would have required the amputation of a leg, which he refused to do.)

Dear Larry,

Please answer a question for me. I can't decide whether to buy a trunk or a freestanding wardrobe to store leather clothing. I heard you have to hang leathers in order to retain their shape. How do you store leather clothing?

John, Wisconsin

Dear John,

Although leathers will take a lot of abuse and still come up smiling, I prefer to hang them—especially if there is a chance of their being put away with any moisture on them. When you travel, of course, those steamer trunks can present a terrible problem.

Interesting how standards can change in a relatively short time. In the early 1980s we were much more concerned with keeping our leathers pristine—and black. Today many guys are going in for used garments—the scruffier the better, including brown WWII aviator jackets. Reminds me of the time a crazy friend of mine stripped naked in the men's room of the old No Name *in San Francisco, and stretched out in the trough urinal, screaming for everyone to piss on him. Most of the leather-clad clientele held back because he was splashing water onto their leathers. Then the whole thing broke loose from the wall, and water sprayed everywhere. Did they ever panic to avoid that!*

Dear Larry,

I'm into cock torture with matches and cigarettes, and I read someplace that there are groups of men who are into branding. Can you give me an idea where to contact them?

Also, are there any pictures of branding being done, or of matches and cigarettes being used in sex play? I'm a white male, age thirty-six, into shaving and all types of cock torture. Final question: Can testicles be pierced, and if so, what are the long range effects of it?

B. H., New Jersey

Dear B. H.,

You pose several questions; let me try to answer them in order. Cock torture with matches and cigarettes is not the best SM technique because repeated use can cause such extensive damage. I'm sure there are guys who are into it, however, since it is difficult to name any activity that isn't being done by somebody, someplace. As to an organized group, I don't know of one that is specifically oriented toward branding. Rather, you will find guys in most of the larger SM clubs who are interested or experienced to one degree of another in the subject. (I did a little piece on branding in my last column—*see Chapter 2.*) As to testicle piercing, I can tell you that it is done. *Dungeonmaster* had an article on it several issues back (early 1984). The guys who were involved in this particular sequence seemed to suffer no long-term ill effects, and the piercing was done with fairly elaborate antiseptic precautions. Just how much damage you are going to do by extensive repetitions is hard to say; in fact, it is difficult to define the term "excessive." The guys who are doing it say it's harmless. My medical adviser threw his hands in the air and said: "What are these nuts going to get into next?" I'm not sure if his pun was intentional, and I was afraid to ask.

Lest there be any doubt, let's establish that piercing one's testicles is a fairly extreme form of symbolic castration, and done improperly can prove to be the real thing. I would suggest that anyone bent on trying this start off with a man who knows what he's doing, preferably one with medical training. The dangers are manifold.

Dear Sir:
I have often read in *Drummer* about the use of electrical torture. While you have mentioned that it should always be applied well away from the chest, and have mentioned devices such as the Relax-A-Cisor, I am still in the dark. No one I have ever talked to has heard of that device. I would probably be able to build an appropriate substitute, but don't know where to begin in the way of voltage or safeguards—and something tells me that guessing wouldn't be a good idea. Do you have a source of plans? Would you be willing to publish them? If you can help me in any way, I would appreciate it. Thanks for your help and your great mag.

Brian, CT

Dear Brian,
Any of us who write on SM, knowing we'll be read by a general audience, are reluctant to encourage certain forms of experimentation. Electricity is one of these, because of its lethal potential. On the other hand, making too great a mystery of it can be an even greater stimulus to experiment. The machine

you're asking about was taken off the market by the feds in the 1960s, because it was a device to electrically stimulate the large muscles that are most frequently exercised in a gym or during calisthenics. It consisted of contact pads that were placed at either end of the muscle to be stimulated, then controlled through a "black box" for strength of current and frequency of impulses. Its application in an SM situation is obvious, but the potential for misuse and injury is also apparent. If you want one, you'll just have to hunt through flea markets and junk shops. Marketing such a machine, or reproducing its plans would—in my opinion—be unethical, and probably illegal.

In more recent years, I have seen ads for machines that look (in the pictures) suspiciously like a Relax-A-Cisor, but I don't know whether the feds are doing anything about them. I have seen the original in operation, and the guys seem to get quite a charge out using it. (Couldn't resist that!) But remember that possession of the device might be illegal in certain jurisdictions. Advertising for someone to share in its pleasures could get you into trouble with the local guardians of public morality.

Dear Larry,

I'm an older man who enjoys the piss scene. Some time ago, my prostate enlarged and I was put on self-catheterization. In time I found it enjoyable to pee and to masturbate using a catheter. Now I've had a prostate operation and can have only dry ejaculations. My questions are:

1. Will other men be turned off, due to dry ejaculations?
2. I would like information on the catheter scene, if there is such a thing. Are other guys into this, etc.?
3. Do you know of any company that sells videotapes of men pissing and drinking piss?

C, Florida

Dear C,

To take your questions in turn: (1) Some guys are going to be turned off, others not. In the present health crisis, it might be a good selling point. Besides, how is the other guy to know until after the fact? (2) There are a lot of guys into catheters, as there are into almost any scene you can think of. I haven't heard much about this going on in Florida, at least not large groups of guys with this interest. Of course, Key West seems to have a little of everything. I do know that the scene is well established in New York City, San Francisco, Los Angeles, and Chicago. (3) I have seen a number of videos which show men pissing, but drinking piss is a no-no for commercial productions.

This drinking of piss is an activity that has been debated widely, both as to its safety factors and its status as normal vs. perverse. Ranging from those who advocate drinking one's own piss for health benefits, to those who consider any interest in the scene as evidence of a "morbid and licentious fascination with excrement," we have many opinions and attitudes. I'll include a few more examples—later on in this chapter—before attempting any more profound comments at this point.

Dear Larry,

I have a question or two about just how much abuse a guy's nuts can take. My other half and I really get into some heavy-duty nut-crushing sex. On several occasions we've gotten out sterilized needles and several large tubes of K-Y and fill each other's scrotum as full as possible with K-Y. That heavy tugging sensation at our balls with a big scrotum is just totally unbelievable! My sac measured seventeen inches in circumference the last time it was filled up, and I might add it really gives the impression of one hell of a *huge* basket! Another fantastic feeling is having your own huge sac slapping against your ass during JO. I would really like to correspond with other guys who have done similar things to themselves or their partners. But I'd also like to know if you think we're risking serious harm by playing this way.

Bret, Oregon

Dear Bret,

Every time I become complacent and think I've heard or tried it all, someone like you comes along and stops me cold. It's a most intriguing idea, but I have to admit I don't know how to answer you. My two medical advisers are both out of town. The first question that comes to my mind is, what happens to all that K-Y? Does the body eventually absorb it? Since it's a sterile gel, I'm assuming it won't hurt you, except that it does tend to dehydrate the tissues. I don't know what this might do to your balls over a period of extended use. I'm sure that some ball-torture aficionado will supply the answer, and when he does I'll pass it along. We've got enough mad doctors "out there" that you'll surely get a number of responses.

The responses that came in on this were surprisingly supportive, both from other guys who played the game, and from doctors. My own medico assured me I had answered correctly and that the body would, indeed, absorb the foreign material with no immediate dire consequences; but over a period of time, such abuse could seriously dehydrate the testicles. An even more popular sport appears to be injecting air in the scrotum, using the cans that are supplied for cleaning delicate electronic equipment. Some guys have also used this to inflate an uncut dick after infibulating the foreskin. None of this is totally safe, of course, but it seems far less dangerous than many of the other things we do to ourselves. All of these activities will create a temporarily enormous endowment, of course, and this can be a thrilling experience. (Yes, I have personally tried the air, but not the K-Y.)

Dear Larry,

Where can I buy real police boots—either CHP or SFPD style? It seems all I can find are English riding boots. Thanks for your help.

Ed, Tiburon CA

Dear Ed,

I can't give you a specific address in the Bay Area, but in Los Angeles I discovered the most obvious answer to be the correct one. Check the metropolitan yellow pages under "Uniforms." It's proved the right move in several areas.

Major changes, again, in the last few years. San Francisco has several great stores selling leather gear, including Mr. S Leathers *and* A Taste of Leather *just for starters. In New York, it's* The

Leatherman *in Greenwich Village; in New Orleans* Second Skin Leathers, *in Los Angeles* The Pleasure Chest. *There are lots of others. Look them up in the* Gayellow Pages, *and if there isn't a listing in your area for a supplier that caters to our community, then go back to my original advice and try the regular yellow pages.*

Dear Larry,

For some time I have been very interested in the uniforms worn during World War II by Nazi soldiers and the SS. Can you tell me where I might find some of these uniforms (even reproductions)?

B. B., Irving, TX

Dear B. B.,

What am I becoming, the local shopping service? But I have to admit some fascination with these materials—more with the brass and insignia than with the actual uniforms, however. In the United States, I have seen various items at large swap meets, and in dusty corners of secondhand shops that specialize in war souvenirs. If you don't mind getting your name on their mailing list, the various "American Nazi Party" groups also run ads in their local publications for people offering the items for sale. You won't find them sold openly in Germany, but I have seen quite a few items in London. There is one shop that specializes in them, plus a number of dealers who hawk their wares at the Portobello Road flea market. I've also seen some at the *Nastmarkt* in Vienna and the Sunday flea market in Madrid. Almost any large city has costume-rental companies, and they will usually have reproductions of many uniforms. If they won't sell them to you, they might put you on to their supplier.

Dear Larry,

In re: Letter from C in Florida, a couple of issues back, about the catheter scene. I've found a new twist, using a round ball chain like the one used to hold the plug for a bathtub. I sterilize it in a pressure cooker, then push it into the urethra, down to the prostate, then jerk off lightly to

a great climax. But don't pull it out too soon, as all valves are closed. Go slowly. It bends every which way and doesn't injure anything inside. (It's about twelve inches long.) Thanks—just had to share this.

Master Ringo, WI

Dear Ringo,

For many years I refused to sell catheters through my mail-order business because I was afraid someone would hurt himself with one. Then I realized that without genuine catheters being available, guys were shoving all sorts of weird devices up their dicks and subjecting themselves to far greater danger. Your comment only enhances my previous conclusion. Those chains are plated; if the plating flakes, you've had it! To say nothing of the possibilities of the chain breaking inside you. I can think of several other dire results, but it's your dick. Enjoy it while you've got it.

Oh, some guys are absolutely mad! Did I ever tell you about the nut with the electric cord and the fishbowl? No, I'd better not. This is the kind of behavior that lands one in a hospital emergency room, with a hard-assed nurse demanding to know how you managed to do this to yourself. I suppose, if you could find a chain that was solid (unplated) steel—nah, forget it! Read on to our next contributor:

Dear Larry,

I am a bottom, and really into "ass stuffing." I've stuffed almost anything you can think of, and I've never had any real problem either while it's in me, or in getting it out. However, I have recently come into possession of some steel balls, in graduated sizes. I've used the smaller ones, but would like to try the largest. This is a little over three inches in diameter. I've taken things that are this big before, but the object has always been something that protruded from my ass, so I could get hold of it and pull it out. I know I can get this ball in, but my question is how to make sure I can get it out. I don't want to end up in the hospital emergency ward and have to explain how it got up there in the first place. Can you help me?

John, Tallahassee, FL

Dear John,

If you were to end up in the hospital emergency room, the doctor would probably use an anal speculum (one of those duck-billed steel dilators) to get it out. I don't like to recommend do-it-yourself medical treatment, but these devices are available from several suppliers. If your ass is as loose as it sounds, you might also do the job with a good dose of castor oil. Just don't sit on the john when you're ready to drop the bomb. New toilet bowls are expensive.

One of my video producer friends recently told me of an interesting incident that happened while he was shooting a flick in Holland. The bottom arrived on the set in an apparently agitated state, questioning how long it would be before he was on camera. When the great moment finally arrived, and he was strapped down, naked, by the Top in preparation for some heavy action, the kid popped a pair of billiard balls out of his ass. He had been carrying them for over an hour, waiting to surprise his Master. I haven't seen the finished video, yet, but I understand his scheme resulted in some appropriate on-screen punishment—and, all in all, a heavy, exciting video.

Dear Larry,

A couple of years ago I had a great pair of leather pants made to order by a San Francisco outfit that's no longer in business. I've now worn them so often that they are all stretched out of shape, particularly at the knees and around the ass. I know I can't shrink the old one back to size, so I'm going to have to buy another pair. The first ones were a pretty heavy leather, and I'd like to try a lighter weight this time. But knowing how badly (and quickly) the originals got out of shape, is there anything I can do to make the new ones last longer?

Alex, Los Angeles, CA

Dear Alex,

Leather is going to stretch when you wear it, no matter what you do. And the lighter the weight, the more it's going to do this. However, I have found two alternatives that seem to lessen the problem. One is to have the pants made of a moderately heavy leather, really fitted tightly to your body and cut to ride low on the hips. This seems to eliminate much of the stretching in the ass area, and if the legs are tight enough, the slight bagginess at the knees does not amount to much. This works out better if you're slender, of course. The other way is to use a lightweight leather and have it lined in a slick (silky) material. This keeps the leather from sticking to your skin and does not allow the sweat to soften it so that it stretches as much. Of course, this also eliminates the sensation of having hot leather directly against your body. If you really love it, and love the feel of it, you may just have to lay out the bucks for a new pair every few years.

Dear Larry,

I have found a Top to end all Tops! The guy is terrific, and I love every second of the time I'm with him. But he makes me pay for my pleasure by cleaning up his dungeon and polishing all the leather toys. This is okay by me, except that he makes me use a boot polish on the leather that gives me a rash. I don't want to be a blubbering bottom, so I haven't said anything to him, hoping he'd notice the problem. He hasn't, because our sessions are just far enough apart that I heal up in the meantime, at least so far. Is there some way to tell him without seeming to be a "cry baby?" Or is there something I could suggest instead of the boot polish?

Would-be slave, Phoenix, AZ

Dear Would-be,

Buy him a big bottle of Neet's Oil. It's much better for the leather than polish, and it probably won't cause a rash.

This is another case where time has worked in our favor. Most of the leather suppliers I've mentioned (several letters back) have a variety of leather-preservation products on their shelves, and in some cases available by mail order. Again, I suggest you check the Gayellow Pages for listings in your area.

Dear Larry,

As a hot-assed, fist-loving, AIDS-conscious bottom, my buddies and I have been getting off on using latex surgical gloves for mutual protection. They are cheap and come in various sizes. I have never known one to break, and they not only offer the fister protection from disease-causing germs, they give the fistee protection from rough nails, skin, etc. Best of all, latex makes entry easier and, if you are into any sort of medical/rubber scene, they are *hot*. I just thought your readers should know about them. Any suggestions you could make regarding readily available germ-killing disinfectants for dildos, buttplugs, ass spreaders, etc., could be useful to all of us, although keeping your toys to yourself is obviously the best protection.

Jeff, NYC

Dear Jeff,

Your ideas are interesting and certainly better than flesh-on-flesh. Still, I wonder about how one gets the gloves off after they are covered with questionable secretions without getting the stuff on himself. Well, I guess if you're careful, you can do it. Fisting, in this era of high risk, still scares the hell out of me; I don't care how you try to protect yourself, it is still one of the most risky things you can do. For disinfectant, use a 75 percent Clorox solution.

Again, looking back on a 1986 answer from the prospective of 1994, the advice seems inaccurate; although, as usual, I erred on the side of caution. Fisting, in and of itself, is less dangerous than many of the other activities that guys who are into fisting are apt to do; i.e., use dope (which impairs judgment), fuck without a rubber, take fecal material into the mouth (sometimes by careless-ness or accident), play more esoteric games involving blood, scat, etc. A good friend of mine from this general era was also a fister, using latex gloves, and feeling almost smug about having outsmarted the virus. As of this writing, he has active AIDS and is not in very good shape. But, again, he did other things that he shouldn't have done, and the medical establishment still can't offer 100 percent assur-ance—"yes" or "no," for many of these fringe activities. It's no wonder a poor columnist is often at a loss, afraid to say, "Go ahead, it looks okay to me," when tomorrow someone is going to find a reason not to do it. On the other hand, if one advises caution in too many situations, you have the sexually active guys on your ass, complaining that you're needlessly scaring off their potential partners. In my own defense, I can only suggest that (I hope) a number of guys are still alive because they listened to me. The next letter is a good example, as is the ambivalence of my answer. (He makes reference in his response to my request that we support the Mariposa Foundation in its research on condom safety and development of antiseptic lubricants.)

Dear Larry,

At your suggestion I am sending a donation to the Mariposa Foundation, but at the same time I would like to tell you about another aspect of the AIDS problem. Recently a doctor was interviewed on our local PBS station, regarding his book, *Maximum Immunity*. He stressed the value of nutrition and vitamins—exercise, etc., mentioning one clinic in Virginia which had sixteen cases of AIDS in remission via this kind of treatment. The reason this struck home to me was that I was diagnosed as "going blind" a year ago, and through a strict regimen of this sort, I was able to totally reverse the process until my eyes are nearly back to normal—all this without other medical treatment. Does this imply that AIDS might also be treated successfully in a similar manner? No M.D. seems to want to admit that this sort of approach can work better than his AMA-approved treatment schedule, but I now really have my doubts. Maybe I'm a kook, maybe the doctor on TV was, but don't you think it's worth exploring?

Jim, Alaska

Dear Jim,

You are not the only one to express this sort of opinion, and my own inclination is to agree with you. Unfortunately, once a guy comes down with a disease like AIDS, he doesn't have the leisure to try one potential cure, and if that doesn't work, to go another route. I'm very much in favor of using megavitamins as an immune-system bolster before the fact. But I would really hesitate to advise a guy who has been diagnosed with AIDS (or any other life-threatening disorder) to ignore the doctors' suggested treatment. I guess it's really difficult to empathize with someone who has come face-to-face with the ultimate diagnosis.

As in my comment on the previous letter, no one can give you a clear, unequivocal answer, although we certainly know more today than a few years ago, when this letter was written. AIDS has been around much longer, now, so it's possible to see where some "long-term survivors" appear to have zeroed in on a regimen that works. Unfortunately, what works for one may do no good for another. And I think this goes for vitamin therapy, as well. Some guys seem to thrive on it; for others it makes little or no difference.

Then there are the crooks and the quacks who are out to make a fast buck on people who are desperately ill. I'm on a multitude of mailing lists, so I get to see most of these phonies in action. Just recently, for instance, I received an ad from a nut who claims to cure AIDS with hydrogen peroxide. It makes you wonder, but I'm sure he's had many takers. How did P. T. Barnum say it?

Dear Larry,

I am getting into "catheter fucking"—that is, fucking the urethra of my cock with small tubes, thermometers, etc. I'm really interested in stretching the urethra to a point where I could fuck it with one of my own fingers. Do you have any suggestions, advice, warnings about this? Am I the only person into this? Am I nuts?

A Fan, San Francisco, CA

Dear Fan,

To answer your questions, not necessarily in order: The dangers are present, as I'm sure you must be aware. Inserting any foreign material into the penile meatus risks bladder infection because whatever bacteria you carry in can find their way upward. In my own mail-order business I declined to carry catheters for many years, but changed my stance gradually because I had received a number of letters like yours in which guys described the really frightening assortment of items they had inserted into themselves—everything from ball-point pens to plastic tubing from an aquarium pump. I decided that if they were going to do it anyway, far better that they use something that was at least made for the purpose. So my first suggestion is that you not use anything except a proper catheter or—if you can find some knowledgeable person to instruct you in its use—a sound (metal tube used by doctors to probe the canal). By using gradually larger catheters, you can expand the size of the meatus, and I have seen guys who could get a finger into the opening. But it took them several years to accomplish this, and the two guys I really had a chance to interview both admitted to having caused various problems along the way—infections, some internal bleeding, prostate irritation, a period of impotence (for one guy), plus various periods of aches and pains. While I cannot in good conscience advise you to do this, I do advise that *if* you are going to do it, find yourself a partner who knows what he's up to and can guide you along the way.

Dear Larry,

I am very interested in piercing, although I don't think I'd ever have the nerve to actually get one. And I don't live where it would be a good idea to have a piercing, since I go to a public gym for workouts. But I really used to enjoy the articles by a guy named Doug Malloy. They were in quite a few different publications a couple of years back, and then suddenly nothing. Can you tell me if Doug is still writing anything and, if so, where I can find them?

(Name withheld) Ames, IA

Dear Withheld,

Doug was a friend of mine and I greatly admired him both as a person and as an expert in his field. Unfortunately, he passed away a couple of years ago from a sudden and unexpected heart attack. His surviving partner now runs Gauntlet Enterprises, which publishes a magazine called *P.F.I. Quarterly.* You can contact them at: 8720–1/2 Santa Monica Boulevard., West Hollywood, CA 90069.

I've substituted the current mailing address for the one in the original reply. In the meantime, they have also opened a store on Market Street in San Francisco, just around the corner from Castro. "Doug" was a very interesting man, who had made a substantial fortune in regular commercial enterprises (and under his real name), which had given him the time and leisure to investigate many places in the world where a variety of bodily adornments were invented and done commonly. He had just about every piercing known to mankind, and was extremely knowledgeable. This tradition is maintained by his surviving partner at Gauntlet.

Dear Larry,

Two short questions: (1) How long should toys and leather be exposed to a bleach solution to ensure their safe use in subsequent sessions? (2) Do you know of any home remedy for ridding leathers of a urine odor?

Norm, Canada

Dear Norm,

For metal or other nonporous materials, the bleach solution should kill the microorganisms within a few seconds. For rubber or plastics (like dildos, buttplugs, etc.), I'd let them soak for ten or fifteen minutes. For leather, I wouldn't use bleach at all, because it can cause damage. Regular rubbing alcohol works just as well. I've simply been cleaning my items with it by wiping them down with a fair amount and letting them dry naturally. If a whip draws draws blood, I soak it in alcohol, let it dry out in the sun, and let it lie for a month or so before using it again. I should also note that the above reference to metal objects does not refer to needles used for piercing, etc. These should be discarded, or at least never used on more than one person. Getting the urine odor out of leather is more difficult because most things that will remove it are not good for the leather. The old home remedy is tomato juice. There are also several products on the market to get "pet odors" out of carpets and furniture, but these may leave a residue which will irritate the skin. Besides, what's wrong with a little extra aroma? (Unless you intend to wear them to the opera.)

We are, of course, being supercareful in the precautions we take, not to spread HIV. In truth, the virus has a very short life span after leaving the cozy warmth of its human host. But, the very idea of being smacked, punctured, or otherwise subjected to contact with an object that may have been contaminated is spooky. Besides, think of all the other maladies we are protecting against.

Dear Larry,

I recently bought an unusual cockring at a "garage sale," when a small leather shop went out of business. It still had its original silver box, but there were no instructions with it. It is plastic, rectangular with rounded corners, and has metal embedded on either of the short ends. There is also a little catch on it, so it can open and swivel to make it easy to put on. I have worn it several time, and it really feels great. My question is two-sided. Can you tell me something about it? A couple of my friends would like to get one, so do you know who sells them?

F. R., New Orleans, LA

Dear F. R.,

It sounds like you found an "Energizer." They are cockrings with unlike metals embedded top and bottom. The theory is that they pick up the minute galvanic (electrical) impulses from the skin and discharge them into your genitals. They are made in England, and as far as I know are still available there. Unfortunately, the manufacturer made some spurious health claims, which resulted in the FDA banning their sale in the United States. Some places sold them anyway, but stocking them presented a problem because they are expensive and come in about a dozen different sizes. If you make it to London someday, try one of the larger dealers. I have one, and I like it, except that it does tend to irritate the skin if you wear it for extended periods.

Dear Larry,

I am interested in exploring foot torture (others', not mine)—but there doesn't seem to be much "out there" on the subject. I am particularly at a loss when it comes to tools. Can you help? Two appliances occur to me. One would be something like a thumbscrew, to be used especially on the big toe. Do you have any experience or advice on this? What do I need to watch out for? Is there a possibility of breaking bones with such a device? Where would I get one? The second item is vaguer to me. I have a faint recollection of reading that the Spanish Inquisition used something—perhaps parchment—which, when wrapped in strips around the foot, shrank and compressed the bones until removed. Do you know anything about this? I also wonder if you can give me any tips/cautions/instructions about putting on plaster casts and how to get supplies.

Albert, Ypsilanti, MI

Dear Albert,

The foot fetish seems to be less common than it once was, but there must still be a planet of people "out there" who dig it. I don't know of anyone making thumbscrews/toescrews, per se; but I have seen several wooden nutcrackers which have to be exact replicas of the old torture devices. Try your local gift shoppe. They are, or course, dangerous. The purpose in using one was to break the victim's bones if he didn't confess, or whatever. The Inquisition wrapping technique was not restricted to just the feet, but might have been used on almost any part of the body—the skull being a favorite place. It consisted of wrapping several layers of wet material around the hand, foot, head, what-have-you, and letting it shrink as it dried. I think that parchment was used, but untanned leather or even animal gut was probably more common. Again, the old inquisitors were not particularly concerned about their victims' welfare, so these techniques are dangerous. They will not only break bones, but may cause vascular or neurological damage, even gangrene if left in place too long.

Plaster casts are easy. You can buy the stuff over the counter at most pharmacies, and if you check the medical section of your favorite bookstore, you'll find more than you ever wanted to know about application. Of course, the bigger problem is getting it off, and they don't always tell you as much about that.

More recently, I have discovered that there is a much larger foot-fetish community than I previously suspected. My friend Bob Jones has been making videos, tailored to the tastes of this subculture, and has met with great success. (Bob Jones Productions, 1026 Folsom Street, San Francisco, CA 94103.)

Dear Sir—

I am writing you this letter in regard to something that totally puzzles, yet fascinates my Daddy and me. When my Daddy and I start to play, naturally I get very excited! During foreplay, when he begins playing with my ass, it starts to get moist. It's almost like the wetness a woman's vagina secretes during foreplay. Then when he penetrates my ass and starts anal intercourse, I become very hot and wet. I've never encountered this before. I think it might have something to do with the emotional set I have for my Daddy, in addition to the fact that I just love to get fucked! My question: Is this normal or not, and should I have any worries?

Daddy's Boy, Cleveland, OH

Dear Boy,

Although not a doctor, and unable to speak with that authority, I certainly can respond with some assurance on the subject of fucking ass. I don't think that "self lubricating" assholes are all that rare, although it is unusual for a guy to prep himself without at least a few drops of some moisturizing agent—spit, if nothing else. Remember, though, that K-Y has been a very popular lubricant for as long as I can remember, and it dries out quickly if you try to use it as a JO gel. In anal (or vaginal) intercourse it works well, because the body supplies the moisture after the initial few strokes. The membranes of the rectum are "mucous" tissues, and so by definition are secretory. In your excitement, you probably also tend to sweat. What's happening is probably perfectly natural to your particular butt-hole. If there is anal pain, bleeding, or excessive discharge of mucus later during a bowel movement, however, you should have a doctor take a peek up there.

Dear Larry,

In some of your past commentaries, you have advised guys not to wear cockrings and ballstretchers when they go to bed to sleep. I wear a leather cockring all the time, taking it off only when I shower. After years of doing this, I don't see that it has had any adverse effects. Comment?
Ralph, Detroit, MI

Dear Ralph,

My advice about not wearing ballstretchers to bed was merely to avoid the possibility of someone hurting himself by having his circulation curtailed when he was not awake and able to do something about it. A regular cockring does not pose the same danger, especially if it is well fitted and not too tight. In fact, it can sometimes help produce some wonderful dreams.

The Energizer we discussed several letters back makes a wonderful bedtime companion, especially in warm weather when the skin is going to sweat a bit and cause the little currents to flow more freely. Try it, if you can find one. Sweet dreams!

Dear Larry,

When I torture myself at night, I can't wear my contacts. I want to start wearing gas masks, slave hoods—leather, latex—when I torture myself. Is there a type of prescription eyeglasses that I can wear under a gas mask or a slave hood without the pressure breaking the glass?
John, Wisconsin

Dear John,

I don't know why you would want to wear glasses under a slave hood, since it is supposed to act as a blindfold. The only way I can think of your getting them to work with a hood would be to get a pair of athletic glasses made up (like basketball players wear), and strap these onto the outside. As to the gas mask, most of these have circular glass or plastic lenses which are inserted into a groove in the rubber. I suppose you might remove the originals and take them to an optician, who should be able to make prescription lenses that are the same circumference. You could than replace the originals with these.

Dear Larry,

In recent years I have gotten very skilled in performing exotic acts of masturbation, mostly because I'm afraid to seek outside sex partners. I particularly enjoy C&B bondage-torture, and often do a real job on my nuts. I use all kinds of leather stretchers, rope or rawhide, metal rings in graduated sizes, and just about anything else you might imagine. (In fact, if I haven't already thought of it and you mention some new device, I'll probably try it.) I've developed a fairly large black-and-blue spot on my scrotum from all of this, however, and I'm sure it happened because I ruptured some small blood vessels in the sac skin. I tried to poke it with a needle and drain out the blood, but it came right back. Is this something a doctor could repair in his office, or do you think they'd want me to go to a hospital to have it done? It's embarrassing enough to think of facing only one man, but I don't think I could face a whole nursing staff, to say nothing of the expense. I know it isn't a life-threatening situation, but it bothers me every time I see it, and when the time comes that I find a safe-sex partner, I don't want him to see it, either.

J. L., New Orleans, LA

Dear J. L.,

My medical adviser reminds me that without seeing your nuts it would be hard to say exactly what you're done to yourself. I do have a friend who had a similar thing happen to him, however—or at least what sounds like a similar thing—and he did have it taken care of in a dermatologist's office. He also remarked, though, that the good doc called in his giggly young receptionist to help hand him things during the little surgical procedure, so that was also embarrassing. But, just think how much more humiliating it's been for people who have to race to the emergency room with "foreign objects" stuck up their asses, or wrapped around their dicks and/or balls that they couldn't remove on their own. It always pays to look on the bright side. You'll probably get off easy—and cheaply.

I included this in the chapter on SM techniques, because I liked his description of SM/JO materials—something that interests more and more people these days.

Dear Mr. Townsend, Sir!
   i am a slave with a Master who controls my orgasms as well as my hard-ons. He says that sometimes i must experience orgasm, only so that i can remember how good it feels, and more deeply appreciate the deprivation when i am not allowed to cum for days or even weeks at a time. But during these periods of deprivation i still have to serve him and his friends, who all sit around naked, sometimes stroking my peepee, then punishing me if i get a hard-on. i sometimes cry because i know i may have to go for such a long time without an orgasm, even though i am living in a house where sexy, handsome men are running around naked and having sex in front of me that i can only watch, and never enjoy personally. i know i must be totally owned by my Master, but i still wonder (and here is my question) if i am going to experience some physical harm from having my load of cum bottled up in my balls for such extended periods of time. Please answer me, and i hope my Master reads your reply.
                          slave billy hard-on masochist cocksucker

Dear sbhmc,
   You are lucky to have a Master who holds you in high enough regard to put you through your paces. Although my medical adviser tells me that consistently holding back one's orgasm can, over a period of time, cause an inflammation of the prostate, there is no empirical evidence that men experiencing this problem (which usually occurs in later life) would not have had difficulty anyway. It seems a cheap price to pay for the privilege

of your present existence. There are a great many guys who would change places with you right now!

My answer brought forth an angry response from another reader. (Note the "Dear Mr. Townsend." It's the salutation I get from respectful slaves or irate correspondents.):

Dear Mr. Townsend,

In *Drummer 149*, you responded to a letter asking about whether having a Master restrict a slave's ejaculations for a long period of time would pose long-term health problems. You dismissed the potential for later prostate problems with an airy "It seems a cheap price to pay for the privilege of your present existence. There are a great many guys out there who would change places with you right now." Really. And how many will want to change places with him when he goes through prostate cancer in twenty years? It is time the Leather Community grew up, and realized that although sex is important (and for some seems to be the only significant element in their lives), sex is not worth death or serious illness. (The letter then goes on at some length about a local doctor who gave faulty AIDS advice.)

A. C., Springfield, VA

Dear A. C.,

Do you really believe that restricting a guy's freedom to shoot his load in his twenties is going to assure his getting cancer in his forties—or fifties, or sixties? I hardly think that is a valid assumption. A Master's controlling his slave's ejaculations is one of the oldest and most universal games in the SM repertory. It also tends to be one of the activities that takes place during the earlier phases of a relationship, and to slack off as the initial passions cool. In other words, it is seldom that a slave is restricted for such extensive periods that you really have to worry about long-term effects. Prostate concern—like most forms of the disease—results from a multiplicity of factors in a person's life. Admittedly, if we all played it completely safe, we might all live a little longer. But by the very nature of the games we play, we do run a greater risk in a variety of areas then the vanilla practitioners. I believe, in answering any of the questions posed by our readers, that we ("we" being either myself or the *Drummer* editors) have to respond within the context of a leather lifestyle *(a term I really don't like, but appropriate, I think, in this situation)*, and to take into account our tendency—as a community—to act out a little more on the brink. Because I've been playing these games for so long, and have watched so many others play them, I guess I tend to read more into a situation than may be expressed in the words of a letter, and therefore assume the practitioners are using at least a modicum of common sense. You are, aren't you?

This controversy also brought to mind the old-time require-ments of abstention, foisted so fondly upon all young men by the various puritanical churches that seem so all-pervasive in our history, and up to the present time. If we were to follow the dictates of these moralists, and deprive ourselves of even a good JO session until we were safely married into a proper heterosex-ual union, would we be asking for prostate problems in later life? It would be interesting to generate some statistics on the good Christians who have been so deprived. Of course, accurate percentages would assume that they didn't violate the rules by jacking off in private when they had the chance. Anyone want to take bets on this?

Dear Larry,

I often read your "Leather Notebook" in *Drummer* maga-zine. Your opinions frequently supplement my own experiences. My current interest is branding. Having learned to endure—then enjoy—the pain of fisting, I think I am now ready to progress to this additional step, which leads to several questions: Where do I get a branding iron? Is it possible to have one made with my initials on it? How does one heat it enough to leave a good scar or welt? What sani-tary precautions should be taken? Should the guy be tied up, or chained down?

Frankly, I wouldn't mind being branded myself by the right hot dude. And he'd *better* tie me up! If you publish this letter, please tell all those hot men out there that I'm looking for their responses to my *Drummer* ad

(Master, Venice, CA.) Thanks, and let's get the irons hot!
Michael, Venice, CA

Dear Michael,

Because branding was a harsh and hated punishment in the
Old World, most American jurisdictions have statutes against it.
Remember that in making public solicitations for a partner. As
to obtaining a customized branding iron, anyone who works with
metal, like wrought iron, can make one for you. It's just a matter
of finding a guy who's willing to do it. Regular cattle irons are
often on sale in antique and specialty shops—even junk shops.
Remember, though, that branding a human is very different
from putting the iron to a cow. Your skin is much thinner. If
you're serious about doing this, I hope you get a response from
someone who has experience. There have to be many pitfalls. If
you just tie a guy down and shove a hot iron against his skin, you
may very well cause a far greater injury than either of you
bargained for. But it *is* an exciting idea, isn't it?

Hello, Larry,

I've belonged to the Leather Fraternity since the days when
they issued membership cards. I've enjoyed the free ads associated with the Fraternity and used to advertise for a "trim pain
slave." My fetish is squeezing the hell out of the slave's waist
and gut, gouging fingers under the rib cage, some hard torture
on the cock and balls. I might hold and control the slave by
his hair or other means of bondage. With the slave on his
back, tied and blindfolded, I will lay with my face on his gut
and get myself off. Needless to say, when I answer my letters
this way, the letters stop, especially when I add that I like to
make love during the process. Do you think there are slaves
around who would dig my scene? Have I just missed connecting with the right guy(s), or am I too far off base?

Respectfully,
Mr. Jones, Coon Rapids, MN

Dear Jonesy,

You also mention in a postscript that you are: fifty, 265

pounds, 6' tall, and modestly endowed. In all honesty, I would suspect that your physical dimensions have more to do with the rejections than your behavior. It's a cruel world out there, more so the older and fatter you get. Most of the things you like to do are a bit out of the mainstream, but not so extreme that you shouldn't find someone willing to give you a try. Of course, I'm not sure exactly where Coon Rapids is. If a guy lives too far out in the toolies, he may simply be inaccessible. I might suggest a diet and good workout routine, followed by a few trips to the leatherbars in your nearest metropolis (Chicago?) on Friday/ Saturday nights.

Dear Larry,

I note both in our column (some time back) and more recently in an advertising blurb in your mail-order brochure, you advise guys not to pop their chrome anal eggs out, into the toilet. You point out that this can shatter the porcelain, etc. (I would also note that it can lead to the loss of the egg, if it gets down the pipe before you can retrieve it.) I'd like you to know that my friend and I overcame the problem by purchasing a "portable bidet." These are plastic inserts that fit over the toilet bowl, and are only a few inches deep. They are quite inexpensive (about $11.00), and can be purchased in most major drug stores. Perhaps you will want to pass this along.

D. B., Indianapolis, IN

Dear D. B.,

Thanks for the info. Like your eggs, it's being passed.

In reading over the letters I selected for this chapter, I realize that several of them could just as easily have fit into other categories. Well, so be it. Techniques come in many shapes and disguises, many times consisting of practices we do not necessarily identify as such. (Much like "philosophy.") I do think that we can profit greatly by studying the experiences and mistakes of others, especially if we take time to think about them before we fall into the same traps on our own.

CHAPTER 5

Parents, Friends, and Other Relationships, Including Role-playing (Sexual and Asexual)

Regardless of a man's specific sexual desires or requirements, he must still cope with people who are interacting with him on various levels, not necessarily sexual, although this may also be a factor. I'm going to include some Daddy-son letters in this section, and not all of these tell a strictly platonic story. Nor do the questions concerning role-playing, but this is often of paramount importance in an SM relationship—especially in its initial stages, when the specific modes of interaction are still being established.

Dear Larry,

I am writing this letter to thank you for writing *The Leatherman's Handbook*, which has influenced my life greatly, but also to ask you a question. You seem to indicate that a guy should start out in the leather scene as a bottom and eventually work his way into being Top. I'm only twenty-one and I haven't had too much experience, but I find that I am always Top in the few scenes I've had. After moving to the Midwest from Oakland, I have been trying to experience every aspect of leather life, and have been hitting the bars, looking for the bigger, rougher, tougher men. I find that I cannot and will not be bottom. I am very aggressive and can dish it out extremely well, but can not take it. This is what bothers me. Also, being 6' and 210 pounds doesn't help, either. Occasionally, I have the urge to be passive as bottom in Greek, and that is as much of a bottom as I am able to be. As a result, I am very puzzled and feel somewhat isolated. Can you offer some helpful advice?

Blue Monday, Nebraska

Dear Blue,

Although I have written extensively on various aspects of the leather scene, it is impossible to describe every case that every individual is going to encounter. Each of us is unique in his sexuality—a point I think I made more strongly in the original *Leatherman's Handbook* than in the sequel. Although I have tried to depict the basic attitudes that most guys reflect in their approach to SM, or to the specific sets of activities that interest them, there are always going to be exceptions to the "main-stream" modes of behavior that I mention in my various books and articles. Your situation would appear to be one of them. If you are happy being Top, and the guys who get it on with you are satisfied with your performance, more power to you. As you note yourself, you are very young and have a good many years ahead of you. I would suspect that somewhere in your future contacts you will find a guy who is capable of topping you, and whom you will wish to have do this. But even if this never happens, it should not be of any great concern. Good Tops are certainly in great demand; if you can qualify as such without ever having been bottom…enjoy!

One of the difficulties in writing about human behavior is that people have such an infinite variety of possible responses and atti-tudes that there is no way to set up categories that include everyone. I have tried to point this out, certainly in both Handbooks, *as well is in this column. I am very opinionated as regards my own attitudes and standards of behavior, and I have definite feelings pro and con on the things other people do. But I try (not always with complete success) to respond to questions on a nonjudgmental level, unless I think the guy is on a course of destruction. I may debate a guy on many points, but I also do this with the proviso: I'm telling you what I think is right, and what's right for me. It may not be right for you.*

Dear Larry,

I live in Los Angeles, and I frequently go to the more popular leatherbars in the area. I have recently encountered a situation that bothers me, and I wonder if you'd like to comment on it. There is a bartender in one of the busiest bars who dresses all in leather, even to a stud in his left ear. At first glance he looks like everybody's fantasy of "Mr. Leather." But when he opens his mouth, he is all girl—even carrying on as to how he can't wait for Halloween, because he has his drags all ready to go. Now, I know that everyone is entitled to his own "thing," but this isn't what I go to a leather bar to hear. Am I out of step? Old-fashioned?

Rob, Los Angeles

Dear Rob,

I think many of us would agree with your reaction to this situation, at least at first impulse. Of course, our house has many rooms, and there are some pretty heavy SM scenes going on that involve transvestites, transsexuals, etc. I guess I'd say: However, if the guy can make a decent drink, he's doing his job. If too many of the customers feel as you do, it might be a smart move on his part to butch up his act a bit. If he can't do this, there are plenty of fluff bars where he'd probably be more in tune with the customers. On the other hand, if the majority of his present customers are happy with him, you'll just have to grin and bear it.

Again, we respond to the stereotype and get upset when someone doesn't come up to our expectations. Even a queen can buy leathers; it takes a man to wear them to full advantage.

Dear Larry,

I'll try to make this brief. I'm forty-eight with a reasonable number of the required attributes to pick up a twenty-two-year-old kid off the streets about six months ago. The kid moved in with all his worldly possessions (on his back), and I've since sprung for some decent clothes, chow, and found him a fairly basic job that pays him a little more than minimum wage. I came home last night and found dinner ready (as usual), the apartment cleaned, etc. The kid was naked and kneeling in complete silence in a corner of the living room. He crawled across the floor, licking my shoes, and said, "Thank you for coming home, sir."

I've been unable to get any kind of explanation out of him, and over dinner (which I ate by myself; he would not join me, but sat and watched) he gave me a copy of a Master-slave agreement and asked me to sign it with him.

You guys got me into this. What the fuck do I do now? The kid apparently typed his document on my typewriter to have it ready for my arrival. All I could do was tell him I would consider it. I don't think I would know how to put him through his paces. I've always bought and read *Drummer* with sort of an academic interest and a certain amount of awe and admiration. Now I find myself in what appears to be the middle of a very heavy thing. Can you offer some guidance, please?

A Master?, Peoria, IL

Dear Master?—

What a marvelous thing to have happen! It's really too bad you don't feel able to handle the situation; it might really be fun for you. However, I'm sure there must be a suitable Master living in your part of the country, who would be more than willing to take the unwanted slave off your hands. I'll pass their responses along to you. The other solution, of course, if you really like the kid and want to keep him, would be to take a few lessons yourself and pass the knowledge along.

If I remember correctly, this situation worked out well, with the reluctant Master overcoming his inhibitions and eventually doing a reasonable job with his kid. How long it lasted, however, I never discovered. It was a case of the role of Master being more or less forced on the guy.

Dear Larry,

   After some time lapse, I have started buying an occasional *Drummer* because I find a portion of the material a turn-on. However, the heavy stuff has the opposite effect. In trying to categorize my sexual interests, I have to say that these center mainly on fucking—love it either way, except that I do like to do things that some of my past partners have thought weird. For instance, I might want to wear a hat when I'm fucking or get fucked with a dildo. I'm thirty-six, and a really good fuck. Since reading the last issue of *Drummer*, I have really been fantasizing about finding a Master, but I'm afraid of getting into a situation where I give up everything else and suddenly find myself dumped because the Master has gotten tired of me, or where I walk out because be can't satisfy me in a monogamous relationship. I've been tied down and found it boring; I've been spanked and beaten and it turned me off. We have one bar here in Austin that caters to the leather/Levi group, but most of the guys look seedy and unhealthy. I'd love a well-bred Master with some class and self-respect, who took care of himself. Does such a rare bird exist? One other question: Some guys in the *Drummer* classifieds list a number such as "Interchain 1234" or "LF" number. Can you explain? Thanks a lot.

HIM, Austin, TX

Dear HIM,

   I have cut your letter down considerably, but hope I've retained the essence of it. You are in the status I have always classified as "fringie" to the leather scene. That is, the idea turns you on, but the heavy action does not. In this you are certainly not alone, and on this basis finding a partner should not be very difficult. However, I also detect the underlying problem as being twofold. First, you want a Master, but you want to call the shots. Secondly, you are so compulsive (and maybe bitchy) that it's going to be hard for anyone to live with you. What you need is a good Master who'll tie you down and show you who's boss, fucking you silly in the bargain...then leaving you in bondage until you cry "uncle!" If you're ever lucky enough to have that happen to you, it might awaken the latent qualities that will make you acceptable to your well-bred, self-respecting Master. As to the codes, both *Drummer's* Leather Fraternity (LF) and Interchain offer a postal forwarding service for their members. The numbers are their identity codes.

This sounded like one more pushy bottom in-the-making. It's just too bad there aren't enough solid, no-nonsense Masters to go around—men with the experience and the patience to straighten'em out.

Dear Larry,

Having originally "come out" in the SM scene with your *Handbook*, I figure you're the guy to ask about my heaviest unfulfilled fantasy. I really want "animal training." I want it so bad I can almost taste it. I have read numerous articles about "dog training," but these are just a mind fuck. I can't find any qualified Top who is seriously interested in turning me into a pig, ass, horse, dog, or...? What I really want is a guy who can make it such a mind trip that I can imagine myself actually undergoing a metamorphosis into whatever animal he has in mind. I picture myself being placed in a really unclean stable, completely under the control of the man who is going to train me. The few people I've discussed this with think I'm just perverted, or maybe not sincere. With respect to SM standards, am I way off base? Is there any chance of my finding the kind of Master I need, or am I condemned forever to fantasize over a situation I can never obtain? (Please don't suggest an ad. I've already tried many of these without success.) Awaiting your reply, I remain married to my can of lube.

Frustrated, Milwaukee, WI

Dear Frustrated,

You are seeking not only a highly specialized situation, but you also need a man who has the facilities to carry out your dreams. While this is one of the more popular themes of SM fiction, I have to confess that I have never met anyone who has actually lived it—from either side. This is not to say it cannot, or has not happened. I'm sure it has, but the fact that I haven't encountered it makes me believe it has to be very rare. I do not feel that you are outside the reasonable bounds of SM behavior, but you are certainly not in the "mainstream." If some rugged farmer type writes in and wants you, I'll certainly be happy to pass along the invitation. (But don't hold me responsible for your saddle sores or fleabites.)

Fantasies like this make me wonder if any of these wonderful situations might have taken place when our western culture was considerably younger, and everyone lived with livestock, riding horses instead of driving cars, and possibly keeping their slaves in a genuine barn. Or out in the Wild West, where men were men, and there weren't many women? We'll never know for sure, but the idea kinda helps to keep your spirits rising, doesn't it?

Dear Larry,

I am a married man. My wife and I have been together for over five years, so I think it's a pretty stable relationship. Both of us are into SM; my wife is dominant, and some of our sessions have gotten fairly heavy. I am complete bisexual, however, and recently my wife has agreed that we should seek some outside interests—three-ways and the like. She is perfectly willing to have the third person be a man—prefers a man because she has no interest in other women. We've run ads a few times, but it doesn't work out well for us to get it on with another couple or with a straight man. At least, it isn't satisfactory for me, because he only turns on to my wife, and I end up being tied up in a corner while she does her thing with him. The few gay men we've contacted are so uptight about "safe sex" there isn't much we can do with them, even if we get over the hurdle of accepting a female Top. Would you have any suggestions for us?

Horny in Dallas

Dear Horny,

For starters, I think you and your wife should begin having some concern about safe sex, yourselves. In Africa, where our current health crisis apparently started, it's regarded as a heterosexual disease. As to gay men getting it on with a woman, it takes a fairly sophisticated bottom to dig this. After all, the reason a man seeks other men is because he isn't turned on to women. I don't know what you look like, but I would suppose that you would have to be the one to attract the guy into your relationship, and hope that he's so hot to get it on with you that he'll also accept your wife in the balance.

I didn't know what else to tell this guy, as I really felt myself on "thin ice." In fact, as a thoroughly hard-core, confirmed queer, it is difficult to empathize with a bisexual. Like so many of my compatriots, I am simply not interested in a woman in any kind of a sexual situation. I know that this condition is far from unique, and is very likely at the heart of the rejection many women find in trying to share our bars or other "space(s)." I can appreciate a woman's plight in these social situations and sympathize with her, as is discussed elsewhere in this book. But on the more intimate level, I find myself in tune with the hard-liners who have no desire for a woman in the place of sexual interaction. This attitude— which I suspect is a majority attitude among gay men—is very likely at the core of Horny's problem. I have noticed, however, that our very youngest contingent (those who are under twenty-five) seem much more willing to share their space with women. Whether they would also be as quick to share their beds is more to difficult to say, but it might provide a starting point for someone in Horny's position. (Unless Horny and his wife would be too old for them, and then he'd be right back to square one.)

Dear Larry,

I've got a good thing going with a really hot man. He has been bottoming out to me since we started, about a year ago. But I really want him to work me over, at least some of the time. I've hinted at this, but he just doesn't pick up on it. I don't know if he has really been missing the point, or whether he just doesn't want to understand me. I'm afraid to press the point too hard, for fear I'll fuck up what I've already got. How do you think I should go about it?

Ready to switch, DC

Dear Ready,

I would guess that your friend is completely aware of what you're trying to tell him, and simply doesn't want to ruin a good thing by changing roles. As we've said a good many times, "A good Top is had to find." If you're playing that role and doing it well, there is probably no way to change the situation without just coming out and stating your case. I think you have to evaluate the risk, and either tell him or let things go as they are.

We keep coming face-to-face with that old reluctance of a man to admit he wants to be bottom. I'm sure it stems from our childhood conditioning, where we are taught that a real man is aggressive and in essence a "Top"—although it is never expressed in such explicit terms. I hate to conjecture on the number of wonderful exchanges that have been missed simply because a lusty potential bottom was unable to admit his true desires. But there does appear to be a slow, gradual shift toward a more honest self-expression, as discussed by and with our next correspondent.

Dear Larry,

There seems to be some discrepancy in your writings about the number of Tops vs. the number of bottoms. In the original *Leatherman's Handbook*, you seemed to imply that the ratio was much higher in favor of the Ms than you did in the sequel. Do you think the numbers have shifted over that ten years or so between the two publications, or has your perception changed? I like to play both sides, usually not with the same person, but consistently one or the other with various, specific partners. What does that make me?

Switch-hitter, MD

Dear Switch,

I don't think there has been a great shift in the number of guys involved in each respective role. Rather, I think, it is my interpretation (more than perception) of what classifies as what. Originally, I adhered to the then-current theory that if a guy played bottom at all, he should be classified as a bottom. Later, I came to believe that these categories should not be defined so rigidly. Many guys enjoy both sides, either alternately or as a set preference over varying periods of time. Because of this shift in perspective, I utilized a "middle category" in my later writings, and now feel that it probably comprises the largest group. It is probably also true that our evolving perceptions and practices have softened the previously harder definitions. All of this, of course, is sheer speculation, since there is no way to make a scientifically valid measure of our population.

This is also why I have started using the term "SM" to describe our community, rather than "S&M" or even "S/M." I have come to accept the fact that there is part of each in all of us, and even if we never (or rarely) act out more than one side of the Janus mask, the second face is still there. The M side is probably the most consistent, resulting in the "M component," which I first described in my novel Masters' Counterpoints. *It is my feeling that no matter how firmly a man may be entrenched as a Top, he is going to have his "M moments." These may be mere flights of fantasy, or some self-bondage done in private in the course of a JO session, or simply springing a hard-on in vicarious enjoyment of a bottom getting his just reward.*

The converse is no less universal, but it tends to have a "lower end," wherein the man experiences relatively weaker impulses (or lusts) to be a Top. There are some guys who are total bottoms and have no overt inclination to be anything else. What elements of Top reside within such a man, they are seldom if ever expressed. Except that, once in a while, even the most confirmed bottom will have a flicker of desire to inflict a modicum of punishment or extract revenge. And when he does act, his behavior may be far more extreme than a man who functions generally as Top. But in this, we are discussing the extreme ends of the spectrum. Most of us fall somewhere in between, having at one time or another functioned in both roles. And, if anything, I see more of this today than twenty years ago. At least, many guys are more open about it.

Dear Larry,

Here's another "Dear Abby" type question for you. My folks are coming to visit in a couple of months. My friend (lover) and I live in a two-bedroom apartment. My folks probably know I'm gay, but it's never been discussed, and they don't know I'm living with another man. They are going to be with me only for three or four days, and they are driving across country with a motor home, and will go on to the West Coast from my place. I really want my lover to stay with some friends (just down the hall in the same building) while my folks are here, but he won't do it. He says if I make him move out, he won't come back. If I could just be sure of my parents' acceptance, I wouldn't care, but I'm afraid to risk it. They're "Bible Belt" people, and I don't want to be "estranged" from them. But I don't want to lose my lover, either. What should I do?

Worried, Phoenix, AZ

Dear Worried,

First, turn off the panic switch. Lots of single people who aren't gay share apartments. Unless your lover's a flaming queen, they probably won't think anything about it. You say you've got two bedrooms; that would seem a perfect cover to me. As to your lover's attitude, he's perfectly right. I'd tell you the same thing. You might send the sling down to stay with the neighbors, though.

It's hard to believe the terror so many guys experience when they think their parents are going to discover they're gay. Most know about their kids, anyway, but may prefer to ignore it. Others may find out and have a bad initial reaction, but will come around eventually. Those who would actually disown their children for being gay are few in number and short on perception. However, worse than facing some possible rejection is the desire on the part of many guys not to "hurt" their parents. But again, everybody goes through a variety of "hurts" in their lives, and discovering that one has a gay child is simply one of them. It's better to get the truth out in the open, one way or another—better, too, to do it on your own time continuum than to leave it to chance or gossip.

Dear Larry,

There seems to be a trend lately for guys to bring women into their SM sex games. I've found this particularly true in

New York and along the East Coast. Leatherwomen now seem to be welcomed in most bars, and if there is an after-hours party they are just as likely to be there, as well. I, for one, don't like it, and I know there are a lot of leather-men who feel as I do. I've read some of your more liberal comments in the past, but don't you think we're entitled to have our own bars and parties without some cunt being foisted on us?

M. R., Baltimore, MD

Dear M. R.,

You're stirring up that old shit again, and ten or fifteen years ago I might have agreed with you. As it is, I still agree to some extent. As one who has not the least interest in women sexually, I certainly feel that I have a right not to perform with one. On the other hand, we are living in a society that is evolving more and more toward a "no-barriers" situation, where membership in a club or patronage of a business (bar or otherwise) cannot be restricted on the basis or sex, age, race, etc. This trend can only spell a positive benefit for us as gay men. At least the general attitudes favor us. Furthermore, the women who show up at our bars or attend our parties are almost certainly friends—friends of specific leathermen, and hopefully friends of the Leather Community in general. And, believe me, we need all the friends we can get. No one is forcing you to have sex with a woman; and, if you keep the door closed, you won't see and neither will she. When you're at someone else's party, you have to put up with the guests he chooses. When you give one your-self, if you don't want women, don't invite them.

I guess my argument is that you get what you pay for. And in terms of social progress toward our own greater freedom, we some-times have to give a little to gain a lot. I spent a couple of years as president of a California Democratic Council political club. It was the first such gay club in the Los Angeles area, and I found the expe-rience a real eye-opener. A number of social causes that had been very peripheral to my life space were suddenly set in front of me. Issues on which I had been more-or-less negative—or, at best, indif-ferent, were now causes I was expected to endorse. By doing so, our own causes were then espoused by some of the people who had previously been oblivious to them. In a sense, some of our own social interactions carry the same sense of "you-scratch-my-back-and-I'll-scratch-yours." And at this point in my life, I couldn't care less if a few women want to share our bar space. Besides, in most larger cities, the women are setting up their own places, anyway; so I have a feeling the problem is going to resolve itself without any great confrontations. Especially among the younger set, as I noted earlier, you find an increasing "unisex" movement coming along with a tendency for an "anything goes" attitude, where burgeoning leather/SM guys are sharing the bar with drags, fluffs, women—just about anyone (except us old guys—oh, well, you can't win 'em all.)

Dear Larry,

I grew up in an "SM household," in that my parents were very much into a variety of bondage-and-discipline activities—both between themselves and occasionally with other singles or couples. They were very careful during my early years, so that I was never aware of the situation until I reached high-school age. We lived in a fairly large house, so they were able to restrict their games to a remote room in the basement. I had seen things that should have tipped me off before this, but it had never even occurred to me that people might do things like this—certainly not my parents. But I believe that some semblance of these urges must be hereditary, because as a teenager I began to fantasize about being tied up and forced to obey the commands of another boy. Looking back, I guess I was always turned on to the idea of bondage. Anyway, despite my naïveté regarding my parents' activities, I was an only child and very close to them. So, when my father finally came to that day when he thought he should explain the birds and the bees—a bit late by current standards, because I was fourteen and ready to start the tenth grade—I confessed my guilty secret. It must have really taken him by total surprise because he obviously didn't know how to answer me. He was supportive and understanding, though. I think he wanted to discuss it with Mom before going any further with me. The long and short if it was (is) that my dad was the submissive partner in his sexual relations with my mother, although you'd never know this otherwise. He is very masculine, now in his mid-forties, and successful in business, etc. Most of this activity between my parents was in the past; I don't think they were doing much of anything—certainly not with outsiders.

So all of this long tale brings me to the question I want to ask. First, do you think SM urges are or can be hereditary? Second, I'm very turned on to the idea of making it with my father, but I'm afraid to say anything to him. I think he's bisexual, but I'm not 100 percent sure. He's really kind of "proper" in his relationship with me, although he did finally admit to the substance (but not the details) of what he does with Mom. Although I'd really like to have him Top me, I'm willing to play the other side, if that's the only way I can make it happen. Just for the record, I'm now nineteen, so I guess that means I'm of legal age, and physical attractiveness isn't a problem on either side. I know I can't foresee all the questions that might arise in your mind in trying to answer this, but I really would appreciate your thoughts. Respectfully,

(Name withheld), East Coast

Dear East,

Your situation has the makings for a wonderful novel! But let's try to examine some of your thoughts in the light of cold reality. Your first question is on that the "experts" will debate forever, although in the current medical literature there are various discoveries being made that imply genetic factors in a number of behavioral areas. The last one I read about involved an apparent chromosome address for a gene that may or may not determine a proclivity for manic-depressive illness. I'd say the conclusions are now so uncertain that you'd be safe to believe what you wish to believe, and no matter what your position you would have ample academic support. (That's the approved scientific way of saying, "I don't know.")

As to getting it on with Dear Old Dad, you really present a dilemma. First, assuming he is bisexual, he may still have strong feelings about an incestuous relationship with his son. You must also recognize that you could be placing yourself into a competitive situation with your mother. Either or both of your parents might respond negatively because of this. There are so many social taboos and undefined sexual valences in this three-way relationship that I have to come back at you with the same answer my computer might give: "Insufficient data." If you are really lusting after your father, I think your best course would be to sit him down in a quiet, private moment and discuss it with him. He sounds like an intelligent, reasonable man. Let him make the decision. I have a feeling that nothing is going to happen immediately, but maybe—over time, who knows? As in so many cases of conflicting human desires, the best answer can be found through truth and openness, rather than inhibited and secret longing.

The lust of the son for the father is very popular in gay SM lore—a twist on the old Oedipal complex, it forms one of the most prevalent fantasies in our community. How different men handle it is always interesting—sometimes fascinating. You'll find another few examples as you read on. Instead of grouping them all together, I have left them scattered in sequence, because the chronology sometimes determined my answers.

Dear Mr. Townsend,

As an avid reader of all L.T./*Drummer*–type material, I find myself wondering if it is ever possible for a man to achieve the lifetime status of slave to a single perfect (or at least acceptable) Master. Outside your fictional productions, have you ever encountered such a relationship that could be considered a lifelong commitment on the part of both Master and slave? Or, if you have not actually observed it, do you think it is possible for such to exist?

Hopeful, NV

Dear Hopeful,

A lifetime, barring accident or fatal disease, is a long time, indeed. I have encountered situations where the two men have been together (not always living under the same roof), and have maintained their relationship(s) well into the "golden years." However, what started out as a hot-and-heavy sexual bond had—in each case—become something very different. The love and commitment remained, but whether I would still call them Master and slave is questionable. However, this is true of any long-term relationship, whether it be gay, het, SM, or whatever. The lust that originally brings two people together will always diminish over the years. It is something else that keeps a couple united. Even in fiction, I never try to tell you that the glorious sex is eternal. It isn't, and it can't be.

So many stories—my own included—will end with the young, lusty couple bound together by love and devotion that the implication may seem that their physical relationship is going to be forever. It makes for a nice feeling in the reader's mind, and there is nothing wrong in implying that a couple may have a goodly amount of time ahead of them in which to enjoy their sexual exchanges. Some do last for a number of years. There may even be one here or there to disprove me. If so, I wish them well.

Dear Larry,

This is kind of personal, but I don't care if you publish it as long as you don't identify my by name or location. I am now twenty-two year old and very interested in the leather scene. In fact, my first introduction to the subject happened when I was in high school. I found a copy of your original *Handbook* stashed away in the back of my father's closet. It already had a "well-read" appearance when I got my hands on it, and it was in even worse shape when I finally put it back. My question: Do you think that my finding the book is sufficient evidence of my father's interest that I might somehow approach him? He never punished me much when I was a kid; in fact, looking back on it I think he sort of avoided physical correction even when I did things to deserve it. I'd love to have him make up for lost time now that I can appreciate it. He's been separated from my mom for a long time and lives alone in the house where I grew up. I really

want to get it on with him, but I love him very much and
don't want to take a chance of fucking up that relationship. What would you do?

Name withheld

Dear Withheld,

I'd go after it! (But then, I'm a confirmed pervert.) You
don't have to lay it all out at once; play it cool and hint around
a bit. If the only evidence you've seen is the book, the old man
might be on a guilt trip and not appreciate your "catching him
at it." On the other hand, he may have a whole existence you
know nothing about. Or, he may be a bottom, and that might
be why he never whupped you. That could also be the place to
start; i.e., ask him why he didn't punish you more severely and
see what he says. This could really be fun! Be sure to keep me
posted.

*The kid's been topping Daddy, now, for going on six years and
the relationship seems to be a happy one—except, that Daddy has
never given my correspondent the good old-fashioned woodshed
treatment he really wanted. At least, he hadn't the last I heard, a
couple of years ago. (And I'm only assuming that the relationship
has remained as it was for the four years I know about.) I never
cease to be amazed at the number of gay men who want to get it on
with Daddy!*

Dear Larry,

I am twenty-four years old, and have been SM/gay for
about five years. I moved away from my folks when I went
into the marines at eighteen; i.e., I never went back after
I was discharged. So they are not aware of my sexual
proclivities, and I'm sure they are not very sophisticated
to anything that is sexually exotic. I tested HIV positive
about two years ago, and now I'm beginning to exhibit
some symptoms. I don't want to be on my deathbed before
I tell my parents, but I'm not estranged from them and still
have a feeling of love and closeness—all except for my
sexual life. I just don't know how they would take the
news at this stage. I imagine you have known a lot of

people in my situation. What has worked out best for them?

Rick, Washington D.C.

Dear Rick,

It's a lousy dilemma, no matter how you cut it. And there isn't any set answer. Every one of these situations is different, because no two sets of parents are the same. Neither are their kids. My own feeling is that it's probably best to hold off telling them when you only know that you're positive because you still have a chance of never getting sick. But once you have a definite diagnosis, you've got to bite the bullet and just do it. It is a heavy enough trip to lay on them right now—far worse when you're further along.

However, you should remember that people will often believe only what they want to believe. If you simply tell them you have AIDS (or ARC), you really don't have to tell them everything else, at least not immediately. If they want to believe that you contracted it other than sexually, so be it. I'm not suggesting that you lie to them; but if they don't ask, you don't have to lay it all out—at least not on the first encounter. I have to say, though, that very few parents have turned their backs on their sons. They've been grieved and upset; but after the initial shock, their concern has centered far more on the guy's health than on his sexuality.

Dear Larry,

I am sorry to write you such a letter, but I answered an advertisement a few months ago. The man said he was a Master and when I answered from Denmark, he wrote back from New Jersey and said he would accept me as a "slave by mail." I said I would like that, and then he started sending me these letters that got more and more awful. He said he would reach across the ocean and punish me if I did not obey. He told me to do some terribly painful things, like wrapping my balls in rope and pulling it off fast to make them spin. He mailed me a big plastic buttplug and told me to wear it all day when I was at work. He said his friends would come and get me on their motorbikes if I did not do it. I think he is very dangerous, but I don't know what to do about it. I wish I had never written to him.

K., Copenhagen, Denmark

Dear K.,

I think you have simply run into a man with a lot of imagination who is enjoying himself by expressing his fantasies in his letters. You know he isn't really going to do anything to you. He's playing the game he probably thought you wanted him to play.

This Master must write quite a letter. This is the second bottom who has written me in abject terror, and I strongly suspect it was the same "by-mail" Master in each instance. It's interesting how much more badly someone else's fantasies can frighten us than our own—when it's our own that carry the potential to harm us.

Dear Larry,

I have become involved in a strange situation, and I'm not sure how to handle it. I'm forty-three, in pretty good physical shape, and making a better-than-average income. I have a nice apartment, but not much time or interest in the chores necessary to clean it, etc. I replied to an ad in a local gay throwaway and hired a young guy to clean my pad once a week. About a month ago, he called me one evening and asked if he could work on Saturdays. Of course, that meant having him there while I was at home, and at first I wasn't too cracked on the idea, but I finally said we could give it a try. Now, the kid is a very hunky guy (I'll call him "Bob"— not his real name), and he works in just a pair of cutoffs. Well, to make a long story short, the inevitable has happened. Except that Bob is into all the *Drummer*-type of action, and he's been getting me into it—as the bottom. I love it, of course, and really dig everything he does to me.

Now we come to the dilemma. I'm hiring him to do what is essentially grunt work, but he is becoming my Master. It's awkward to tell the guy who's just tied you down and whipped your ass that you want him to wash the windows or scrub the kitchen floor. On the other hand, I certainly don't want to get into the very situation I hired him to remedy. So far, the issue hasn't come up (between us), but I know it will have to. Suggestions?

Name withheld

Dear Withheld,

You are in a situation with so many possible variables that it is hard to foresee exactly how things are going to develop. I'd suggest a couple of possibilities. Tell him of your concern and suggest that he do the apartment work on a day when you aren't there. This way, there isn't any employer-employee exchange, at least not face-to-face. You can then play your games under circumstances which are separated from his work. Or, if your relationship is developing into a play-for-pay situation, and that's what you both want, hire someone else to do the housework and have your sex with Bob when and where it's convenient. In any event, I agree that the present arrangement is going to become awkward, and you are wise to try planning ahead.

It does sound like fun—just the sort of relationship people dream about. But this situation also goes to show how reality has so many more valences than fantasy.

Dear Larry,

Here's another of those controversial-type questions, but maybe you'll feel up to answering it. I'm thirty-eight years old, and I've been around the leather scene for most of my adult life. I've got lots of friends who are also into everything I am, but when it comes to sex I'm sort of a loner; i.e., I go out on my own, and I don't really discuss my affairs with anyone else. Although I am basically a Top, I really dig an occasional workout as a bottom. Nothing unusual in that, I know. However, the guys who turn me on as Tops are always smaller than I am, sometimes sort of puny, sometimes even effeminate—certainly not the masculine muscle builders one reads about in *Drummer*-type stories. In fact, I'm really not turned on to this kind of guy as a Top—maybe as a bottom, okay. (I'm six feet tall, average build.) I've never really discussed these preferences with my friends, mostly I guess because I'm the typical 90 percent Top who doesn't like to admit he swings the other way. Anyway, what would your explanation be for a guy's having tastes like mine?

Anonymous, East Coast

Dear Easterner,

It's another case of "everyone to his own taste." Just as no one can dictate our sexual orientation, neither can conventional wisdom tell who is going to turn us on. If you are looking for an explanation of why you dig a "lesser man" as your Top, my guess would be that you are seeking a degree of humiliation. After all, what could be more humiliating than to submit yourself to a guy who would not be able to subdue you on the basis of relative physical strength? I've seen similar situations where an older man likes to submit to a younger guy (not just because he's pretty); or a wealthy man to street trash; or an intelligent professional man to an uneducated punk. It's all part of the reverse psychology that underlies SM sex. In this context, it is quite normal.

As I've noted before, that's why "they" call it perversion. The ultimate humiliation is to be forced into submission by someone who has no apparent claim to the status of Master. If that is your particular game, how better to play it? Remember my friend Cliff's adventure in the original Handbook? *When he was forced by his Master-of-the-evening to suck off the pair of fluffs who lived in the adjoining apartment, he was totally humiliated. But he loved it!*

Dear Larry,

I praise the quality of both the photographs and written content of *Drummer*. Too bad we can't get it over-the-counter here in Canada, but don't worry. We always manage to get our hands on it one way or another.

I have two questions for you. The first concerns the extra-submissiveness of bottoms. I have found that every bottom who has really turned me on, later turned me off because he was so willing to do whatever I wanted him to do. Sometimes they have even gotten ahead of me and started leading the action into heavier areas than I would otherwise have gone. Is this normal, or have I just happened to hit on a biased sampling?

Secondly, I wonder if I am "out of step" with the main-stream, being a twenty-nine-year-old Top, and always finding older men as my subjects. (Guys in their late thirties, early forties.) I'm also about average size, but my bottoms always tend to be physically bigger than I am. I enjoy getting it on with these men, but it would be even more exciting for me to find some bottoms who are my own age and size, maybe even smaller.

So, what are my chances of finding a resisting bottom, and one who is more a brother than a father image?

D. B., Montreal, Canada

Dear D. B.,

Pushy bottoms have been around since the dawn of SM history. Although they can fuck up a scene (or relationship) by making the Top feel inadequate, they may also encourage him to get into more interesting or heavier areas than he would on his own. (As happened to you.) If you don't want this inter-ference, it's easy enough to assert your control by punishing or threatening to punish the verbal expressions. If the guy still won't shut up, gag him. A lot of times, though, the bottom may be attempting to lead because he doesn't think you are experienced enough to do it on your own. Proving your "right to be Top" is something you may find necessary because your bottoms are older, and need to be convinced of your compe-tence. As to finding younger, smaller bottoms, good luck. Most guys don't get into the more interesting aspects of SM until they are your age or better. It just takes that long for most of us to recognize and act on our deepest desires. But there are a few younger ones around, and they'll be exactly what you want, because by and large they will be less experienced than you, and probably more willing to trust your judgment.

To some extent, this may be the other side of the humiliation coin, with bigger, older men seeking a smaller guy to top them. Of course, it could also be a matter of supply and demand. Now, here's a Daddy who reports the obverse of a problem we discussed a couple of letters back.

Dear Mr. Townsend,

I've recently found myself in an awkward situation involving my eighteen-year-old son, who has lived with his mother since he was six—but stayed with me one weekend per month. I've suspected for some time that he was gay because his mother has spoiled him rotten, and he has always been a sissy. Although I have tried to be firm with him, I haven't whipped his ass since puberty, because nothing makes me hotter than busting ass. A month ago, on his eighteenth birthday, his mother called to "warn" me that he had told her he was gay, and that he indicated that he was also going to tell me. About a week later, he came to stay with me for five days, but said nothing. He then returned to college leaving a note for me on his pillow, marked "Daddy."

The first thing I saw was a photo of him, shaved and wearing pink panties with little white hearts all over them.

The letter said in brief: "Daddy, I've written this for you," and a second envelope contained a first-person story: "I knew I was a pussy...my Daddy caught me wearing my panties and beat my ass for it, and made me lick his boots, etc." I don't know how he had picked up on my own fetish, because in truth the whole thing got me so hot I damn near shot without touching my dick. I've used the boy's letter and photo for daily JO sessions ever since.

Now, he's coming home from college in a few weeks, and I don't know what to do. Am I sick, crazy, or what? How do I handle the situation? This isn't something I can write Dear Abby about. Appreciatively,

Daddy in Distress, IN

Dear Daddy,

I suppose it's the moral aspect of the situation that bothers you, and this is a question I really can't answer for another person. If establishing a physical relationship with your son is going to cause you such severe mental anguish that it outweighs the pleasure you derive from it, then you'll have to leave it alone. However, it's been my experience that the only sexual relationships I have ever regretted were the ones I let slip through my fingers. A few issues back, I answered a letter from a son in the reverse perspective of your situation, and I told him to "go for it." I don't know how this worked out, but I'm really inclined to say the same thing to you. If you pass up the opportunity, I think you'll regret it for the rest of your days, because you'll never know how it might have been. There are lots of guys who'd give their left nut to be faced with your choice (or your son's); and, from my admittedly jaded perspective, I don't see anything wrong with giving it a try as long as both of you are willing participants.

Oh, this fascination with Daddy and by Daddy is such a big thing with our group! (You'll note that at the time I answered this guy I hadn't gotten reports on my earlier correspondent. It turned out well in the first instance, hopefully in this one as well.) Here's another interesting parent/child situation in a slightly different vein.

Dear Larry,

When I was a kid and living with my parents, I did what many kids do, and rummaged through their closets and dresser when they were out of the house. I found a number of items that didn't mean anything to me at the time, but which I now realize must have been SM sex toys—ropes, dog choke chains, long narrow strips of rubber, etc.—all stuck in boxes on the back shelf, or under clothing in a drawer. Looking back on it, I also realize that my folks must have gone to SM gatherings with other people, always making sure they neither did anything nor said anything in front of me. I've now twenty-four and living on my own, and just starting to involve myself in SM activities, which I enjoy very much. Since I appear to be developing the same interests as my parents—although mine are gay and theirs were not— I'm wondering if there could be an inherited trait. They certainly never did anything to influence me into SM, and to this day there as never been any communication between us on the subject. What do you think?

Curious, Bangor, ME

Dear Curious,

You know, of course, that you are asking a question that has been debated ad nauseam by professionals, semiprofessionals and cocktail-party psychologists for years. *(And that I tried to answer a few letters back.)* There is no proof one way or the other, but there is some interesting speculation (and some inconclusive evidence) to support either a "yes" or a "no" answer. The truth is that no one really knows. Your own experiences might appear to be evidence that there is a genetic connection; on the other hand it might be argued that your finding the "toys" somehow triggered an emotional response within your own psyche—that, plus some other unrecognized stimuli that existed in your childhood home (your "family of orientation.") Over the years, my own beliefs have tended to swing back and forth on this subject until I no longer have a set opinion. I lean slightly toward the environmental explanation, since it seems most logical. But I do not have a firm enough conviction to argue about it.

As with so many aspects of human behavior, it is all but impossible to make up rules that will fit even a majority of cases—one of my reasons for rejecting the efforts to make psychology a science. At best, it's an intuitive art form. (You can tell by the different tone in my second response, as contrasted to the earlier letter/answer, that my own feelings are quite ambivalent.) Here's another case of a guy wondering why he gets the urge, and the explanation—at least superficially—would appear to be largely environmental. Or is it?

Dear Larry,

I was in prison for three years, and because I was so young when I went in (twenty-two), I became a "punk" in order to survive. The guy who became my "protector" was rough as hell, and he used to do things with me (or to me) that would certainly qualify as SM. He tied me down, whipped my ass, threatened to castrate me if I didn't do whatever he wanted. Now, when I first went into the joint, I had never made it with a man, although I had thought about it. Now that I'm on the outs, I've done it *only* with men, and the few women I know I could get just don't interest me. I've lately started to go for some *"Drummer-type"* action, which I enjoy if the other guy is rough enough with me. Although I hated what was happening to me in the joint when it was actually going on, I think back on it; and if I don't have a sex partner available, I jack off to the memories. My question is whether you think I was this way all along and didn't know it, or did my experience in prison change me?

Ex-con, Kansas City, MO

Dear Ex,

According to the most currently accepted psychological theories, a person's sexual personality is formed in the early stages of his life. Thus the seeds were sown, so to speak, before you ever knew what your pecker was there to do. However, the experiences we have later in life will often open windows for us that would otherwise remain closed. I would guess that you carried the latent abilities to enjoy SM sex long before you entered prison. Your experiences there simply gave you the opportunity to realize them. Now, you have to decide if this is the route you wish to follow. I might note, though, that however much you may have enjoyed being forced to have sex, this is not the real essence of SM.

Yet it's a fantastic fantasy. Rape, as they say, is fun only when you want to be raped. Of course, it's also frustrating when you want it to happen and it doesn't. But is it an hereditary or a socially conditioned urge? Will we even figure that one out? Now, here's another Daddy to tell us how he handled a situation similar to our Daddy of a few letter back:

Dear Larry,

Just a daddy who was in the same boat as "Daddy in Distress IN," Issue 127. Just wanted to tell him: No, he's not sick or crazy. My son was twenty-two years old when I received the envelope addressed "Daddy" with a short letter and quite a few photos of him completely nude except for the leather harness around his hard cock and balls, and a set of titclamps on his nipples. He had also picked up on my very own fetish (smarter than we give them credit for) and I *did* shoot my load without touching my very hard cock. The short note was: "Daddy, i want to be Your slave and pussy." Today he is my slave and pussy, and neither of us has ever regretted it. Daddy's word is law. My son's obedience is the best it has ever been in our entire relationship. This Daddy says, "Go for it!" No regrets.

Daddy, Detroit, MI

Dear Daddy,

Old Horatio Alger never found a happier ending. I wonder if this trend might be the answer to our current drug and gang problems. Read on.

Dear Larry,

I don't really have a question, but just wanted to tell you my story and to thank you for planting some seeds of thought in the right place. I'm now nineteen, but a couple of years ago I was a kid heading for certain destruction. I was heavily into drugs, including coke and alcohol, and was running with a gang of other punks whose greatest highs came from trashing other people's cars and property. My parents finally had enough and shipped me off to a private rehabilitation hospital. It didn't take the first time, so they threatened to send me back. When they went out one night, I went over to my older brother's apartment to try to get him to help me persuade them not to do it. He was just as unrelenting as they were, and when I realized I wasn't going to get him on my side I went into a blind rage. He beat the shit out of me, tied me down, and kept me in bondage for several weeks. (He's an auto mechanic who lives behind his shop, so he could look in on me from time to time during workdays.) He told our folks that I was staying with him while he tried to straighten me out. They were so glad to get rid of me they didn't ask many questions. Well, the long and the short of it has been that I became my brother's slave, and I love it! In the beginning it was the fear of having to go "cold turkey" again in bondage that kept me straight. Now it's my fear that he'll throw me out and never whip my ass again that does it. All through this, it was your *Handbook*s that he made me read like they were the family bible. Thank you, Sir; you helped to save my ass for better things.

slave, Eugene, OR

Dear slave,

I don't know what Dr. Spock would say about all this, but it certainly indicates that there's sometimes a better way to use an ass than to simply pat it and send it on its willful way.

I have long maintained that discipline is the answer to much of our current juvenile crime problem. Not all kids are going to respond as our last correspondent did, but sparing the rod has certainly not resulted in fewer spoiled brats on the streets of our major cities, killing each other, spraying graffiti on every available surface, and generally creating the greatest crime wave since Al Capone and John Dillinger. Since the Singapore incident (Michael's caning), several local politicians have jumped on the bandwagon and sponsored bills that would bring corporal punishment back into our litany of legal remedies. I doubt that any of these will become law, but we can always hope. In the meantime, I know there are a few responsible Masters "out there" keeping their sons and slaves in line.

CHAPTER 6

Accoutrements, Bodily Improvements, and Adornments

Many guys have written to ask how to improve this or that aspect of their bodies, or how/what to wear to enhance what they already possess. Interestingly, some men want their kinky tastes to "fit in"; others would rather shock the uninitiated. We can take solace in the knowledge that we are fully integrated into our genre when nothing surprises us anymore, and "shock" is a thing of the past. After all, as the great sages have told us, it's kinky only the first time you do it.

Dear Larry,

About a year ago I read an article (I think in *Drummer*), that extolled the wonders of tits. It stated that one could work the tits into fantastic little pleasure points, with a little work, and that they would grow and develop as a result. Well, I began working and they have truly been a major source of erotic sensation for me. However, the damned things are still as flat as pancakes. Nothing—suction cups, clothespins, lead weights—nothing seems to make those little tips stand out. Can you or some of your readers help?

Flat in Indiana

Dear Flat,

If you're getting the sensual responses, you've really achieved the most important goal in titplay. (By the way, a lot of guys would prefer what we refer to them as "nipples," feeling that "tit" applies more aptly to women and cows.) Be that as it may, I'm not sure there is any absolutely certain way to build up the nipple that is going to work for everyone. Even a seemingly flat nipple will form a little point when it's excited, though, and I suspect yours are probably doing it, too, except that you can't really see it when you have something clamped onto it. Obviously, heavy usage over a long period of time is the best prospect for bringing on a permanent physical change. If you do some exercises, such as push-ups or prone bench presses (in a gym), you will improve the muscle tone underneath. Then, frequent use of a small-tipped clamp with a moderate weight attached should produce results. Be careful not to leave the clamp in place for such a long time as to cause circulatory problems. Frequent short sessions are best. If some real nipple expert would care to comment, I'd be glad to pass on his advice.

More guys seem to be concerned with enlarging and shaping their nipples than almost any other aspect of physical alteration, except for foreskin restoration—this so frequent I've given it its own chapter. But enlarging the nipples remains a serious project for many, many men. We can blame part of this on the Hun, who draws nipples that look like small penises. Of course, we do like to suck on 'em!

Dear Mr. Townsend,

My lover and I are both men in our thirties, who have been together for a number of years, and have at least experimented with most phases of SM. We have now come to a point where we would like to be branded by each other. We have designed the pattern we would like for the brand, but don't know where to get it made, or how it should be applied. Specifically, we would like to know: What metal is best? How long and at what pressure should it be applied? Are the sanitary setups the same as for piercing? What immediate and long term care is best to treat the wound? How long is the healing process? What other special things should we know?

Thank you for your help, and for your book for which the leather community, especially the novices, are eternally indebted to you.

J. W., Norfolk, VA

Dear J. W.,

I checked around with a couple of people who are into branding and found some diversity of opinion. However, the most reasonable answers seem to be: Exercise some care in how you inquire and where you do it, because branding is specifically outlawed in a number of states; and, for ethical reasons, I cannot suggest that you do it in such a jurisdiction. It can also present problems if one of you requires medical attention. As to the type of metal, any good conductor is going to work. Copper was mentioned as first choice by one expert, but another said it may tend to be too soft and can warp in the heating process. Whatever is used should have enough mass to retain the heat. Likewise, the design should be fairly bold—not an intricate filigree, because it will tend to blur the outline. For the same reason, contact with the skin should be just a tap. It is better to cause just a light scar that retains the pattern, which may fade and have to be redone later, than to cause an ugly smear that will last as long as you do. The sanitary precautions are mostly concerned with treatment afterward, and these would be the same as with any burn and would depend on the severity,. If you have ever burned yourself accidentally, you know how long it took you to heal.

I don't know if these guys ever did the actual branding, but I know that many more guys are turned on to the idea than actually do it—more because of the pain, I suspect, than because they chicken out on having the scar. Several people have asked me why so many jurisdictions have laws against branding of human flesh, when they neglected to enact ordinances prohibiting many other, more common forms of behavior. The answer is simply that branding was one of the more detested penalties inflicted on convicts in England. This punishment was outlawed in the New World, as were some other basics of British common law. Unfortunately, in several of the original thirteen colonies, the standards of the Puritans prevailed, leaving us with a superfluity of antigay, antisex regulations that should have been dumped with the other "blue laws." Someday, maybe. (But don't hold your breath.)

Dear Larry,

Being an avid fan/reader/collector of *Drummer*, I know you have given some excellent advice. But you have never discussed the problem that applies to me, and that concerns my lacking one particular piece of equipment, which I've especially enjoyed on other men. I got ripped off early in life; my balls are very small and undescended. They seldom come out; and when they do, they are very tender if someone tries to suck on them. I've tried hormone pills, but all I got was a slight change in voice and more hair. I also tried weights attached to leather cords, and still no luck. Any advice from you is worth the effort—or do I just forget about it and try to enjoy other men's balls and cocks down my throat to make myself and them feel good?

Low-slung gear, S.F.

Dear Low-slung,

I'd say you were high slung, and that's a medical problem which you have probably already investigated with an M.D. (I'm assuming this, since you have tried hormones that would require a prescription.) At any rate, you appear to have tried the two most logical approaches to the problem. Beyond this, and short of surgery, I don't think there is very much you can do. The "tenderness," of course, is a direct result of your nuts' failure to descend normally. I know of guys—and have discussed the problem in this column—who wanted their balls to hang lower, and have accomplished this successfully with a series of increasingly long ballstretchers, wearing these over a long period of time. However, I hesitate to suggest this in your case, because you could do yourself some harm. You live in San Francisco, where there is a plethora of gay doctors. If they can't help you, I guess you'll just have to enjoy the low-hanging equipment on other guys.

Since I answered this one, a number of our leather suppliers have come out with "bull's balls," that are fun to wear and might be a partial answer for Low-slung. These are soft leather pouches with some weighted material (sand?) sewn into the lower end. The devices come in various sizes and, when fitted over the sac and secured around the base of the cock and balls, swing heavily between the thighs for a truly fantastic sensation! It might be enough to make a guy temporarily forget that he doesn't have much in the nutcase.

Dear Larry,

I'm writing about a letter in your column, several issues back, which refers to a man who can't seem to enlarge his nipples. You asked for some real nipple expert to comment; and while I'm not really that, I have come experience and would like to pass it on.

You suggest a clamp with a minimal weight as an enlargement technique. My experience is that the weight will stretch the pec area, not just the nipple. Suction cups simply do not provide a lasting effect. Since my nipples are cross-pierced, they are now solid and stick out all the time, roughly a half inch. To make them larger, I'm going to try a plastic ice-cream scoop, with the handle cut off and a hole in the center of the globe. If the nipple is stretched out to the hole, and barbell piercings used to hold it in place, it should stretch the part you want to enlarge, while the mouth of the scoop will hold back the rest of the chest. The assumption, of course, is that anything stretched long enough (time and length) will eventually assume that shape.

Thanks for your past advice, and I hope you get several more responses on this subject.

T. G., Palm Springs, CA

Dear T. G.,

Your idea is quite ingenious, and it might work well for guys with pierced nipples. For the rest, they still seem to be left with clamps, weights, and suction cups. Although there is really no substitute for a Master's fingers—applied hard and frequently—

these other techniques can (and do) work. I'd be interested in knowing the results of your experiment, since you seem to indicate that you haven't actually tried it. If you'll recall, I did suggest previously that push-ups and prone bench presses are recommended to firm the pecs and help prevent their being stretched along with the skin.

One of the human universals, it seems, is a drive to improve whatever it was we received as a body. The enormous cosmetic industry, worldwide, is one certain proof of this. And among gay leathermen, the enlargement of one's nipples is often a prime area to try for something more. I wonder sometimes if this isn't carried a little beyond reason, when a guy comes out looking as if he had a miniature penis growing on each side of his chest. However, if that pleases him, it's his business. As mentioned before, check out the Hun's artwork. He really glorifies these beauties. If that's what turns you on, go for it.

Dear Larry,

I always read *Drummer,* and am intrigued by the leather/SM scene; but despite a few excellent experimental experiences, I am reluctant to get further into it. I am chubby, and do pretty well with the chubby-chasers. But my reasoning on the leather scene goes this way: The chubby-chaser scene represents at most 1 percent of the gay world. If the leather world is 10 percent of the whole, then that doesn't leave me with a helluva lotta men to find. I see a group of chubby leathermen in one of our local bars, but they are scraggly-bearded, heavily tattooed, and look more like the villains in motorcycle movies than gay leathermen. They appear totally unapproachable, seem only into each other, and never come on to or leave with anybody else. I don't want to be like them. I was wondering whether you could shed some light on this. Are there more chubbies and chasers in the scene than I imagine?

S. B., Los Angeles

Dear S. B.,

Although you ask some well-framed questions, you left out

a couple of important points, so I'll have to make a few assumptions. First, you are inexperienced, so you are probably looking to be a bottom, at least in the beginning. Second, you say you're "chubby." This might mean you are twenty pounds overweight, or that you're mountainous. I'm going to assume that you are somewhere in between. I'm also going to assume that your age is something less than senior citizen.

All this being the case, I'd have to say that your chances are going to be about the same in our scene as any other. Most guys are not turned on by fat, but there are a lot who don't seem repelled by it—especially if the chubby has a reasonably enticing personality. The "chubbies" you saw in the bar are fairly typical throughout the leather scene and they seem to do all right—functioning in a variety of roles and different scenes. Overweight Tops, of course, do better than overweight bottoms—for obvious reasons. If you want to try it, I don't see why you shouldn't. After all, it isn't a one-way street. If you can't find partners among the leatherguys, you can always revert to the scene you know. However, I would strongly suggest that you not be too quick to reject the guys you describe in your local bar. They are probably much less formidable than they appear. If you talk to one or two of them it might serve to break the ice.

While in the process of pulling this book together, into its final form, I had to break off and go to New York for the grand leather/fetish fest and celebration of Stonewall's twenty-fifth anniversary. I have to note that among the thousand-plus leather attendees, fat did not seem much of a deterrent in a great many liaisons, either casual or full-term Master/slave situations. If our chubby friend is still around, I'd definitely tell him there's hope aplenty. I must note, however, that there were many more fat Tops than bottoms.

Dear Larry,

I was told by a friend of mine that one night he slept with an American guy who had an 11" cock; and although my friend was small in body size, he claimed that he was able to take the whole 11" prick inside his ass. My question is

whether this is possible and, if so, what is your advice for me to be able to take such a huge tool: techniques, materials, creams that help me in taking such a large penis inside my hole. Your advice is well appreciated. Please let me know as soon as possible, because I would love to try it, but without pain. Thanks for your help.

Ali, Singapore

Dear Ali,

I think your first problem is going to be finding that 11" beauty, but you'll have to solve that one for yourself. As to taking a large cock, this is not particularly difficult if you are able to make yourself relax. In this sense, the problem is more mental than physical. A really good lubricant is going to help, of course. There is a new one on the market called Astroglide, which is the best ass-fucking product I've ever found. (It's not viscous enough for FF, but otherwise ideal.) I don't know how much time and effort you want to expend in training for this great event, but you can certainly condition your sphincter to relax through some homework with dildos of gradually increasing size, assuming the real thing is not available. Body size has little to do with a guy's ability to take it up the ass, although the danger of rupturing the rectal lining is greater if the length of the anal channel is shorter (distance between the asshole and the point at which the tube bends to enter the colon). Good hunting!

Good old Astrolube. *It's still around, and it's still one of the best, although it has gotten very expensive. There are now other products in the market that may be better for safe-sex usage because they contain Nonoxynol-9 (a spermicide that's been found to kill HIV), and still provide good lubrication. Check your local adult bookstore for the latest in these products—or the ads in mags like* Drummer. *Just the thought of Singapore gives some of us a surge of excitement these days, so if Ali is still looking for American meat, he may find it more readily available than in the past.*

Dear Larry,

I have been an advocate of yours for many years, ever

since the first *Leatherman's Handbook,* so it is natural that I turn to you for advice. I want to have my right nipple pierced. The problem: the areolar diameter is 1¼", but there is no nipple protruding from it. I have tried small elastic bands, but they do not stay on. What equipment, exercise, etc., can you recommend to develop a decent nipple size for piercing?

Bill, Maryland

Dear Bill,

Enlarging any part of the body's external "soft" tissues can be accomplished by constant, regular stretching. However, your degree of success is going to depend on several factors, including the genetic characteristics which make your body what it is. The most dramatic changes I have seen in nipple size have resulted from the use of titclamps with increasingly heavier weights attached to them. In doing this, one has to be careful not to use overly tight pressure for long periods of time, thus cutting off circulation and running the risk of gangrene. But a regular, several-times-per-day regimen should accomplish your purpose. Don't expect results overnight. It will surely take months, maybe longer. The massage you give yourself after each session is also going to help. Is it going to hurt? Of course—but pain is pleasure, isn't it?

Despite its redundancy, I included this letter, because the passage of time between it and the earlier question (about a year) reflects some change in my ideas on technique, but a consistency in the final answer, despite comments by others along the way. The subject is also one of such importance to so many of my readers, it deserves some extra attention.

Dear Mr. Townsend,

I have a dilemma that I hope you can help me with. I have very insensitive, nonerotic nipples. It really upsets me to work over another man's nipples and have him writhing in sheer ecstasy; of course, I really get off on this. But when a man attempts to do the same to me, I get no erotic response. So I try to fake it as much as possible in order not to disappoint him. Is there something I an do to get my nipples to become erotic to touch and torture as I feel a man's nipples should be? I will appreciate any information you can give me. Respectfully,

Chuck, Los Angeles, CA

Dear Chuck,

Yours is probably a neurological problem, and I would suspect that you are also a person with a high pain threshold, or at least with a less sensitive skin than the average. If that's the case, there isn't a hell of a lot you can do about it. You might try "sensitizing" your nipples with an emery board or very fine sandpaper. Used judiciously just before, or even during a scene, you may be able to increase the feelings. The flip side, of course, is that doing this too often is going to result in the skin toughening still further; so that without the artificial assistance, you'll be even less sensitive. The other possibility is a psychological "block." Some guys subconsciously fight their homosexuality so desperately that they (again subconsciously) refuse to respond in any way that they construe as feminine. This is going to be even harder to overcome, but could be symptomatic of an entire syndrome. To solve this you'd probably have to find the right therapist and try to work it out with him.

Back when I was counseling I worked with a couple of young guys who would have been perfect subjects for exactly the kind of therapy this writer needed. Fun, too! Of course, a good heavy scene with some temporary piercings might also help to stimulate a greater sensitivity in the titties.

Dear Larry,

I know you have indicated in past columns that you feel you have done a sufficient number on ballstretching in past columns. Unfortunately, I missed them, and I really want to know how to make my balls hang lower in the sac. Are ballstretchers safe? I love the feel of wearing one, especially under my clothing while I'm out in public. Sometimes it hurts me, but that's okay, too, as long as I know I'm not doing some permanent damage. Won't you please discuss this subject again?

Pete, Detroit, MI

Dear Pete,

Okay, I'll do it again. If they fit properly without cutting off the circulation, ballstretchers can eventually elongate the skin of the scrotum. You want to be careful not to herniate yourself by using too long a stretcher. Start with a modest size and build it up gradually. Wear it for shorter times in the beginning, building up the length of the sessions with the length of the stretcher. It may take a year or two before your efforts really pay off. If you try to go faster, you could easily do some damage. Some guys like to wear stretchers at night, but I really think this is more dangerous than doing it during the day when you are awake and can feel what is happening. Besides, eight hours is really too long a time for a beginner. Leather stretchers are fine, but should be made of softer, garment-weight skins. Latex stretchers are even better because they are more elastic and less apt to injure you. Do not use some hard, inflexible material; and if you feel a pain up the side of your body, you are probably pulling your balls down too severely. Remember that some leather dyes are toxic and can irritate the skin. Don't put the stretcher back on, atop a sore—especially an open sore.

Here's another guy, several months later, asking basically the same question. I included it, because my answer had a slightly different emphasis. If you're into ballstretching, read on. If not, skip to the next letter.

Dear Larry,

I have a question that may sound silly, but it's been a problem for me—and I have observed others who seem to encounter the same difficulty. Unless I am fresh out of a hot shower, my balls want to climb up and rest tightly against the base of my cock. This makes it difficult to put on even a cockring, much less a more exotic device that is intended to spread the nuts or stretch them. Is there anything I can do to train my balls to hang, the way we always see them in the illustrations for an erotic story?

Richard, Los Angeles, CA

Dear Richard,

A lot of guys have balls which seem destined to be ever curled up in repose against the underside of their endowments. This is a matter of physiological construction, and it seems to vary greatly from the extreme of deep, low-hanging balls, to the type you describe. Heat will tend to make the balls descend, whereas cold does the reverse. I have known several guys who tried—with varied degrees of success—to solve this "high-rider" problem. If you want to embark on a full-fledged campaign, you might start using modest-length ballstretchers (such as are sold in most leather/toy shops), and wear one for as long as you can bear it during your waking hours. It will take quite a long time—maybe a couple of years—but if you are persistent and keep doing it, you will eventually stretch the tissues until your balls hang lower than they do today. You will probably never have real Tom of Finland deep-hangers, but who has a cock like that, either? (A word of caution: do not wear a stretcher when you are asleep. If you should cut off circulation when you can't feel it, you could do yourself some injury.)

In addition to the space given over to this subject here, I fielded a few similar questions in Chapter 8, where I have put most queries dealing with the cock and balls. However, this is one is asked so frequently, it can't hurt to have it both places. If there really were a merciful God, don't you think she'd have given us all big thick cocks with foreskins resistive to surgical removal, plus a pair of heavy, deeply suspended balls? It's enough to make a man question his faith! And here's another guy with the opposite problem:

Dear Larry,

I have a slight physical problem, and there probably isn't anything to be done about it. I thought I'd ask, though, since you may have run into it before. I have about an average-size cock, but my balls hang very low—always, even in cold weather or under circumstances where you would expect them to pull up. For this reason, I can't seem to wear one of those heavier metal cockrings that have gotten so popular. Even if it seems tight when I put it on, the weight makes it slip down so that it rides low enough to cause the skin of my dick to fold over. Eventually, I end up with an abrasion. Is there any solution?

Randy, Phoenix, AZ

Dear Randy,

Nice, low-hanging balls are certainly set off beautifully by a heavy metal ring, so I can appreciate your dilemma. A friend of mine had a similar problem, and solved it by putting on the metal ring first, then pulling on a fairly narrow latex ring beneath it. The rubber tends not to slip, and (at least for him) it held the metal ring in place. Give it a try.

Dear Larry,

I read your column regularly, and have for—I guess—as long as you have been writing it. Over the years you have answered a lot of people who wrote in about enlarging their nipples or having a reconstructed foreskin. These seem to be the most popular physical problems. But I have a different one. How does a guy get his ass in shape? I mean the buns, not the center of activity. I'm just over thirty, and in the past I've been quite a bit overweight. Now I've lost the flab, but I can't seem to get my butt into that nice, tight shape that looks good in a pair of well-fitted Levi's. I go to a gym, and I'm embarrassed in the shower room by my dimpled asscheeks. The exercises recommended by the instructors just seem to make the muscles bigger, particularly my thighs, which are big enough already. Can you make any suggestions?

Mike, Des Moines, IA

Dear Mike,

As one who has fought the battle of the bulge for most of his life, I can certainly sympathize with you. Most weight-lifting regimens are designed to increase the bulk of the large muscles; the heavier the weights you use, the more this tends to be true. At your age, though, reducing the buttocks should not be too difficult. The most simple exercise is probably going to do the most good. Try a good long walk every day, plus lots of climbing stairs. Ride a bicycle, again going uphill as much as possible. Get a book on ballet exercises, since these tend to emphasize stretching as opposed to heavy lifting. Despite its being an oldie, one of the best systems is the USAF pamphlet on isometrics. Whatever routine you decide to follow, don't expect success overnight. Remember, it took you years to get out of shape. It's going to take some time to repair the damage.

Dear Larry,

I have always liked big nipples on other guys and recently started working on my own—nothing serious, just clothespins and snakebite suction cups. However, one of my nipples seemed to blister a bit almost immediately, and consequently I stopped working on them. I can handle a little blood, but this was a real turnoff. My questions:

(1) Is this normal? (2) Does blistering mean an infection is present? (3) Could I resume working on them, and do you recommend any different techniques?

Confused in LA

Dear Confused,

I get so many questions about enlarging tits and replacing foreskins, I'm afraid my regular readers are going to get tired of hearing about them. There is no way to enlarge your nipples quickly; and because of individual differences, there is no one method that is going to be best for everyone. Blistering as a result of the mild methods you describe is unusual, so you probably have a more sensitive skin than most—maybe an allergy. Only a doctor's examination is going to tell you for sure. A blister usually becomes infected only if the skin is broken. I recently received a long, detailed letter from a guy who claims to have used a vacuum pump on his nipples, then tied them after they were greatly enlarged. Over a long period of time (probably a couple of years), he produced permanently enlarged nipples. However, compared to you, he probably had the skin of an elephant. I know of other guys who have fucked around with their tits until it required surgery to repair the damage. If you skin is as delicate as you indicate, you are probably better off admiring the big nipples on other guys and leaving yours alone.

Big tits and low-hanging balls—somehow the mark of true masculinity for so many guys. It is impossible, really, to assess the reasons for these particular concerns. In the end, I suppose, those of us who produce the books of pictures and stories are to blame. I'm reminded of a session I had a few years ago with a more-or-less novice, who became quite agitated when I hung a pair of moderately heavy titclamps from his nipples. "You're going to give me breast cancer!" he protested. That's one I hadn't heard before. (And hope I never hear again.)

CHAPTER 7

Financial, Legal, Health and Household Problems

Surprisingly enough, a lot of questions have come my way from guys who don't know how to cope with some rather mundane situations, made unique—or at least different—by the fact that they are gay leathermen. Managing money, investments, or estates are very serious considerations, and from time to time I've tried to help. Although I am not a doctor, I have received many questions relating to health problems, and I have tried to answer them—often with the help and advice of an M.D. So let's take a short break from the bizarre and the purely sexual to consider a few of the problems that can result from an SM sexual orientation—or, sometimes, simply from life.

Dear Larry,

I live in a small "Bible Belt" town where everyone knows everybody else's business. My problem is that I have anal warts—six of them, as best I can count. (Those little white nubs, just on the inner edge of the mucous membrane.) I know they aren't going to kill me, but I want to get rid of them. What I want to know is, are they strictly something you get from anal sex, or could they have come from some other source? If our local sawbones sees them, is he going to know how I got them?

Please, no name

Dear No Name,

I can't think of any way you might have gotten them other than by sexual contact, although your doctor may. In any event, even if it means a trip to a larger city, you should get them removed as soon as possible. If you don't, they are likely to increase in number and eventually require more than a quick session in the doctor's office. You could also infect someone else. Warts are not *highly* contagious, but they *are* contagious. They're also a pain in the ass!

Since writing this, I watched a good friend go through hell with anal warts that really got out of hand. He had full hospital surgery twice; and, at last count, there were still some of the pesky things appearing. But the doctor thinks he can get these with simpler office procedures. If you get them, be sure to have them taken care of as quickly as you can. Apparently, there have been more virulent strains coming along lately. (Where have we heard that before?)

Dear Larry Townsend,

To become a complete slave to a Master—to comply with all his demands, and to do exactly as he commands—and still maintain a semblance of one's own mind so he can continue to work and assist in support of the Master—How does one become trained to do both? Is there a good course to be taken? Try as I may when attempting complete servitude, I find I tend to lose my presence of mind, which I require for my job. Do I have to wait to retire to be the complete slave I desire to be?

In brotherhood, Miami

Dear Brotherhood,

Since your servitude to your Master presumably takes place in a different time and place from your work situation, I don't see why this should be so much of a problem. Most gay men learn early on to lead a sort of double life, and this is not necessarily exclusive to us. There are many het workers who take a lot of shit on their jobs, working as low men on the company totem pole, but who remain "masters" within their own families once the door of their homes closes behind them at night. You may be living the reverse of this, but I know a lot of guys who sit in a seat of command in the office, aware at all times of their true status because their Masters' marks can be felt on their asses, even as they issue their commands. I suppose this is more difficult for some than for others, but as you get used to the idea it should become easier for you to carry it off. Just remember that, even as you perform these seemingly unrelated tasks in your work space, you are actually carrying out the commands of your Master.

I don't know if this guy was trying to give me a little sarcastic poke in the ribs, or not. I chose to take him seriously and answer him accordingly. One of the most interesting of the SM convolutions is the tendency for men to who hold command positions in their businesses or professions to be subservient at home—sometimes to blue-collar types (real or simulated).

Dear Larry,

I would really appreciate your making some comments on AIDS, especially offering what advice you can to a bottom, like me. I'm not into fisting or scat scenes, but I would like to know what to watch out for. Is it realistic to have a Top wear condoms? What about using amyl? I am quite new to the scene, so I am concerned about what extra precautions should be taken.

Mike, Washington state

Dear Mike,

In the past, I have not written a great deal about AIDS, because every gay publication in the country was running extensive articles, and it seemed superfluous for me to do so. Lately, however, the true horror (and potential horror) of the disease has been brought home to me more directly as I learn of more and more people coming down with it. As you probably know, I do a mailing every two months. I used to get back one or two mailers marked "deceased" each time or two I mailed. On my December 1984 flyer, I had fourteen such returns. In mid-December, I had a long conversation with Dr. (Ph.D.) Bruce Voeller, who formerly ran the National Gay Task Force, and who is still serving on almost every major health project committee in the country. His remarks were so disturbing that it really sent me into a funk for several days. At the risk of doing the same to your New Year's expectations, I'd like to reiterate the highlights for you. If it frightens you, maybe it will save your life.

At the present time, there is no cure in sight, despite the frequent reports of a "breakthrough" in one area or another. The researchers are learning more about the theoretical causes, but each remedy they have tried—even if it worked in a test tube—failed when used on an animal or human. The virus tends to mutate so rapidly that the eventual cure may require a unique, specific vaccine for each patient. Transmission of the disease is thought to be via the exchange of bodily fluids, and these appear to include saliva and sweat, as well as semen, blood, urine, and feces. Although we have assumed, on the basis of intelligent logic, that the use of condoms would help prevent transmission of the virus, there has never been a properly controlled experiment to verify this. Although amyl is still suspect, it is not as prime a suspect as it was a year ago. Much of the "safe-sex" advice is based on common sense and past experience with other diseases, but there is no clinical proof available that it will protect you from the AIDS virus.

There was a good deal more said, but there isn't space to go into it here. Specific recommendations for guys into SM should probably include a reminder to clean your toys after/before each use. A solution of 70 percent bleach (like Chlorox) and 10 percent alcohol appears to be 100 percent effective in killing the virus. Remember that a whip which has absorbed an M's sweat—and certainly if it has drawn blood—should be disinfected thoroughly. Likewise dildos, gags, pinprick cockrings, and other such devices. Obviously, a guy who has not yet come down with the disease can still transmit it if he has been exposed and infected. Whether or not his ability to transmit it means that he is going to get it is still uncertain. A recent survey of gay man in San Francisco found that over 70 percent had antibodies in their blood, but no one knows if this means that any appreciable number of them is going to come down with it. It does mean they have been exposed.

Frankly, facts such as these just scare the shit out of most of us, and they should. When even the supposed experts can't tell us for sure what is safe and what isn't, you can't blame a guy for staying home with the latest *Drummer* and doing it by hand.

How depressing to think that I wrote those lines in early 1985, and they are almost exactly what I would have to say in June 1994. We know a little better which bodily fluids are apt to carry HIV, and we know that a guy with antibodies is unlikely to escape the disease. But the elusive cure seems as far away as ever, while our friends and lovers continue to fall all around us. Bruce Voeller himself passed away earlier this year, having put up a long and valiant fight with the disease that had so occupied his life. As head of the Mariposa Foundation, he had been involved in some very extensive research on the retentive properties of various condoms, and was responsible for several production changes. Although Bruce became a victim, his warnings probably saved my life, and I will be eternally grateful to him, as should those who heeded my advice—based on his guidance—and have also remained HIV negative.

Dear Larry,

About seven months ago I met my lover, who is attractive enough to have had his picture in *Drummer*. At first, we hit it off very well. I prefer Top, and he bottom, but we trade off. He had done a lot of SM things with his former lover while on drugs. All of this excites me, although I don't like to use dope. He says it's impossible without it. As a result, our sex life has dwindled down to just jerking off once every couple of weeks. He now claims he can't be fucked, due to outside venereal warts (that have lasted over four months, despite doctor's treatment). Any mention of SM is dropped promptly as impossible, yet he fantasizes about it. Despite his claim of pain from fucking, I know he uses a dildo when I'm away. Here is a chance for a great monogamous relationship, but I don't know how to make it work. We've reached a point where we can't even talk about it anymore. Got any ideas, before I drop out of this unsatisfactory situation?

Brad, NYC

Dear Brad,

It sounds to me as if you have gotten together with a guy who's been spoiled by his own beauty. If he really had any regard for you, he wouldn't put you through this mental anguish. On the other hand, you have probably given in to his whims until he thinks he can walk all over you—as he is. Bitching at him isn't going to help. And until life kicks him around a few times, he probably isn't going to accept the fact that he could be at fault. You don't have that much time invested. Why don't you tell him to play with his dildo while you go out and find the real thing? After all, the only reason to have a lover is to improve the quality of your life. When the relationship fails to do this, it's time to bail out.

Dear Larry,

I know you don't like to write about AIDS, but I just have to ask you if the information I got was right. A local health counselor told me that sucking cock was not really dangerous if you spit out the load instead of swallowing it, and rinse your mouth immediately with a good antiseptic mouthwash. I'm only twenty-four, and in perfect health. I don't even smoke or use drugs, so I don't want to fuck myself up.

Young and healthy, NYC

Dear Young,

The procedure suggested by your adviser is partially correct, and is certainly better than merely sucking and swallowing. However, this is not a surefire protection. Research has not yet determined how fast the body can absorb HIV. All you would need would be a tiny cut or sore in your mouth, maybe a spot along the gum where you brushed too hard, or where you nicked the inside of your mouth in chewing or in your sleep. Nor is there any firm proof that you can't simply absorb the virus through the mucous membranes of the mouth. Stomach acid will destroy HIV, but saliva will sustain it. That's the best I can gather from all the advice I've received and all the mountains of paper I've read. When you come right down to it, no one is 100 percent sure of anything; so if I err in the advice I give, it is always on the side of extra precaution.

And, of course, they now tell us that saliva will "tend" to suppress HIV (whatever the hell that's supposed to mean).

Dear Larry,

I have a really terrible problem. I am just twenty-one years old, and I have been living with an older man for almost five years. In fact, he picked me up on the streets and gave me a place to stay when I was in such a mess I didn't know where my next meal was coming from. He's been really good to me, and I've tried to make it up to him by doing the housework and also carpentry and stuff I'm fairly good at. I've had sex with him many times, because I figured that was part of the price for everything he was doing for me. I don't mind having sex with him, but it never really tuned me on. Now, just as I've met someone I'm very much in love with, and want to live with, my older friend has been talking as if we were lovers. I've afraid to tell him about this other guy, because I know he really cares for me and I care about him. It's just I don't love him in a sexual way. What can I do? I'm afraid if I don't move soon, I'll fuck up the relationship with my new friend.

(Please don't print my name or location.)

Dear Unnamed,

Yours is a fairly classic dilemma. You want to do what you perceive as "right," but that is going to deprive you of what you really want. In the long run, you are not doing your older friend a kindness by staying with him when your heart's not in it. You are going to be unhappy, and in the end it will make both of you miserable. Tell him the truth and make your move. If you handle it properly, you can probably remain friends and, after a time, the passions will die down.

Dear Larry,

Since the advent of the current health crisis, I have done what many of my gay brothers have done, which is to load up on hot mags and videotapes, and jack off to the fantasies I am afraid to enjoy in reality. I have gradually expanded my horizons (or at least my sensations) by using a variety of sex toys. I really like to stretch my balls down with one of several devices, and manipulate myself slowly. I've actually gotten good enough at this to keep it hard and randy, but just short of ejaculation, from the beginning to the very end of a 90-minute video tape. Then, when I finally let myself cum, oh man!—what a blast! It's almost as good as the real thing. But now I've got a problem. I've noticed that my cum has started to get a sort of rusty color to it. It happened once before, but went away after a few days. Now it's started again, and it's lasted over two weeks. It scared me enough that I went to the drugstore and bought one of those kits designed for testing if your shit has blood in it. My sperm tested positive, so I know I'm bleeding internally. Because I live in a small bible-belt town, I'm afraid to go to a doctor and tell him the whole story. What should I do? Have you ever heard of a similar case? Please write directly, if you can, so I can get the answer without waiting for the next issue of *Drummer* to be published.

Frightened, (near)Des Moines, IA

Dear Frightened,

I'm writing to you directly, but I'm also sharing your dilemma with our readers. The November 1985 issue of the *Mayo Clinic Health Letter* contains a timely answer. It states that whereas blood in other bodily secretions is often cause for alarm, "...appearance of blood in the seminal fluid after ejaculation rarely is a hallmark of significant disease." The article goes on

Dear B. D.,

I fear that by this time all the harm that can be done has already happened, insofar as your personal situation is concerned. However, just for the record: A person who tests positive for the AIDS antibodies is already at greater risk than someone who tests negative. Unlike most common diseases, our best evidence indicates that HIV mutates so rapidly that each exposure increases your risk dramatically. This results from the fact that your body has already produced antibodies against the particular mutation to which you were originally exposed. When struck by a second, third, or further exposure, your system will eventually reach a point where it can no longer produce the requisite varieties of antibodies, and you succumb to the disease. That, at least, is one of the more popular theories. So I would answer your question with an emphatic "yes, you should use a rubber." As to your second question, to the best of my knowledge, there is no such thing as "industrial-strength" rubbers, (Few machines seem to require them.) There are a couple of brands (maybe more) that do come in larger sizes. Go to a pharmacy and ask for them. Then ask your Daddy to use plenty of lubricant and to stop letting that big thing go hog wild when he gets it into you.

As with so many of these AIDS-related questions, I am constantly reminded (and discouraged) that my answers of several years ago would have to be substantially the same if I made them today.

Dear Larry,

My lover and I are both AIDS-negative, and we are strictly monogamous. Do we still have to practice "safe sex"? (We have for a long time, but it's boring as hell.)

Billy, Dallas, TX

Dear Billy,

If you haven't been exposed to a disease, you can't very well pass it on. However, we are living in such a state of hysteria that it makes me hesitate. Are you sure you're negative? Have you each been tested several times over a period of six months or more? Do you really trust each other not to engage in extracurricular activities? Remember, it's your life and his.

And, of course, it's that last question that tells the tale. Two guys can get into a supposedly monogamous relationship, each verify that he's HIV negative, and start having unprotected sex. So far, so good. Then, as the initial passion begins to wear thin, one (or both) have a quickie here or there, and the rest of the story hardly needs to be stated. There has to be real trust and total devotion in a relationship before I'd suggest unprotected sex.

Dear Larry,

With all the concern about AIDS, no one is saying or writing anything about some of the problems that have plagued us for years. I recently got it on with a "street person," whom I allowed to sleep overnight with me. I should have known better because I've now got a bad case of crabs and I can't get rid of them. Because of the area I live in, I'm embarrassed to ask a doctor, or even a pharmacist. What should I do?

R. C., Davenport, IA

Dear R. C.,

This problem is solved much more easily than it used to be, but you've let it go long enough to need the full treatment. Pull off all your bedding and wash it on "hot," and use some bleach in the water. Don't neglect the blankets and bedspread. Wash them, or have them dry-cleaned. Get a "flea bomb," such as is advertised for controlling pet parasites and fumigate your bedroom. While your bed is stripped, turn the mattress. Be sure to give your bathroom a good Lysol cleaning—especially the toilet—and wash the rugs, bathmats, and towels. That should get them out of your environment. To get them off yourself is easier. There are a number of preparations sold in pharmacies to kill the bugs on your body. But if you're afraid to ask for one, your local-pet supply store is the answer. Get a flea bath and flea spray that are recommended for puppies and kittens. These are gentle enough that they won't hurt you. At worst, you may get a little skin irritation from them. Just read the directions carefully, and follow the safeguards such as how much to dilute it and keeping it out of your eyes, etc. If you go

through all this, and still have them, you will have to break down and see a dermatologist. Even in Iowa the guy will have seen it before; and if you have some exotic kind of bug, he should be able to help you get rid of it.

I wonder, sometimes, why people are so afraid to seek professional help for problems resulting from their sexual activities, when these are the same problems a heterosexual could have. Sometimes, the cause need not even be sex-related. After all, didn't your mother warn you about papering the seat in a public john so you wouldn't get "germs"?

Dear Larry,

I am very concerned about the "health" program, embarked upon by one of my best friends. He is so terrified that he will come down with AIDS that he is not only dosing himself with handfuls of vitamins, but has gone down to Mexico and bought a supply of AZT. He is taking this along with everything else. He's had the AIDS antibody test twice, and has been negative both times. He's so afraid of infection, I don't think he's had sex in five years. I'm sure he must be doing himself far more harm than good, but I can't convince him. Would you comment, please?

Worried Friend, Los Angeles CA

Dear Worried,

The use of vitamin tablets/capsules as food supplements has always been a basis for argument among medical authorities. Some swear by them; others claim they are a waste of time. My own unprofessional opinion is that a well-balanced regimen of vitamins can be beneficial. However, too much of certain vitamins can be toxic. You should work with a professional to establish the dosages, etc., which are right for you. (Sometimes the person in the health-food store will be as knowledgeable as anyone you can find.)

So much for vitamins. As to AZT, your friend is doing about the worst thing he possibly could. This is material which I would classify as a "drug of desperation." For a person who has been diagnosed with AIDS—which is a fatal disease—AZT offers the hope of his survival until something better comes onto the market. But it also has severe toxic side effects, the most serious of which (as of present knowledge) is a debilitating anemia. In fact, the last report I read indicated that 25 percent of people taking it develop these symptoms early on, and have to be taken off the drug. Others don't begin to show signs of anemia for a year or more, but most will eventually do so. In his paranoia, your friend is seriously endangering his health.

In filling his system with AZT, he was also using up the limited time he would be able to use it if and when he should really become ill. But then, in later times, it appears that the medicos have solved part of the problem in using AZT by cutting down the dosage to eliminate these harsh side effects. But now they're beginning to question the drug's overall effectiveness. And to think I grew up believing that doctors were possessed of omniscience!

Dear Larry,

Because I am very turned on by young Latin types, I have had a succession of live-in houseboys—one from El Salvador, the rest Mexican. I'm sure that all of them have been illegal aliens. Now, with the new amnesty law in effect, I'm afraid of getting into trouble if I continue this practice. And wouldn't you know it—I've got the hottest kid yet, ready to move in with me. What do you think? I don't know where to go for advice, since most of the clinics seem to be run by the Catholic church.

L. R., San Diego, CA

Dear L. R.,

Don't sell those padres short! Some know more about young boys than you do. But you really should get proper legal advice. Why not try a gay lawyer? Contact your local gay-lesbian organization for a referral. My own reading of the law leaves me with the impression that you actually have to employ the person to be in violation. However, knowingly harboring an illegal may be a violation under the old laws—probably is, but whether anyone is going to bother enforcing it is another question. If they did, I think we'd have half the population of Southern California in the slammer.

He was referring, of course, to the amnesty law that came onto the books in 1987. Interesting how prophetic my comments were, however. Into the 1990s, we are certainly beginning to find out just how many priests have been exploring the exotic with their altar boys. And the number of illegals swarming across the border into California has become monumental. If I had a nickel a head, I could retire a rich man! As to busting guys for harboring illegal house-boys, I haven't heard of any great purges, even to this day. They'll nab the kid if they can catch him, though, and ship his hot little ass back south of the border. Unless you've been nominated for the Supreme Court or some other high governmental office, it's unlikely anyone is going to check on you.

Dear Larry,

I think everyone is getting tired of constantly talking and reading about AIDS. Still, in any social gathering the subject continually crops up, and understandably so, because it remains a constant element in determining our behavior. So, I have two questions that have been subjects of discussion in recent social encounters. (1) As far as you know, has anyone ever been cured? (2) If two guys have enjoyed a monogamous relationship for a number of years, how far back does this have to go for them to feel completely safe?

Steve, Los Angeles, CA

Dear Steve,

I agree. This miserable disease is threatening all of us; and, like the prospect of nuclear war, it hangs over us with such menacing implications we can't ignore it. But to try answering your questions: (1) I am not aware of anyone's being cured, once he has actually contracted AIDS. I do know several guys who have managed to get it under control by a combination of drugs, vitamins, proper health regimen, etc. AZT, despite its harsh side effects, seems to offer the first real glimmer of hope. And there are other drugs in various stages of development. I am hopeful that it will soon be possible to treat a person with AIDS as they do a diabetic: i.e., put him on a standard schedule of medication that will sustain him in a reasonably normal condition until he can be cured. (2) The general consensus seems to be that 1977 is the cutoff point, prior to which the virus was not around. Remember, though, that it took a while to spread into the Community. Thus the chance of meeting someone who was a carrier was fairly remote until 1980 or 1981—greater, of course, in Los Angeles, San Francisco, and New York than in less-populated areas.

Now, several years later, we find a number of "long time survivors" who seem to go along with no problems. I know one guy who was diagnosed with active AIDS almost ten years ago, and he's just fine. Of course, he is one of the very few for whom interferon seems to be working. And as to the length of a relationship before you can be sure? I'd now tell you: "No cutoff point. Get tested!" A little over a month ago I lost a very close friend who had been in a monogamous relationship for about twelve years, but without either partner being tested. They went to Europe with us a couple of years ago, with no suspicion on the part of any of us that they were infected. Then suddenly, both guys manifested symptoms, and our friend was dead in about six months. His partner is still in fairly good shape, but they were surely the last people we ever expected to lose.

Dear Larry,

I have been reading the story in *California Magazine* (Oct 87) about the Air Canada steward who is suspected of being responsible for spreading AIDS all over the United States in the early 1980s. In the course of the article they mention Zaire as a source from which some other people may have contracted the virus and carried it into Europe. Just as a matter of curiosity, knowing that you obviously keep up on the current theories, where do you think it started? I read another piece (I forget where) that seems to imply that it actually started in New York.

Alfred, San Diego, CA

Dear Al,

There are so many fanciful explanations that it is hard to

know which to believe. Some people think it came from Haiti, others that it was a Russian chemical-warfare experiment. The Soviet disinformation mill claims it was a CIA project gone awry, and still others who pretend that it isn't caused by a virus at all, but: (1) the result of using poppers, (2) God's vengeance on a sinful population, (3) a psychological indisposition resulting from mass hysteria...and on into the night. I tend to favor the theory of the (mostly) French researchers, that it did originate in Central Africa, as a mutation from a virus infecting other primates. It may or may not have been introduced into the United States via Haiti. I also read the article, which I strongly recommend to everyone. The part about the airline steward is certainly a classic example of how one irresponsible man can injure innumerable other people.

This asshole became Randy Stilts's "patient zero," who gleefully, and deliberately infected hundreds of men with "gay cancer." He's dead now, himself. May he roast in hell.

(And the Band Played On, *by Randy Stilts.*)

Dear Larry,

I read your column regularly, as well as most of the other major gay publications, and I am frankly puzzled over some of the cautions you (and others) give re: keeping your toys free of the AIDS virus. You tell us to take all of these elaborate measures to clean anything that might draw blood, even down to the prickers on some cockharnesses. Yet the best authorities seem to indicate that the virus can't survive for more than a few hours outside the body. Is all this nonsense really necessary?

Alex, Los Angeles, CA

Dear Alex,

Put yourself in the place of someone who is trying to give responsible advice, and maybe you'll understand why we recommend all these precautions. We are not advising on how to avoid a dose of clap that can be cured with a shot in the ass, or a bout of crabs that can be knocked off with flea spray. This disease is both deadly and incurable. If you take extraordinary measures to avoid it, that is far preferable to running even the slightest risk. I, for one, am not about to advise people "not to worry about it." Besides, the extra precautions should be observed, anyway, because there are all sorts of microorganisms that may be transmitted by dirty toys. If my advice helps someone avoid hepatitis or herpes, I don't think I'm doing him a disservice.

And think how desolated I would be if I told people "not to worry," and a few months down the road, some researcher discovered that a heretofore-unknown mutant strain of HIV was able to survive being frozen, boiled, or whatever. It may be unlikely, but with this miserable disease, I wouldn't say it's impossible.

Dear Larry,
I am an AIDS victim, in my mid-forties. Although I am currently doing okay, I know that my life expectancy is limited. I have a lover of many years' standing, and I want to leave all my property to him—not a great fortune, but the culmination of a working man's life. This includes a small house, as well as bank account, insurance, etc. I have purchased a standard form from a stationery store and made out my will. Living where I do, I don't know of a lawyer I would feel comfortable going to. My question, simply: should this be enough, or do I really need a lawyer to draw up a formal will?
Name Withheld, ID

Dear Withheld,
You slip me a curve, because I don't know how things are going to work in Idaho. In areas where there have been more openly gay relationships, with proportionate numbers of wills going into probate, there have been holdings (higher-court decisions that are binding on the lower courts) which better establish the rules. I really think you are going to be forced to consult a lawyer in order to be sure. In addition to making certain you have executed a valid will, there are also tricks of the trade that only an attorney is going to catch—such as establishing an executor who is to serve with or without having to post

a bond, etc. There should be a gay service organization in Boise that can help you find a lawyer. Try *The Gayellow Pages*. Their listings should tell you were to start looking.

The passing of an estate to the desired gay heir can be an "iffy" proposition in even the most liberal jurisdictions. I've seen family members suddenly forget the acceptance they had accorded a relationship for many years when they realize that the lover is going to get the dough. You can also find conservative judges doing their best to obstruct the wishes of a gay deceased. Always consult a lawyer to draw up the papers in any estate planning. I've noticed that many of our gay attorneys are offering very reasonable—some even free— assistance to people with AIDS. And don't wait until you're on your deathbed to do it. Not only can it be nip-and-tuck whether you get it done in time, it also leaves your will subject to challenge later, in such grounds as mental incompetence or "undue influence" by the person you designate as heir. And, by the way, The Gayellow Pages *is a great source for all kinds of listings in all areas of the country: P. O. Box 533, New York, NY 10014.*

Dear Larry,

I have seen several ads asking guys to send (or offering to send) used rubbers—sometimes with the cum still in them. This raises several questions in my mind. First, how can you send a sample of cum in the mail without getting it damaged? Then, wouldn't this be a possible way to spread AIDS or some other disease? Doesn't it get rancid?

E. E., San Francisco, CA

Dear E. E.,

Raunch has long been a major fascination for a lot of people, and what could be raunchier than a little rancid semen arriving in your mailbox on an otherwise dull and dreary afternoon? I don't think that mailing a used rubberful of cum is going to harm it, particularly. It might get squashed in the canceling machine if you try to send it in a regular envelope, but a little box would probably work quite well. As to spreading disease, that's hard to say. Most microorganisms would expire before the package arrived, but there could still be danger of contamination. I guess that would depend largely on what you intend to do with your newly acquired treasure. Hopefully, it will remain outside of any bodily orifice.

I should probably have put this in the "Outrageous" chapter, but health considerations were foremost in my mind when I first read the letter. I shudder to think what someone might do with such a piece of homemade exotica.

Dear Larry,

I see ads in a number of magazines, from people offering vitamins or other food supplements which claim to "boost the immune system." While they don't say that these products will help prevent a person's getting AIDS, that is the clear implication. Would you give me your reaction to this? Do you think there is any possible value for a person who is not presently infected?

John H., Los Angeles, CA

Dear John,

I have always been an advocate of vitamins, mostly because I personally find them beneficial. I have a great deal more energy when I take them, and generally feel better than otherwise. From this respect my answer would be: Sure. Go ahead and take them. Like chicken soup, "they can't hurt" (unless you overdo the oil-soluble ones—usually A, D, and E). As to their effect on the immune system, I think this is probably negligible. Being in the best shape possible, of course, is going to permit you to better handle any disease that comes along. But this requires more than just vitamins. There is an entire underground at this point, of people who have either tested positive for HIV, or who have been diagnosed with AIDS or ARC, and who are taking all kinds of vitamins, minerals, home and/or folk remedies. This information is regularly passed through the grapevine, and much of it is done with at least the tacit consent of a doctor. I have talked to a few guys who are involved with this, and they swear by the positive benefits. Nobody really has the answer, I would suppose, but a number of people who are in these holistic programs are beating the odds and are holding their own. You can't knock a winner.

Which is not to say that there aren't plenty of scam artists about, trying to make a dirty buck on the fears and frantic hopes of men who have been infected with HIV. It's disgusting, and unfortunately it's becoming ever more prevalent. I strongly advise anyone with a positive HIV test to contact one or more of the legitimate AIDS service groups. Subscribe to their newsletters and study them for information on whatever is new and/or currently seems to offer some help.

Dear Larry,

I have been reading your column since it first appeared in *Drummer,* and I seem to recall your answering a couple of questions about anal warts. My impression (although I can't find the back issues to refresh my memory), is that you seemed to feel they were fairly common and fairly easily treated. I had never met anyone who had this problem until recently, but just within the last six months I've encountered three guys who have them. Is this another epidemic, or is my triple experience merely coincidence?

Charlie, NYC

Dear Charlie,

I read an interesting article in the April 4 issue of *Time Magazine (1987—ed.):* "Another Sexual Blight to Fight." There is apparently a "new" virus called HPV that is causing genital warts in both men and women, and the writer seemed to feel that if it were not for AIDS getting all the media attention, this would be perceived as a major health crisis. This HPV (human papilloma virus) seems to be a really miserable bug which resists conventional treatments, and in some instances has proven incurable. It just isn't safe to stick your pecker anywhere, these days, to say nothing of your asshole!

Shortly after answering this letter, I met a really beautiful little guy who was rendered almost asexual by this condition. Surgery hadn't done it, and he still had them. It made him so miserable and self-conscious that he couldn't have sex, except to suck someone off without removing his clothes. He couldn't stand the thought of someone inadvertently touching his anal area, much less seeing the disfiguration. I think he was cured, eventually but has scars that will never disappear. If you get them, have them treated immediately, before they get out of hand.

Dear Larry,

I have always enjoyed amyl, or "poppers," when I have leathersex, or even when I just jackoff (which is about all ones dares to do these days). Unfortunately, one place after the other has made them illegal, and now I can't find anywhere to buy them. When my present supply runs out, I've had it unless you can suggest an alternative. Will someone mail them to me from someplace? Also, how harmful do you think they really are? *(Letter received Spring 1987—ed.)*

P. H., Atlanta, GA

Dear P. H.,

I can't help you buy the stuff because I don't know where it may still be legal to sell it. As to the dangers, they have remained a bit nebulous. I think that heavy usage in a situation where one or both of the partners might be an AIDS carrier could heighten the risk of transmission. Using it at home when you do a solo JO session is, of course, not putting you at immediate risk of infection. However, some health experts feel that even this can be dangerous, because prolonged use may cause permanent damage to your red blood cells.

Since this time, there have been more extensive studies which show a suspicious correlation between the use of amyl and depleted resistance to viral infections, including HIV. But these surveys involved men who used the materials very heavily. I still doubt that occasional, moderate usage is going to hurt the average otherwise-healthy guy. However, with their typical governmental logic, the feds first outlawed amyl nitrite, then all of the butyl concoctions (like Rush) that came along later. The real amyl was by far a safer product than butyl, which in turn was far less harmful than the junk now being sold under various labels— not yet outlawed, simply because the feds haven't gotten around to it.

Dear Larry,

I was recently nosing through an old issue of *Drummer* and came across a letter in your column questioning the need for "extreme" safer sexual practice. I volunteer at a free clinic which handles a lot of sexually transmitted diseases. In my work I deal with men both straight and gay. While doing an interview, I will explain various infections—then, in the case of gonorrhea, ask which sites need to be cultured. I can't force a rectal culture, but usually get consent for throat cultures. Even on routine exams we are seeing an alarming increase of *pharyngeal* GC (clap of the throat.) The same activities that put us at risk for gonorrhea, syphilis, and venereal warts also put us at risk for HIV infection. As with any advice columnist, sometimes I agree with you and sometimes not; but your advice to the side of caution is vital. You hit the nail on the head. As gay men, with an incurable, life-threatening disease facing us, we have a responsibility to ourselves and our partners to learn about our bodies and the infections that go along with our sexual practices. We have accomplished a lot in teaching persons about risk reduction, but we still have a long way to go. Thanks for using your column for this important purpose.

David, Richmond, VA

Dear David,

Thanks for your note. It's nice to know that someone is paying attention.

Sir:

When I suck a Topman to orgasm and he shoots his load into my mouth, it's thrilling for both of us. But unless I swallow his cum, my effort to give him a good, loving blowjobs seems pointless. To make him withdraw his cock from my mouth before he shoots off, or to spit out his cum, turns what should be a thrilling mutual encounter into something incomplete, disappointing, unsatisfying. It's like leaving a good play before the last act. But I'm afraid of contracting AIDS from swallowing cum. How concerned should I really be about this? Won't stomach acid destroy any virus that might be present in my Topman's cum? Also, I hear that a person can contract AIDS through a sore in his mouth, but suppose after taking my Topman's load I quickly rinse out my mouth with a solution of hydrogen peroxide or some other antiseptic? Shouldn't that reduce the danger considerably? Isn't there any way to give head without major risk to the bottom?

Concerned, Boca Raton, FL

Dear Concerned,

Cocksucking, as opposed to assfucking, is a *relatively* low risk activity. However, when you are dealing with a disease as deadly as AIDS, even a very-low-risk situation is placing your life on the line. If you have any kind of sore in your mouth, there is no way to get an antiseptic solution in there fast enough to assure sterilization. If you insist on taking the risk, you can cut the odds a bit by following the ejaculation with an immediate rinse, gargle and/or swallow of vodka or whiskey. But this only decreases the risk, it doesn't eliminate it. Swallowing the load seriously increases the danger, because the stomach acid is in the stomach, not in the esophagus. It's your life; you have to decide, but you should treat any unknown partner as if he were HIV positive. You may not want to miss the last act; but if there's a fire backstage, you'd better get your ass out of the theater.

I know that these AIDS questions are redundant, but they are so damned important! Besides, I like the way this guy asked for advice. (I liked my answer, too.) I always try to take a little extra time for a man who is obviously a dedicated cocksucker.

Dear Larry,

My biggest turn-on is getting into a hot scene with a serviceman, especially a marine, or maybe a sailor. It's even better is the guy seems to be hustling. I thought this would be safer, too, because I understood that everyone was tested for the AIDS virus when he was inducted. Now, I hear about the disease being a problem in the service. Are there statistics on this? Is a serviceman just as apt to be infected as anyone else?

Jock, New Orleans, LA

Dear Jock,

Because most guys in the service are also in the most statistically vulnerable age group, you have no guarantee. After all, if he plays games with you—and especially if he does not observe the rules of safe sex—you can figure he is doing it with other guys, as well. After all, how does he know you aren't a carrier? Are you playing by the rules? You might be a greater danger to him than he is to you. Remember, a negative HIV test today does not preclude your picking up the virus tomorrow.

Dear Larry,

Two of my close friends have been lovers in an SM relationship for a number of years. One of them (the bottom) has a name which could be either a man's or a woman's (like "Lee," although that isn't it). This gave the Master the idea of simply claiming that they were married, and using his friend's proper name on the forms when they filed income taxes. I keep telling them that they're crazy, because they are going to land in jail, but they won't believe me. They claim that they have been together long enough (over seven years) to have established a "common-law" relationship, and are therefore entitled to do what they're doing. I can't believe they're right, but maybe I'm the one who's crazy.

Name and area withheld

Dear With,

No, you're not crazy, although your friends are a little mad. The feds simply do not recognize gay marriage, even if performed by a church which is willing to do this. However, the most silly aspect is that they are actually cheating themselves, since the tax breaks are generally better if two people file separately. Not being a lawyer, I can't quote chapter and verse as to the legal consequences when they get caught, but it is my feeling that nothing too terrible is going to happen to them. They are probably paying more tax than they have to, and in that case Uncle Sugar isn't going to be overly peeved. If you can nudge them into it, however, a trip to the local mouthpiece is probably a good idea.

Dear Larry,

I'm a Master who has taken on a permanent live-in slave for the first time. I'm almost twenty years older than he is, so I know that he is probably going to survive me. We both work, and he turns his paycheck over to me every week, never asking what I do with his money. I have set up an investment fund in my name, with him as beneficiary in case I die. He doesn't know about it, and I'm afraid to say anything to my lawyer—who's kind of a redneck, as are most people in our area. My family knows I'm gay, and have more or less disowned me because of it. Since I don't know where to go for legal advice, my question is whether or not my family is going to be able to grab the money if I die, or will my designation of the kid as beneficiary be sufficient?

Concerned Master, Fresno, CA

Dear Master,

You really should pop down to Los Angeles one of these days and talk to a gay attorney. You can get a referral very easily from the Gay & Lesbian Community Services Center in Hollywood. My gut feeling is that you're probably okay, since California courts seem fairly sophisticated to these kinds of arrangement; but there may be some very simple things you could do to make sure.

Again, the questions become somewhat redundant when pulled out en masse and grouped together by category. But I would remind the reader that these questions were spread out over a ten-year period. I tend to go overboard in advising on AIDS-related questions, because I want to prevent as many guys as possible from contracting the disease.

CHAPTER 8

The Cock & Balls: Circumcised vs. Uncut, Penile Enhancement, Foreskin Restoration, Castration

I think no other subject has so preoccupied so many men as this one: the shape, size, and general appearance of a man's penis. The issue of circumcision is of particular interest to Americans, I suppose, because so few male babies escape the knife in this country. In most other civilized lands, the human male is allowed to grow up with the sensual feel and aesthetic enhancement of a foreskin. Here are a few of the most interesting questions and observations on the subject of this great source of male pride and concern.

Dear Larry,

I have heard about a process for enlarging the penis, similar to what they do for women's breasts—using silicone injected under the skin. Do you know anything about this, and if so can you tell me how to go about having it done? I was not gifted with much meat, and I'd like to try the process.

Terry, Fort Worth, TX

Dear Terry,

A few years back, there were a few doctors in Nevada who provided this service. In fact, it was called the "Las Vegas Treatment." Recently, I haven't heard anything about it, probably because it was not very satisfactory. I've known two guys who had it done, and both of them were unhappy with the results. There does not appear to be any way to keep the silicone distributed evenly along the penile shaft, with the unfortunate result that it tends to gather like a large doughnut behind the cockhead during use. The injection of silicone, of course, can only make your dick larger in girth. It does nothing to lengthen it. One guy did remark, however, that the added pressure and weight was a sexy feeling. If you really want to try it, you might send an inquiry to the Nevada Medical Association. As far as I know, this was the only state where it was done—possibly the only one where it was legal.

Fortunately, this procedure never became very widespread, judging by all the problems women have developed from silicone breast implants. I have, however, never heard of a man having similar results; i.e., cancer, etc. I have noticed ads in many major newspapers recently, under the heading "Men Only"—medical groups offering surgical penile-enlargement services. I don't see the local authorities going after them for fraud or malpractice, so perhaps they have finally found an answer to the problem of a small dick.

Dear Larry,

You have answered several letters about ballstretching, with the intention of making them hang lower. But I'd like to know if there is any way to make them bigger. My nuts swing low enough, but they're so damned small that I'm embarrassed when someone takes hold of them. I've even been told they look like two bird's eggs that fell out of the nest. Have you any suggestions?

J. R., Seattle

Dear J. R.,

No. As long as they work, use them and enjoy them.

There are some guys you just can't help. I might have referred him to that crazy exercise from an earlier letter (see Chapter 4), where the guys pumped their sacs full of K-Y, but since I suggested to these guys that they might dehydrate their nuts by doing this, a guy with little ones to start with might end up with desiccated husks, down to the size of a Spanish peanut.

Dear Larry,

My lover and I have been together for almost fifteen years. He is quite a bit older than I am, but I still love him very much. He has recently been diagnosed as having cancer of the prostate, and he is very much afraid that he is going to end up being castrated. I've tried to tell him that bad as it might be, it wouldn't be the end of the world; but he seems to believe that he'll never be able to have sex again if they have to remove his nuts. I can't convince him otherwise, and I'm really not too sure exactly what his physical condition will be. Do you have any knowledge of guys who have been through this?

Worried, Seattle

Dear Worried,

Short of death, itself, the prospect of losing his balls is probably the most terrifying situation a man can face, largely because of all the symbolism of "balls making the man," etc. However, life does not end with this, if a guy is determined enough to overcome it. By the use of hormone therapy, it is possible to retain a reasonable degree of sexuality. They also have "falsies" that can be inserted into the scrotum after everything's healed up. They seem to be a big psychological boost for a lot of guys. I don't envy you your situation, because you are going to have a heavy burden in helping your friend overcome the emotional repercussions. But you're right; it's not the end of the world. The globe is just going to tip a little, and you'll have to tip with it.

Terrible as the prospect may be, a lot of men have survived it and gone on to lead reasonably normal lives, although sex was no longer a major factor. There is no denying the tragic aspects of this situation, but there are support groups in most major cities, and they can help ease the way.

Dear Larry,

The guy I've been having an affair with for several months used to be married to a woman, and they had several kids. I have often wondered why he never seems to have a very big ejaculation, and he just told me he had had a vasectomy in order not to have any more kids. Since he's probably not ever going to do it with a woman again, can he have the operation undone? I'd really love to take a big load from him. Otherwise, he's the hottest man I ever met.

Ben, NYC

Dear Ben,

For starters, it is probably not the vasectomy that is causing him to have small ejaculations. His semen is simply devoid of sperm cells. The bulk of a "load" is produced in the prostate and other parts of the system, which are not affected by the operation. You might try getting him to take heavier doses of vitamins, especially B-complex and E. These seem to help increase the size of a man's ejaculation. To answer your question about reversing the vasectomy, there are now microsurgical techniques to do this, although a man will usually not produce as much sperm as he did before. There is an interesting article on this in *The Health Letter,* published by News America, P. O. Box 19622, Irvine, CA 92713 (Jan 10, 1986 issue). The suggestion regarding vitamins is mine, however, not theirs, and is based on personal observation rather than professional medical opinion.

Dear Larry,

With all of the current concern about Arab terrorists, there seems to be an increasing interest in these guys as sexual objects. I guess the syndrome is sort of similar to someone wanting to be whipped by an SS storm trooper. In a recent discussion, a friend of mine kept telling me I shouldn't be so turned on to them because I like uncut dick, and he says all Arabs are circumcised. I don't believe him. Will you please enlighten me—us?

Barry, Portland, OR

Dear Barry,

Unfortunately, your friend is right—at least 99 percent so. Moslem law requires circumcision, much as Jewish law. However, several Arab sects leave a portion of the foreskin, or may only take a nip out of it. And, of course, not all Arabs are Moslem, so the rite of circumcision may or may not be performed on these men. (The Christian sects in Beirut, for example.) With an Arab, you still have the same problem you'd have with an American. You've got to pull his pants down to find out.

Or lift up his skirts. Since answering this letter, I've been to North Africa, and all the ones I saw were cut—but most Arab men seem to be quite generously endowed. Of course, I never had a chance to do a proper empirical survey. Don't laugh! I couple of years back my friend, the late Dr. Bruce Voeller published a most interesting paper during the course of his surveys on the effectiveness of various condoms. In this he provided some fascinating statistics on the relative sizes of penises on college men, hard vs. soft. He would never describe his methodology, but it must have been a classic case of devotion to one's duty.

Dear Larry,

Reading your material, and looking at the pictures in publications like yours and *Drummer*'s, I really feel I've been shortchanged. I was circumcised as a baby, and have never had the opportunity to feel what it's like to have a foreskin, or (apparently) the extra sensitivity that goes along with it. Every time I think about it, I get furious! It's my parents' fault, because they could easily have waited until I was old enough to decide for myself. All this crap about "it's cleaner!" What bullshit! There isn't a single advantage that I know of in having half your dick chopped off. If they had any money, I'd sue my parents!

Cut and pissed, NM

Dear Cut,

I really feel guilty about contributing to such unhappiness. In reality, it doesn't make much functional difference one way or the other, although an uncut cock probably does have a little greater sensitivity. I simply find it more aesthetic, as do many others. However, when I did a survey a few years back, the vast majority of guys didn't care one way or the other. As to the positive advantages of being cut, there actually are a few. For one (at least the last time I was able to check on it), there was no case on record of a circumcised man getting cancer of the penis. Likewise, it appears that it is less likely for a circumcised Top to contract AIDS from anal sex because he is less likely to have the tiny lesions that often develop under the foreskin of an uncut man. It is also fairly common for an uncut man to be circumcised if he develops prostate cancer, in the belief that the buildup of smegma can contribute to a spread of the disease. Although these are statistically remote arguments for circumcision, they are arguments I have gotten from several different doctors over the years. Although I still think it's much prettier with skin, it's difficult to tell the difference in the dark, when it's up and ready for action. And don't sue your poor parents, even if they win the lottery. Some damned doctor convinced them that it should be done, and they believed they were doing it for your own good.

The idea that a circumcised cock is "cleaner" is the most common argument given by the doctor who expects to make a few extra bucks by doing it. This attitude, of course, harkens back to our puritanical forebears, who believed that anything to do with sex was "dirty." You'd think, after a couple of hundred years, our culture would have progressed a little further.

Dear Larry,

I have a physical problem that I can't seem to get the answer to. When I get a hard-on, my dick develops a severe downward curve that makes it difficult to use as I'd like to use it. I've been like this as long as I can remember. A nurse friend-of-a-friend told me I have something called "Peyronie's disease." I asked my doctor about it, but he didn't seem to know what I was talking about and said I had just been circumcised too tightly. He didn't offer any solution and, in fact, seemed a little uncomfortable discussing it. Can you tell me anything about it? (I can't

find the damned nurse anymore; I think he's long gone.)
Arc'd in Utah

Dear Arc'd,

Consulting my files, I found a reference to Peyronie's disease in a correction to an article that appeared in the *Mayo Clinic Health Letter*. They called it "an organic disorder of the penis," and went on to note that there is medical disagreement as to whether or not it should be treated with radiation. They also seem to suspect that the condition can be brought on by certain "beta blocker drugs" (such as Inderal) which are frequently prescribed for people with heart disease and/or high blood pressure. The article in question is in the January 1986 *M.C.H.L.,* if you can run it down. However, my feeling is that your doctor was probably right. If you have had this problem since puberty, you may very well have been cut without enough slack in the skin of your penis. (And if your present doctor is the same one who did it, I don't wonder that he's uncomfortable talking about it.) Why don't you go to a sex clinic if there is one in your area, or talk to a plastic surgeon? I should think they would be able to correct the problem.

In this kind of situation, "let your fingers do the walking." You can generally find a listing in the yellow pages for a doctor or a clinic that can help you—either directly, or by referring you to the proper professional.

Dear Larry,

This letter is in answer to the guy who was pissed at his parents for circumcising him and to all cut guys who are mad about it. I am uncut, and it has not been a great pleasure for me.

(Point 1) The so-called pleasure of greater sensitivity is a myth. I have been so sensitive that I have been unable to be touched on the exposed cockhead until the past few years. (I am forty-five.) I could not enjoy getting sucked because one or two touches of the teeth would either abrade me or cause a very unpleasant jolt. I had to be very careful selecting "fuckees," because an overly tight asshole caused pain when the skin was pulled back.

(Point 2) I have a slight phlimosis, a nonelastic ring which clings too tightly when I skin back, so it is a constant problem. I should have had this taken care of when I had the time, but I was not willing to go through the pain and discomfort of adjusting to what might have turned out to be a mistake. As one doctor said; the result might have been to overtraumatize it. My uncut cock has not been a source of pleasure, and although my experience is not a normal one, I want to say to all unhappy cut guys to get over it and enjoy the positive aspects of their equipment, not dwell on the things they think they're missing.

(Point 3) Real sexual pleasure and cock sensitivity are generated from the mind, anyway. Maybe these cut men should reflect back on the times when they were most sensitized in the cock, and remember what they were thinking or who they were with. I know that I and many other "uncuts" can't get over the top just on penis sensitivity alone. You need a good fantasy. Good luck to all pissed-off cut men. You are really just as well off as us uncuts.

K, NYC

Dear K,

I guess you've said it all. I'm just glad that Michelangelo left the skin on David. It's so damned pretty!

At the time, I didn't want to say much in answer to this guy, because he was kind enough to write and share his problems with us. However, I did get a number of angry responses from other uncut men, telling me how far off-base this man was. I do think he was the exception to the rule, but I also think his statements were true. (And my response about Michelangelo and David simply reflects awareness of David's status as a Jewish religious hero— and King—who by all rights should have been circumcised.)

Dear Larry,

After a couple of years of wanting to get into an SM situation, I finally contacted a guy through a *Drummer* ad and submitted to him. Although he was attractive and seemed to know what he was doing, the scene was a disaster. I was so nervous that I couldn't even get a hard-on, as much as I wanted to. Finally, my Master tied me so I was standing up and he sucked my cock. At least, he tried to suck it, but I couldn't get it up and he broke off the session, suggesting that we might try again when I could relax more and feel more comfortable. I really do want to try it again with him, and I guess he'd be willing, but I'm afraid to call him, because I'm afraid it will happen again. I haven't had this kind of problem before, so I know there isn't anything physically wrong with me. Can you suggest an answer?

Nervous, San Diego, CA

Dear Nervous,

Impotence can stem from a variety of physical and emotional causes. In your situation, the cause is fairly obvious. I say "fairly obvious," because you may not be reacting just out of fear or anxiety. There can be a fair amount of guilt associated with the beginning of SM behavior, just as there can be when you have your first gay sex. Regardless of the cause (assuming it is emotional), the more you worry about it, the more hopeless is it going to get. Conversely, the best cure is to be in a situation where it doesn't make any difference. Many Tops simply don't care whether their bottoms get hard or not; some will even punish them if they do. Bearing this in mind, why don't you call your Top and ask him for another session. If he agrees, he is accepting you as you are, and probably will take a different approach with you. If he is willing to talk about it on the phone, see what he has to say. He might be insightful enough to set up a less-stressful situation for you. In any case, you have nothing to lose but your cherry. And if it doesn't work out with him, San Diego is not such an SM desert that you can't find another potential Master.

Impotence is a strange condition that has so many connotations, it is difficult to make a definitive statement that applies to a single individual, let alone a group of men. It is uncommon to find a physical cause, especially in a young man. Almost inevitably, the source will turn out to be psychological. But the myriad potential sources of the emotional trauma are innumerable and often elusive. Worse, the condition is self-perpetuating because anxiety over its possible occurrence (or recurrence) is often a factor in perpetuating the problem. In a sense, it's like a person with high blood pressure going to the doctor for a test. He's so afraid the reading is going to be elevated, his very fear causes it to be.

Dear Larry,

I was interested in the letter from K, NYC. I agree with him that there is nothing great about foreskins, though I find no fault with those who like them. What puzzles me is why K hasn't simply had his removed. Putting one back after it's been removed may be difficult, but removing it isn't. I never found mine to be in any way pleasing to me. In fact, I didn't like it; so when I was about twenty-two, I had it removed. I am now fifty-seven, and I have never regretted it for a moment.

R. C., Minneapolis, MN

Dear R. C.,

No one can say you've never missed what you've never had, can they?

Dear Larry,

As a man who has probably less-than-average cock and ball size, I want to ask you if there are any devices to enlarge one's cock? How about devices to make the balls hang lower? I see items in bookstore, etc., but I'm concerned about safety as well as efficiency.

C. B., La Jolla, CA

Dear C. B.,

This is a question that people ask all the time, and one which I have tried to answer in this column a number of times. There really isn't much you can do about your cock. The penis enlargers you see on the market are usually plastic tubes with a vacuum pump. These can force your cock up to a larger size temporarily, but they can also cause permanent damage by rupturing the tiny blood vessels in the erectile tissue. Then you'll have not only to say that it should prompt a visit to your doctor, but that the source of blood is rarely found unless there is really a problem in the prostate or testes. In other words, there are often minor sources of bleeding from the surface blood vessels in the lining of the sperm-storage sites. These generally tend to heal themselves after a period of time. So, while I am telling you that you probably have no great cause for alarm, you should get yourself checked by a doctor. You don't have to tell him about all your toys, since your condition can easily happen without their use. The chances of serious problems are remote, but don't take a chance. Besides, the doc can probably prescribe some medication to clear up the condition and make sure it doesn't become serious.

Dear Larry,

I am just downright disgusted by some of the people who are supposedly leading this "AIDS Crusade," giving people advice on how to avoid getting the disease and attending meetings about it, always with a cigarette hanging out of their mouths. Don't they realize that they are running a much higher risk of premature death and disease than the people they are trying to help? How can they pretend to be dedicated to better health and welfare when they place their own lives in such deadly jeopardy? I hope you will say something about it one of these days.

Peter, San Francisco, CA

Dear Peter,

What can I say as I sit here puffing on a cancer stick and trying to produce some sensible comments? You are, of course, absolutely right. The addiction to nicotine is every bit as deadly as the sexual addictions that lead people to disregard the rules of safety. But this is really the essence of the problem—in both cases—because it is an addiction, and very difficult to break. The AIDS deaths are simply more immediate and more frightening, because we see so many young people succumbing to AIDS after being sick for a short period of time. Cigarettes don't usually get us until much later, and there is always the idea in the back of your mind: "I'll quit before it's too late." Let's hope we can.

Well, at least I can report having gone over five years without a cigarette. I guess I'm healthier for it; at least people say I smell better, and I can walk up a flight of stairs without palpitations and a coughing fit. But am I safe from the ravages of too many years' indulgence? Who knows?

Dear Larry,

I really enjoy reading your column in *Drummer*. I would like to ask a question that may sound silly, but a lot of guys seem to believe that anal intercourse may possibly shrink hemorrhoids by strengthening the muscle tissue around it. Is there any truth to that, or would it be harmful to hemorrhoidal tissue? I would appreciate your comments.

(Name Withheld)

Dear Withheld,

This is an old wives' tale that has been circulating for years. But, like many such O.W.T.s, there may be a modicum of truth to it. If you can get a doctor to take you seriously enough to answer your question, he's likely to tell you that getting fucked in the ass is certainly not going to cure your condition, but the stretching action may help to stave it off. However, if you're prone to the malady, nothing is really going to prevent it. But there are things you can do to slow it down (such as not pressing down hard and regularly to evacuate the bowel.) On the other hand, if you need a good rationale for getting fucked, that one's as good as any. Hemorrhoids are such a pain in the ass!

Dear Mr. Townsend,

I am in the United States Navy. Recently they conducted a Navy-wide HTLV-3 test, and lo and behold, I tested positive. Through the navy's program I met my Daddy, who had also tested positive. Our question is: since we are both positive, is there any need for Daddy to use a rubber? And if there is, where can I find heavy-duty, industrial-strength, jumbo-size rubbers? He has tried several brands, including the "natural" (sheepskin) rubbers, but the damned things always shred. Thank you.

B. D., East Coast

a small cock, but a limp one. As to making the balls hang lower, you can lengthen the scrotum over a long period of time by use of increasingly longer "ballstretchers," but this also has potential dangers. *(See detailed answers in previous chapters—ed.)* For all practical purposes, you are far better off learning to live with what you have. As long as it works, don't try to fix it.

Dear Larry,

   I have been reading the concluding articles on the Stockholm AIDS conference (Spring 1987), and I see they're at it again! Dr. King K. Holmes of Seattle is reported to have implied that uncircumcised men may be at greater risk in contracting the virus than men who are cut. I have heard this BS before, and it makes no more sense to me now than it did a couple of years ago, when that San Francisco quack alleged the same thing. Why the fuck should I be at greater risk with a foreskin than some guy who doesn't have one?

                                         Guy, Los Angeles, CA

Dear Guy,

   I'm assuming you read the same *LA Times* article that I did, and if you had read it to the end you would have gotten your explanation—at least the line of reasoning followed by Dr. Holmes. His contention is that men with skin can develop small lesions (cracks in the skin) underneath the foreskin. These may be so small they go unnoticed, but any tear in the skin is sufficient to admit the virus. Apparently, the studies that sustain these conclusions involved native Africans. I can appreciate the logical basic of the good doctor's concern, although I might have some reservations in translating an African study, where hygienic conditions may be considerably different from ours, into recommendations for behavior in American/Western European society. Still, there is a possibility that the risk exists, and it certainly behooves an uncut man to be aware of it. In order to enjoy both the aesthetic and sensual advantages of possessing a foreskin, you should take responsible precautions to assure your own health and well being. I don't think these medical observations are sufficient to justify a mass stampede into the local circumcision parlor, nor is this implicit in the recommendations coming out of Stockholm.

I don't know how closely related it may be to Dr. Holmes's observations in 1987, but in the last couple of years, we have seen a frightening epidemic of AIDS all though Central Africa. This is apparently exacerbated by a secondary venereal disease, which causes lesions to appear on the genital areas of both sexes. This becomes a perfect avenue for the transmission of HIV—with or without foreskins.

Dear Larry,

I have a question concerning immobilizing of the penis. I have heard that rapists can be treated so that they cannot obtain erection. There is supposed to be an operation. What is actually done?

Name withheld (Europe)

Dear Anonymous,

Although I keep up pretty well on this type of material, I have not heard of any operation specifically designed to immobilize the penis (by which I presume you mean to render it impotent, incapable of erection.) In our Western societies, there is such universal abhorrence of any legal penalty that involves physically depriving a man of his sexuality, I doubt that such an operation is on the books in any country. There have been experiments with female hormones, but these tend to be so destructive to the testicles that heavy, prolonged treatment is tantamount to castration. (See my answer to the next letter.) There are drugs, of course, that will render a man impotent, but again these are not considered acceptable within the limits of our current attitudes on "cruel and unusual punishment."

Dear Larry,

Although I know that castrating a man is supposed to leave him incapable of sexual performance, I have heard so many conflicting stories that I'm curious to know what

really happens to a guy who gets nutted. How about remov-ing just one testicle? Does it take two to tangle?

H. C., Phoenix, AZ

Dear H. C.,

The removal of both testicles, without the man's receiving hormones to compensate for this loss, usually results in a signif-icant reduction of his sexual drive and interest. However, in our society, it is rare for a man not to receive hormone treatment, and almost anyone (usually a cancer patient) who loses his balls is on a program of medication that allows him to retain a fairly normal array of "secondary" male sexual characteristics; i.e., his beard continues to grow, his musculature remains masculine, he does not grow breasts, etc. I am personally acquainted with several guys in this situation, and all claim to be capable of erec-tion and many of the pleasant sexual sensations they had prior to their operations. They cannot ejaculate, and this is the great-est frustration (sexually). For the sake of appearance and psychological satisfaction, it is possible for a castrated man to have "flashes" inserted into his scrotum. In ancient cultures, particularly Persia, where eunuch were employed as harem guards and servants, there was—of course—no hormone treat-ment available. Histories of this period indicate that if a man was castrated prior to puberty, he was capable of intercourse, but could not procreate. However, this satisfied the ancient kings, since they were less interested in the fidelity of their multi-spouses than they were in ensuring that any progeny were legitimate. Eunuchs were noted for their effeminate mannerisms, however, and a tendency to become fat. Losing one testicle will have little or no effect, except that—as in the case of full castra-tion—there is bound to be an emotional as well as physical impact. How a man copes with this is going to vary greatly according to the other factors that determine his personality and mental outlook.

Although we often hear angry people opining that all rapists should be castrated, the effect of this would not alleviate the prob-lem—in fact, might even make it worse. Not only can simple drug therapy maintain the culprit's ability to spring a hard-on, the

*guy's anger over being castrated might well cause him to become
an even more angry, desperate man, seeking to revenge himself
on society in general, and women in particular.*

Dear Larry,

I'm writing because I hope you can resolve a question that
has been the source of some contention between me and a
close friend of mine. We are both admitted size-queens,
and despite the safety precautions we have to take, both of
us just love to suck cock. Of the European races, I maintain
that the Italians are the best endowed. My friend claims
that this honor belongs to northerners, like the Germans or
Scandinavians. I know you have spent a lot of time in
Europe—probably more than both my friend and me
combined. Could we solicit your opinion on this debate?

Cal, Philadelphia, PA

Dear Cal,

You must understand that there has never, to the best of my
knowledge, been any scientific research into the relative sizes of
European pricks. However, I do recall reading some silly,
supposed survey a number of years ago that gave the prize to the
English. On the basis of my own observations, I have to say
that there are gems to be found in almost every country, but also
a great diversity. I have certainly observed some Italian beauties;
but, having spent more time in Germany than any other country, I can testify from firsthand experience that these gentlemen
have nothing to be ashamed of. Then there are the Spanish and
Portuguese...and the Greeks...and the Poles. Oh, it is very hard
to choose! Why not simply enjoy what you can get and quit
worrying that there might be a bigger one someplace else?

Dear Sir,

I hope you can help me. My Master requires me to play
with my cock as punishment, continuously, sometimes for
hours on end without allowing me to cum. I'm not
concerned about the blue balls, but since I have a foreskin,
the constant thrusts and retractions occasionally create

what looks like blood blisters around the slit of my cock. My Master told me to write you about it. He says they're nothing to worry about.

Slave Tag, No Hollywood, CA

Dear slave,

They probably are blood blisters, and you probably deserve whatever pain they are causing you. My medical adviser says to put a little antiseptic on them after your session.

Dear Larry,

Some months ago I started a subscription to *Drummer;* and, after reading several issues, I realize that there is a great difference in your (Americans') attitude toward circumcision, and that of us Frenchmen. Whereas most Americans seem to have had the operation, it is very unusual in France. In all my active sex life (I'm fifty-nine), I have met only two guys who were circumcised. Although both were beautiful men, I felt badly for them that they had been cut off. To play with one's skin is a real pleasure, and for a man not to ever be permitted to do this is a terrible loss. Why does this happen so consistently in America? A number of years ago, I discussed this with a friend of mine, and he suggested that it might be because of the many Jews in your medical establishment. But, among Jews, circumcision is not a medical act. Can you satisfy my curiosity?

J. B., Paris, France

Dear J. B.,

It is indeed difficult to understand how routine circumcision was able to become so well entrenched a practice in the United States. Obviously, our medical establishment has been responsible for convincing American mothers that their sons would enjoy a "cleaner" existence with their foreskins removed. Perhaps some doctors honestly believed this, although I would question whether, in many cases, it wasn't simply a matter of selling additional service for a few extra bucks. Of course, with our long-standing puritan ethic, our masses have continually regarded anything sexual as "dirty"—and this would certainly help explain how it all happened. And as to the Jewish influence, who knows? Most of my Jewish friends believe in circumcision, although a few do not. I doubt that Jewish influence within the medical profession would have been enough, in and of itself, to turn the tide; but it may have been a contributing factor. Your guess is as good as mine.

The most eager circumciser I ever met was a woman, who almost drooled at the prospect of taking the skin off a newborn babe, to say nothing of the unmitigated joy she expressed the one time she told me she was about to perform her art on an adult man. It had to have been a true symbolic act of castration for her. Of course, this woman was such a hidebound male-hating lesbian that she wouldn't even let her lover have a male dog, for fear she might have to see that "awful little red thing sticking out once in a while." It takes all kinds.

Dear Larry,

I'm a young guy—twenty-two, and not bad-looking. I really want to be a slave, although I know from reading your things—and comments by others—that I have a lot to learn before I can claim that status. In fact, I've had leathersex only a couple of times. But that's just enough to know that I really want to go for it! I've even got the Master picked out, and I think he's interested in me. (I've been going to a bar near where I live, and he's in there a lot of times.) I've got one problem, and I'd like to know how you feel about it. Despite my having a decent face and body, I've got a really small set of cock and balls. They are so small, in fact, that I'm embarrassed to have anyone see them. I go to a gym, but I never take off my jockstrap, not even in the showers. Do you think this is going to make a difference to a Master? After all, a slave isn't supposed to use his cock for much of anything, and I'd really be willing to do anything else he wanted. I mean, like getting fucked and taking care of His cock, etc. What do you think? Is the size of a slave's cock of any importance?

Tiny, NYC

Dear Tiny,

It's hard to say how important the size of a slave's cock is going to be to a specific Master. Even if it is just a matter of aesthetics—i.e., something pretty to look at—there is going to be a great deal of difference between the reactions of one man and another. But what do you have to lose? The worst that could happen would be for the guy to toss you out after the first session—and he might do that, anyway, for any number of reasons that have nothing to do with the size of your dick. If you want this particular Master, I'd say, "Try for it!" And I'd be interested to know what happens. Drop me a note and let me know—assuming, of course, that your Master gives you permission.

To some extent, guys like yours truly have helped to promote the myth of big cocks being the most desirable standard. While most guys would prefer to read about big dicks, and to see them in pictures, the truth is that a nice average-size cock is the most practical in use. The bottom can take it without any massive trauma, in either end. Even an exceptionally small cock is not necessarily a bar to sexual enjoyment. When I look back on the many sizes, shapes, and textures of the dicks I have known intimately, it makes me realize how little difference these variations can make. I've enjoyed them all!

CHAPTER 9

Censorship, Travel Tips, Travel Restrictions, and Other Outrageous Repressions

Although we enjoy a far greater degree of freedom today than was the case a couple of decades ago, this tends to vary greatly by geographic area. There are still many horrific roadblocks dropped in front of us—sometimes by people or organizations (or governments). One's ability to cope with these, either to live with them or to ascertain a way to circumvent them has been of prime concern to a number of correspondents. I think I have been helpful in many cases, simply because I have heard from such a wide variety of guys that I have been able to pass on the knowledge gained by the hard lessons of one, to another who may thence be spared. At least I tried.

Dear Larry,

I have an opportunity to travel in the USSR this summer, where I will probably stay for a month or so. I realize that the chances of an SM encounter are remote, to say the least. But what about regular sex? I really dig uncut meat, and I'm sure this must be the norm in Russia. What are the legal consequences if I get caught, and how likely is that to happen? Are there gay bars? And what about AIDS? Has it

gotten across the Iron Curtain? *(Note that this was asked and answered in 1986.—ed.)*

Curious Tourist, NYC

Dear Curious,

I would suggest that you keep your pecker in your pants once you cross the border into Russia. Because Soviet housing standards generally allow an individual very little living space, there are few gay men who "have a place to go." A lot goes on in parks and other dark, secluded places, but it's transitory sex. The penalties are quite severe if you're caught; and, as an inexperienced outsider, your chances would be much higher than a native who knows the ropes and the language. (Although in the case of tourists, they are most apt merely to deport you.) I have heard of several bars or other social gathering places where gay men go to meet each other, but no gay bars as such. If you discovered one and went to it, you would be conspicuous and subject to harassment. Unless you're a special case, such as a potential political activist or spy, there is not much chance of your being tailed. But a foreigner trying to make personal contact with a Russian citizen can bring himself to the attention of the police and may get his Russian friend into difficulties. As to AIDS, the Soviet authorities deny it, but there have been cases in Moscow and Leningrad—probably other places, as well. I'm not telling you that sex isn't there; just that the risk is probably not worth the quickie you might get. Save it up until you get back to Germany or Sweden.

There's sure been a big change in this situation, although I have a feeling that old ideas and attitudes die hard in the eastern countries, just as they do here. Although the Russian laws have changed, it is going to be a while before sexual freedom is commonplace. After all, they're years behind us, and we're still fighting the puritanical attitudes which survived the demise of many local "anti-sodomy laws"—to say nothing of the jurisdictions where gaysex is still illegal.

An interesting example of Russian attitudes toward gays in general, happened in West Hollywood a couple of years ago. The city has a large number of Russian immigrants in residence—mostly Jews, whom we in the Movement have always thought of a friends and allies. However, these people reflect a much different orientation. When some of the new residents discovered that the gay band was rehearsing on a regular basis in a public park, a group of these men descended on the location one evening, with the intent of beating up some queers. Their first surprise came when the gays fought back. The second—and most shocking—revelation was when the sheriffs arrested the Russians. I take this incident as indicative of a Russian—as opposed to a Jewish—attitude toward homosexuals.

Dear Larry,

Several times, now, I've tried to order SM publications from Europe, and only about one out of three get to me. The others are seized by U.S. Customs, which sends me a rather frightening letter and tells me that if I sign an authorization for them to destroy the material, they won't do anything else to me. I'm just wondering if: (1) what they are doing is really legal, (2) what they would really do to me if I refused to sign the authorization, (3) what criteria they use to decide what is "obscene" and what is not. Are the mags that get through to me officially "passed," or is it just that no one bothered to look at them?

Bob, Boston, MA

Dear Bob,

Yes, isn't our government wonderful? In this time of austerity, you'd think they would have better things to do with their time. But to answer your questions:

(1) Unfortunately, the U.S. Custom activities are legal under federal statute, and will remain such until someone takes them to court and persuades a judge otherwise. (2) If you refuse to sign the destruct authorization, you will get a frightening document in the mail which is a Xerox copy of the lawsuit they file against the magazine (not the publisher, but the mag itself). Because there is seldom anyone to step forward and offer a defense, they win by default and destroy the questionable mate-

rial. Their sending the copy to you is supposed to alert you to this impending actions and give you a chance to appear in court to oppose them, if you wish to do so. This always comes by registered or certified mail, and often gives a first-time recipient heart palpitations. But it doesn't mean anything; just shit-can it and that's the last you'll hear from them.

(3) It is difficult to guess what criteria determine "obscenity." Many of the European mags have photos of water sports, heavy SM (that draws blood), fisting, and even scat. These are for going to get it banned for sure if the snoops see them. Plain old fucking and sucking also seem to qualify, however, even though you can buy this in any neighborhood porn shop. If your mag gets through, it is probably because they didn't open it. You are in the worst district for this nonsense, so your proportion of loss is going to be higher than in most other parts the country.

Sad to say, the censorship picture has not improved much since this letter was answered in 1986, although Boston no longer seems to be any worse than the rest of the country. Of course, we're still better off than some other English-speaking nations. In Canada the RCMP have been known to seize incoming porn, then get a search warrant to invade the guy's home. They confiscate whatever they find and can charge the victim with importing obscene materials, on the assumption that any mags, etc., he has that were not produced in Canada must have been "imported" by him. In England, I have had customers write to tell me that my first-class mailings (flyers in a regular envelope, not merchandise) have been opened by postal inspectors and confiscated. And trying to mail into New Zealand—forget it! One would have thought these stupid restrictions on an adult's reading material would have gone out with Adolf Hitler, but obviously not so. See the next item.

Dear Larry,

I have a couple of friends in England, and for several years I have been sending hot books and magazines to one of them—things they can't get over there. Recently, my friend asked me to stop sending anything, and offered only a rather strange comment about "police searches" as an explanation. Is he being realistic? I can't believe that a

person could get in trouble because someone in a foreign
country sends him something in the mail. After all, there is
no proof that he asked for it.

Al, Pacoima, CA

Dear Al,

For some reason, the English authorities have developed a
peculiarly paranoid attitude toward porn in recent years. They
seem to classify its destructive power as something akin to an IRA
bomb. As a result there have been several nasty instances of
their obtaining search warrants and ransacking the homes of
suspected "importers." These occurrences are mercifully few
and far between, but even one is so outrageous it brings into serious question the sanity of Maggie's minions. Still, the situation
has spooked your friend, and you can't really blame him.

*This is a situation that has not improved over time. I have had
several English subscribers to my mail-order service request that I
cease mailing to them, because their customs have opened and
inspected (and in one case confiscated) my flyers, which were sent
by first-class airmail. That is really outrageous!*

Dear Larry,

I know that you're a devotee of European travel, so I
just thought I'd ask what you think about all the terrorist
shit that's going on over there. I've finally saved enough
pennies to go, and I'd like to get in on some of that hot
action before the dollar drops so low I'll have to save up for
another couple of years to pay the tariff. Has it altered
your plans—or would it?

Gene, Miami

Dear Gene,

Since I'm not really interested in Greece, Israel, or the other
countries in that general area *(where the terrorism was happening at this time—ed.)*, I'm not greatly concerned for my personal
safety. If they're going to get me it can happen under the wheels
of a taxi in Beverly Hills just as easily as on an air-bus. Frankly,
it's the Lufthansa-type seats and grub that would discourage me

much faster than some Arab with a pocketful of plastic. But a word of caution: I see guys who are afraid to practice unsafe sex in the United States doing all sorts of things in Germany and Holland. *That* is dangerous!

And I've been "over there" a number of times since. The dollar exchange rate has gotten worse, and the conditions aboard the aircraft have definitely not improved. The only conditions that have changed in my favor are: First, I've got my "frequent-flier" ball rolling so that I can usually fly something other than tourist. Secondly, I have enough friends in various strategic places that I'm never lacking for native guides (or a place to stay). And Europe is still wonderful! If you like'em uncut, it's definitely the place to take your next vacation.

Dear Larry,

People are always sending you questions about medical things, and you have to go research the answers with doctors. But in the long run, I think most of us encounter day-to-day problems that are more in your own line: psychology. I'd like to know what there is in the "average man's" makeup that causes him to hate gays. I moved to San Francisco to get away from the shit I had to take in my hometown (in Kansas), only to find that it isn't safe to walk on the streets at night, because there are gangs of teenaged punks out there "fag bashing." I know I was passed over for promotion in my job because the boss knew (suspected) I was gay, and just the other day my lover and I were in a good restaurant, properly dressed and not camping it up, when I overheard a man tell the waiter he didn't want his family seated next to "queers." I should think that if there is any place in the world where a gay man can live his own lifestyle in peace, it would be in San Francisco, but even here they dump on us!

Outraged, San Francisco, CA

Dear Outraged,

As I have noted before, the nice thing about prejudice is that it requires no logical basis. It's a condition from which all of us suffer to one degree or another, whether these feelings are directed toward people on the basis of age, sex, color, religion, behavior, or whatever. And everyone is the recipient of prejudice in some form or other. No one's immune. Unfortunately, we are one of the more popular targets. Telling you that some men hate us because we remind them of their own sexual inadequacies doesn't take the sting out of their overheard remarks, or lessen the pain and injury from their physical assaults. On the other hand, I have asked waiters not to seat me at a table near a family with obstreperous kids. Prejudice can cut both ways—and does. We all need to feel superior to someone, and we all have what they call "social distance" from one or another group. I don't say it's right, and don't say we shouldn't be trying to do something about it. But you didn't ask me how to fight back, merely why it happened.

Man's cruelty to man is certainly to be found on every level and in every part of the world. When I see TV newscasts or read reports in the newspaper about all the mass killings that result simply from one ethnic or religious group hating another, it only serves to deepen the mystery.

Dear Larry,

I'm middle-aged and pretty well off financially—in business, etc. I feel that my basic interests are better served by the goals of the Republican Party than the liberal big-spenders on the other side. Recently, though, the actions of Ed Meese and others in the administration have begin to scare the shit out of me. As a gay man, I don't want to end up in a concentration camp, or have my property confiscated because I am what I am. I remember your comment on this type of situation in the *Leatherman's Handbook II*. What do you foresee? Are we really in as much trouble as I think we are? *(Received May 1986—ed.)*

(Name withheld)

Dear Withheld,

I hear you loud and clear—more so, because I've been up-front for so long, and have a couple of million words in print on

the very subjects "they" consider so negatively. So far, the
powers that be have only been able to rack up real victories
against the purveyors of kiddy-porn (as opposed to mainstream
erotica.) I think that Georgia's sodomy case was probably a
setup, poorly conceived and done at the wrong time. Although
the Supreme Court made a rather narrowly defined decision, it
was still a terrible blow psychologically. It is all very frightening,
with most of the cards seeming to fall into the wrong hands.
There were a lot of Jews in pre–World War II Germany who
thought "it can't happen here," and some actually voted for
the National Socialist Party. I think we have to realize that it *can*
happen here, if we don't support the people and organizations
who are trying to prevent it. If that means voting for a neoso-
cialist in order to elect a man (or woman) who possesses a
modicum of humanity, so be it. If we all sit back bemoaning our
fate and doing nothing, we will have no one to blame but
ourselves.

*Curious, and frightening, how little some things have changed,
even under a more benign administration. The hate is coming
largely from outside the government at the moment, but the far-
right nuts have more money and seemingly more power than ever.
Even as I write these lines, I know that a snoop from the LAPD
Administrative Vice Unit has been poking around my post-office
box. It's unlikely he'll do much more than that, but why should he
even be interested? I have come more and more to regard the police
as the tools of the right-wing repression that seeks to destroy us.
And that's frightening! When a criminal threatens your person or
your property, you call the cops for help. When it's the cops threatening you, who can you call?*

*As I was writing these lines, I had the TV news on in the back-
ground, and I must share this with you. A few minutes ago, I
hard a teaser for the late (11:00 P.M.) newscast: "Tune in for the
story of Daring Police Action." They just did the story. The daring
police action was to raid a whorehouse, bust the whores, and put
policewomen in to entrap the customers. That's daring? How many
police man-hours are lost on such nonsense, when every jurisdiction
in the country is poor-mouthing the voters and begging for the
funds to fight violent crime, dope, gangs, etc. When I was president*

of HELP, Inc., back in the mid-seventies, we were doing our best to provide legal services for guys who had been preyed upon by the local police. The organization was disbanded about ten years later, because supposedly it was no longer needed. Are we going full circle? I hope not, but—again—only time will tell.

Dear Larry,

Among the many disadvantages of censorship is that it suppresses information which may save a life. As a specific example, drinking piss is a forbidden subject. I would like to know if drinking piss is a way to extend life at sea in a lifeboat.

George, Los Angeles, CA

Dear George,

Although I doubt that the navy will ever publish this as a survival technique, it is certainly true that drinking piss is one (sometimes the only) way to obtain essential fluids in an emergency situation. Of course, we know that a person suffering from a serious viral infection can also pass this to the recipient via his urine, since the body uses this as one way to eliminate undesirable microorganisms. But you knew that all along, didn't you?

I'm sure this question was intended to bait me into a more ribald response, but I resisted the temptation at the time. I should have painted the mental picture of half a dozen hunky young sailors, cast adrift in a lifeboat, each taking some fluid sustenance from the source in a sort of circle-suck. But, I guess that will never make one of the navy rescue manuals, either. Too bad, it might save a life someday.

Dear Larry,

I just read a news magazine account of the problems some of our gay brothers have been giving Jerry Falwell. One guy even programmed his computer to call the Moral Majority's 800 number once every half hour, which cost them a buck a shot. I'd like to do the same thing, and maybe get others to join in, but I'm concerned that there might be some federal law against it—telephone harassment, or some such. Can you enlighten me?

Peter, NYC

Dear Peter,

My legal adviser indicates that although he is not an expert in this field, he would incline to the opinion that programming one's computer to bug somebody would probably constitute harassment; but it is doubtful that anyone would bother to prosecute. Individuals calling an 800 number and expressing their opinions of the services offered are perfectly within their rights, although there are statutes prohibiting profanity over the telephone.

You know, I answered this guy's question in early 1987, and would you believe that sick bastard (Falwell, not my correspondent) is still at it? More recently, he started sending out videotapes to show how evil the gays and lesbians really are. What a psychopathology must be driving such a thoroughly evil mind!

Dear Larry,

I am gay (and into leather), but I am also politically conservative on most issues. I don't believe in the old Democratic Party idea of "tax and spend," and I don't believe in "welfare rights" or a lot of other bullshit ideas that are espoused by organizations like the ACLU. On the other hand, groups like this are the only ones that seem to support our rights as gay citizens. I seem to detect a slightly conservative philosophy in a lot of your writing, so I wonder how you feel about this.

M. H., Atlanta, GA

Dear M. H.,

You have to give a little to get a little. The American Civil Liberties Union supports several causes that I don't necessarily agree with, and a lot more that I don't care one way or the other about. However, they do support our causes, and for that reason I donate to them regularly. I also give to People for the American Way (Norman Lear's group which is fighting the

Falwell ilk.) If by so doing, I am also helping some poor slob get a few bucks out of the county treasury, so be it. God knows, the politicos are taking enough away from me every year to feed their multitudes of pork barrels that I am happy to see a little of what I earn going to support projects that I want to support. And when you mention the Democrats' "tax-and-spend" philosophy, I'm not too sure that Reagan's "spend without taxing" makes any more sense, not when the national debt is going into the trillions.

Similar, I guess, to my response to the question just a couple back, I can't go along with the conservative philosophy when the people espousing it are our sworn enemies. I'm certainly no wild-eyed radical, but no politician gets my vote unless he (she) expresses some sympathy for our problems (first time out), then does something about them once he's in office. Of course, I live in an area where the politicians have been forced to give us some attention. In the states of the Old Confederacy, Bible Belt, etc., I wonder how long our brothers and sisters will have to wait.

Dear Larry,

Before I became personally involved in SM, I guess I shared the opinions that seem to be so commonplace: that everything remotely associated with bondage or such was just plain bad—"sick"—and anyone who thought differently was way out in left field. Now that I've done most of these things myself, and met a lot of other men who do them (and more), I realize how stupid these public attitudes are. Even the Meese report on pornography, with full sanction of the federal government, seems to assume this without even finding it necessary to explain why. Do you think we are ever going to be able to overcome this attitude? The mainstream gay groups seem to be just as rejective as the Moral Majority. *(Letter received in October 1987—ed.)*

J. B., Philadelphia, PA

Dear J. B.,

The entire gay community once suffered from this type of social attitude, and that is gradually changing. (Although, thanks to AIDS, we have slipped back a few steps.) If you read any number of books that were written 150 years ago, you will find that blacks were considered to be universally inferior. Social attitudes are shaped by a great many variables, and we are all victims of this. But to answer your question: Yes, I do think that social attitudes toward SM will eventually change. Whether we will live to see it is another question altogether. The fledgling organizations that are working for us are not making much headway within the community as a whole, but their efforts are eventually going to produce results. As per my favorite maxim: The nice thing about prejudice is that it requires no logical basis in fact.

Dear Larry,

As we gradually see every bathhouse in the United States being closed, I wonder what you—as a liberation activist in addition to your expertise in SM—what do you think about the situation? *(Letter received mid-1987—ed.)*

Lars, Miami, FL

Dear Lars,

As one who worked for years to help establish our right to our own bars, baths, and other businesses, it upsets me greatly to see the authorities closing down the bathhouses. On the other hand, it upsets me even more to think of the number of guys who have literally fucked themselves to death on these premises. I don't buy the argument that "they'll just go somewhere else." There isn't anyplace else where a guy can lie on his belly and get fucked by a dozen men a night. I think the bathhouses should close until this crisis is over, but they should close because we all have sense enough not to patronize them.

I note that more recently, we have seen a resurgence of bath-houses in most major cities, but they are opening with the claim of far-more-responsible management than before. I don't know how realistic this is, but supposedly they now serve as centers for the distribution of health information, and have strict rules of conduct. I hope so.

Dear Larry,

I'm a gay man, holding enlisted rank in one of the U.S. armed services. I have been trying to follow the Perry Watkins case because his circumstances are somewhat similar to mine—except that he apparently admitted to being gay when he originally enlisted, whereas I did not. However, the local newspapers in my area are not giving very complete coverage. I know his case went to the Supreme Court, but I don't know what happened. I live on a military reservation, so I'm afraid to have much gay material sent to me. A friend does get *Drummer*, however, and if you answer this, I'll see it. My main question is simple. If he succeeds in his appeal, will that mean I'm safe from being bounced out of the service? I've got twelve years in, and I'd like to make it twelve.

Name and location withheld

Dear Soldier/Sailor/Marine/or Airman,

I can tell you what happened on the Watkins appeal, but I can't advise you regarding your own status. The fact that Watkins admitted his sexual orientation when he enlisted, and you did not, would probably make your case just different enough from his that, whatever eventually happens to him, you can't count on its being the same for you. You'll have to consult a specialist in military law for a definitive answer. As to Watkins: For the benefit of our readers, let me explain that this is a man who has been in the U.S. Army since 1967. When he originally enlisted, he admitted to being homosexual, and apparently has never attempted to conceal this during his years in the service. In 1981, the army promulgated a new set of regulations, which stated that being homosexual—regardless of whether the person was having sexual relations—was sufficient grounds for involuntary discharge. Despite an apparently brilliant, unblemished career record, Watkins got caught up in this. When they tried to discharge him, he sued and lost his case. On appeal (which went to the Ninth Circuit Court, not to the Supreme Court), he won a reversal because the court held that the army regulations violated equal protection. However, I doubt that this is the end of it because the Army is sure to file an appeal and this time it will go to the Supreme Court (if they agree to hear it.) No one knows what the Reaganquist court is apt to do, but in the meantime I'd suggest you play it cool. Lots of gay men (and women) make it through to retirement/pension time, despite the government's hypocrisy and bullshit.

Although they eventually managed to discharge Perry Watkins, and destroy his life, his case is a landmark and will be a stepping-stone for future cases, where people fight this injustice. For a full account of his case and many others, read Randy Shilts' Conduct Unbecoming, *St. Martin's Press.*

Dear Larry,
I am going to Australia on vacation later this year [1988]. Are there any special precautions you can think of that I should take, either from the standpoint of health or otherwise?

R. P., San Francisco, CA

Dear R. P.,
Although I have never been "down under," I have several Aussie friends who assure me that their country is at least as civilized as ours. They may be a few years behind us when it comes to such social innovations as crime rate, drug addiction, and juvenile gangs, but otherwise they are quite like us. AIDS has reared its ugly head there, of course, but since Aussie physical attributes are quite similar to ours, your behavior should be about the same as you are currently doing here. Actually, they are less puritanical in their porno laws than we are (for the moment), but that is probably not of great concern to you.

Dear Larry,
I want to take issue with your comment about wanting to see the bathhouses shut down, if not by the law then by us "because we have enough sense not to go there." I have spent years of my life as a gay activist, and being able to go freely into our own bars and baths has been the surest mark of our having gained the freedom of self-determination.

Now you want to surrender this hard-won right voluntarily, and allow the bigots of the Right to impose their restrictions on us all over again. After all, this health crisis isn't going to last forever, and then we are going to have to fight the old battles all over again.

Paul, Seattle, WA

Dear Paul,

Although I stepped out of the limelight of Movement politics a number of years ago—mostly because I got tired of wasting my energies scrapping with other gay men and women—I also have a considerable investment of time, emotion, etc., in the achievement of our civil rights. I feel no less strongly about this today than I did at the height of my Movement activities. However, I can not condone the potential danger a man faces in a bathhouse on the basis of these previous activities and beliefs. When the health crisis is over, I'll be right there demanding that the baths be open again. Right now I see them as a terrible danger to the lives of the very people we are supposed to be "leading." As I stated before, I don't like to see the authorities shutting down any of our businesses; we should be doing it ourselves by refusing to patronize them.

I included this response to the earlier letter, because I know that the Community has been seriously divided on this issue. Maybe I feel as strongly as I do as a result of being forced to watch so many close friends die.

Dear Larry,

You have apparently been to Europe a number of times, so perhaps you can advise me. I am going to London over Christmas, and because of the current health crisis, I want to take some personal items with me, such as dildos, etc. What are the chances of my having an embarrassing incident going through customs? And if they do make me open my bag and find the things, are they apt to take them away from me?

S. D., NYC

Dear S. D.,

Assuming you look like an average tourist, the chances of having to open your bags going into England are remote. Even if they do open them, it is unlikely they will take a dildo away from you, since it is not an illegal item. Do *not*, of course, attempt to carry any controlled substance (dope). If you are concerned about having your private sexual tastes bared before the customs inspectors, I might suggest that England is quite a civilized country, and London has a plethora of adult bookstores that sell all kinds of "marital aids." You can buy them there easily and save the potential embarrassment. Coming back, U.S. Customs agents are more likely to inspect your baggage, although lately they are also too busy to be bothered unless you look like a doper.

Dear Larry,

I am a foreigner who is looking to apply for permanent residence in the States. Now, one of the questions asked on the form is: Are you afflicted with..."sexual deviation"? I won't make any comment on the fact that this "deviation" is paralleled with "psychopathic personality" and "contagious disease," but I am concerned about what I should answer to this question. Should I lie? And, if so, do you think I should have my name removed from the mailing lists of several gay artists in order to erase my "public" evidence of homosexuality? If I tell the truth, do you think it will jeopardize the outcome of my request?

C. D., Houston, TX

Dear C. D.,

Heaven forbid that I should ever advise anyone to lie on an official federal questionnaire! Of course, if you don't lie, you won't get the permanent-resident status you want. As to having your name taken off gay mailing lists, that's pure nonsense. Being on a mailing list is not a crime; hence, there is no way for the government to acquire the names, even if they were interested enough to try—which they aren't.

This question arrived in 1988, and despite my being aware of our government's frequently stupid attitudes, it surprised me. I don't know if the form has been changed, but if it hasn't it sounds like a good job for the GLACLU or People for the American Way. It's incredible what our bureaucrats can get away with!

Dear Larry,

I am going to be in Japan a few months from now, and I'm just wondering if you know the names of any leather bars in the Tokyo or Osaka areas, is there much of a leather scene in Japan? I haven't seen much about it in any publications.

Paul, San Antonio, TX

Dear Paul,

Never having been there, I am not an expert on Japan. However, I put your question to a friend who returned not too long ago *(Jan 1990—ed.),* and he wasn't very encouraging. He found that the Japanese are almost paranoid in their fear of AIDS and, as a result of this, my friend found himself excluded from any homosexual contact, other than hustlers. (And he's HIV negative.) In fact, the women seem almost as fearful as the men re: having sexual contact with foreigners, especially Americans. There has never been much of a leather scene there, anyway, as far as I have been able to ascertain, although a few Japanese Masters have displayed remarkable abilities in imaginative and elaborate bondage. You would probably be best advised to leave your leather gear at home, and concentrate on the normal tourist activities.

And bring plenty of money. Japan is expensive!

Dear Larry,

I live in Tennessee, and I really want to participate in leather *Drummer*-type activities. I have few enough opportunities to do this, and I just can't understand why none of you guys are willing to even send your catalogs to me. If I can't do the real thing, why deprive me of the chance to get some vicarious pleasure from reading about it and looking at pictures of guys who are doing it? We're not all rednecks, you know. As it is, I'll probably have to travel out of state to pick up a copy of *Drummer* to see if you deign to answer me.

B. W., Nashville, TN

Dear B. W.,

Unfortunately, your neighbors have decided to pass local ordinances that restrict your right of communication, and mine. I certainly have no desire to see my fellow leathermen cut off from the mainstream of thought and fantasy. But the censorship ninnies have gained control of the legal mechanisms in your area, and there isn't anything I can do about it. At this point, I don't think even the *Advocate* will ship into your area, will they? I think your protest is better directed to your state legislators. They're the ones who are denying your rights. (I'll run off an extra copy of this and mail it to you, since you may have trouble finding a copy of *Drummer*.)

Tennessee is one of the most dangerous areas for a porno mailing. The authorities have set up entrapment situations that have caused some serious problems for the unwary smut peddler. I mean, when the locals demonstrate outside a 7-Eleven because they have Playboy on their magazine rack, you get an inkling of the mentality one has to deal with. I hate what they're doing, but I don't want to be the test case.

Dear Larry,

I wonder if you would have any theory to explain the great difference between leather interests in Northern Europe (Germany, Holland, England) versus such southern areas as Italy and Spain. Whereas the north has a lot going on, there do not seem to be any bars, clubs, or other activities in the south. I don't think it's racial, since I've met a lot of hot SM men (Americans) who are of Italian or Spanish descent. Is it the Catholic church influence, or the warmer climate, or what?

Rex, San Antonio, TX

Dear Rex,

Your question is one that many of us have pondered, and which is not easy to answer. The lack of current interest in SM is particularly curious in Spain, which was certainly not known for her aversion to torture. Just think of all those fabulous tales about the Inquisition, and the wonderful imaginations it took to construct some of their instruments. Nor was Italy particularly backward in this discipline, starting with Imperial Rome and going through the Middle Ages. And much of these later activities were church inspired. Of course, there is no one more adamant in his (her) morality than a reformed whore, so perhaps this can explain some of the current attitudes. If you count the number of gay bars in southern Europe, the puzzle becomes even more complex. Looking at the *Spartacus Guide*, for instance, you'll find more listings in Madrid than any place else. I'm sure the reason is cultural, but I am really at a loss to explain it in more detail.

In defense of the south, however, I have to say that I have quite a few customers in both Spain and Italy. They are simply more closeted, afraid not only of the heterosexual world, but fearful that their other gay friends will find out their guilty secret. Many guys also manage to hold it in at home, but let their hair (or whatever) down when they travel. One Italian friend of mine made such a spectacle of himself over several weeks at the old Mineshaft in NYC, that they presented him with a loving cup when he went home, inscribed "To the Italian Pig." That has to say something.

Dear Larry,

Back in *Drummer* issue 130, you advised a guy from Texas who was going to Japan not to expect gay encounters here. Of course there is fear of AIDS so much as in the United States, but we have not closed our door to foreigners. There are a few places for Westerners to enjoy. When you are in Tokyo, try a visit to the bar "G.B." in Shinjuku Nichome (phone: 352-8972). This is a bar for both Japanese and Westerners, and the best place to start a night. Most people there can speak English, and many Japanese like Westerners. Unfortunately, we do not have so-called leather bars, but we do welcome guys in leather. So come and enjoy your stay in Tokyo!

Leatherly yours,
Toshi, Tokyo, Japan

Dear Toshi,

As a native, you are certainly much better informed than I, so I thank you and pass along your helpful suggestion. However, I have heard from too many guys who have had problems to simply abandon my previous caveat. By your own admission, Japan is not anywhere near as open as either the United States or Europe when it comes to leather. When it comes to SM activity, your closet door is closed much more firmlythan ours, and an outsider had better have a personal contact, or he is likely to come away without any scars to show for his efforts.

My earlier informant was back just recently, this time living in the country for several months. He says that for Westerners, not much has changed. And this guy speaks the language, has many Japanese friends, etc. I'm sure that a native is going to have a different perspective, as this correspondent had. For Americans, I still say, "Don't expect too much by way of leather/SM activity." Whatever there is will be hard to find. Japan has many other positive things to offer. Why not enjoy them, and play your erotic games in more fertile territory?

Dear Larry,

I am a serviceman, just returned from the Persian Gulf. During the course of my time there, I received an award for valor, and was in every way an exemplary soldier/sailor /marine/airman. (I won't say which, because it might serve to identify me.) I am gay, of course, and a loyal reader of your materials, as well as *Drummer,* etc. My question regards what you think about my coming out. I'm not interested in any real long-term service career, but I do want the various benefits that I have earned. And I'd like to enjoy them without any big hassle. On the other hand, I have done my duty as a man, and feel I have proved myself as such. I'd love to rub some of those pompous noses in it, by openly admitting that I'm gay. My question(s): Do you think I should do it? If I "out" myself, will I lose my benefits? Could I get into any serious legal problems, like being imprisoned for lying on my application form? (I didn't admit I was gay when I enlisted.)

Serviceman, East Coast

Dear Serviceman,

I know how you feel, and I can certainly respect your desire to rub some noses in the crud of their own hypocrisy. If you really want to do it, I'd suggest that you drop by the nearest office of the ACLU, and see if they'll let you talk to one of their lawyers. Although there isn't much chance of the government's tossing you into the brig anymore, they might give you trouble getting an honorable discharge, and this would directly effect your eligibility for benefits. If you wait until you're out of the service, you'll preserve the benefit rights, but you will also have lost the impact of a serviceman seeking his rights as a gay man. Before I stuck my neck out, I'd definitely talk to a lawyer, and preferably a civil-rights lawyer, who will know what he's (she's) doing in advising you. If you want to take a public stand, more power to you. Just make sure you know what you're getting into before you commit yourself.

Although I admire a man (or woman) who has the guts to stand up to the establishment in any of these myriad situations (military and otherwise), I don't like to encourage anyone to get himself into more difficulties then he is ready to handle. Some people love to fight the good fight just for the thrill of the contest. Others get talked into taking a stand that they later live to regret. I don't want to be in the position of having encouraged someone to make a serious—or possibly destructive—mistake.

CHAPTER 10

Organizations, Publications, Businesses, and the Things They Supply

I have often been asked to provide information to assist a man in finding the help he needs from a support group, or more basically how to find the type of literature that keeps his libido from withering from lack of stimulation. In this age of instant communication, it is often feast or famine; but if you don't know where to look you may miss out on the most wonderful reading/viewing materials that are practically under your nose—or at least under some protruding part of your body. Where to find your leathers or your toys can also be a problem, and I've tried to help with this, too.

This first letter dates from 1983; but despite my uncertainty at the time, this group is still with us, a good decade later—going strong:

Dear Larry,

In reading your remarks in *The Leatherman's Handbook* regarding the *Chicago Hellfire Club*, I wonder at your absence of comment on San Francisco's *The 15 Association*. My Master and I are both involved in this club's activities, and we (all the members) try to be for San Francisco what *Hellfire* is for Chicago. Although we don't claim as many associate members around the country and the world as they, we do have associate members in about a half dozen states and several foreign countries.

Michael, San Francisco

Dear Michael,

Afterthought, in all things, is easier than preplanning. When I wrote the particular chapter to which you refer, I was more concerned with illustrating a point than in giving any specific group a pat on the back. I would have mentioned The 15 Association, except at that point I wasn't sure if they were still in existence. The last letter I had sent to their P. O. Box address came back as undeliverable, and no one of my acquaintance seemed to know what had become of the group. Naturally, as soon as the manuscript was typeset and edited, I began to get all kinds of information about The 15. If there should be a *LM's HB III*, I'll certainly remember you—that is, if we all make it through the 80s.

Well, we all made it through into the 90s, and both organizations are still going strong—each a center of male-to-male SM activities in their respective areas (and each with many more resident and associate members than when I answered this letter). Just for the record, the mailing addresses for each is listed below. If you can convince them that you're man enough (and legitimate) you may get invited to participate:

Chicago Hellfire Club, P. O. Box 5426, Chicago IL 60680
The 15 Association, P. O. Box 421302, San Francisco CA 94142

Dear Larry,

Although I used to run into you fairly often, back in the old days of HELP, Inc. in Los Angeles. I had not seen you until I attended the Gay Press Association meeting in North Hollywood last May. At that time, the organization was again debating whether to add "Lesbian" to its name. I was curious that you made no statement on this, and did not even attend the meeting where the vote was taken. Knowing how outspoken you could be in expressing your sexist values, I just wondered why.

A Lesbian Admirer, L.A.

Dear Lesbian,

Like the advent of 9-digit ZIP codes and talking cash registers in supermarkets, we are continuously faced with societal changes that we accept because we can't do anything about them. I didn't attend the discussion on the name change because I've long since given up trying to fight the half-men/half-women rule that the Movement people have imposed on themselves for all committees, boards, etc. If there isn't enough mutual trust to make it possible for a man to represent a woman, or vice versa, then this is probably the only way to handle it. Of course, I remember you from the HELP, Inc. days and I'll bet you still haven't learned to cook. Sexist indeed!

Despite my rather flip reply to this woman, who was always (and still is) a good friend, I am quite serious in my dislike of this balancing act we used to be called upon to observe, trying to make it half-and-half, men-to-women. I have no objection to being represented by a woman, as long as she is going to do the job. The big problem that arises for an organization locked into this 50-50 rule is that they may have a superfluity of qualified people of one gender, but few of the other. Of course, AIDS has changed a lot of this, having killed off so many of our qualified men and leaving their organizational positions to be filled by women. And some of these are pretty tough cookies who have accomplished what they were supposed to do without wasting time on bullshit names and titles.

Dear Larry,

I heard most bars in San Francisco were closed, that the leather scene is dead! I don't mean to be vicious, but New York is again Number One in leather. All those pictures of leather contests and stories of California are always in *Drummer.* Why not cover a story of what just happened in NYC, the big leather contest at Alex's in Wonderland and the others—twenty-three in all, with over 2,000 people in attendance? I do hope *Drummer* can up-beat a story from NYC, or are you afraid?

Shining in Leather, Brooklyn

Dear Shining,

I know that *Drummer* has a photo coverage in the works that will be "Mr. Leather 1984 New York City." As of this writing, it is scheduled for Issue 80. As the *Drummer* editors have indicated before (and as I've reported in this column), *Drummer* is always looking for copy worldwide, and is open to submissions from reporters and photogs on the East Coast and elsewhere. Issue 79 has a big spread on the Mr. Europe leather contest, etc. As for the SF leather bars closing, this is news to me. They were certainly packed when I was there a couple of weeks ago. I might add that you personally should have no complaint, since I have published more letters from you than from any other individual. You may submit them under different names, but I recognize the scrawl.

Fortunately, sectionalism does not seem to be a big part of the leather/SM scene. In fact, there is a certain universal feel in places where leatherguys gather, whether in this country or in Europe. Except for jingoists such as this guy, I have found very little of the regional rivalries that are so common in other gay situations, where guys from West Hollywood speak disparagingly about "the queens from Silverlake." What nonsense!

In the midst of putting this book together, I was asked to attend the Leather/SM Fest in NYC, to commemorate the twenty-fifth anniversary of the Stonewall Uprising. As part of this, I sat on a panel discussing the past and future of SM, where I was appalled to hear one of our lesbian leaders decry the sectionalism between East and West Coast organizations. I didn't agree with her, but I wasn't interested in getting into a shouting match. One gentleman in the audience made a rather telling comment about "inflated egos" being at the source of the problem, but I think this went over her head.

(The whole scene served to remind me of why I had gotten out of active involvement in Movement activities.)

Dear Larry,

I'm a long-time reader of *Drummer* and your books, and just about anything else that's halfway literate in the leather/SM genre. The trouble is, there isn't enough published that is really novel length by someone who understands the scene like you guys do. It seems to me that a few years back (maybe mid-70s) there was a lot of good stuff being put out by Olympia Press in New York, and whatever that outfit was in San Diego that used to publish stories by you and Durk Vanden, and a few others. What's happened to all of them? I thought things had loosened up to a point where they could publish almost anything they wanted to. After all, the leather scene is certainly a lot more visible than ever before. Isn't the reading audience here, and ready made for them?

Chuck, Indianapolis, IN

Dear Chuck,

I'm with you! But the story I get from the guys with the money and distribution outlets is that the increase in publishing costs has grown even more rapidly than the potential audience. I've seen a number of promising talents appear on the scene in the last few years, and I'd really enjoy reading them in longer formats. It's too bad no one struck while the iron was really hot. Now, the likes of Gloria What's-her-name and others who think some man might want to rape them (though God only knows why), are trying to get local governments to pass laws to cut back what's already available. I'm afraid we're heading into a state where bible tracts will be all that's left. Of course, some'a them guys were pretty kinky!

That was answered in mid–1985, just before several new gay publishers came into being. Today, of course, a number of major publishers have discovered the gay market and are attempting to exploit it. However, in their classic pseudo-intellectualism, some of these are almost as provincial in their attitudes toward sexually explicit writing as the censorship advocates of fifteen years ago. There are a number of us who are simply too vulgar for our contemporary gay literati. However, even our more liberal publishers feel

some constraints. I was recently told that my novel The Long
Leather Cord *could not be republished in its original form, because
it contained incest. Thus my most explicit novel of a daddy getting
it on with his sons is not going to see print without some editorial
deletions.*

Dear Larry,

  **I used to buy quite a bit of stuff by mail order, but I
am now in a (living) situation where it is awkward to have
these promotional materials coming in to me. I've tried
everything to get my name off the various mailing lists.
I've written letters to a couple of places, and they've stopped
sending things. But I still get mailings from places I've
never bought from. Lately I've been scratching off my name
and address and sending this shit back marked "refused,"
but it still keeps arriving. Could you suggest some way I can
stop this? I don't want to go to the post office and ask
them to "protect me," but I don't know what else to do.**
                                      KC, Albuquerque, NM

Dear KC,

  None of us in mail order want to waste our time or postage
on people who are not interested in our materials. If a supplier
knows someone wants off his list, he will generally take him off
right away. Unfortunately, some places are not very efficient.
However, the worst thing you can do is to obliterate your name
and send the stuff back. How are they supposed to know who
is asking to have his name taken off the list? It sounds to me as
if you have gotten onto a list—probably from a larger outfit—
which has been whored around until everybody's got it. The only
way you're going to get off of it is to send back each address label
with a demand to be removed from the list. Eventually, you'll
be scratched off. As for the post office "protecting you," forget
it. All they can do is send a letter to the company that sent you
their flyers, after you've received them and complained.

  *One of the most difficult problems for someone dealing mail
order with erotic materials is keeping his mailing list current, free
of guys who don't want to be on it, but up to date for those who do.*

Computers have greatly eased the problem, but you still have to deal with former customers who suddenly find Jesus and decide that writing "Return this filth to sender" on the outside of the mailer, and dropping it back into the mails is going to cleanse their souls. Worst are idiots like this guy, who obliterate their names and addresses, then return the mailing piece expecting to have their names removed from the list—later responding in fury when they aren't.

Dear Larry,

I am very interested in original art, particularly from guys like Tom of Finland, Sean, and the Hun. I've been able to pick up originals from time to time, and over the years I've built up a pretty good collection. I think I'm also making a good investment, but several of my friends tell me I'm crazy, that I'll never get my money out of the pictures I already own. What are your feelings about this? I know you handle a lot of original art in your own publishing, and I assume you keep a good part of it. Do you feel you are investing in this?

Jan, Philadelphia, PA

Dear Jan,

Any investment in art is a risky proposition; and if you're doing it strictly for the money, I'd recommend municipal bonds or mutual funds. But you are obviously collecting these items because you enjoy owning them—the same reason most of us collect the things we do. Whether it's art or postage stamps or antiques, most of us buy at retail and when we try to sell we find we're selling at wholesale. That's not the way to make a profit. Still, if you think about it logically, the money you put into art would probably go for something far less tangible if you didn't buy the drawing—like a few drinks, or a new suit, or something else that isn't going to be around a few years hence. So, whatever you can realize from the art some time down the road is going to be more than you'd get for a pile of old clothes. And, you've had the pleasure of owning it all that time. I hang on to as much original art as I can in my business, but mostly because

I simply enjoy owning it. If it helps bail me out of the old folks' home someday, so much the better.

SIR!
Do you know where I can find brown-hankie videos? I know you're into both selling and commenting on gay tapes, so I thought you might know.

Paul, Northern, California

Dear Paul,

By "brown hankie" I assume you mean scat. I think it is safe to say that there are no commercially available tapes that depict this, although there undoubtedly are some available in private editions. Since this activity is somewhat removed from my areas of interest, I haven't sought them out, and don't know who might have them. There is a scene in one of the Christopher Rage tapes where they do a number with chocolate drops. It think it was in the one he called *Toilets*.

Since my answer to this letter, I have seen some absolutely outrageous tapes from Christopher Rage, but he was an AIDS casualty a couple of years ago, and I don't know if his successors have kept these tapes in their catalog. (Live Video, Inc., New York City.)

Dear Larry,
I have been reading *Drummer* for eight years. I am black and want to get more into leather, besides just using *Drummer* fiction as the best JO material I have read. How do I get involved? Also, are there any precautions I should take when answering an ad in *Drummer*? Also, why aren't there more blacks and other Third World gays in *Drummer* fiction?

Robert

Dear Robert,

Unfortunately, when the editors forwarded your letter to me, they did not send the envelope; and since you did not indicate a return address on the letter, I don't know where you live. This makes it more difficult to answer your first question.

If you live in a city with any sizable gay/leather community, it is mostly a question of going wherever they hang out and socializing. If there are clubs in your area, they will usually have runs, beer busts in local pubs, or open meetings when they install new officers, etc. Attending these can put you in touch with active leather guys. As to precautions, you should make sure you are submitting—I assume that as a novice you intend to start from the bottom—to a man who is neither drunk nor gone on drugs, and who expresses enough sense of responsibility that he assures you of his intention to play it safely. And safely applies both to health ("safe sex") practices and sane SM behavior. You can never be 100 percent sure, but if you make it clear that these comprise your limits, most Tops will respect your wishes.

Your last question is very interesting, because I've never thought of American blacks as Third World people. In this sense you are asking two questions. I have read (and written) several stories concerning Third World characters: Vietnamese, Central American guerrillas, Arabs, etc. Many of these have been printed in *Drummer* or *Macho*. As to blacks, per se, I have to admit that I don't recall a story where one of the main characters was black, but there have been several with blacks as secondary protagonists (as in my recently serialized *Court Martial*). Maybe we should look into this.

In fact, I think we have all looked into this in the intervening years, since there seems to be a fair amount of literature with black characters available these days—some by black writers, too. I have recently reissued my Court Martial *story, by the way. It's in the* Dream Master *collection (LT Publications, ISBN 1-81684-00-8, $11.95.)*

In looking back on this answer, I realize that I did not address the underlying question: prejudice. Robert was probably afraid of being rejected because of his race. For those of us who live in areas like Los Angeles, where we see blacks (and any other race) frequenting the bars and club meetings without anyone even thinking about it, it is hard to realize how different things can be in other areas of the country. Whereas my advice would have been valid in such an area as ours, it would not have been in a redneck commu-

nity. But, in such an area, we aren't likely to find the gay bars and clubs operating with the same degree of openness. When "they" oppress one group, they usually don't stop until they've victimized us all. So, if Robert were to follow my advice, he might have had to travel outside his area of residence. But a lot of our guys have done that, haven't they?

Dear Larry,

I am writing this before the Gay Pride Weekend (1987), when all the parades will take place. I have seen a number of articles in both local and national publications that indicate there will be a lot of freaky people taking part in the demonstrations and parades. I really cringe when I read these accounts and see the accompanying photos of what is going to appear in public to represent our "community." I understand who they are and where they're coming from, but I just can't believe that the average Joe American is going to be swayed to our viewpoint by having these negative stereotypes flouncing across his TV screen. What do you think?

A. D., Los Angeles, CA

Dear A. D.,

I don't feel that the Gay Pride demonstrations do much, one way or the other, to mold public opinion. It is the action behind the scenes, going on all year long, that results in changes of law or social acceptance. The celebrations are really more for us than for others because we're the only ones who pay much attention to them. It gives the men and women who are actively involved in services on behalf of the Community, a moment in the limelight. Let them enjoy it, and be thankful for their efforts in activities you never see. I take my hat off to anyone who can sit through those interminable meetings that occasionally result in some positive gain. If they want to kick up their heels (or their skirts) on Gay Pride Day, more power to them.

More recently, of course, our enemies of the far right—those with the herniated cerebrums—have used videotapes of the more outrageous characters in the parades to show middle America how dangerous we are. "Lions and tigers and queers, oh, my!"

Dear Larry,

I'm a video collector, but I'm much more interested in films like *Caligula* and *Sebastian* than in the usual run of porn flicks. I think it's much more exciting to have the sex, overt or implied, pop up between the other activities in a real story. The most interesting situations seem to occur in historical settings, and I don't know very much about these periods. How accurate do you think they are, specifically the two I've already mentioned?

Pete, Albuquerque, NM

Dear Pete,

As an amateur historian, my word should not be taken as gospel, but I think *Caligula* was based in large part on fact. They took a great many liberties in filming it, but most of the major occurrences are inscribed in the historical record—his turning the palace into a brothel with senators' wives as the whores, sending the army to whip the sea in his war with Neptune, making his horse a senator, the incest with his sisters, etc. Caligula was mad as a hatter, and he had absolute power. *Sebastian*, on the other hand, is almost pure fantasy. This stupid bastard almost got himself executed once, was nursed back to health by a widow woman, than had no better sense than to present himself to the Emperor Diocletian all over again, and this time they got him. It's a gorgeous film, nonetheless.

So gorgeous, in fact, one might almost forgive Derek Jarman for producing Edward II.

Dear Larry,

Of the names we see as bylines on leather/SM stories—not so much in *Drummer*, but on porn novels, etc.—what percentage are really SM guys, as opposed to old queens just out to make a fast buck? And, is there a kind of "in group," where you guys sort of all know each other?

Bob, Astoria, NY

Dear Bob,

Whereas I know many of the guys who write for *Drummer*,

Mr. SM (Sweden), etc., I don't know who most of the people are who write the novels, or who write for some other publications. I would suspect that many of the "novelists" are not leathermen. In fact, if you read some of these stories, you know damned well the guy has never bound or been bound. The magazine writers, however, are at least gay men in 99 percent of the cases. The SM may be pure fantasy, but if the stories are produced by a pair of aching balls, it can often ring true, regardless. I think the readership of our periodicals has become sophisticated enough in recent years that the publishers can no longer get away with the old Mafia-style operation, where some nongay hood would be placed in charge to turn out some "crap for the fag market." As for an organization of writers, no. There is no formal organization other than *The Gay and Lesbian Press Association,* which is a mixture of everyone and has a strong orientation toward Movement activities.

Again, times have changed to some degree. Most of us who have been around for any length of time know each other, or at the very least recognize each other's name. There have also been some literary groups formed in the last five or six years, and most of them put out periodic reports or newsletters. The best known of these is Lambda Rising, *which publishes a quarterly magazine and also conducts the annual awards for gay and Lesbian writers. (Lambda Book Report, 1625 Connecticut Avenue., N.W., Washington, DC 20009.)*

Dear Larry,

For some time I have been receiving mailings from an outfit in New Jersey, which I will not mention by name, because I don't want to give them any publicity. (Although I am enclosing their latest flyer for your information.) You will note that I have highlighted a couple of sections on their book ads, where they claim that their books are more psychologically insightful than yours, and also compare themselves favorably to *Drummer* and others. I was curious, so I ordered a couple of items, which I found dull and poorly conceived. I just wondered if you were aware of these sleazy advertising practices, and what your reaction is.

Phil, NYC

Dear Phil,

Yes, I've been aware of this advertising for quite a while, but took it as a compliment that they felt the need to compare themselves to me. Someone sent me one of their publications some time ago; and, having read it, I did not feel greatly threatened. It reminds me of the old adage: It is better to be stolen from than to need to steal. Of course, I was just sufficiently offended that I have declined to handle their products on my own mail-order list.

I guess one should not speak ill of the dead. The source of this correspondent's ire bit the dust a couple of years ago, and most of his stuff has faded away without much fanfare.

Dear Larry,

I'm just looking for your opinion. I'm a sports car-enthusiast, but I've got no interest at all in motorcycles. I've recently been subjected to several derisive comments from bikers when I pulled up to the local leather bar in my hot little buggy. What makes these clowns think they're more butch than I am, just because they ride bikes? I wear leather because I've earned the right to wear it. Some of these big biker types don't know what it means. How do you feel about it?

Phil, Houston, TX

Dear Phil,

Tell 'em to fuck off! I can appreciate the thrill of having something interesting between your legs, but—like clothes—the machine does not make the man.

In more recent times, the mystique of the motorcycle has become less of a potent fetish within the leather/SM community, I think for several reasons. First, a lot of motorcycle guys are not into SM sex, although they may wear leather. Now that the cycle club runs are not the only places to get together for some good B&D action, their presumed leather/SM leadership status has suffered. There is also the arrogant attitude as decried by my correspondent, which many nonbikers found offensive. By rejecting others, the bikers have abdicated the position they once held, or at least tarnished the image.

*Of course, some bikers are still into it and make very hot part-
ners, as appears to be the case with our next correspondent.*

Dear Larry,
   As a young (twenty-seven) bike rider, I have really gotten
into leather clothing. I think I look good in it, and I
certainly enjoy the feel against my skin. I love to go out
naked, except for my leathers. Just knowing that there is
nothing between me and all that black leather is a real turn-
on. Over the past couple of years, I have seen several
beautifully designed and fitted outfits, but I've never been
able to find similar things in any of the stores I've gone
to, and no one seems to know how to make them. The
things I like most are maybe not made in the United States.
One of the most distinctive things about them is a little
band of red leather along the seams of the pants and jackets. Do you know where I might go, or write, to get a
catalog of these really hot leathers? I'm pretty standard
size, so if they come ready made I should be able to buy them
"off the rack."

                                              Randy, Detroit, MI

Dear Randy,
   Although there are plenty of leather shops in this country
which can make about anything you want, I think the items
you have seen are probably European. The red seams are a sort
of trademark. Try Hein Gericke, Expressverstand, Spedition-
sstrasse 1-3. D-4000 Dusseldorf 1, Germany. They are a large
mail-order outfit, and offer all kinds of leather clothing. Their
catalog is about the size of a small telephone book, so they'll
undoubtedly want a few bucks to send it. One caution: A lot of
the better leather clothing made in Europe is lined, often with
silk or nylon. This might not satisfy your desire to be "naked in
leather."
   *I received a flood of protests on this answer, mostly from Amer-
ican leathermakers. But, as I noted above, whereas our locals can
make anything you want, the red stripes are typically European. At
this stage, my first domestic choice would be Mr. S Leathers, 310*

Seventh Street, San Francisco CA 94103. *The original Mr. S has retired, and the business is now affiliated with Fetters of London. There's also The Leatherman, 111 Christopher Street, NYC, which has a huge stock of leather clothing. There are, of course, many others. Again, I'd refer you to* The Gayellow Pages *for a relatively complete listing.*

Dear Larry,

I have been employed as a technical writer for most of my working life, and I enjoy what I am doing. But for a long time I have had a yen to do some SM stories. I don't know much about the market, whether I'd make much money at it, assuming my things were good enough to get published. I really don't care so much about that, since my greatest pleasure would just come from seeing my stuff in print. My biggest concern is whether the reelection of a conservative administration—with its power to appoint judges and thereby twist a number of laws—is going to put me in legal jeopardy if any of my things get published. Can you advise me on this, at least from the basis of your own experience, not as a lawyer—which I know you are not?

Jerome, Tampa, FL

Dear Jerome,

The powers that be have not succeeded in busting the written word since the infamous James Joyce persecutions several decades back—which isn't to say they might not try again, and might not pull it off. However, the danger to a writer seems to me to be minimal. It's the guy who publishes the material—especially if he illustrates the publication with photos—who is going to be in greatest danger. Even so, there is some very gross material up-front that no one does anything about. I don't see that a guy who simply writes an erotic story should have much to worry about. But I can tell you, you won't get rich.

Dear Larry,

Several weeks ago, I met a fellow in a bar and had a long discussion with him about SM devices, particularly antique things. He said that they used to have a machine in the Old South to whip disobedient slaves. I asked him what it looked like, and how it worked, but he said he had never actually seen one. I'm just curious, and wonder if you know anything about them.

M. H., Minneapolis, MN

Dear M. H.,

Although I have never actually seen one of the originals, I noted a reference to them in (Rev.) William M. Cooper's classic *History of the Rod* (which has, incidentally, been reprinted and is currently available through Barnes & Noble.) Several years ago, a friend of mine showed me a contrivance he had made, and which he said was modeled on some kind of antebellum drawing he had seen. It consisted of a 3½ to 4 foot upright, to which he had attached several leather straps, about the heft of a wide workman's belt, and ranging in length from about 18" to 30". He had installed an electric motor in the base, that spun the dowel and made the straps fly out to strike whatever was within reach. He had also added a rheostat to regulate the current, and hence the speed. He then found it necessary to weight the base, to keep the whole contrivance in place, and to make it deep enough to contain a substantial length of dowel. In the Old South, of course, they would have had to use some kind of foot pedal to turn the thing, probably utilizing the same principle as a spinning wheel.

But what a shame to rely on mechanical devices, when the real thrill of whipping a recalcitrant slave should come from the heft of the whip in the Master's hand—his sense of fulfillment as he hears the impact and feels the leather cling to naked flesh, before drawing back his arm for another blow. The machine, like the wearing of lined leather clothing, deprives you of the true sensation.

Dear Larry,

If anyone would have advice to give on my question you will. Where would I seek information on breaking into the world of nude modeling and videos? Is it a hard field to break into? Are there plenty of would-bes waiting in the wings? I have looks, a good trim body, and a nice-sized piece of meat. A second question. If I want to put together a portfolio to send people, how do I go about it? Home cameras just don't do it, and if I did get some good shots I don't know how to get them developed—surely not at the local drugstore.

Hot Shot, Midwest USA

Dear Hot Shot,

I think you have a somewhat glamorized perception of the porno modeling business. With the few exceptions like Jeff Stryker and Al Parker, who have had the business acumen to put together their own companies, most of the guys you see in photos and videos are not making a living out of it. Many are hustlers who pick up a few bucks by posing or acting. Others are just guys who have regular jobs, usually in situations where their employers don't care about their outside activities. On the other hand, if you want to model/act in order to satisfy some inner craving, and aren't going to be happy until you've done it, I'd send a home photo (Polaroid if need be) to any of the larger video outfits and ask if they'd be interested in you. You'll probably have to get out to the coast on your own, but most of these places are always looking for new faces (and whatever else you have to offer), because the name of the game is to keep up a steady flow of "new discoveries." Just be sure you have a return ticket in your jeans. As to getting film developed, I know it is probably difficult in an uptight community. When I shoot pics, I simply take them to a local commercial lab, and they do anything I want with them. But that's the difference between one area of the country and another.

Interesting changes in the porno industry since I answered this in 1989. Now, we have a few genuine stars who seem to be in demand all over the place. Some even last for a couple of years. But the market is fickle, and even the best fade much more quickly than actors in regular movies or TV shows. Unfortunately, there aren't many parts for aging actors in the porno industry. But the ones who are on top are making much better money these days than even a couple of years ago. The secret (for them) is to hang on to it, and have something to sustain them into a postporn career.

As to the general run of porn-flick actors, most of these are still hustlers, except that the business has become much more sophisticated, with the more successful carrying beepers or cellular phones to keep in touch with their "clients." The name of the game, now, is "escort," although "masseurs" still dominate the personals. A good following as a porn star will generally assure a fairly successful hustling career—if dope or disease doesn't cut it short.

Dear Larry,

Over the last few months I've gotten solicitations from three different organizations, all claiming to be "SM contact" clubs. Two of them had fairly extensive questionnaires, and all three wanted me to send money for membership. I know that responding blindly to this kind of advertising might cost me the bucks—which doesn't amount to very much, and is of minor consequence. But I am concerned that I might be getting into more than I bargained for if I answer them, especially if I fill out the questionnaire.

Pete, Fort Lauderdale, FL

Dear Pete,

I make it a rule never to fill out a questionnaire for anyone, unless I know exactly where it's going, who's going to see it, etc. I don't know what variety of scenes you might be into, but there have been some nasty government stings that start off just the way you describe them. They haven't been after SM people, per se, as far as I know. The main targets seem to be people who can be lured into buying kiddy porn. Just because "they" tell you "they" don't have the manpower to properly prosecute the savings & loan thieves, don't believe for a minute they can't find the agents to hassle "vice crimes." After all, the savings & loan creeps are friends and relatives.

I got so carried away in my rage at the government's handling of the crooks who took so many elderly people for their life savings, I used up my space and didn't get into the secondary source of anger. It was during this same period that the Feds had pulled off one of their most outrageous scams. They had busted some ditzy bimbo who sold nude photos, including those of underage kids. Using her mailing list, plus names they picked up from ads placed under her trade name in various periodicals, they used the mails to solicit the sale of photos depicting nude children. As best I could ascertain, the kids weren't doing anything naughty; they were just naked. In their test case, some poor goon responded after several of these solicitations, and was promptly arrested. To me, it was a classic case of entrapment, in which the government had committed a far more serious crime (solicitation via the mails) than the victim. Years later, the courts agreed and tossed out the guy's lower-court conviction. But the cost to him in cash and emotional distress must have been appalling. I wanted to warn off my correspondent in case they were at it again. And, of course, there are other scams "out there," run by plain, ordinary crooks without the trappings of our federal government. Always remember: knowledge is power. If you give away intimate information about yourself, you may well live to regret the manner in which some unscrupulous people use it.

Dear Sir,

When I was in London a couple of months ago, I bought a copy of your *Leatherman's Handbook,* marked "3d Printing—Complete original text, Le Salon, San Francisco." The book contains fourteen chapters, and no appendices. It ends on page 246. In reading the book, which is excellent and most interesting, I found references to such things as: Appendices A & B, Chapters 15 & 16, lists of suppliers, etc. The binding shows no sign of tampering, so I would like to know if there is some way I can exchange my copy for a complete edition.

A Loyal Reader, Hong Kong

The answer I gave this guy in 1991 is no longer valid, so I will answer it as I would today. I received several such complaints from people who thought they were buying my book in England. There was obviously a rip-off edition, with the last portions missing. In the interim I have reissued the original Leatherman's Handbook *under my own L. T. Publications imprint. You can find it in most gay bookstores in the United States, or you can order it directly from me. Also in most stores is my* Leatherman's Handbook II, *now in its 3d printing from AmCam Inc. (publishers of* Honcho *and* Mandate), *NYC. As of this writing, I have about twenty titles in current print (or reprint), from four different publishers. You can get a listing by sending your name, address, and statement that you are over twenty-one: Larry Townsend, P. O. Box 302, Beverly Hills CA 90213—Fax: (213) 655-7314. How's that for crass commercialism?*

Dear Larry,

I have been one of your loyal readers—fan, whatever— since you first started getting published (thereby making both of us older than either would care to admit, I'm sure.) Be that as it may, I would like to ask why you are willing to ship materials to South Africa, through your mail order business? I'm sure the apartheid-ruled society must be just as repressive for gay men as it is for nonwhites. Don't you feel you are contributing to this repression, in the same manner—although on a smaller scale—as any other company that does business with that crummy country?

Proud Gay Man, NYC

Dear Proud,

In view of your stated long-term loyalty, I shall resist the temptation to label you in any derogatory terms. If you hadn't already displayed such superior taste and judgment, however, I'd say you were guilty of true dumb-thinky. Who the hell do you think is ordering from me in South Africa? De Klerk? Or maybe Botha? It certainly isn't the Johannesburg Public Library. I'm in communication with a small, select group of gay men, who would otherwise be completely out of touch with our community. I am certainly not contributing to the strength or welfare of the South African government. This is also an area of the globe where our gay brothers are in danger of being forced to wear the pink triangle. Should we refuse to communicate with them because their unrepresentative politicians repress them?

Of course, things have changed in South Africa during the last few months. Let's hope that the new black leaders will remember their own oppression and liberate the gay community as well—as they promised to do before the election.

CHAPTER 11

Philosophical Considerations

With the evolution of our SM subculture, some of us have been concerned with defining the basic philosophy that determines and/or justifies our various modes of outlandish behavior. As with any ideas, our most salient thoughts involve deeper levels of consciousness than some guys wish to explore, but for many of us it is necessary to consider who we are, and why we function the way we do. I have probably engaged in the most serious arguments in this arena, but that—after all—is what makes it all worthwhile. Central to much of this argument is the conception/definition of Master and slave. I have therefore included most of these questions in this section.

In my opinion, religion also belongs in the general category of philosophy, so I have lumped it all together under this one heading.

Dear Mr. Townsend,
    With the permission of my Master i am writing for your advice. My Master thinks that i should be totally shaved. we have a good relationship and i have never refused him anything he wanted to do to me, except on this one issue.

i have an extremely hairy body. My Master is not particularly hairy, and he believes that slaves should not be permitted hair on their bodies, which he maintains is the sign of a Master. i do not believe that hair means anything except that is the way i am. He wants to take me to a Master Barber, where i will be totally shaved, even my head. Afterward, my Master wants me to keep my body clean (of hair). i have tried to be a good slave, and want to please my Master. However, i don't agree with him that i need to be shaved. What advice would you give to a slave in my position? i don't want to lose my Master, but i don't want to lose my hair, either.

Hairy, but sincere

Dear Hairy,

You write, claiming to be a slave; yet your mental attitude is not in keeping with that title. A slave obeys his Master, even when he doesn't want to obey. He doesn't whine, he doesn't protest, and he certainly doesn't argue. If you're just an M, playing at being a slave, that's a different story. That is the fundamental choice you have to make.

The more I've read these letters from supposed slaves over the years, the more I've realized that 99 percent of them don't realize what a slave really is. The writings of Kyle Onstott (Mandingo, Drum, *etc.) describe in great detail what it means to be a slave; and, to some extent, this is brought through into the two movies that were made from his titles. Unfortunately, the racial overtones tend to cloud the issue; but if you can imagine the entire cast(s) of characters as being all of one race, it will illustrate the true status of a slave. Naturally, for us—under our Constitution—such a status must be voluntary, but that does not obviate the basic definition. Can you imagine one of Hammond Maxwell's slaves questioning his Master's right to shave any part of his body?*

Dear Larry,

I have been reading your writings on SM since the advent of the original *Leatherman's Handbook,* back in the early 70s. As my own experience has grown, I have come to agree with you on most points, disagree on a few, but I find one area where you never quite say what I keep waiting to hear. This had to do with religion. I think you put down religion in a sometimes-nonconstructive way. If it were not for the built-in guilt feelings engendered by religion, I wonder if there would be as many men seeking to be disciplined or have their endurance and fidelity tested. Without men in these states of mind, I wonder if there would be enough bottoms to go around.

Paul, Southern California

Dear Paul,

Just as I try not to put anyone down for his particular sexual interests, I am also a bit wary of delving into one's religious beliefs. I have to agree with you as to the high incidence of guilt feelings engendered by organized religion—and, most specifically, the self-anointed leaders of various religious sects. It is the pressure exerted by these groups that force society in general to accept the standards of behavior that create guilt feelings in the guy who is unable to abide by them. When all is said and done, your true religion is not the ritualized formulae espoused by the priest/minister/rabbi/ayatollah of "your" church. It is the belief that you hold within your own mind. Even if you never express this openly, the difference may well be the basis for your feelings of guilt. So, do we thank the fundamentalists for giving us all those hot little bottoms? I suppose we should, much as we can, thank Anita Bryant for bringing our community together a few years ago.

Although I have always tried to avoid any direct criticism of specific religious beliefs, I have to confess that I am personally so turned-off by organized religion that it is difficult for me to be objective about it. I find most of the Judeo-Christian dogma to be totally illogical, to the point of absurdity. It is all but impossible for me to understand how otherwise intelligent people can accept this material without question, and in so many cases without exercising their own intellectual powers in trying to interpret the supposed truths being presented to them. Reading the Bible and memorizing its passages is a far cry from an honest attempt to analyze the stated facts and to reconcile them with ones' own real-ity. The pompous air of superior godliness assumed by so many of our religious "leaders"—especially the TV demigods—is little more than a front to convince the unwary of their presumed holiness, more often than not in an effort to shake loose some big bucks—or, even more dangerous, to acquire power. In this, several have been success-ful beyond their wildest dreams! If you have some sincere religious beliefs, good for you. Hold them and cherish them; share them, if you wish, but don't try to convince those who disagree with you that yours is the only path to salvation. If such there is, it must have many access routes, judging by the number of people who are honestly convinced that their form of belief/behavior is the right one.

Dear Sir,

Let me assure you from the outset that this letter is writ-ten out of curiosity. I am not judging or finding fault. However, I do not understand why you are so rigid in your definition of "slave" vs. "M" or "bottom." I am reacting particularly to your comments on the letter from the slave who didn't want his Master to shave him. You didn't ask if the guy might have had a job where he couldn't appear completely shaved, or whether this shaving might have violated some basic set of limits. Likewise, to carry this line of logic to its extreme, would you also say that a slave should submit if his Master comes home drunk with a hammer and bag of nails and says he wants to do a little piercing? I think that this attitude on your part may tend to keep a lot of people from getting into the scene, for fear of having to give up all control, including the right to safe-guard his own well-being. Comment please?

Curious, Anaheim, CA

Dear Curious,

Your letter was quite long, so I hope I've paraphrased it to include the most important points. I think you have failed to grasp the true sense of a Master-slave relationship. (But don't feel bad; you have lots of company.) When a guy responds to a "Master seeks slave" ad, he really is not responding as a slave, but rather as a bottom who may or may not become the slave of this Master. Until he has convinced himself that this man is qualified to be his Master, he has no business offering his total, unqualified submission. Likewise, a Master assumes the responsibility for his slave's welfare. Since the contract is completely voluntary on each side, it can be broken at any time by either partner. But if the slave demands his freedom, it will generally result from an overall deterioration of the relationship rather than fear for his well-being. A man who is qualified to be a Master would not come home drunk and commit mayhem on his slave. A true Master-slave relationship involves a very deep, long-lasting affection on both parts. But it also demands complete submission on the part of the slave. If the Master shaves him, and he loses his job as a result, the loss is actually the Master's. There are, of course, very few of these relationships that ever develop into the complete "ideal" because there are not very many men who are fully qualified on either side, to say nothing of the difficulty in finding a proper matchup. For most of us, the conception of full and complete submission is as elusive as the conception of infinity. You can accept the idea intellectually, but you can't visualize it. And if you're not cut out to be a slave, it really doesn't matter.

Oh, Hammond Maxwell, where are you when we need you? It's so difficult for a person brought up in any of our Western societies, with our strong teachings about liberty and individual freedom, even to conceive of what it is to be a slave. And this very condition contributes mightily to the fact that so very few men ever achieve the mind-set to be one of these truly wonderful creatures. In actuality, a true slave is just as rare as a fully qualified Master. This means that most of our discussions on SM involve Tops and bottoms, not real Masters and slaves. For this reason, most of our basic perceptions have to do with this majority group. And there's nothing wrong with this, as long as a guy doesn't try to convince himself that he's something he is not, and probably can never be.

Dear Larry,
   Your comments in the "Leather Notebook" are always

interesting and provocative. However, one of your recent replies to an inquiry puzzles me. In your advice to "Curious" (*Drummer* # 79), you insist (rightly) that the slave offers his "total, unqualified submission" to the Master. You also write that since the "contract" between the Master and slave is purely voluntary on both sides, it can be broken at any time by either partner. These two viewpoints seem inconsistent.

Puzzled, Boca Raton, FL

Dear Puzzled,

Although these concepts do appear inconsistent, you must remember that we function within a society with very specific laws against involuntary servitude. Therefore, the slave must at all times be free to break the contract and demand his freedom. However, this is his ultimate recourse; and, in doing so, he is relinquishing all the positive aspects of a relationship that he presumably cherishes. In fact, the greatest threat the Master can make is just this sort of termination. It is the reverse of this—i.e., the slave's threat to terminate—that should remain unspoken, although a sensitive Master will recognize it. In other words, the slave has the choice of accepting whatever is demanded by his Master, or breaking it off. All or nothing. If a guy is truly (emotionally) a slave, his Master will have to be really gross before he (the slave) will take this extreme step. Remember that the true Master/slave relationship is a rare occurrence. To survive for any length of time, there has to be a bond of love and understanding between the two guys involved. It's not a contest to see how much shit a slave will take before he splits.

Dear Larry,

Perhaps you can settle something for me. My Master, who is quite a bit older than me (I'm just a young punk) got pissed off at me the other day, because I stopped for a few beers on the way home from work and didn't let Him know where I was. For punishment, He went out and picked up a street-dog slave. He ordered us both to strip and kneel at his feet, while He fondled His big cock. Then He ordered the dog-slave to suck on it while I watched. Then He had the slave onto his knees and fucked him. I was nearly out of my mind seeing this. Master blew a heavy load up the punk's ass and pulled out. The punk licked his cock clean. Then Master asked me if I'd like some of His cum, too. I couldn't figure what He was up to, but naturally I said "Yes." He then ordered me down behind the dog-slave and made me eat it out of his ass. I almost vomited! Then it went on from there, Master doing everything he could to humiliate me in front of this street punk and giving him all the action that should have been mine. He even ordered the punk to whip my ass. I think I am right in feeling that this was cruel and unfair punishment. I know I was way out of line, but the punishment didn't fit the crime. A good old-fashioned ass whipping would have been more in order. I feel this is the lowest I could ever sink, but I think Master was wrong. Please help me settle this matter, because I don't want it ever to happen again.

Slave, Huntington Park, CA

Dear Slave,

If you were merely claiming to be an M or a bottom, I'd answer you differently. But you claim the status of a slave, and this is a very rare and honorable condition. However, a real slave is just that: the complete and unquestioned property of his Master. So long as you maintain that you are a slave, you have no recourse. Your Master's word is law! The only aspect of the whole scene which I see as questionable has to do with the health risk to which your Master subjected you both, but this is also his decision. I might also suggest that your Master instruct you in the proper use of the pronoun "I" (vs. "i") when he permits you to write a letter.

I have to admit that I was somewhat taken back by this Master's poor judgment in having his slave eat out the ass of a street hustler, in light of the ongoing health crisis. However, in my opinion, he was marginally within his rights to do it. But it wasn't an easy call; and if the slave chose to break off the relationship as a result, I could understand it.

Dear Mr. Townsend,

In your response to "Puzzled," you speak of involuntary servitude and the fact that both Master and slave can ask for termination (freedom) in regard to our societal laws. The true Master/slave relationship, although rare, is based on voluntary servitude, and usually a Master cannot get rid of the slave no matter how hard he tries. But a true Master with a true slave would not envision freedom at all; they both endeavor to perfect their commitment together for life.

I find it ironic that so many pushy bottoms are looking for a "real" Master. By their attendant attitudes, they are begging for a bruising. They deserve whatever happens to them! Hopefully, nothing. They deserve frustration, an empty life and no release or fulfillment. Most of them are all talk, anyway, and are submissive only to what they are into...real pussy slaves. Don't you feel they should be taken up on their challenges to teach them some respect? Afterwards, they can be discarded, being the piles of shit they really are—no real slaves at all.

A true slave is worthy of a Master's love; all else is pig's scum.

                                        Iron Rose, San Francisco, CA

Dear Rose,

In a way I agree with you, in that a guy has no business calling himself a slave if he isn't willing to assume all the elements inherent in the role. However, for the most part, I am called upon to answer questions for the would-be slave; and when I do this, I am ever hopeful that I am addressing my words to a man with some degree of potential. Perhaps I retain a more optimistic attitude than you; at least I hope so.

It was always nice to hear from guys whose conceptions of a slave's proper role were even more rigid then mine. It served as a nice counterbalance to all the bleeding hearts to accused me of excessive cruelty. Bah! Humbug!

Dear Larry,

You keep writing about the right of a Master to use his

slave any way he wants, and conversely the slave's duty to obey. Well, I served one Master for almost twenty years, and now the bastard has thrown me out with little more than the clothes on my back because he's found a young punk to serve him. I think that even as a slave, I have a right to something better than this. I suppose you'll tell me otherwise, but I thought I'd write anyway.

Dispossessed, Cleveland, OH

Dear Dis,

I never said that all Masters were nice guys, and within the Master-slave relationship it is quite acceptable that his behavior be less than kind. However, I have always emphasized the responsibility of the Master to care for his slave, and to see to his well-being. This includes making some provision for him when he may no longer be wanted. If all you say is true (and by necessity I have condensed your letter), you got a raw deal, although this is one of the risks a slave must be prepared to take. Don't let it destroy you. You're no worse off than many women who are divorced in their middle years and must face the necessity of picking up the pieces and starting all over again.

Although fate seems to have dealt cruelly with this guy, we must remember that he did have twenty years as the slave he apparently wished to be. The fact that he was so badly treated in the end might not be a worse fate than a truly masochistic slave would expect— maybe even desire.

Sir:

As a novice to leathersex, I have very little by way of experience to draw upon other then the little I've learned over the years as an observer on the sidelines. My problem is this: I have met a Man whose boy I want/need to become. I have very little knowledge of what it involves aside from my readings of *Drummer*-type fiction. Part of this appeals, part does not. The Man says that the part I have problems with does not belong to the makeup of a personal slave. But I can't see this complete lack of self-esteem that is always written as a slave's mind-set in fiction. I can't fathom why a man would want to be someone who considers himself a piece of garbage for the world to walk on. What is the challenge of ownership in that? He suggested that I read one or two of your publications, but I would appreciate it if you could offer something by way of additional help/guidance.

Would-be-slave, New Jersey

Dear Would,

You are one of a large group who would like to think of themselves as other men's slaves, but who really do not have the mental set to do it. If you were true slave material, you would be willing to submit completely to the man whom you want to love as a Master. If you can't do this, you are not a slave; you are a bottom, an "M." In this status, you retain the elements of self-determination that seem so important to you. Nor is there anything wrong with this, since it is only a very small proportion of Ms who can really be slaves. As long as your Master will accept you as such, you can function in the sexual role as bottom to the mutual satisfaction of both. But if he demands more, you simply will not be able to give it unless you undergo a severe emotional reconditioning. In fiction, this is frequently accomplished by a skillful Master holding his subject in involuntary bondage and "training" him. As the Horatio Alger of male-to-male leathersex I have written about many of these "ideal" relationships—some of which were pure fiction, some based on reality. But your reality has to be just that: *yours*. I can't do more than define the alternatives.

Dear Mr. Townsend, Sir:

i want to tell you, in all due respect, Sir, that i feel you are too hard on us slaves. i have a Master i have been with now for almost four years, and we both are very much settled into our respective roles. But my Master is not much of a businessman (that by his own admission), and he isn't good at handling money. He leaves all of this to me, and just lets me take care of all our financial dealings, where i have done a good job and both of us are very happy with the results. If we had followed your advice, He would have been doing this and we would not be as well off as we are. What answer do you have for this?

slave johnnie, CT

Dear slave,

If you had really studied my materials, as you should have, you would know that I always advise the slave to obey his Master. If your Master wants you to manage the household finances, that is his decision to make. I just hope he's rewarding you with a good thrashing for every buck you bring in. (Get snotty with me, will you?)

It's hard to put across the point, I guess, although I seem to have gotten through to most of my readers. Let me state it in more specific terms: I see a slave as a man who is completely subordinated to his Master, but the form of this subordination must be determined by several factors. The first of these reflects the way the Master wishes the relationship to be structured. Secondly, can the slave accept these conditions? Once there is mutual agreement at the beginning, the relationship can progress from there. It is, naturally, going to evolve into something different from what it was at the starting point. But the Master must continue to set the parameters, and in doing so he has a great deal of latitude. Some Masters enjoy physically subduing their slaves, and in so doing proving their "right" to command. If that's the way they want to do it, that's up to them. Other Masters want a slave who offers no resistance. Still others like a wise guy, who gives them the pleasure of correcting and punishing the transgressions. But in all of these, the roles are defined and understood, and in the end the slave obeys the rules as determined (verbally or otherwise) by the Master.

Dear Sir,

I am an eighteen-year-old-high-school student. I live with my Master, who supports me with the agreement that I serve him as his slave. At first everything was great, but now the public humiliation he forces on me is getting more and more extreme. I NEED YOUR ADVICE! My Master keeps me naked around the house all the time, even when friends come over. During one bondage session he shaved my body, pierced my navel and put a ring in it, fastened so I can't get it out. This is especially embarrassing in gym class, where I can't keep myself covered. My Master forces me to wear a G-string–type swimsuit to the beach. Once I almost got arrested for indecent exposure, but I talked myself out of it since my pubic hair was shaved and that's the main thing they look for. This is just a sample of what my Master required, and if I don't cooperate I usually get punished with long periods of naked bondage. Lately he is threatening to shave my head for backtalk. I can't give you a return address since my Master doesn't allow me any mail, but he does get every issue of *Drummer*. You are the only one to whom I can turn. Please help by answering in your next issue.

Scott

Dear Scott,

Shades of "Slave R"! *(Chapter 2—ed.)* Here we have another young man, getting exactly what most would-be slaves can only dream about, and he's unhappy. Again, this poses the question: Are you really (emotionally) a slave, or merely a bottom who has submitted to a slave's condition because it puts a roof over your head and food in your mouth? You don't mention the type or degree of affection that binds you to your Master; neither do you ever refer to yourself as "slave" (beyond the initial statement), although there are several references to your "Master." This leads me to question exactly how your perceive yourself. If you do think of yourself as a slave, and wish to retain this status, I would say you have no choice but to submit to the will of your Master until such time as it becomes impossible for you, and you dissolve the relationship. If you are a bottom who is functioning as pseudo-slave in exchange for your bread and butter, you should then renegotiate the covenant, so to speak. In the latter situation, if you are unable to reach a mutually satisfactory agreement, you face the choice of either going along as you have been, or seeking another source of support. I know that's rough, but it's the same problem faced by most of us at some point in our lives where we consider the option of keeping a job with which we're not completely happy, or seeking other employment.

It's the hard realities of life, but in this case, the Master had no obligation to support this kid, except under the terms of their understanding/agreement. As usual, my position on this issue brought some angry responses:

Dear Larry,

I am a twenty-one-year-old male, just learning about SM, and would like to be a slave. But, reading about the kid named Scott who was acting as a slave for the guy who supports him, I got really angry. I believe you must first be respected as a human being, whether you are a Master or a slave. It sounds like this kid is really scared and feels trapped with no place to go. I know I'd have felt bad having to go to gym class with a pierced navel. I was told by a good friend, "Don't do anything that doesn't feel right. Go with what your gut instincts tell you." It sounds like this kid doesn't have any choice about what happens to him. I don't know about you, but I don't want my first experiences to be bad, like this. I'd just like to tell Scott, "If you have no say and don't like what's going on, get out of there and live with friends or anyone else."

Don, Minneapolis, MN

Dear Don,

In the broadest sense, you're right, and this is what I told Scott to do. But remember, he didn't say he was a live-in lover; he called himself a slave, and it was apparently on this basis that his Master took him in. That creates an entirely different relationship from the one you apparently visualize and desire. I've ruffled a lot of feathers by holding to this position, but those who understand the meaning of the word "slave" agree with me. Let me give a couple of examples to illustrate my meaning: If I offer to allow a young man to live in my home and agree to support him in exchange for his sexual favors, I have created a situation wherein he has the right to refuse anything he considers to exceed his limits (be these SM or whatever). Of course,

I also have the right to tell him to leave if he refuses to satisfy me. Conversely, he has the option to leave if I make him unhappy. This is clear-cut and understandable to anyone. Now, add the element of a Master-slave situation. In this, the kid is abdicating his right of choice, and placing himself completely under my control. He does this voluntarily and knowingly. I may then call upon him to do whatever I require of him, until such time as either of us decides we are unhappy with the situation. The choice of going on together, or breaking it off, is still within the purview of either partner. My argument in Scott's case was that he called himself a "slave," but refused to accept that status. If his Master was too rough on him, his choice was either to accept it or to leave. If he had no other place to go, that's tough; but it's also life in the big city. His Master was not under any obligation to support him; it was only by mutual consent that they were together in the first place. Read on.

Dear Sir,

My Master allowed me to write You. Like Scott, i am eighteen years old, and a student (junior college), but i am a slave. i live with my Master, who supports me with the agreement that i am his slave. My Master has shaved my crotch, pierced my tits and cockhead. i don't care what anyone in gym class thinks about this. These are the will of my Master, and that is all that matters. We often go to the beach, and my Master always puts a cock-and-ball harness on me that causes me to get a hard-on. i am then ordered to wear a brief bikini, which leaves little to the imagination. (And I'm very well hung.) If my Master ordered me to wear a G-string, i'd do it because He wanted me to. i am also given to the winner of the monthly poker game for a day, with strict limits set by my Master as to what my temporary Master can do to me. i love all of this, and love my Master for allowing me to serve Him and His friends. i hope Scott gets his act together and serves his Master. He must learn to submit to his Master's will.

slave mike, Mt Clemens, MI

Dear slave mike,
    you sound like a man who is worthy of the title. Congratu-
lations!

Dear Larry,
    From your past comments i know that you have strong
feelings about the differences in status between a true slave
and a bottom, even if he is in a permanent relationship. i am,
in my opinion, a true slave. i have lived with my Master
for three years, and he has completely taken over my life. It
is a situation i like very much, and do not want to lose.
However, my Master has allowed me to continue working
full time, and i have been doing this for most of the time we
have been together. i make very good money—more than he
does, in fact. But he takes my paycheck and puts it in his own
bank account, then uses any excess to make investments
which are completely in his name. i don't object to any of
this, except that i also know he has not made any financial
provisions for me in the event he should die, or decide to
kick me out. (He's late forties and i'm twenty years younger.)
Although i don't want to sever the relationship—not by
any stretch of the imagination—i also don't want to end
up a homeless bum on the street, when i've been bringing
home a good paycheck all these years. What would you
suggest?
                                        Name and area withheld

Dear slave,
    It is obvious that you have a legitimate concern. While I
might question whether you are a true slave or a bottom in a
permanent relationship, I cannot in good conscience advise you
simply to "obey your Master." If all you say is true, he appears
to be taking unfair advantage of you. On the other hand, he may
have done something to protect you that you are unaware of—
such as making a will in your favor, buying securities jointly in
both your names, or whatever. In this case, he could be said to
be testing you. If that isn't the case, you simply must order
your priorities and take whatever action is going to be most

appropriate for you. A Master does have the obligation to look after his slave, and on this basis—if everything you believe is true—he is not fulfilling his end of the bargain. You'll have to let him know your feelings, even if you get severely punished for it. But that wouldn't be so bad, would it?

Dear Larry,
I know that the word "sadist" comes from the Marquis de Sade, but where do we get the word "masochist?"
Phil, Houston, TX

Dear Phil,
You obviously have not done your homework, as this is explained at some length in both my *Leatherman's Handbook*s. The term is derived from the nineteenth-century novelist, Leopold von Sacher-Masoch. He wrote such books as *Venus in Furs,* in which he extols the pleasures of submission. Although they deal with heterosexual protagonists in settings much less graphic than we find in contemporary novels, you might still find his works tantalizing. His prose is very elegant, even in translation.

In issue 139, I answered a letter from a man who was incensed over the scat activities that were (are) so common in Europe, particularly in Holland. This elicited some equally outraged responses. I included these letters in the chapter on philosophy for reasons that will become more clear as you read them. (Note that when they address me as "Mr. Townsend,"—as in the second one down—it's usually because I've hit a raw nerve):

Dear Larry,
I just took a trip to England and Holland, and I was shocked to discover the prevalence of SCAT activities in Amsterdam. They actually have parties that attract several hundred guys, and they're all participating, because they won't let them in if they don't. In addition to the idea being complete repulsive, I can't understand how so many men can be attracted to it. Isn't it just about the most dangerous thing a guy can do? Were you aware of what's going on? If you were, why haven't you said anything about it?
Outraged, NYC

Dear Outraged,

I have many friends all over the Continent, and I receive most of the publications from northern Europe; so, yes, I am aware that scat has become amazingly popular during the last few years. It's a phenomenon that I must confess I find difficult to understand, especially since it can be very dangerous. Aside from the health implications, however, I haven't made many comments about it in print, because it happens to be someone else's "bag"; and even if it's just a bag of shit, in my view it is going to be perceived very differently by those involved. Knowing that my own sexual preferences (leather/SM/bondage) are surely repulsive to many outside my own clique, I try not to put down the practices of other people, simply because they don't turn me on. Frankly, many of the things my heterosexual neighbors are doing would be equally as abhorrent to me, but as long as they are willing to leave me alone I have no argument with them.

Dear Mr. Townsend,

"Outraged, NYC" (Issue 139) has no reason in the world to be outraged at the giant scat parties in Amsterdam. He exhibits the very same behavior as Jesse Helms does when confronted with things he is not personally into. Personally, sex scenes involving women, knives, candles, and mutilation, among other things, are all turnoffs to me. Big deal. I'm not "outraged" by them. On the other hand, I have been to lots of fantastic scat parties in Amsterdam (and Germany) and have never had so much fun. Lots of us guys in the general population (and about 20 percent of *Drummer* classified ad writers) are into scat. By and large, *Drummer* stories ignore that. ("Ass Full of Molasses," Issue 139, is a welcome exception, although it was basically an enema story, not a scat story.) A lot of us would prefer stories involving huge, hard, foot-long, beer-can-thick turds. To say scat is dangerous is as dumb as saying sex is dangerous. Obviously, some things are safe, others are not. That goes for scat as much as anything else. There is safe scat play and unsafe scat play.

D. H., Maryland

Dear D. H.,

Your point is interesting and well taken, starkly in contrast with our next respondent.

Dear Larry,

I was glad to see that someone else found the increasing interest in scat within our community to be just as disgusting as I do. I don't care if some freak wants to shove his face up some other creep's shitty asshole. I just don't want to be subjected to pictures of it in my favorite leather/SM publications. I compliment the *Drummer* editors on their taste in not printing the kind of revolting muck that now dominates the pages of *Mr. SM* and *Toy,* two European mags that used to be my eagerly awaited imports. I don't know why this type of material should be included in a book that is supposed to be for leathermen, anyway. What has shit got to do with mainstream SM? And isn't it just about the most dangerous thing a guy can do, from an HIV standpoint?

Chuck, Denver, CO

Dear Chuck,

Although my personal inclination is more to your side than to that of D. H., above, I have to correct you on one point. If we accept that de Sade was the father of SM, which he most assuredly has to be, then we must—at least on a philosophical level—admit that scat is a legitimate element of SM. De Sade's stories are filled with it—which is not to say that *Le Grand Marquis* was necessarily full of you-know-what. (Sorry, I couldn't resist that.) I really have to admit that I don't have the answer to all of this. The arguments from either side have merit, and my own fecalphobia is going to color any response I make. However, I don't think we're going to see the kind of pictures in an American publication that are coming out in Europe. Our laws are more restrictive. As to scat being dangerous, I have to admit that D. H. is right. To those of us who aren't into the scene, it seems so gross that one's visceral response is that it has to be a sure path to HIV infection. I'd say, depending on exactly what you do, that the danger is considerably less than getting fucked without a rubber, probably about on a par ("danger-wise") of sucking a stranger's cock.

In examining the writings by and about Le Grand Marquis, we should take several obvious facts into account. First, he was a spoiled rich man in an era when spoiled rich men could (quite literally) get away with murder. By almost any standards—but most certainly by our own contemporary rules of acceptable behavior—de Sade was an unmitigated maniac. Although his most outrageous ideas were fictional (to the best of our knowledge), he was tossed into prison more than once, and finally ended his days in an insane asylum. He apparently thought nothing of engaging in forced sex—either outright rape (of either man or woman) or rendering a voluntary subject helpless, then proceeding to do whatever he wished, regardless of the victims' protests.

In no respect, can we consider de Sade's behavior to bear any relation to our latter day "safe-and-sane SM." Of course, it was this propensity for the outrageous that made his writings so popular. I have had people read my own stories and accuse me of a similar disregard for humanist considerations. However, in my own defense I note that my fiction is obviously not a prescription for overt behavior, any more than Agatha Christie's murder victims are supposed to be models for would-be killers. During the time he was free to do so (especially in his later years), de Sade tried with varying degrees of success to put his fantasies into action. Anyway, that's why I categorized the scat discussion as a philosophical subject. It really stimulated some heated controversy, and while I have some qualms about devoting so much space to the subject, I guess these strong feelings justify it. I'll give you just a couple more:

Dear Larry,

I have been reading with some amusement this running, three-way discussion between you and the shit-lovers vs. the shit-haters. I can appreciate your reluctance to come right out and say you disapprove of scat, but it does bother me that you haven't been more specific about the dangers these sorts of games have to entail. Come on, be honest. A guy can't go to a party where he's shit on by a dozen other guys, and not be in some kind of jeopardy. **Pardon the pun, but to say otherwise is pure bullshit!**

Mario, Munich, Germany

Dear Mario,

In responding to previous correspondence, the emphasis has been on the danger of contracting AIDS from playing scat games. The risk is there, but in all honesty (and according to my highly respected medical adviser)—despite the fact that shit is dirty and smelly, etc.—the chance of contracting an HIV infection from it is much less than, for instance, letting a stranger fuck you in the ass without a rubber. The greatest danger from an AIDS standpoint is that there might be blood in the material, and this could infect the bottom through a tear in the skin, mucous lining, whatever. However, we should not allow our preoccupation with AIDS to make us forget the other diseases that have been out there for a lot longer time. Hepatitis is a real possibility, as is good old clap, syphilis, and a whole litany of exotic amoebas. If both Top and bottom are healthy, noncarriers of any microorganism, they don't need to worry. But when you go to a big party, how can you know? The one guy I used to run into periodically, and who used to give me all the arguments about scat being safe, died of AIDS a few months back. But he was into a lot of other things, too. And maybe that's the real danger.

Dear Larry,

It is very clear from your remarks in the last several issues of *Drummer* that you do not approve of scat. I think you're behind the times. As one of your earlier correspondents pointed out, a good 20 percent of the *Drummer* advertisers are interested in these activities. You have also made reference to disease other than AIDS which can be transmitted by fecal material. We all know about hepatitis, and try to be careful not to expose ourselves to it. I'd like you to name just one other microorganism that can *commonly* be transmitted by fecal material.

Party goer, NYC

Dear Goer,

The fairly obvious fact that I dislike scat still leaves we with the 80 percent majority who are also uninterested in it. To say that I "disapprove" of these activities is to state the case more strongly than it really is, however. I am accepting of the circumstances—namely, that a lot of guys enjoy scat activities. If that's their bag, it's their business. In other words, if I had the power to stop them, I wouldn't. Lots of people disapprove of SM, and I don't want to be told I can't engage in these activities anymore. (As recently happened in England: read on.) As to diseases transmitted by fecal material, the medical journals have recently done several articles on *shigellosis*. This is a type of dysentery caused by bacteria commonly transmitted by "poor toilet hygiene," and is rivaling *salmonella* as a health threat. For more detailed information, contact the Centers for Disease Control in Atlanta, GA.

Now, that's enough for scat! The next letter was the beginning of my acquaintance with the infamous "Spanner" case in England, which has now become a cause celebre *with leatherguys in the United States and Europe.*

Dear Larry,

I don't know how much of this you can squeeze into your column, but I am enclosing an account from a London newspaper. They have actually put eight men in jail for having private SM sex! I think this is outrageous, and I think your readers should be warned about it.

Concerned Reader, U.K.

Dear Reader,

The clipping you sent is indeed a shocker, but I suppose it can best be understood as an end result of Ms. Thatcher's neo-Nazi attitudes. I was especially disturbed because one of the victims is an old friend of mine, and make no mistake: these men *are* victims, in every sense of the word. The judge described their sexual activities as "degrading and vicious," and sentenced several defendants to jail terms of four-and-a-half years. Even the newspaper which carried the story *(The Independent)* felt compelled to run an editorial in the same issue, criticizing the court's action. These men were not child molesters, nor were they even accused of any active proselytizing. The youngest was thirty-seven, the eldest a man in his sixties. By the time they reached this stage in their lives, one would think they should be entitled to engage in whatever private consensual sexual behavior they wished. But you see, this is why I am very reluctant to condemn another person's activities, unless I think they are a danger to life and limb. If we do it to them, someone is going to do it to us. And in contemporary England, Maggie's *Gestapo* already has. Amnesty International, where are you when we need you?

This case has now gone on for several years, with the British appellate courts holding that consent is not a defense to battery. Amnesty International, by the way, has finally taken an interest in the case, as has the International Court of Human Rights in the Netherlands. In the meantime, eight men's lives have been ruined to placate the biased sense of propriety within the ultra-conservative English judiciary.

And don't think that our right-wing nuts wouldn't love to do the same thing in the United States! That's why it behooves us all to support the various organizations that oppose them.

Dear Larry,

I am a university graduate student, working on a doctorate. Although psychology is not my field, it is for several of my friends. Thus, on these cold winter nights, we have had a number of discussions involving our diverse fields of endeavor. (All involved are gay men, by the way.) I was appalled by the recent assertion of one psych candidate, to the effect that "women are basically masochistic," going into some detail to argue his point: that their "normal" position in sex, for instance, is subservient, and therefore any woman who enjoys sex must at the same time enjoy submitting, etc. I was so surprised by this statement that I did not know how to answer him, and even after giving his remarks some thought I find it difficult to counter them on the grounds of his own logic. Would you be able to enlighten me?

Still Learning, NYU

Dear Still,

Although I have stated on many occasions that I know very little about women, my own reaction to this type of statement—which I first heard several years ago—was much the same as yours. I was sure it couldn't be true, yet found it a difficult point to argue in light of Freud's having expressed the same opinion—based on much the same logic as your friend (who was probably quoting him). Well, any prominent shrink who expressed such views today would certainly be in deep shit. I would remind you that Freud lived in Austria during an age when women's place was summed up as "KKK" (German for "church, kitchen, and children"). He never had to face a Gloria Allred, or even a Nancy Reagan. While one might argue that the reversal of roles, wherein the woman dominates the man, is simply a perversity of our society, I think that this same social evolution has worked its effect on both men and woman. We know for sure (as *Drummer* readers if by no other means) that not all men are sadists (Tops); thus it is difficult to claim that the reverse of the coin is also going to be true. For a good argument on this, try Paula Caplan's *Myth of Woman's Masochism*. Or drop a note to Pat Califia; she'll straighten you out!

Dear Larry,

I have encountered the word "androgynous" several times recently, in various pieces of gay writings, and I've looked it up in the dictionary. So, I know it means having the char- acteristics of both sexes. But I'm wondering if the writers are using it correctly when they apply the term to a person who is physically normal; i.e., he has all the proper male parts and none of the female. Doesn't the term also imply that the subject is hermaphroditic?

Curious, Milwaukee, WI

Dear Curious,

I think most writers in using the term are making reference more to the person's psychological makeup than to his physical being. The *androgyne,* of course, were the bearded women of Greek myth, so by this very narrow definition one might expect some physical anomaly as well. I just don't think the general usage implies this any more, and words mean only what the users perceive them to mean.

Dear Larry,

Over the years I have noticed—in your writing, as well as others—that the motorcycle is less of an SM fetish object than it used to be. In fact, in your second *Handbook,* when you discussed fetish objects you never mentioned cycles. As an old-time biker I find this both strange and discouraging. Is this just my imagination, perhaps a symptom of old-age paranoia, or has the bike lost its fascination within the leather community? I'd like to know your honest opinion.

Bruce, Santa Fe, NM

Dear Bruce,

To some extent, I think the bike and bikers have lost a bit of their glamour because so many guys have discovered that they don't need to ride a bike in order to wear the clothing associated with it. And, in all honesty, I think it was the costume more than the bike itself that turned a lot of people on. To be a real biker takes a lot of time and effort, in addition to its being expensive—as I'm sure you must realize. A few years back, the only social functions with an SM undertone were organized and run by the bike clubs. Now there are many others doing this and, as a result, the bikers no longer control the action to the extent that they did formerly. Then, deserved or not, there was a certain amount of antagonism on the part of some guys who were not interested in cycles, but were very much into SM. Some of the bike clubs were so clannish that outsiders were made to feel like poor relations when they went on a run. I think this has all combined to tarnish the image, although there are still a lot of guys who fantasize over being tied down to a bike and…whatever.

Dear Larry,

I've got a very serious moral problem to put to you, and I'll understand if you don't want to go on the record about it. My lover and I have been together for over ten years, and both of us have been HIV positive for almost three. My lover has now become symptomatic, and has just come out of the hospital after his first bout with *pneumocystis*. He has asked me to make sure that he doesn't have to go through the really terrible things we have seen happen to so many friends, especially if the infection gets into his brain and he is unable to take care of himself. Quite apart from the legal implications, which I know and understand—and would be willing to risk, I just don't know if I could bring myself to actually end it for him if the time comes, as I know it will. Can you give me some support, one way or the other? What would you do in a similar situation? I really love him, and I don't want to desert him at the very time he is going to need me the most.

(Name withheld) San Francisco, CA

Dear Friend,

I find myself almost at a loss to respond to you, because the same conflicting emotions which are tearing you apart have to form the basis for any reply. Our society has developed such a rigid attitude when it comes to keeping a person alive, one would think they would also be as concerned with the quality of the life they are preserving. You see evidence of this in so many situations: antiabortionists insisting that the kid be born into the bleakest poverty, but being totally unwilling to help support him afterward. Medical institutions refusing to "pull the plug" on someone who is long gone and has no hope of ever regaining consciousness, much less a functional life. People being locked up "for their own good" because they are suicidal, but later being released with no follow up to help them solve their problems.

But this is of little help to you. If you were talking about a family pet that you had loved for many years, the answer would be relatively simple. But we can't do that with human beings. All

I can tell you is that in your shoes, I would say to my friend: "When the time comes, I'm not sure I will be able to do it, although I know it means failing you in your hour of greatest need. I'm not even sure I would know exactly when it should happen, because I can't bring myself to deprive you of even a few moments of life. But I know how you feel, and why. Even in the worst of circumstances, you are going to have a few moments of lucidity, when you can still decide this for yourself. And if it comes to that, I won't interfere." This may not be the right thing for anyone else, maybe not for you. But that's what I would do.

At least, that's what I think I'd do. Who can really predict such a decision when the time is fairly far in the future?

Dear Larry,
   I'd like to pose a historical question for you. I've recently done some reading about St. Sebastian, whom I notice you have called "the patron saint of SM." Was he supposed to have been gay, as well as being the ultimate M? There is no mention of the possibility in any of the standard reference material I can find, and I'd be curious to know.
                                        C. R., Milbrook, CT

Dear C. R.,
   Other than the fact that he was obviously not too bright, it is difficult to glean much from the written history to enlighten us on St. Sebastian's personality traits. Of course, he lived during a period when the western Roman Empire was in its latter stages of decline, and when bisexuality was really the norm. But, our Beloved Saint was a Christian, which is what got him into all the trouble in the first place. The early church seems to have been less concerned with teaching guilt than has been the case in more recent times, but by the same token the basic tenets of the faith were even more strongly based on Jewish laws and beliefs. Hence, a good Christian man should not have been getting it one with other men, even then, even if Roman law and custom permitted it. My own impression has been that Sebastian's masochism outweighed any other facet of his personality,

and I suspect he was not greatly concerned about sexual orientation, simply because it was not a matter of much concern to his society in general. (Just for the benefit of those who are unfamiliar with the story: Sebastian was an officer in the Roman army who made such a nuisance of himself in trying to convert his fellow soldiers that the emperor Diocletian order him shot to death with arrows—the scene depicted so widely in both church and SM art and literature. He survived miraculously, and was nursed back to health by a widow woman. After months of recuperation, he once again presented himself before the Imperial Throne. This time, Emperor Diocletian ordered him beaten to death. We love him, I suppose because of all the wonderful paintings and sculptures showing his handsome young body skewered by numerous shafts.

Dear Larry,

I am new to the world of leather/SM. I have been away from the gay scene (i.e., celibate) for about four years, because of dissatisfaction with behaviors, relationships, and sex in the gay community. It seems to me that more should be shared between two men than an orgasm. I'm not sure just what.

I see in the leatherman qualities I want to develop in myself and have found no way in our culture to do so. I see in the leather scene and its rituals a strong sense of community and a path to self-discovery. Leather seems to involve the whole man; physical, mental, psychological and spiritual. Am I deluding myself as to what this is all about? Is it inappropriate to expect to learn discipline, perseverance, loving, and just plain masculine toughness at the feet of a Master?

Marty, Boston, MA

Dear Marty,

Like so many of life's rewards, the potential benefits of "a leather lifestyle" are not going to float into your eager hands without your putting forth a considerable effort to acquire them. You probably have a great deal to learn at the feet of a Master, if you can find one who is willing to put up with you.

This guy sounded so overly idealistic, I wasn't sure I should take him seriously. But, I had to give him the benefit of the doubt, although I'm still not sure I really understand everything he was trying to say.

Dear Larry,
What happens to a slave when the Master dies suddenly? Can the Master leave a will bequeathing his slave to another Master, or does the slave have to be released? What arrangements should be made in case a slave's Master dies? This is an issue that should be brought into the open for the sake of the slave.

slave, south of Mason-Dixon line

Dear slave,
The fourteenth Amendment ended legalized slavery in 1867 (final adoption). It therefore follows that any Master-slave relationship that exists today is strictly voluntary on the part of both parties, and can be terminated by either at any time, regardless of what "legal" documents may have been drawn up by or for the participants. However, for people involved in this kind of relationship, their own set of rules (written or otherwise) are just as real as if they had the effect of law to sustain them. Unfortunately, when a Master dies he can only "will his human chattel" to another Master if both the slave and the new Master are willing. The Master should, however, assure that his slave is provided for to the best of his ability—especially if the slave has not been employed outside the house, and therefore has no immediate financial or employment prospects of his own.

And thus, as best I can, I have expressed my opinion on the Master/slave situation, as well as a number of other issues that tantalize the imaginations of the leather community. I've been asked if I'm really as serious as I make myself out to be. Am I? Maybe. You decide.

CHAPTER 12

Outrageous!

Many of the subjects I have covered in other chapters may well fall into this category in the minds of the less-well-instructed. In fact, there is not much left out there that the majority of my readers would find difficult to accept. Yet, just when it seems I've heard everything, here comes someone with something you literally wouldn't believe—or at least you wouldn't believe he'd say it—not like that!

Dear Sir,

I am not sure if you can help me directly or not. I have a project in mind and would like some guidance. I want to make a reasonably believable dog costume for a man; i.e., by adding such items as fur, paws, tail, snout, to make him as close as possible to a dog. I want to do this to allow the enactment of an SM theme, with a guy who really wants to play the part of canine in training.

Trainer, San Francisco, CA

Dear Trainer,

Yours seems to be a case where the mind, rather than the physical being, is going to play the more important role in establishing the fantasy. You run the risk of making a burlesque of your scene if you get too deeply involved in this type of costume. I do recall hearing a very amusing story of a guy who was bound, blindfolded, and turned into a werewolf on a night of the full moon—this with the cooperation of an Old English sheepdog, a pair of shears and a bottle of Elmer's glue. However, the story is amusing rather than sensuous, at least in retrospect. In your case, the costume is going to be more effective from the standpoint of the Top (who can see it) rather than the bottom, who is only going to feel the effects of the accoutrements. But if you're determined to try it, I think the loose fur and glue is going to be more effective than something which is going to totally enclose the body.

I met this silly fucker a few months after answering his letter, and he was indeed every bit as crazed as he seemed in his letter. He got so ripped one holiday weekend—I think it was Memorial Day—that he stripped naked and ran along 15th Street, chasing a cat at one or two in the morning. By some miracle he didn't get arrested that time, although I understand he did spend several months (incarcerated) in drug rehab. He was young and quite attractive, and I'd have enjoyed getting it on with him, except that even at this stage, before AIDS had become such a preoccupation, I was afraid of whatever other diseases he probably had. I heard that he had died a year or two after the naked nocturnal foray—from hepatitis and/or?

Quite incidentally, I know that my fear of infection seems strange to many guys. I've even been compared to Howard Hughes, whom we know was a fanatic on "germs." I've never reached that stage, but I always had a terror of contracting hepatitis, and assiduously avoided contact with anyone, or any behavior, which I thought could expose me to it. Since some of the same practices can transmit HIV, I credit this phobia with sustaining me through the early stages of the epidemic.

Dear sick pervert,
   I've read your filthy trash, and I hope you and all your friends and readers get AIDS and die and go to hell.
                                    A brother in Christ
                                    (Postmark, Oklahoma City)

Dear Brother,

Thanks for your Christian charity. May God reward your noble sentiments.

Although answering this asshole was relatively simple, it gives one cause to wonder at the degree of hatred directed against us. Our attempts to educate the "Great Unwashed" still have a long way to go. It also makes one wonder at the hypocrisy of the whole thing, since he obviously had to have acquired and read a copy of Drummer *in order to know about my filthy trash.*

Dear Larry,

Do you know of any honest-to-God chain gangs I could volunteer for? Outfits involving legitimate outdoor work, with guys loaded down with chains? Have heard rumors that they exist, but can't get any leads. I assume if anyone has the space and privacy to operate such a gang, he'd be very publicity-shy. Still, if you can tell me anything I'd appreciate it, maybe in a note instead of in your column if you don't want to give away a good thing.

Bill, VA

Dear Bill,

If I knew of such an outfit, I'd tell you privately. Unfortunately, I do not know of any place at the moment. There was a "work farm," run on a sort of old-plantation style, a few years back, but it was located near an area where dope smugglers began dropping their shipments (from aircraft). The feds thought the slaves were part of the gang. I don't think anyone actually got busted for it, but the publicity fucked up the works. There have been a couple of attempts to get things started in other areas; but, to my knowledge, no one has really gotten it off the ground.

One of my advisers is nagging me about putting this letter in the "outrageous" chapter, telling me that wanting to be in a chain gang is a perfectly normal desire for a boy to have. Perhaps, but to most of us it seems a bit far out. In the intervening years, interestingly enough, there have been several places that offered good, solid slave-labor situations for those who wanted to play this partic-

ular game. As far as I know, none of them lasted, although a good friend of mine does have a wonderful military prison all ready and waiting for the right men. Don't write and ask for a referral unless you're interested in a little screening exercise first.

Dear Larry,

Can I say something to all the men who place ads? Why, oh why, when I send you additional revealing photos after the first time, do you write a short note back with no information about yourself? Are you collecting photos or looking for action? I'm wondering if anyone out there is actually serious about meeting or corresponding. I should own the local postal center! Hell, I'll be wanting a hot-assed slave here in the near future and I want to spend serious time reviewing and interrogating potential slaves. But 99 percent of all you assholes out there just want my hot photos and JO letters. Fuck, I've got much more than that to offer! Shit or get off the pot, fuckers!

Greg, Miami, FL

Dear Greg,

Okay, you said it. I hope you get a chance to whip some of those elusive little asses.

This was just one of many letters that came in expressing much the same sentiments. This guy just seemed to sum it up succinctly. Is he really outrageous? Maybe not. I guess it would depend on your perspective.

Dear Larry,

My roommate and I are having a dispute, which maybe you can settle. I know from reading your *Leatherman's Handbook* that you disapprove of having sex with animals, and I agree with you. But my roomie (not my lover) likes to play around with our dog. We have both been tested for the AIDS virus, and he is positive. (I'm negative.) I'm concerned that he could transmit the disease to the dog. He says it's not possible, because it's a human disease. Can you tell me?

A. R., San Francisco, CA

Dear A. R.,

My medical adviser says, "Probably not." He went on to cite the lab experiments he knew about where they had used animals—specifically monkeys, but the virus used in these experiments is not exactly the same as the human variety. He said he was sure that a lab technician or someone else involved directly in lab research could answer you off the top of his head. If such responds to this column, I'll let you know.

It is curious how cautious our learned medicos can be in answering questions about HIV infection. Although this question is from 1985, the supposed experts were still hedging their bets because the final answers were still evading us. (And are evading us!) And that's outrageous!

Dear Larry,

I'm twenty-three years old, and I'm fatter that I should be. In fact, I have kind of big breasts and wide hips that some guys laugh at. Not long ago, some guys at our local bar got to teasing me, and they started calling me a "morphodyke." I tried to look this up in a dictionary, but I couldn't find the word, and I don't know what it means. I'm afraid to ask anyone. Can you tell me what it means?

Overweight, Atlanta, GA

Dear Overweight,

Your detractors are expressing their own ignorance, because the word they probably meant to use was "hermaphrodite." This is a person who has the sexual equipment of both sexes. Unless you have a pussy between your legs, in addition to a penis, I wouldn't worry about it.

Dear Larry,

Many years ago (and I'm not going to tell you how many years ago), but well before the AIDS crisis reared its ugly head, the wildest and most exciting sex always involved a big cock up my ass. Of course, my wildest fantasy involved being the guest of honor at a heavy SM session, culminating in a gang bang. In fact, I did take as many as eight guys at a party arranged by a friend. Not too long ago, I was talking to another friend whose tastes are similar to mine, and he claimed to have taken twenty-six. This brings me to my question. I doubt you'll find the answer in Guinness, but what's the most guys you've ever heard of getting into a single "fuckee" at a gang bang? Then, too, I strongly suspect that my shopworn friend was exaggerating. Aren't the tissues of the anus and rectum too fragile for this kind of abuse?

Jim, San Francisco, CA

Dear Jim,

Tender anal tissues seem to deter only the sane and sensible. Although twenty-six is certainly a respectable accomplishment, I doubt it is a record. Back in the pre-AIDS bathhouse days (and hopefully not continuing into the present time) I knew—or knew of—many guys who loved to lie facedown on their cots, allowing all and sundry to fuck them for hours on end. From these specialists I have heard estimates that went over forty. It is indeed unfortunate that Guinness refuses to maintain statistics on such socially significant events, since I'm sure the record would appall even you and many others.

It would also have encouraged more damned fools to try breaking the record. Oh, Messalina, where are you now? I'm sure that your spirit must be a guiding light for many would-be record breakers.

Dear Larry,

I recently got into a really weird scene, where the "Top" did things to me that I had seen in some old drawings (I think from Stephen). He took me out to the desert, starting late at night, so we got there about dawn. He tied me facedown, naked, and spread-eagled me by lashing my wrists and ankles to wooden stakes. He whipped me and did a bunch of other things; then he stuck a rubber tube up my ass (like a length of garden hose), and started dropping things into me. He had some little round balls (BB's, I think), and he found a few small round pebbles. But he ended up finding some ants and dropping them into me, too. He scared me pretty badly, because I didn't want him to do this, and he wouldn't let me go until he got damned good and ready. I don't think I've suffered any injuries from it, but although I'm really turned on to the guy, I'm afraid to go out with him again. He's called me several times, and he's promised he won't get so carried away again. (But he does want to go back to the desert with me.) I don't know what to do. What do you think?

Randy, Los Angeles, CA

Dear Randy,

If you think you can trust him, okay, On the other hand, it sounds like you don't feel you can. I don't know the guy, so you'll have to make the judgment. However, in my own life's experience, it's the things I didn't do that I regret more than those I did. (His technique could use some decided refinement, regardless.)

Although this Top's behavior certainly exceeds most reasonable boundaries of "safe-and-sane SM," it is also an exciting, barbaric ritual he performs. It is understandably intriguing for a young, lusty bottom. In afterthought, I might have suggested that the guy insist on a "turnabout" arrangement, where he gets his crack at playing Top. This might help to keep his partner from getting too excessive in his torments.

Dear Larry,

You guys keep advocating "safe sex," and that might be okay for some old guy who's done his thing and now only goes out for sex once a month or so. But for someone like me, who is still under thirty, it's another story. I'm hot and ready all the time, and let's face it: safe sex is dull! It's dull and boring. If I can't touch the guy I'm making it with, I might just as well stay home and jack off.

Randy, Seattle, WA

Dear Randy,

I hear you, and to some extent I can appreciate your feelings.

It's rough to have it up and dripping and have your prospective partner slide a rubber over it, or insist that you not cum in his mouth. Nor is this attitude in any way confined to your age group. There are a lot of horny old goats out there who are used to getting it often and completely, and don't enjoy "safe sex" either. But this isn't something that's being foisted on you by your enemies or detractors. The people who are trying to advise you are trying to tell you how to stay alive. We're only telling you what is supposed to be safe, and what isn't. Unfortunately, I can't just say, "It's your life. Take my advice or leave it." You have to consider the other guys you are apt to infect if you are careless in safeguarding your own health. However, I've known too many guys who have died of AIDS to take it lightly. You are better off to stay home and jack off. At least you'll live to bitch about it.

I can really sympathize with a young guy in his twenties, feeling all that lust and being unable to fulfill so many of his cravings. But HIV is nothing to play with. Unlike the diseases that threatened most of us at this age, AIDS can't be cured by a simple shot in the ass. We've all had to learn to live with it—at least, all of us who are still around to complain.

Dear Larry,

There is a rumor going around that AIDS was really started, either by accident or on purpose, by the CIA experimenting with germ-warfare materials. Have you head about this, and do you think it could possible by true?

J. M., Miami, FL

Dear J. M.,

Anything is possible, but I really think we're looking a little far afield to accuse an agency as ineffective as the CIA with doing such a thing. The evidence would suggest otherwise, since there seems a pretty clear path from Africa to Haiti to here. Besides, I'd prefer to believe it was the KGB.

And yet, I have a friend who swears he's discovered the "smoking gun," connecting experimental government labs in Puerto Rico to the epidemic. He won't tell me more than this because he wants to write his own book on the subject. I don't believe him, but—who knows? I'd like to read his book when and if he ever gets it written.

Dear Larry,

Although I know from your answers in the past that you are against sex with animals, I have the following question to ask, and hope you will answer. I am a very experienced bottom into FF, dildos, W/S, etc. For the past few years I have wanted to expand my experiences to include Great Danes and horses. Is there an organization that you know of that could help me with this?

Mark, FL

Mark:

No.

'Nuff said to that clown!

Dear Larry,

I was recently given a birthday present that I think came from your mail-order catalog. It is about a 9" long cylinder made of gray rubber, almost 2" in diameter. It has a hole running lengthwise through it, and has a plastic tube attached. I can't figure out what to do with it, and I'm embarrassed to ask the guys who gave it to me. Can you enlighten me?

Perplexed, Seattle, WA

Dear Perplexed,

Oh, how I have wanted to say this to various customers for years! *Shove it up your ass!* (Then attach it to an enema bag or other water source, and do your thing.)

Recreational enemas have become such popular sports that it's hard to imagine a guy not recognizing such an obvious piece of equipment. (This letter actually came to me through my business mail, but I couldn't resist sharing it in the column—as I have several others.)

Dear Larry,

When I was younger and doing all the things no one dares do any more, one of my favorite sexual exercises was to get with another well-endowed guy, and we would mutually fuck each other—both at the same time. It was tricky to do, and a bit awkward, but an awful lot of fun. Now my major enjoyment has to come from videos, but I've never seen one that shows this kind of action. Can you tell me if there is such a tape? If so, where can I get it?

Pete, Fort Lauderdale, FL

Dear Pete,

Just when I think I've heard them all…. No, I must confess that this is not only a type of action I have never seen, it is one I find difficult even to conceive. (But it does sound like fun.)

This seemed like such a wild idea that I got one of my video producer friends to have a couple of his actors try it. However, despite their each being quite a talented sexual athlete, they weren't able to bring it off. I'm not sure if my correspondent was funnin' me or not, but if he actually did it, he and his partner(s) must have been double-jointed—over ten inches, that is.

Dear Larry,

I have been having an argument with a friend of mine, who insists that you can get AIDS from a toilet seat—just like you can get syphilis. I told him you can't. Who's right?

J. L., San Antonio TX

Dear J. L.,

AIDS, like syphilis, can by contracted from a toilet seat only if you sit down before the other guy gets up.

Dear Larry,

One of my greatest fascinations is with impalement. I know that you are knowledgeable on this because I saw several stories and articles that you wrote a number of years ago—also noted somewhere that you had done a novel on Ivan the Terrible, when this sort of punishment was fairly common. AIDS considerations aside, is there any safe way to actually have a scene involving impalement? Since I would like to be bottom on this situation, the safety factors are of particular concern. (And by "impalement" I mean being put up on a greased pole, or stake, so that you have to stand with the end up your ass, high enough that you can't lift yourself off, balancing yourself on tiptoe.) Shit, I'm getting a hard-on, just writing this!

Pete, Dallas, TX

Dear Pete,

Since impalement was invented—apparently by the Mongols—as a punishment intended to result in a humiliating and painful death, it is not a game that is easily played with any degree of safety. I suppose you might lessen the odds by constructing a blunt-ended pole with a "stopper" on it, which would prevent it from entering your gut beyond 6" to 8". However, the entire situation is going to be fraught with peril, and I do not recommend it. Of course, I get a bit squeamish when I see some of the heavier electro-play and warm-weather mummification, as well; and these bottoms always seem to survive their ordeals. I am simply concerned that we not negate our own assertions that SM play can be safe and sane by engaging in foolhardy experimentation. See the next letter.

I might interject that I did an impalement story as one chapter in my early novel Leather Ad–S, *but I have to admit that I was less experienced then, and not as aware of the safety considerations that later became the watchwords in my writings.*

Dear Larry,

I have been around the SM scene for longer than I'm willing to admit, and in the last few years I have attended a number of "runs" and parties put on by the clubs in various parts of the country. In the course of this, I have seen a number of "exchanges" which I felt were downright dangerous, even though both Tops and bottoms seemed extremely competent, and no harm resulted from their behavior. I don't want to condemn what any other men may do, but it all makes me begin to wonder if your past assertions that the "ultimate" in SM is something other than death. Isn't there a heavy "death wish" on the part of: (1) an elderly man who submits to a whipping which would test the endurance of an eighteen-year-old, or (2) a guy who permits himself to be sealed in a plaster cast with just his nose and genitals protruding, on a day when the temperature exceeds 90 degrees, or (3) a middle-aged man who enjoys being suspended by his ankles and left hanging upside down for half an hour or more?

I could mention other examples, but I think these should be enough to make my point. I would really welcome your comments.

(Name and area withheld)

Dear Withheld,

Although you may be right in projecting a death-wish mentality onto a bottom who skirts disaster in some of his scenes, I can't help but compare his mental set with that of other guys who involve themselves in any number of asexual adventures, which also expose them to deadly peril. Take, for example, the case of a race-car driver, or a mountain climber—to pick just a couple of the most obvious examples. Are these men exposing themselves to mortal danger because they subconsciously wish to die, or are they doing it to prove their own skills—perhaps their own immortality? I have a very ambivalent opinion on this subject, but in this I am certainly not alone. The psychological literature is full of diverse opinions. I'd say that whichever side you choose to take, you would have ample academic company.

I put these last two letters in the "outrageous" chapter, mostly because they bring up the question of the "ultimate" SM scene. I know that many people believe this to be death, or a scene in which dying is a viable alternative. Sometimes this is seen as the "forfeiture," should the bottom fail his test of endurance, or if the Top does not possess the skill to bring off whatever he is attempting to do. I have never felt that this was legitimate SM behavior, at least not on the scale of normalcy. I do recognize that some men can only achieve their ultimate thrill if they risk disaster in the course of prov-

ing themselves capable—in effect, capable of defeating death. In the vast majority of cases, I do not believe that the person taking this risk seriously believes he is going to die as a result of whatever game he is playing. Rather than a death wish, I see most of this behavior as an acting out to prove the man's conception of his own immortality—never for a moment believing that he is going to be killed. In keeping with this, I have seen many more young guys taking these heavy risks than older men. (Although there are certainly enough seniors doing it to prove the rule.) However, one's belief in his own immortality is, understandably, more common among the young. Of course, this is merely my opinion. There are lots of "experts"—shrinks and other behavioral-scientist types— who will take the opposite point of view.

Dear Sir:

i guess i am really what you would all a heavy bottom, not really a slave, or i wouldn't be asking you this. But i am living as a slave in the sense that i have only one Master, and although we don't live together during the week, i usually spend every weekend at His house. While i'm there, i'm always naked and in some sort of bondage. i serve my Master and his guests in any way He requires of me, and i try to fulfill the role he sets for me. Lately, however, he has gotten into dog training. i am required to sleep curled up on a mat beside His bed, etc. The only problem is with the things i'm required to eat. Although i am sometimes allowed to beg for scraps at the table, my main meals are dog food (like Alpo or Kal Kan meat), eaten out of a bowl on the kitchen floor. Is it okay for a human to eat this stuff? Aside from the bland, unseasoned flavor, it really isn't too bad, especially the canned beef or horsemeat. i wouldn't have any reservations as long as i could be sure i wasn't poisoning myself.

slave?, TX

Dear slave?,

The feds do only a half-assed job when it comes to protecting our human food supplies, and while they are supposed to keep an eye on pet food, as well, I wouldn't want to bet on it—certainly not if the wager was my life or my health. On the other hand, there does seem to be a degree of concern on the part of the pet-food producers to maintain the quality of their products. After all, if they kill off the consumers, who'll be left to eat their stuff? I'd say you were probably safe enough eating the canned meat from the major companies, in that it is unlikely to poison you. And since you eat on your own during the week, you can make up for the unbalanced weekend diet. (My Dober-persons love Kal Kan, and I wouldn't give it to them if I thought it would hurt them.) You occasionally read stories of homeless folk surviving on dog food because they can't afford anything else, and they must be eating cheaper brands than you are. Kal Kan is expensive, after all. Your Master could be doing much worse by you.

I almost told this guy that if Alpo and Kal Kan (name now changed to Pedigree) are good enough for my Doberpersons, they're good enough for some miserable slave. But I'm afraid I'll be accused (again) of slave abuse. But isn't that why they become slaves? Oh well, there's an even crazier one coming up a few items down the way.

Dear Mr. Townsend,
I have recently read a couple of your "novels," and I found them utterly disgusting. You have glorified every form of vice and perversion, without ever considering the disservice you do to the beliefs which form the foundation stones of our civilization. How do you reconcile these vile forms of behavior with our established Christian faith? I'm sure that God Himself must blush to read such blasphemy.
A Christian, St. Louis, MO

Dear Chris,
If the Bible were set down in contemporary English, I think most people would find it quite sensual. In fact, many seem to get a charge out if, even as it is usually presented. Be that as it may, my writings—and those of my contemporaries in this genre—are not intended as entertainment for the uptight, constipated Bible thumper. Under our constitutional form of

government, there is supposed to be a sharp separation between church and state. This means that my writings—or anybody's writings—are supposed to be free of religious restriction. Likewise, no one is constrained to read anything that displease him. Since you claim to have read "a couple" of my novels, I can't help but wonder why you subjected yourself to the second, having already been appalled by the first. Could it be that some degree of sexual desire has survived your indoctrination in Christian guilt?

Oh, aren't they wonderful—these minions of Christian repression? Someday, I'm going to do an explicit novel on the behavior of a few of our favorite biblical characters. I may have to publish it myself, though; these crazies seem to have intimidated almost every publisher in the country.

Dear Mr. Townsend, Sir,

This might sound weird, but ever since high school I have really gotten off on having pimples popped. As long as I live I will never forget the times my Uncle Eddie popped the zits on my back when I come home from class. Of course, you have to understand I've always had the hots for my uncle. Nothing would excite me more than to have him drop by after work (unexpected) all hot and sweaty, darkly tanned, wearing a tight tank top, and ask me to him a favor and make a cup of coffee. Then I'd get him to "pop" me. I'd stretch out on the couch, and he'd pop away. He had rough hands and took great pleasure in causing me discomfort. I've never been able to find anyone else as skilled as he was, although I'd still get off having someone else pop my occasional pimple. Am I just strange, or perhaps slightly touched in the head? Since I'm out of school and use special soap, I don't have very many zits anymore. But in the summer, when I start to sweat more, I still get a couple of really big sore ones. Is there anyone out there who would consider stopping by for a cup of coffee? I'm sure I can find something useful you can do with your hands while you're waiting.

RLV, Selingsgrove, PA

Dear RLV,

I wouldn't worry about being a little "touched." If all of us had our full range of fantasies exposed for the world to see, there would be too few guys left running loose to care for the rest of us. Interestingly enough, a friend of mine saw your letter and actually drooled a bit. It appears he's into "social grooming," and when he sees a zit on a well-restrained subject he can't keep his hands off it. He says it's not really a great sexual turn-on, just a slight compulsion. Can we do a little paraphrase on Sir Isaac? *For every perverse desire we harbor within ourselves, someone else harbors an equally perverse and opposite desire.* The trick is simply to find the right guy. If you're ever on the West Coast, I'll send you on to my friend.

I also got a few letters telling me how disgusting they found the whole idea. However, they were nowhere near as violent as the pro- and anti-scat guys in Chapter 11.

Dear Mr. Townsend,

Although I have purchased and read your materials in the past, I must now ask that you cease to send any more of your filth to my address. I have found a new Master, and He is Our Beloved Lord and Savior, Jesus Christ. I know that you write a column for that muckraking rag, *Drummer,* so I hope you will have the guts to print my letter so that others may have pause to stop and consider the errors of their way as they rush down the path to hell. Real men don't need pornography, nor should they be polluting their souls by lusting after other men, and engaging in the sins that destroyed Sodom and Gomorrah [sic].

James T., Atlanta, GA

Dear James,

I guess a few of us still eat quiche, too. In any event, I hope your new Master takes good care of you. I would, however, suggest that you do a little more thorough reading of your bible. The "sins of Sodom and Gomorrah" are described quite differently in the "good book" from the misquotes in the printed tract you enclosed with your letter. I hope that the earthly representative of God, who appears to be guiding your current conversion, is better informed than his encapsulated quotes and his spelling would indicate.

So here's another nut who got "saved" just in the nick of time. Isn't it wonderful when they find Jesus? I had one customer who used to write stories for me, then get religion and want them back, only to resubmit them a few weeks later. Last I heard he got busted for sucking off the altar boys. I guess you never really reform an old whore—unless you throw stones at her.

Dear Larry,

On New Year's Day, a couple of years ago, I watched in horror as a group of AIDS activist crazies threw themselves in front of a float, trying to disrupt the Rose Parade. I'm sure that most of our Community would agree with me that this isn't the way to get whatever it is that these people want. In other instances, they have thrown paint on the front doors of Catholic churches, and I understand that in NYC they even invaded St. Patrick's Cathedral and threw the sacred Eucharist onto the floor. I know that in the past you have been involved with several responsible groups within the Gay Movement, and that you have spoken out against this type of unreasonable behavior. What can we do to stop these people before they turn the whole country against us?

Upset, Los Angeles, CA

Dear Upset,

The best way to stop these crazies, of course, would be for the government and Catholic church to make some response to their legitimate grievances. However misguided they may be, or may appear to be (insofar as their behavior is concerned) they are trying to make some changes that would be very beneficial to all of us. The ones who did the number at the Rose Parade were from a group called SANE, which is not the same organization that has been going after the Catholic Church. (That's the ACT UP people.) Whereas I am distressed to see gay activists making fools of themselves by physical attacks on church property, I am even more distressed to hear the supposedly responsible archbishop of Los Angeles condemning the use of condoms as a means of preventing the spread of the AIDS virus. In many respects, both our government and some of our churches are unrealistic, prejudiced, and way behind the times. I'd like to see these attitudes change. Desperate situations stimulate desperate responses. Although I think the kids are going about in the wrong way, I don't think it behooves us to condemn them out of hand.

And yes, this is a change of attitude on my part from the days when I headed one of the larger gay groups in the L. A. area. At that time, though, I think I was more disturbed by the fact that the "radicals" were also very far left politically, and this troubled me more then than it does now. As to the idea that we are making enemies instead of friends by an "in-your-face" demonstration technique, I remember the opinion expressed by the late David Goodstein (owner of The Advocate*) a few years ago. He maintained that we could divide the heterosexual world into three basic groups: (1) those who hate us, and are going to hate us no matter what we do, (2) those who like us and are going to support us no matter what we do, and (3) the vast majority who don't care what we do, and have too many interests of their own to be bothered.*

Dear Larry,

Gay men familiar with water sports might be interested in knowing that urine has also been used as a healing method for thousands of years and continues today. AZT-free PWAs are controlling oral candidiasis, diarrhea, and skin problems with *their own* urine. Disappearance of KS lesions has been reported within the group. Because of the intense taboo against urine, this knowledge is not easily accepted by most people. I suspect *Drummer* readers will be more open minded.

Name Withheld, M.D.

Dear M. D.,

I don't know if there is any validity to your treatment/theories or not. My medical advisers all tell me you're a crackpot and I should ignore you; but that's to be expected, even if you've got something worth investigating. I'll list your address for the benefit of anyone who wants to check you out, but with the disclaimer that neither the *Drummer* editors nor I can make any recommendations one way or the other: Water of Life Institute, P. O. Box 22–3543, Hollywood, FL 33022.

I don't know if this guy is still around, but his theories have the status of long-standing belief among a fairly wide range of people—including, so I've been told, the late Mahatma Gandhi, who was said to have consumed a glass of his own urine every morning. He did last a long time, although an assassin's bullet deprived us of the ultimate answer.

Dear Master Larry, Sir!

Some time ago, you answered a letter from a slave who was being "dog trained," and in the course of this was being forced to eat dog food. At that time you indicated that you did not think Kal Kan or any of the better brands would do him any harm, at least over limited periods of time. i am a weekend slave, and have been being "pussy trained" for about two months. i report to my Master on Friday evening and am allowed to leave early Monday morning. When i arrive i am stripped naked, except for a black velvet collar and cockring, both studded with rhinestones. i am required to crawl on all fours, to sleep on a big cushion at the foot of my Master's bed, to use a sandbox for my natural functions, and i am fed only cat food. Of course, i am also given lots of "pettings," which always get heavier until my back and ass are really red. Anyway, all of this is great and i love it, except that the cat food (Whiskas and Friskies) is making me nauseous a lot of the time, and I'm afraid it might cause me some health problems. I'm a bit of a health nut, and eat very properly for the rest of the week, work out at a gym, etc. What do you think?

pussy-slave, Chicago, IL

Dear pussy,

I'm not sure what to tell you about cat food, because the formulations are apparently very different from dog foods. Cats seem able to digest things that dogs can't handle. In addition to our two Doberpersons, my friend and I have a couple of cats, and I've discovered that the dogs will get sick if they eat any appreciable amount from the cat's bowl. Although I don't like to interfere with a Master's control of his slave, I have to be honest and tell you that he is doing something I wouldn't do; and my reason for not doing it would be fear of endangering my slave's health.

Here's another slave with an even more serious problem over the things his Master is making him ingest than the bottom forced to eat dog food. But if my Doberpersons can't handle it, I don't think it's a good idea to feed it to a human, even a slave.

Dear Master Larry, SIR,

My Master requires me to lick his work boots clean every night. He works at outdoor construction and does a lot of walking in the course of his job. Obviously, he doesn't have time to look where he's stepping. Sometimes his boots are caked with mud, dirt, and construction debris, but he still requires that i lick and clean them spotless for him, using just my tongue. My concern is that i might catch something. Could i get parasites if there is some dog shit mixed with the mud? What about asbestos fibers, or who knows what else might be on them? i am really concerned about this. i do want to please him, but this demand seems like it may be hazardous to my health. Otherwise he is very good to me. i do enjoy having his boots holding me down and he always lets me cum while he's fucking my ass.

A leather bootslave, AK

Dear bootslave,

Although you are one of the lucky ones, having found a Master who has taken you in and appears to be training you properly, you may indeed by exposing yourself to health risks. You have already enumerated the most obvious, so that is not really the question. More to the point are the several decisions you will have to make. If you can verbally express your concerns to your Master, you should do it. If you are afraid that doing this is going to terminate your relationship, you'll have to make your choice. Is it worth the risk you're taking? If not, then approach him even if you think he's going to toss you out. Otherwise you must make the decision, whether to stay or not. No one can do it for you. (As I write this, I have two slaves reading off the screen. One says, "Tell the Master to fuck off." The other says, "Eat his shit if you have to, but do what he wants." That's a big help, isn't it?)

In reading back over this collection of craziness, I still find several points of genuine concern as well as items that make me laugh, even after the passage of several years. The most amazing aspect is the wide-ranging variety of these inanities, and the fact that all of these guys have lived to write their letters. I would conclude with only one more caveat—this to the Tops and Masters: Watch what you're doing! If you accept a slave and make him subservient to your control, you must assume responsibility for his well-being. I don't like to second-guess a Master in his treatment of a slave, but some of the letters I've answered indicate some very poor judgment calls. If you are functioning as Master, or Top, it behooves you to remember that you literally have your bottom/slave's life in your hands.

CHAPTER 13

Subjects That Defy Categorization

I guess you might call this miscellaneous, but I hesitate to label some of these ideas as such. That would tend to relegate them to the category of something less weighty or important than concepts that are more commonplace—and hence easier to assign a name. So here are some odds and ends that simply didn't fit anywhere else—the tune of the proverbial different drummer? Perhaps.

Dear Larry,

I read with interest your response to R of NYC about men into diapers. I'd like to advise you on a couple of points. First, our smaller group of "loners" is becoming less lonely, since this condition stemmed largely from fear of ridicule— a less likely condition as guys become aware of others who share their interests. In addition to *Drummer*, other major publications have also run articles on the subject. There are now a number of clubs and outlets catering to our interests, a couple being: Diaper Pail Society (DPF), 55 Sutter # 457, San Francisco, CA 94104 (membership club); Lil'

Wrangler Enterprises, 484 Lake Park Ave. # 36, Oakland, CA 94610 (paraphernalia supplier).

Generally, there are three categories of diaper lovers: Guys into water sports who have discovered the warm convenience of diapers and plastic pants vs. wet clammy jeans. Men whose fantasies relate to a total regression to an infantile, "baby" state. Daddies/diaper boys; i.e., guys into milder forms of SM who use the diaper as a form of punishment/humiliation. The largest number of guys probably fall into this latter category.

C. T., Washington, D.C.

Dear C. T.,

Thanks for sharing your expertise with us. I know you were the one who invented the diaper "hankie code" as a tongue-in-cheek remark in an earlier *Drummer* article, but I have seen a couple of guys actually using it. Maybe your scene is even more popular than you realize.

The diaper scene is definitely outside the mainstream (no pun intended) of SM activities, and is certainly one form of behavior that can bring ridicule upon the participants. Still, for those who dig it, the activity is just as legitimate as many other, more common forms of expression. It is also relatively harmless from any health or safety standpoint. The above letter/answer date from March 1984, however, so the addresses given may be long gone.

Dear Larry,

Hello Brother! Sitting here at Folsom State Prison, thinking about all the hot times at the Brig and Hot House. This Downed Brother needs some advice. I need to know if *Drummer* will print an ad from a convict. Since I am in the closet, I don't receive any gay publications. Thank you for your time. Ride free and play hard!

A Downed Brother

Dear Downed,

There isn't any problem in running an ad in *Drummer*. In fact, we used to have a column devoted to prison problems and communications. The only reason it was discontinued was due to the departure of the guy who wrote it. Of course, if you do place an ad, I don't know how deeply you may be able to remain in the closet, once the answers start coming in.

Corresponding with guys in the joint has been a persistent problem. On the one hand, we know that many gay men get into trouble because of their sexual orientation and can even land in prison as a result. On the other hand, there have been some real horror stories of men who have tried to help an inmate, sending money and various materials while he's behind bars, then trying to help him along when he gets out, only to be badly ripped off or otherwise stung. Most modern prisons have become more lenient in recent years, allowing inmates to acquire gay printed matter and to correspond with openly gay men. My advice to the potential "pen pal" is: go to it, but be careful until you really get to know the guy. For example, inviting a man fresh out of prison to come live with you can prove disastrous. But we don't want to let our legitimately repressed "brothers" suffer any more than necessary, either.

Dear Larry,

You've answered travel questions for other guys, so I'd like to ask if you ever heard of "The Heath" in London? Is it a bar, or a private club? If the latter, is it SM-leather, and how does a guy get recommended for membership? From the little I've heard, it sounds real hot!

Jake, Detroit

Dear Jake,

You must be referring to Hampstead Heath, which is neither a bar nor a club. It is a large (800-acre) wooded park in northwest London. It has long been a popular cruising ground, with all types, all sizes and shapes to be found. The action can get quite heavy from time to time, depending on who happens to meet whom. It is also somewhat dangerous because the place is so big and so dark that it is easy pickings for the local punks. Police patrols are a less-potent threat, but you have to be on the lookout for them, as well. The biggest problem is getting to and from the Heath, due to the irritating English custom of shutting down all public transportation by midnight. Especially on a weekend night (the busiest, naturally) you really should rent a car unless you want to stay until the first trams start up in the morning. You'd also be well advised to look over the lay of the land in daylight, preferably with a native guide to show you which areas to frequent.

As one might expect, because of the HIV threat, the Heath is about as dangerous as a public sex club. In the days before AIDS, the place was a real blast! I spent one night there, performing just about every act—SM and/or sexual one could think of—and when I left well after daylight it took me a couple of days to recover! If you remember your classic films, the Heath tended to resemble a rather well-tended Sherwood Forest. It was one place no gay tourist should miss. Today? Well, you know the risks, but I'm sure there is still plenty of action if you're foolish enough to seek it out.

Dear Larry,

My greatest pleasure in life is sucking cock. I know it's become a dangerous occupation these days, but I feel I am trimming the odds, so to speak, by cruising areas frequented by men who are largely straight. Sometimes they are what you'd call "rough trade," but that element of danger only makes it that much more exciting. Anyway, please don't caution me about AIDS. It's a risk I guess I just have to take. My real problem is that I have a terrible time controlling my weight. I'm always on a diet, and put on five pounds if I just look at a piece of pie or cake. I have a friend who keeps telling me that the reason I tend to gain weight so easily is that I'm ingesting a lot of fat by swallowing cum. He says that there's as much animal fat (saturated fat, the very worst kind) in a good hot load as in a large, untrimmed piece of steak. Is this true?

A World-class Cocksucker, MI

Dear World-class,

Digging back into my files, I find a notation in the *Journal of the American Medical Association.* (August 1959), in which a doctor replies to a similar question, submitted by a female patient: "...Even assuming an ejaculation of 10 c.c. of semen were all fat, this would be only 90 calories. It is extremely doubtful that this would have a significant effect on inability to take off weight unless, of course, it was practiced several times a day...." So, I would say that unless you are making a complete pig of yourself, it's not the cum that's doing it. Even if it is, you could always jog around the truck stop a couple of times between loads.

No sooner do we get one fatty taken care of, when here comes another:

Dear Larry,
   Slightly different problem here. You know that "lipo-suction" that is going on? Well, I've seen a guy get rid of about twenty pounds—I don't know how many inches. Now the guy is hot, about forty-five, able to fill a mean pair of 501s, in every sense of the word. There is a gay dude doing this "liposuck" in private. If you could turn me on to him, I'd be eternally grateful.
                         Slightly Overweight, Hollywood, CA

Dear Slightly,
   My first random response: Why the hell didn't you ask the guy who lost the 20 lbs? Okay, so you're bashful. I have been aware of this procedure for some time, although I understand that most medical authorities do not approve of its being used to remove large amounts of fat. The technique was originally devel-oped to remove small fatty deposits from the face as a part of cosmetic surgery. (For those who don't know what we're talk-ing about: this is the technique of inserting a needle into a deposit of fat, then suctioning it out.) I have heard about a couple of doctors who do the type of thing you want done, but I don't know how to contact them. Neither do I know how expensive or how ethical they are. I'm sure someone will write and tell me, and I'll pass it on. In the meantime, I strongly advise against a nonmedical person being allowed to slurp your fat. (Doesn't that have a wonderfully kinky sound to it!)
   Of course, since I answered this letter in 1986, liposuction has

become a rather common procedure, although many doctors still recommend against it. I guess you have to be in good physical shape to get through it—not for the weak of heart, etc. It leaves you swollen and in considerable pain for a couple of weeks afterward. Then, you may have folds of loose skin to get rid of. And finally, you'd better stop overeating because the fat will not build up again in the areas where you had it removed. Instead, you may grow enormous hips, tits, or God-knows-what-else. (No, unlikely down there, where you'd like it.)

Dear Larry,

You have written quite a bit, from time to time, about the use of music as an essential background during an SM scene, and you seem to prefer classical to pop. However, have you ever considered the value of silence? To me, there is something much more "mood setting"—maybe even eerie—to a completely quiet room, except for the sounds made by the participants. I'd be interested in your comments.

A Topman, Houston, TX

Dear Top,

As I've also indicated many times, the choice of particulars is completely up to the individual(s). I did not do a great piece on silence because there really isn't much to say about it. It is also difficult for most of us, in this busy, noisy world we live in, to find a place that is completely quiet. However, if that's your preference, and you are able to achieve it, more power to you. My comments on music were merely an attempt to express my own feelings and preferences—based on reactions by my partners and myself in the course of many encounters. I recall one visit to another guy's dungeon, where I entered to find the bottom hooded and secured in a great void of sound. It was effective.

And looking back on several more scenes since answering this guy, I am even more impressed by the fact that there can be a certain eeriness to a truly silent room. However, it almost requires that the place be soundproofed to achieve this condition. As I noted above, our world is really a noisy place. (I discovered this most pointedly

when I tried to make some audiotapes of my books. Every time I
started to read, a car went by outside, or something else disturbed
the silence. Of course, the fact that my friend collects clocks didn't
help.)

Dear Larry,
I'm a real fan of yours, and I also read a lot of other
male-to-male erotica. I find the written material much more
interesting than pictures. But I find a number of writers like
to describe a guy getting fucked, ending up with something
like: "He could feel the hot rush of cum shooting into his
bowels." In the first place, I don't think the word "bowel"
is very sexy; and secondly, I know damned well you can't feel
the cum shooting into you. I've never read anything of
yours where you say this, so I think I'm safe in asking you
to comment on it.

J. B., Chicago, IL

Dear J. B.,
Obviously, those other writers never got fucked with anything
less than a fire hose.

Dear Larry,
I read somewhere that you are against sex with animals,
I'd like to know why. Is it for health reasons, or is it ethics?

Chuck, Baltimore

Dear Chuck,
Although Our Heavenly Mother certainly knows that I'm
no moralist, this is one area of sexual behavior toward which I
have very negative feelings. I really can't give you a completely
logical reason for this, because it's a matter of personal prejudice. (The nice thing about prejudice, of course, is that it doesn't
require a rational basis.) I really love animals. At the moment I
have two Doberpersons and a Siamese cat. But to have sex with
any of them would be (to me) on a par with molesting a child.
I simply couldn't do it. Nor do I like to think of other people
doing it with their animals. I know they do, and they enjoy it—

and the animals apparently enjoy it. I don't think here is any particular health problem, nor do I find it "disgusting" in the sense of being appalled by raunch or slime. So I guess I'd have to answer your question by saying that for me it is a matter of ethics.

As you may note, this is the third letter I've answered on this subject, that I included here. My attitude has generated a lot of controversy over the years, ever since I mentioned my attitudes in the Original Leatherman's Handbook. *We all have our own boundaries of behavior; this happens to be one of mine.*

Dear Larry,

I remember reading someplace, some time ago, that you were an opera buff, in addition to your involvements in SM. I thought that was a funny combination of interests, but I just came back from a trip to Germany and Holland, and half (or more) of the guys I met there in SM circles were opera fanatics. Can you explain this? Is there some common ground between the two that I just haven't been able to perceive?

L. R., NYC

Dear L. R.,

No, I guess it just reflects the fact that having good taste in one area will often mean one has good taste in another. Or should I say "exquisite taste"?

Dear Larry,

I know that you, as most everyone else at *Drummer*, is very gone on leather—the way it looks and smells, etc. But I honestly can't tell the difference between leather and a good piece of vinyl imitation. In fact, I've seen a couple of my leather friends go through quite a bit of feeling and sniffing over a good imitation before they were sure of what it was. Can you honestly tell me that you can tell the difference at first glance, so if someone walks in with a black jacket that might be one or the other you really know?

Barry, London, England

Dear Barry,

In the dark, all cats are gray (or in England, I guess it's "grey"). No, I have to admit there have been times when I've been fooled. But I'd know in a hurry if I were the one wearing it. You can't fake the feel—and certainly not the smell—when it's on your own body. And I don't really care what someone else might enjoy wearing, unless I'm called upon to make love to it. If you can afford it, take the real thing. If you can't—well, we can always make do if we have to.

The love of leather is such an all-pervasive element in our lifestyle that it is hard to imagine not having it. But I have to acknowledge that not all the Drummer *people were into leather, per se. Some were simply into SM or some specific kink that didn't involve skins. I have also found that a number of my English friends and acquaintances tend to play some wonderful SM games, but most of them don't seem to care much about its being done in leather. Again, a matter of taste, I guess.*

Dear Larry,

This isn't really a gay or sex-related question, but having read your books and articles I know you own Dobermans and must know a lot about them. My friend and I live in an apartment (we own the building) and have decided we need a dog for security reasons, as well as wanting to have a pet. We both love the elegant appearance of a Doberman, but are concerned that if we get one that will scare off the burglars he might do the same to our friends. And vice versa, if he's friendly, he won't do the guard-dog number. Also, is it fair to keep a big dog like that in an apartment? Are they destructive? Could we trust him not to tear the place apart?

Bert, New Orleans, LA

Dear Bert,

I am naturally very prejudiced in favor of the Doberperson. If you get one from a reputable breeder, and bring him up with a lot of affection, you'll have a wonderfully friendly pet. Most burglars will simply pass on a home with a Dobie; just his presence is enough to discourage them. He doesn't need to be a real guard dog, although this seems to come naturally to a Dober-person. If you have a place to take him out for a run, or even a good long walk several times a week, he'll do fine in an apartment. Of course, any puppy is going to chew; but once he's six months old, or so, you should have been able to convince him not to tear things up. I leave mine alone with the complete run of the house when I'm out, and the worst thing they do is to pull trash out of the wastebaskets. But pay the price for a good puppy; show lines are bred for disposition as well as appearance. The $100 pups advertised in the throwaway papers might or might not be from good lines. Try to see both parents, if you can, and evaluate their dispositions.

Dear Larry,

I have been reading your novels and stories for years, and think I have a nearly complete collection. I note that you have written on a number of historical characters, including kings and emperors. I just wanted to ask if you had a list of gay kings, emperors, etc. Or do you know where someone might obtain such a list? I'd particularly like one that listed SM types.

R. W., Montreal, Canada

Dear R. W.,

I do not have a list which I have personally compiled, nor do I know of one which can be considered complete. There is also the problem of one guy putting a name on the list which he thinks belongs there, only to have it disputed by another person of equally substantial credentials. You also have the problem of bisexuals—to count them or not. For instance, Gibbon noted that of the first six emperors of Rome, only Claudius was completely normal (sic) in his sexual practices. This would imply, for instance, that Augustus was not completely heterosexual. He probably wasn't, but I wouldn't classify him as gay, either. Anyway, if someone out there has a list I'd love to see it, and if someone sends me one I'll Xerox it and send it along to you.

This has always been a popular sport with us amateur histori-

ans. There actually have been a couple of books published in recent years dealing with this subject, but I have not found any of them attempting to give a comprehensive list. Neither have the authors solved the problem I mentioned in my original answer: How do you classify the bisexuals? Then, trying to list SM types creates another nightmare of confusion. Ivan the Terrible, for instance—a man whom I have studied extensively—was certainly one of the greatest torturers in history. He had six, possibly seven wives. (Historians aren't sure.) But from my own studies, and reading between the lines of writers who would have committed hara-kiri rather than speculate on the tsar's homosexuality, I'm convinced that he—and a good part of his court in the latter part of his reign—were so ambisexual that they defied categorization. They fucked anything on two legs (and possibly on four), and you can't tell me that all that dungeon action was going on without some of the Tops playing bottom from time to time. The trouble was that most of their dungeon activity was very serious, generally ending in the death of the subject. It also took place when the torturers were very drunk. Playing bottom with this crowd was more dangerous than picking up a spaced-out street hustler today. But it's still fun to speculate. When I get my book on Ivan published, you'll see that I mean.

Dear Larry,

As a "late bloomer" in your garden of SM'ers, I only recently read your *Leathermans' Handbook*s (both volumes). Realizing that *HBII* was written five or six years ago, I can't help but wonder what has happened to your little character, Penishead? Is he still alive, or has he succumbed to his vices, and been carried off like Don Giovanni?

A Fan, Philadelphia PA

Dear Fan,

I have to confess that Penishead was actually a composite of two different people. Both are still alive. The one who was 75 percent of the Penishead character is on the verge of being put away for dealing drugs, and has never altered his behavior. How he has remained healthy is a mystery to me, and to everyone else except him. (And he's too stupid to slow down long enough to think about it.) It's too bad there is no way for medical science to study this type of individual, because bodies such as his must contain the answer to immuno-longevity.

Well, we've had another six years since I answered this one, and Penishead Major has gone to his great gang bang in the sky. But he lasted a lo-o-o-ong time! All of his friends—the guys with whom he shared needles, douche tubes, and tricks—all predeceased him by several years. I talked to him shortly after he had (finally) gone in for an HIV test, and had turned up positive. I felt sorry for him because he was genuinely terrified and alone. But there was no helping him. I saw him in an after-hours spot a few weeks later, and he was busy lining up his FF companion for the night. He lasted a couple more years, then suddenly was very sick, and gone. Penishead Minor, surprisingly, is still alive and HIV negative—mostly, because he has so many other things wrong with him that he is constantly at doctors' offices, and they have apparently scared him into a new mode of behavior.

Dear Larry,

I am on your mailing list as well as being a subscriber to *Drummer*. I note that both of you are using computers to manage your lists, so I thought you might be able to advise me on a couple of points. I am in the market for a computer, and I'm especially interested in being able to communicate with other leather-oriented men through one of the "bulletin board" services. I'm a little hesitant to ask the salesmen about these, for obvious reasons, but I want to be sure I get a machine (with modem) capable of accessing the ones that cater to our tastes. Any suggestions on brand of computer, modem? Can I expect to make interesting contacts?

Technical novice, San Antonio, TX

Dear Novice,

You can access the bulletin boards with almost any computer/modem, because they automatically translate the signal into a universal machine language. My experience is limited with the bulletin boards, simply because I'm not interested in them. Nor am I inclined to play much with the computer. I want it to do its work, and beyond that I have other things that interest me more. I'd say that your choice of computer should be based on your pocketbook, plus consideration for the other things you want it to do (graphics, desktop printing, word processing, records management, etc.) I would recommend a Hayes modem, however.

Interesting, I'd say about the same thing today. I do know that the bulletin boards have expanded greatly, however, and with the prospect of interactive CD-ROM just around the corner, they should be even more fun. I still don't play much with the computer, except that I've recently beaten my 486 in a couple of chess games, and that's encouraging. (Of course, on the easy setting! You think I'm a nerd?)

Dear Larry,

In some of your past columns, you have discussed questions dealing with Nazis, and with the sexual fascination that old uniforms have for many SM guys. I have also been very interested in this phenomenon, and I guess you might say that my greatest hobby is the study of World War II. Hitler, himself, is probably the most interesting enigma of the whole, particularly his sexuality. The few women who have been identified as his sexual partners were all rather immature emotionally. And then, he seemed to have a penchant for the godlike tall, handsome, blond Aryan type of man. Closet case?

Lance, Miami, FL

Dear Lance,

I have thought about this as I read various accounts of Hitler and his time. It's apparent that you are right about his women being immature. Eva Braun was certainly no challenge to his authority; nor was his niece, Geli Rabaul, who died under such mysterious circumstances. One of his greatest early supporters was Ernst Roehm, a "notorious homosexual" whom Hitler eventually destroyed. It's a puzzle that will probably never be solved. In some ways it reminds me of the writings of Casanova, who is reputed to be one of the greatest heterosexuals of all time. Yet, reading his memoirs, he is often at greater pains to describe the handsome male guards or attendants than the lady, herself. It really does make one wonder.

Dear Larry,
With everyone now urging the use of condoms (except the Pope and few other conservatives), it has made some of us curious about where these dreadful little sheaths were first made. Do you know?
Peter, NYC

Dear Peter,
I don't think anyone knows for sure. There appears to be some reference to them in artifacts from ancient Egypt, but if so their use apparently did not continue into subsequent ancient civilizations (Greece, Rome, etc.). They were apparently in use in England during the reign of Charles II (Charles the Voluptuous)—made from animal gut. They were also used in France at about the same time, and no one knows who came first. The theory that they were invented by a "Dr. Condom," after whom they may have been named, also seems to hold no water, since there is no archive record of such a man ever having lived. Bear in mind, however, that the only rubbers we should be using are made of latex, and these were not produced until the 1930s.

Dear Larry,
As a fellow writer, maybe you can help me. I have written a very hot, gay SM novel that I want to submit for publication. I have a couple of ideas as to where to send it, but I don't know how to protect myself from being ripped off. I think my ideas are just different enough that someone might steal them. How can I prove that the manuscript is mine if a dispute comes up at a later date?
David, Albuquerque, NM

Dear David,
Living where you do, I doubt there is a local branch of any major writers' guild. If there is, most of them offer a registra-

tion service, whereby they will take your ms., wrapped and sealed, and lock it in their vault—usually for a period of three years on payment of a single (usually nominal) fee. Failing this, you can follow the old standard of sealing up a copy of your ms and mailing it to yourself as registered mail. Keep it sealed up in a safe place, and you have a dated record of ownership.

Dear Larry,

Have you ever heard of a group (religious, I think) called the *Penitentes*? If so, can you tell me something about them? Also, I recently read that Ramon Navarro, the famous silent movie star, was supposed to have been associated with them. But he was an actor, not a religious type, and gay—no?

P. R., New Orleans, LA

Dear P. R.,

The *Penitentes* are a secret Catholic religious group—not really an "order," as such. A couple of hundred years ago, they had monastic settlements in several places throughout northern Mexico and New Mexico. I know they still have a place on the Rio Puerco, near Albuquerque, but I'm not sure what others remain. There have been many stories told about them, since their beliefs led them to "mortification of the flesh" as an act of spiritual purification. The modern day practitioners deny much of this, and it is difficult to know just how much was true. Ramon Navarro may well have been associated with them, since he came from a part of Mexico where they were (then) functioning. After his murder (by a male hustler), I was contacted by an investigator who was unable to identify some of the articles found in his bedroom (the murder scene). I know that some of these were items reportedly used by *Penitentes* to cause the wearer discomfort (much as ascetics in the Middle Ages would commonly wear shirts woven of horsehair.)

Dear Mr. Townsend,

I don't know if you will want to answer this in your column, but I hope that you will be kind enough to drop me a note if not. I am a twenty-four-year-old woman, and I have

a fairly long-standing (year and a half) relationship with my boyfriend. We have engaged in some light bondage and spanking, always with him as the submissive, so I know that he has some interest in what I guess you guys call SM, but it never dawned on me that he might be gay or bisexual, until I came across a stack of *Drummers* and other magazines in his apartment. I asked him about it, and he admitted that he was "bi," but swore that he wasn't playing around with anyone else, man or woman. I guess I believe him, but it still leaves me with two questions:

1. Am I apt to be have been exposed to AIDS?

2. Is it possible for a man to have an active interest in other men, but to maintain a monogamous relationship with a woman? We have discussed marriage, and that is a possibility. But I don't want it to end up in a divorce court, with me naming a man as correspondent. What are the odds?

Name and area withheld

Dear Ms.,

To answer your first question: exposure to the AIDS virus can happen in almost any sexual situation these days. If you're worried about it, then for your own peace of mind, you should get tested. It can be done anonymously and cheaply. As to your second question, this is much more difficult to answer. Of course, any human being is capable of a monogamous relationship if he really wants it and really loves his partner. You have to be the judge of this and make your own decision. Do you think his affection for you is strong enough to overcome his interest in other guys—other women, for that matter? It's a question you will never be able to answer "for sure," but I don't think that his interest in other men is as much the source of concern as his ability, or desire, to remain faithful to you. After all, many marriages fail because of extramarital heterosexual involvements. It isn't his sexual orientation you have to worry about, as much as his overall maturity and the depth of his feelings for you.

Dear Larry,

I have seen several TV shows which dealt with the subject of rape, always men doing it to women, of course. But there have been passing references to "male rape" in a couple of the statistical rundowns they gave at the end of the shows, and these have made me wonder. I know guys get raped in prison, but there seems to be an implication that this happens on the "outside" as well. But I've never seen any newspaper accounts of it, like they report women getting raped. Do you think it happens very often to men?

Hopeful, Cincinnati, OH

Dear Hopeful,

It probably happens more often than you suspect, although I think it is more likely to be "date rape;" i.e., one guy strong-arming his companion of the evening to do something the other doesn't want to do. As for forcible "break-in" rape or grabbing some guy off the street and making him do the deed, I would think it is fairly rare. Remember, the heterosexuals outnumber us about nine to one. Even though we read about numerous females getting raped, the experts maintain that by far the majority of these cases go unreported. I would expect that a male victim would be even less inclined to come forward, regardless of the circumstances (i.e., date rape or otherwise). There really are no reliable statistics to provide an answer, but you can always dream.

As I did when I wrote Masters' Counterpoints, *my 1993 novel about male rape of Hollywood's most handsome.*

Dear Larry,

My greatest joy in life has been to get fucked, and I mean I really love it! I'm now in my early forties, so I haven't been getting it up the ass like I used to, especially since all the health warnings began to be circulated. Recently, I have started to develop hemorrhoids, and this leads me to ask two questions: Could all the fucking in my younger years have caused the problem? If I go to a doctor, can he tell that I've been heavily fucked? I'm a career naval officer, so I'm naturally concerned, especially about the latter.

Skip, Alexandria, VA

Dear Skip,

My medical adviser tells me that hemorrhoids are such a common ailment, and can be triggered by such a variety of causes—including hereditary factors—it's impossible to tell how yours might have started. Ass fucking is not generally perceived as being causal. You are more likely to bring it on by sitting at a desk for long hours, day after day. Likewise, the tightness of one's sphincter (the only clue a doctor is going to have re: your former anal activities) tends to vary so greatly from one individual to another that it isn't going to provide any reliable evidence or past indiscretions. I wouldn't worry about it.

Dear Larry,

I read *Drummer* and a lot of other gay publications that carry fiction and your type of "Dear Abby" columns, and it seems to me that a lot of what you write about, particularly in your fictional stories, is unconscionable in view of the present health crisis. How can you even suggest that someone go out and have sex when it might mean they end up with AIDS. It sure scares the shit out of me to think about it.

A. R., Houston, TX

Dear A. R.,

Don't think for a moment that these considerations have not crossed my mind, as they surely have those of every other responsible person in the gay writing/publishing field. And there certainly is a division of opinion. Some, like you, feel that only safe-sex stories should be published or put on film.

Maybe you're right, but I see it a little differently. Although we know that there are certain forms of sexual behavior in which we must not engage, the fantasies are still present. Reading about them, or seeing them enacted in a video (where the action may or may not be only simulated), permits a guy to enjoy a vicarious experience that is otherwise denied him. I don't see this as basically different from the stay-at-home who enjoys reading stories of high adventure. I enjoy a good Ludlum-type thriller from time to time, but this doesn't mean I'm going to go out and start mowing people down with an Uzi. Neither are Agatha Christie fans any more likely to poison the local vicar after reading one of her mysteries. Reading fiction is most often done as an escape from the humdrum of our daily lives. Why should stories of sexual adventure be any different? As to us "Dear Abby" types, I don't think that any of us advocate unsafe-sex practices, either from the standpoint of AIDS dangers or any other. Within my own particular genre, it is even less apt to promote health risks. Bondage, whipping, and most of the other more common SM activities do not involve an exchange of body fluids. In this sense, they are the safest form of quasi-sexual behavior.

And that really puts the cap on my thoughts. However far I may have led my readers astray from the pure and holy thoughts our detractors would have us promote, I have done my best to guide my listeners into areas where they can enjoy whatever it is they are trying to find, but to do it in a way that does not injure them either physically or emotionally. If I have succeeded in alleviating even a modicum of the guilt that has been laid upon us, then I have achieved my goal.

So I say to you, my children: Go now, and sin some more!

ORDERING IS EASY!

MC/VISA orders can be placed by calling our toll-free number

PHONE 800-458-9640 / FAX 212 986-7355

or mail the coupon below to:

MASQUERADE BOOKS

DEPT. Z54A **801 2ND AVE., NY, NY 10017**

QTY.	TITLE	NO.	PRICE

Z54A

	SUBTOTAL	
POSTAGE and HANDLING	
TOTAL	

We Never Sell, Give or Trade Any Customer's Name.

Add $1 Postage and Handling for first book and 50¢ for each additional book. Outside the U.S. add $2 for first book, $1 for each additional book. New York State residents add 8.25% sales tax. No C.O.D. Orders. Please Make all Checks Payable MASQUERADE BOOKS. Payable in U. S. Currency Only.

NAME_____

ADDRESS_____

CITY_____ STATE_____ ZIP_____

TEL ( )_____

PAYMENT: ☐CHECK ☐MONEY ORDER ☐VISA ☐MC

CARD NO._____ EXP. DATE _____

THE EROTIC COMEDIES

A collection of stories from America's premier erotic philosopher. Marco Vassi was a dedicated iconoclast, and *The Erotic Comedies* marked a high point in his literary career. Scathing and humorous, these stories reflect Vassi's belief in the power and primacy of Eros in American life, as well as his commitment to the elimination of personal repression through carnal indulgence. A wry collection for the sexually adventurous.

136-5

THE SALINE SOLUTION

During the Sexual Revolution, Marco Vassi established himself as an intrepid explorer of an uncharted sexual landscape. During this time he also distinguished himself as a novelist, producing *The Saline Solution* to great acclaim. With the story of one couple's brief affair and the events that lead them to desperately reassess their lives, Vassi examines the dangers of intimacy in an age of extraordinary freedom. A remarkably clear-eyed look at the growing pains of a generation.

180-2

PAT CALIFIA

SENSUOUS MAGIC

Sensuous Magic is clear, succinct and engaging even for the reader for whom S/M isn't the sexual behavior of choice.... Califia's prose is soothing, informative and non-judgmental—she both instructs her reader and explores the territory for them.... When she is writing about the dynamics of sex and the technical aspects of it, Califia is the Dr. Ruth of the alternative sexuality set....
—Lambda Book Report

Don't take a dangerous trip into the unknown—buy this book and know where you're going!
—SKIN TWO

Finally, a "how to" sex manual that doesn't involve new age mumbo jumbo or "tricks" that require the agility of a Flying Wallenda.... Califia's strength as a writer lies in her ability to relay information without sounding condescending. If you don't understand a word or concept... chances are it's defined in the handy dictionary in the back....
—Future Sex

Renowned erotic pioneer Pat Califia provides this honest, unpretentious peek behind the mask of dominant/submissive sexuality—an adventurous adult world of pleasure too often obscured by ignorance and fear. Califia demystifies "the scene" for the novice, explaining the terminology and technique behind many misunderstood sexual practices The adventurous (or just plain curious) lover won't want to miss this ultimate "how to" volume.

131-4

CHEA VILLANUEVA

JESSIE'S SONG

"It conjures up the strobe-light confusion and excitement of urban dyke life, moving fast and all over the place, from NYC to Tucson to Miami to the Philippines; and from true love to wild orgies to swearing eternal celibacy and back. Told in letters, mainly about the wandering heart (and tongue) of writer and free spirit Pearly Does; written mainly by Mae-Mae Might, a sharp, down-to-earth but innocent-hearted Black Femme. Read about these dykes and you'll love them."
—Rebecca Ripley

A rich collection of lesbian writing from this uncompromising author. Based largely upon her own experience, Villanueva's work is remarkable for its frankness, and delightful in its iconoclasm. Widely published in the alternative press, Villanueva is a writer to watch. Toeing no line, Chea Villanueva's *Jessie's Song* is certain to redefine all notions of "mainstream" lesbian writing, and provide a reading experience quite unlike any other this year.

235-3

MICHAEL PERKINS

THE GOOD PARTS: An Uncensored Guide to Literary Sexuality

Michael Perkins, one of America's only serious critics to regularly scrutinize sexual literature, presents an overview of sex a seen in the pages of over 100 major volumes from the past twenty years.

I decided when I wrote my first column in 1968 that I would take the opportunity presented by Screw to chronicle the inevitable and inexorable rise of an unfairly neglected genre of contemporary writing. I wondered if I would remain interested in the subject for very long, and if the field would not eventually diminish so there would be nothing to review.... Every week since then I have published a thousand-word review, and occasionally a longer essay, devoted to discovering and reporting on the manifestations of sexuality in all kinds of fiction, nonfiction, and poetry. In my columns I cast a wide net (a million words so far) over a subject no one else wanted to take a long look at. It has indeed held my interest. 186-1

LARS EIGHNER

THE ELEMENTS OF AROUSAL

Critically acclaimed gay writer Lars Eighner—whose *Travels with Lizbeth* was chosen by the *New York Times Book Review* as one of the year's notable titles—develops a guideline for success with one of publishing's best kept secrets: the novice-friendly field of gay erotic writing.

In *The Elements of Arousal*, Eighner details his craft, providing the reader with sure advice. Eighner's overview of the gay erotic market paints a picture of a diverse array of outlets for a writer's work. Because, after all, writing is what *The Elements of Arousal* is about: the application and honing of the writer's craft, which brought Lars Eighner fame with not only the steamy *Bayou Boy*, but the profoundly illuminating *Travels with Lizbeth*. 230-2

MARCO VASSI

THE STONED APOCALYPSE

" *...Marco Vassi is our champion sexual energist.*"—VLS

During his lifetime, Marco Vassi was hailed as America's premier erotic writer and most worthy successor to Henry Miller. His work was praised by writers as diverse as Gore Vidal and Norman Mailer, and his reputation was worldwide. *The Stoned Apocalypse* is Vassi's autobiography, financed by the other groundbreaking erotic writing that made him a cult sensation. Chronicling a cross-country trip on America's erotic byways, it offers a rare glimpse of a generation's sexual imagination. 132-2

A DRIVING PASSION

"*Let me leave you with A Driving Passion. It is, in effect, an introduction and overview of all his other books, and my hope is that it will lead readers to explore the bold literary contribution of Marco Vassi.*"
—Norman Mailer

While the late Marco Vassi was primarily known and respected as a novelist, he was also an effective and compelling speaker. *A Driving Passion* collects the wit and insight Vassi brought to his infamously revealing lectures, and distills the philosophy—including the concept of Metasex—that made him an underground sensation. An essential volume. 134-9

GAUNTLET

THE BEST OF *GAUNTLET* Edited by Barry Hoffman

No material, no opinion is taboo enough to violate Gauntlet's *purpose of 'exploring the limits of free expression'—airing all views in the name of the First Amendment.*—Associated Press

Dedicated to "exploring the limits of free expression," *Gauntlet* has, with its semi-annual issues, taken on such explosive topics as race, pornography, political correctness, and media manipulation—always publishing the widest possible range of opinions. Only in *Gauntlet* might one expect to encounter Phyllis Schlafley *and* Annie Sprinkle, Stephen King *and* Madonna—often within pages of one another. The very best, most provocative articles have been gathered by editor-in-chief Barry Hoffman, to make *The Best of Gauntlet* a most provocative exploration of American society's limits. *202-7*

JOHN PRESTON

MY LIFE AS A PORNOGRAPHER
AND OTHER INDECENT ACTS

The erotic nonfiction of John Preston. Includes the title essay, given as the John Pearson Perry Lecture at Harvard University, and the legendary "Good-Bye to Sally Gearhart," and many other provocative writings.

...essential and enlightening...His sex-positive stand on safer-sex education as the only truly effective AIDS-prevention strategy will certainly not win him any conservative converts, but AIDS activists will be shouting their assent.... [My Life as a Pornographer] is a bridge from the sexually liberated 1970s to the more cautious 1990s, and Preston has walked much of that way as a standard-bearer to the cause for equal rights.... —Library Journal

Preston's a model essayist; he writes pellucid prose in a voice that, like Samuel Johnson's, combines authority with entertainment.... My Life as a Pornographer *...is not pornography, but rather reflections upon the writing and production of it. Preston ranges from really superb journalism of his interviews with denizens of the S/M demi-mond, particularly a superb portrait of a Colt model Preston calls "Joe" to a brilliant analysis of the "theater" of the New York sex club, The Mineshaft.... In a deeply sex-phobic world, Preston has never shied away from a vision of the redemptive potential of the erotic drive. Better than perhaps anyone in our community, Preston knows how physical joy can bridge differences and make us well.*

—Lambda Book Report *135-7*

HUSTLING:
A GENTLEMAN'S GUIDE TO THE FINE ART OF HOMOSEXUAL PROSTITUTION

John Preston solicited the advice of "working boys" from across the country in his effort to produce the ultimate guide to the hustler's world. *Hustling* covers every practical aspect of the business, from clientele and payment options to "specialties," sidelines and drawbacks. No stone is left unturned in this guidebook to the ins and outs of this much-mythologized trade. *137-3*

SKIN TWO

THE BEST OF *SKIN TWO*   Edited by Tim Woodward

For over a decade, *Skin Two* has served as the bible of the international fetish community. A groundbreaking journal from the crossroads of sexuality, fashion, and art, *Skin Two* specializes in provocative, challenging essays by the finest writers working in the "radical sex" scene. Collected here, for the first time, are the articles and interviews that have established the magazine's singular reputation. Including interviews with cult figures Tim Burton, Clive Barker and Jean Paul Gaultier. *130-6*

ROBERT PATRICK
TEMPLE SLAVE

...you must read this book. It draws such a tragic, and, in a way, noble portrait of Mr. Buono: It leads the reader, almost against his will, into a deep sympathy with this strange man who tried to comfort, to encourage and to feed both the worthy and the worthless... It is impossible not to mourn for this man—impossible not to praise this book

—Quentin Crisp

This is nothing less than the secret history of the most theatrical of theaters, the most bohemian of Americans and the most knowing of queens. Patrick writes with a lush and witty abandon, as if this departure from the crafting of plays has energized him. Temple Slave is also one of the best ways to learn what it was like to be fabulous, gay, theatrical and loved in a time at once more and less dangerous to gay life than our own.

—Genre

Temple Slave tells the story of the Espresso Buono—the archetypal alternative performance space—and the wildly talented misfits who called it home in the early 60s. The Buono became the birthplace of a new underground theater—and the personal and social consciousness that would lead to Stonewall and the modern gay and lesbian movement. *Temple Slave* is a kaleidoscopic page from gay history—a riotous tour de force peppered with the verbal fireworks and shrewd insight that are the hallmark of Robert Patrick's work. **191-8**

LUCY TAYLOR
UNNATURAL ACTS
"A topnotch collection..." —Science Fiction Chronicle
The remarkable debut of a provocative writer. *Unnatural Acts* plunges into the dark side of the psyche, past all pleasantries and prohibitions, and brings to life a disturbing vision of erotic horror. Unrelenting angels and hungry gods play with souls and bodies in Taylor's cosmos: where heaven and hell are merely differences of perspective; where redemption and damnation lie behind the same shocking acts. **181-0**

DAVID MELTZER
THE AGENCY TRILOGY
With the Essex House edition of *The Agency* in 1968, the highly regarded poet David Meltzer took America on a trip into a hell of unbridled sexuality. The story of a supersecret, Orwellian sexual network, *The Agency* explored issues of erotic dominance and submission with an immediacy and frankness previously unheard of in American literature, as well as presented a vision of an America consumed and dehumanized by a lust for power. This landmark novel was followed by *The Agent*, and *How Many Blocks in the Pile?*—taken with *The Agency*, they confirm Meltzer's position as one of America's early masters of the erotic genre. **216-7**

BIZARRE SEX
BIZARRE SEX AND OTHER CRIMES OF PASSION
Edited by Stan Tal
Stan Tal, editor of *Bizarre Sex*, Canada's boldest fiction publication, has culled the very best stories that have crossed his desk—and now unleashes them on the reading public in *Bizarre Sex and Other Crimes of Passion*. Over twenty small masterpieces of erotic shock make this one of the year's most unexpectedly alluring anthologies. Including such masters of erotic horror and fantasy as Edward Lee, Lucy Taylor, Nancy Kilpatrick and Caro Soles, *Bizarre Sex and Other Crimes of Passion*, is a treasure-trove of arousing chills. **213-2**

SAMUEL R. DELANY
THE MAD MAN

For his thesis, graduate student John Marr researches the life and work of the brilliant Timothy Hasler: a philosopher whose career was cut tragically short over a decade earlier. Marr encounters numerous obstacles, as other researchers turn up evidence of Hasler's personal life that is deemed simply too unpleasant. On another front, Marr finds himself increasingly drawn toward more shocking, depraved sexual entanglements with the homeless men of his neighborhood, until it begins to seem that Hasler's death might hold some key to his own life as a gay man in the age of AIDS.

This new novel by Samuel R. Delany not only expands the parameters of what he has given us in the past, but fuses together two seemingly disparate genres of writing and comes up with something which is not comparable to any existing text of which I am aware.... What Delany has done here is take the ideas of Marquis de Sade one step further, by filtering extreme and obsessive sexual behavior through the sieve of post-modern experience....

—*Lambda Book Report*

The latest novel from Hugo- and Nebula-winning science fiction writer and critic Delany... reads like a pornographic reflection of Peter Ackroyd's Chatterton *or A.S. Byatt's* Possession.... *The pornographic element... becomes more than simple shock or titillation, though, as Delany develops an insightful dichotomy between [his protagonist]'s two worlds: the one of cerebral philosophy and dry academia, the other of heedless, 'impersonal' obsessive sexual extremism. When these worlds finally collide ... the novel achieves a surprisingly satisfying resolution....*

—*Publishers Weekly*
hardcover 193-4/$23.95

THE MOTION OF LIGHT IN WATER

"*A very moving, intensely fascinating literary biography from an extraordinary writer. Thoroughly admirable candor and luminous stylistic precision; the artist as a young man and a memorable picture of an age.*"
—William Gibson

"*A remarkably candid and revealing...study of an extraordinary and extraordinarily appealing human being, and a fascinating...account of the early days of a significant science fiction writer's career.*"
—Robert Silverberg

The first unexpurgated American edition of award-winning author Samuel R. Delany's riveting autobiography covers the early years of one of science fiction's most important voices. Beginning with his marriage to the young, remarkably gifted poet Marilyn Hacker, Delany paints a vivid and compelling picture of New York's East Village in the early '60s—a time of unprecedented social change and transformation. Startling and revealing, *The Motion of Light in Water* traces the roots of one of America's most innovative writers.
133-0

CARO SOLES
MELTDOWN!

An Anthology of Erotic Science Fiction and Dark Fantasy for Gay Men
Editor Caro Soles has put together one of the most explosive, mind-bending collections of gay erotic writing ever published. *Meltdown!* contains the very best examples of this increasingly popular sub-genre: stories meant to shock and delight, to send a shiver down the spine and start a fire down below. An extraordinary volume, *Meltdown!* presents both new voices and provocative pieces by world-famous writers Edmund White and Samuel R. Delany.
203-5

GUILLERMO BOSCH
RAIN

"*The intensely sensual descriptions of color and light, the passionate characters, the sensitive experiences of love and pain depicted in* Rain *moved me a great deal.* Rain *is really a trip...*"
—Dr. Timothy Leary

"Rain *definitely pays homage to the European tradition of an erotic literature which stimulates intellectual and moral questioning of social, economic and political institutions.* Rain *is an important book.*"   —Robert Sam Anson, author of *Best Intentions*

"Rain *is a vivid novel that transcends its genre. Only Guillermo Bosch could blend the political and erotic with such ease.*"
—David Freeman, author of *A Hollywood Education*

"*This book will sear the flesh off your fingers.*"—Peter Lefcourt, author of *Di and I*

"*It was Bosch's poetic language which first attracted me to* Rain, *but his unprejudiced mixing of ethnicity, different sexual persuasions and diverse personalities is unique and most refreshing.*"   —Meri Nana-Ana Danquah

An adult fairy tale, *Rain* takes place in a time when the mysteries of Eros are played out against a background of uncommon deprivation. The tale begins on the 1,537th day of drought—when one man comes to know the true depths of thirst. In a quest to sate his hunger for some knowledge of the wide world, he is taken through a series of extraordinary, unearthly encounters that promise to change not only his life, but the course of civilization around him.   232-9

MICHAEL LASSELL
THE HARD WAY

"*Michael Lassell's poems are worldly in the best way, defining the arc of a world of gay life in our own decade of mounting horror and oppression. With an effortless feel for dark laughter he roams the city, a startling combination of boulevardier and hooker.... Lassell is a master of the necessary word. In an age of tepid and whining verse, his bawdy and bittersweet songs are like a plunge in cold champagne.*"

—Paul Monette

Virtually all of the material in this book was written and published between 1983 and 1993, although it covers all the years I can remember. The focus, of course, is on the post-Stonewall Liberation Years.... I am, like most writers, horrified to read work written as recently as ten days ago, much less ten years ago, but I have bitten the bullet and made few changes, except when some reference is so out of cultural currency as to obscure my own obscure point, or when I can't remember what the hell I meant by something. But what you see here, is pretty much the way it was the first time it appeared in black and white....

—from the Introduction

The first collection of renowned gay writer Michael Lassell's poetry, fiction and essays. Widely anthologized and a staple of gay literary and entertainment publications nationwide, Lassell is regarded as one of the most distinctive and accomplished talents of his generation. As much a chronicle of post-Stonewall gay life as a compendium of a remarkable writer's work, *The Hard Way* is sure to appeal to anyone interested in the state of contemporary writing.   231-0

LOOKING FOR MR. PRESTON

Edited by Laura Antoniou, *Looking for Mr. Preston* includes work by **Lars Eighner, Pat Califia, Michael Bronski, Felice Picano, Joan Nestle, Larry Townsend, Sasha Alyson, Andrew Holleran, Michael Lowenthal,** and others who contributed interviews, essays and personal reminiscences of John Preston—a man whose career spanned the industry from the early pages of the *Advocate* to various national bestseller lists. Preston was the author of over twenty books, including *Franny, the Queen of Provincetown,* and *Mr. Benson.* He also edited the noted *Flesh and the Word* erotic anthologies, *Personal Dispatches: Writers Confront AIDS,* and *Hometowns,.* More importantly, Preston became a personal inspiration, friend and mentor to many of today's gay and lesbian authors and editors. Ten percent of the proceeds from sale of the book will go to the AIDS Project of Southern Maine, for which Preston had served as President of the Board.　　　$23.95/288-4

THE BEST OF THE BADBOYS

"…What I like best about BADBOY *is the fact that it does not neglect the classics…..* BADBOY *Books has resurrected writings from the Golden Age of gayrotic fiction (1966-1972), before visual media replaced books in the hands and minds of the masses…."*

—Jesse Monteagudo, *The Community Voice*

A collection of the best of Masquerade Books' phenomenally popular BADBOY line of gay erotic writing. BADBOY's sizable roster includes many names that are legendary in gay circles. Their work has contributed significantly to BADBOY's runaway success, establishing the imprint as a home for not only new but classic writing in the genre. The very best of the leading Badboys is collected here, in this testament to the artistry that has catapulted these "outlaw" authors to best-selling status.　　　*233-7*

EDITED BY AMARANTHA KNIGHT

LOVE BITES

Vampire lovers, hookers, groupies and hustlers of all sexual persuasions are waiting to entice you into their sensuous world. But be prepared! By the end of this book, you will have not only succumbed to their dark and sexy charms, but you will also have joined the swelling ranks of humanity which understand on a very personal level that Love Bites　　　—from the Introduction by Amarantha Knight

A volume of tales dedicated to legend's sexiest demon—the Vampire. Amarantha Knight, herself an author who has delved into vampire lore, has gathered the very best writers in the field to produce a collection of uncommon, and chilling, allure.

Including such names as Ron Dee, Nancy A. Collins, Nancy Kilpatrick, Lois Tilton and David Aaron Clark, *Love Bites* is not only the finest collection of erotic horror available—but a virtual who's who of promising new talent.　　　*234-5*

KATHLEEN K.

SWEET TALKERS

Kathleen K. is a professional, in the finest sense of the word. She takes her work seriously, always approaching it with diligence, imagination and backbone; an exceptional judge of character, she manages both customers and employees with a flair that has made her business a success.

Here, for the first time, is the story behind the provocative advertisements and 970 prefixes. Kathleen K. opens up her diary for a rare peek at the day-to-day life of a phone sex operator—and reveals a number of secrets and surprises. Because far from being a sleazy, underground scam, the service Kathleen provides often speaks to the lives of its customers with a directness and compassion they receive nowhere else. *192-6*